Claws scraped
brushed up agains
was pushed from
got shoved two
shove, and the dark water closed over his head.

Large furred bodies slid in after him, their pointed heads and naked tails barely rippling the water. Five were dark enough to blend with the night; the sixth gleamed like a corpse-light in the darkness.

Water-sodden clothes wrapped shroudlike around him, Dmitri struggled toward the surface. He lost all concept of up or down. Sleek bodies brushed by him, squeezing him as they passed. Claws raked open chest and back, leaving sizzling lines of pain.

He had to breathe.

Had to breathe.

Had to . . .

Ravenloft is a netherworld of evil, a place of dark-ness that can be reached from any world—escape is a different matter entirely. The unlucky who stumble into the Dark Domains find themselves trapped in lands filled with vampires, werebeasts, zombies, and worse.

Each novel in the series is a complete story in itself, revealing the chilling tales of the beleaguered heroes and powerful, evil lords who populate the Dark Domains.

BOOKS

BOOKS

Scholar of Decay

Tanya Huff

SCHOLAR OF DECAY

Cover art by Robh Ruppel.

First Printing: December 1995
Printed in the United States of America.
Library of Congress Catalog Card Number: 94-68160

9 8 7 6 5 4 3 2 1

ISBN: 0-7869-0206-X

TSR, Inc.   TSR Ltd.
201 Sheridan Springs Road   120 Church End, Cherry Hinton
Lake Geneva, WI 53147   Cambridge CB1 3LB
U.S.A.   United Kingdom

For Carrie and Dave
and a hundred afternoons
spent rolling ten-sided dice.

 **Prologue**

"Aurek?" Taking the heavy tray from the kitchen maid, Natalia Nuikin smilingly dismissed the girl and pushed open the narrow door to her husband's study. It would have been locked to anyone else. That it opened to her touch was a measure of the depths of her husband's love. His study was his sanctuary, his alone until his marriage had opened more than just his heart. "Aurek?"

He was standing in the center of the book-lined room, one hand holding a huge, red, leather-bound volume, the other lifted to shoulder height, ink-stained fingers spread wide. Facing him was a creature out of nightmare. The crest of its misshapen head brushed against the beams in the ceiling. Its skin was gray and pebbled. Its eyes, all three of them, were amber. Two rows of pointed teeth were clearly visible as it opened an enormous mouth and roared.

Natalia screamed. The tray and its contents smashed against the floor.

Aurek whirled around to face her.

The monster vanished.

"Natalia?" Aurek set the book on its pedestal and quickly crossed the room to take both her hands in his. "What's the matter?"

Trembling, she clung to him. "There was . . . I saw . . . It was . . ."

"Illusion. Only illusion." Lightly grasping her chin, he lifted her face until their eyes met. "Don't you remember how I promised you that I would never bring danger into this house?"

Unable to decide if she should be feeling fear or anger and finally letting go of both, Natalia found a shaky smile. "I remember. It just seemed so real." Pulling free of his grasp, she knelt to scoop up the fallen food and bits of broken crockery. "I thought you might want something to eat. You've been in here all day."

He knelt beside her. "I've finally deciphered that last bit on the scroll, Lia."

"And you've added it to the book?"

"I was just about to."

She took a thick piece of buttered bread out of his hand just before he could bite into it and put it back on the tray. "You can't eat that, Aurek. It's been on the floor."

"Then I shall have to eat this instead." Lifting the inside of her wrist to his mouth, he chewed lightly on the soft flesh.

Natalia giggled. She tried not to; it wasn't the sort of thing matrons of good Borcan families did, but she couldn't help herself. "Aurek!"

"Natalia!" Her name emerged considerably muffled as he'd pushed up the full embroidered sleeve of her shirt and was now chewing on the crook of her elbow.

Pulling her arm free, she pushed him playfully away. "Not here and not now," she admonished. "What would the servants think?"

"The servants can't get in," he reminded her with a smile, but he stood and extended a hand to help her to her feet. "I tell you what, give me another hour and I'll be finished for the afternoon. Then I'll come out and have something to eat in the dining room, like a civilized human being."

"You promise?"

"I promise."

She stood on her toes and pressed a kiss against his mouth to seal the pledge. With the tray balanced against her hip and one hand on the door, she paused and glanced nervously over at the book. Even she, with no magic of her own, could feel the power contained between those red leather covers. "I'm not sure you should be adding to it."

"It's perfectly safe, Lia. I have protections . . ."

"Around the book and around the study and around the entire house," Lia said, completing his oft-repeated assurance. "I know." She kissed him again. "You've got an hour, no more; then I'm coming back to drag you out into the sunshine—by your ears if I have to."

As the door closed behind her, she heard the sound of the chair being pulled up to his desk. It was very likely that she'd have to make good her threat. It wouldn't be the first time.

Brows drawn in pensively, she carried the shattered luncheon back to the kitchens. Illusionary monsters aside, she found her husband's research more frustrating than frightening. Aurek believed in knowledge for the sake of knowledge. As he kept reminding her, he was a scholar, nothing more. He thought knowledge was the only thing in the world that was pure and untainted. It never seemed to occur to him that it could actually be used for something.

There was so much good he could do with the knowledge he'd acquired over his years of scholarship—if only she could convince him to do so. She smiled as she thought of him—arrogant and brilliant, inkstained and rumpled—striding out into the world to save it from itself.

Well, maybe not, she decided, setting the tray on one end of the huge old table and nodding at the cook. She'd brought most of the servants with her when she'd come here from her mother's house. Before their marriage, Aurek had been living alone on the Nuikin family's old country estate with only a single manservant. Personally, Natalia thought that Edik, the servant, deserved a medal for enduring the situation.

The sight of a horse galloping past the kitchen windows drew her out into the gardens in time to see Aurek's brother, Dmitri, ride into the stableyard. When he saw her, he spurred his mount toward the house.

He was a handsome, athletic young man—a boy, really, she amended, for there had been fifteen years and four sisters between his birth and Aurek's. Although Natalia saw very little of the rest of Aurek's family—they foolishly preferred town and the court of Ivana Boritsi to country life—Dmitri occasionally made an effort to break into Aurek's self-imposed isolation. Desperate for acceptance by the older brother held up as a paragon of virtue by their sisters, Dmitri had no idea of how to go about gaining Aurek's approbation and no intention of admitting such a need to anyone, even himself. Natalia liked her young brother-in-law and wished Aurek were more welcoming.

Dmitri had never learned to hide what he was feeling, and this afternoon, he looked distressed.

"Natalia." He combined bow and dismount, somehow managing to make them both look graceful. "I have to speak with Aurek."

"He's in his study, but . . ."

"His study." Dmitri's lips thinned. "I might have known he'd be no help!"

Natalia sighed. In many ways, the two were very

much alike. Once one of them got an idea into his handsome head, it practically took direct intervention from the gods to get it out again. Aurek believed Dmitri was an undisciplined fool who thought only of himself, and Dmitri believed Aurek was a cold intellectual who cared for no one. They were both wrong, but Natalia was having a difficult time convincing them of that. "What's the matter?"

"What makes you think something's the matter? I mean, just because Aurek doesn't deign to notice me, that doesn't mean no one does." He threw the words away with such total indifference that it was obvious he had to be in some kind of serious trouble.

For a handsome young man in Borca, serious trouble could mean only Ivana Boritsi.

"I'll go and get him for you."

"If you think he'll come."

She laid her hand on his arm and smiled comfortingly at him. "Yes, I think he'll come."

Leaving Dmitri pacing about the garden, Natalia hurried back to the study. She was so intent on coming up with the best way to win the argument she was about to have with her husband that she never noticed how quiet the house had grown . . . how there were no servants about.

The smell of heated metal drifted toward her as she pushed open the study door.

"Aurek?"

A man with wild gray hair and even wilder eyes stood by the pedestal, clutching Aurek's red leather book.

Natalia stepped over the threshold and stared in confusion at the stranger. "Who are you?"

He smiled at her, and she saw madness twisting the curve of thin lips.

"Fate," he said.

 **ONE**

Hands clasped behind his back, Aurek Nuikin stood in the tower window and watched the light fade over Pont-a-Museau. Dusk masked the worst of the decay, replacing the rot with a patina of shabby gentility. Even the river, flowing sluggishly between the islands and through the canals, seemed less fetid than it had under the light of an unforgiving sun. For those who knew no better, dusk made the city appear a much less dangerous place than it actually was.

Aurek knew better.

The search for knowledge had occupied his entire life; had destroyed his life; could, perhaps, redeem his life. After months of frantic study, of piecing together travelers' tales and rumors for which he could find no source or validation, the search had led him here, to this island city in Richemulot, in the desperate hope that in these mist-created ruins he could find his salvation.

As he watched, dusk gave way to darkness, and the true face of Pont-a-Museau emerged.

In the near distance, someone screamed

His mouth twisted as he pulled the shutters closed. In a very short while he would face Richemulot's greatest challenge. It was long past time to prepare.

* * * * *

A huge, humped form scurried across the slate roof of the Chateau Delanuit and paused outside an attic window. Much larger than the giant rat it resembled—almost the size of a large dog—it dug front claws into the rotting wood of the windowsill and thrust its wedge-shaped head into the house. Apparently satisfied, it squeezed the rest of its ebony body through the opening, the movement so lithe, so fluid, it seemed to be pouring itself into the attic as though it were made of liquid darkness rather than corporeal flesh.

Once inside, it moved purposefully down a steep flight of stairs and along a wide hallway. No lamps were lit, but it moved in the half-darkness of the corridor as easily as it would have in full sunlight. More easily perhaps. Although not strictly nocturnal, it much preferred the night to the day.

It paused for a moment outside a closed door. Rising up on sleek haunches, weight balanced by a hideous length of naked tail, it laid one paw against the wood and appeared to be thinking, notched right ear cocked forward, claws flexed. Some of the reddish brown stains that covered them flaked off to disappear in the pattern of the marble floor. After a long moment, the creature shook its head—as though reluctantly dismissing the dark possibilities gathered about it—dropped to the floor, and continued on its way.

The door it wanted was open. Tail lashing, it slunk into the room beyond.

A few minutes passed, then Louise Renier stepped out into the hall, a red silk robe tied loosely around her waist. Her furious summons brought a servant racing up from the first floor at a dead run.

"Yes, mamselle?" he panted, trying very hard not to stare at the curves of ivory flesh exposed by the gaping robe.

"Nothing works around here," Louise snarled, pushing a thick fall of ebony hair back off her face with a bloodstained hand and tucking it behind the edge of her ear. "The bellpull's broken again, and I want a bath!"

*   *   *   *   *

Hours later, Louise stepped out of her suite in time to see a whimpering servant scurry past, blood dribbling out from under the hand clutched to her cheek. Sighing deeply, she hurried down the corridor, carefully avoiding the glistening drops that gleamed like jewels against the marble floor. A pity, she thought, and not for the first time, that such an enthralling color occurs only in such an . . . ephemeral form. It was never half so pretty when it dried.

She paused with one hand on the door to her sister's suite, smiled almost ruefully, and entered.

The outer room was empty, so she made her way to the inner chamber, her gaze lingering over the furnishings as she walked. In sharp contrast to the chaos in the rest of the Chateau, these rooms were practically empty, the pieces richly simple, the arrangement sparsely elegant. Louise hated it. She remembered when this had been their grandfather's suite—before Jacqueline had killed him—and with all her heart, she longed for the chance to gut the rooms to the bare walls and replace everything with her own, more opulent, style.

At the open door to the bedchamber, Louise paused and stared fixedly at the back of Jacqueline's slender neck. A few steps, a quick twist, and control of Richemulot would pass on—to her. But though she'd grown weary of waiting for her turn to rule, she had not grown weary of living. Jacqueline had to have heard her approach, and to try anything now would be tantamount to suicide. She'd have had a better chance earlier in the evening—better, but not assured, which was why she'd decided, once again, to wait. Her sister's death would be meaningless if she didn't survive to enjoy it.

Arranging her expression into a parody of concern, she asked, "Trouble?"

The woman seated at the dressing table turned. Sleek, black brows rose into a delicate arch. "Concerning what?" she wondered.

"I saw whatever-her-name-is." Louise stepped forward, red kid shoes sinking into a carpet that had a design so complex several children had gone blind weaving it. "It looked as though you two had a disagreement."

Jacqueline lifted one bare shoulder and let it fall in a graceful, minimalist shrug. "Hardly trouble; the stupid woman thought she was permitted to have an opinion on what I wear."

"And she's still alive?"

"I like the way she does my hair." Gleaming braids wrapped round her head in an ebony crown. Glancing up at her twin, she smiled and murmured, "What do you think?"

"Beautiful." It didn't matter what she thought; there could be no other answer. Louise clenched her teeth as Jacqueline's smile broadened. Both sisters recognized the question as the petty test it was. She fought the urge to touch her own hair, artfully arranged to cover her damaged ear. "Are you ready?"

"Not quite." Shaking the folds out of her gown's full skirt, Jacqueline stood. "Why don't you go on. I want to see Jacques for a moment before I leave."

Louise fell into step beside her. "I'll wait. No point in taking two boats when one will serve." No point in arriving anywhere before Jacqueline. Better to share a welcome than to stand and watch her twin's arrival, forced to acknowledge the reception as warmer than hers. Even thinking about it set her teeth on edge. There had been too many times in the past when she'd stood unwillingly in Jacqueline's shadow. It would not happen tonight.

* * * * *

"Mama! You look beautiful!"

"Don't I always look beautiful?" Jacqueline wondered, her voice just slightly edged.

"Oh, yes, Mama, always," Jacques hastened to assure her. "But tonight you look especially beautiful."

"Thank you, my darling." She bent and kissed the soft black cap of his hair. He preened under the attention. "And what of your aunt?"

Staring adoringly up into his mother's face, Jacques shook his head. "Tante Louise is beautiful, but not as beautiful as you, Mama."

Well trained, Louise thought. Jacqueline had spent a careful ten years raising her son so that when he thought of his mother, he thought only of how to please her. Even as she found the results disgusting, Louise had to admire the technique. Unless things changed greatly, this boy would never grow up to wrest control from his mother's dead hands.

Unless things changed greatly.

"Will you bring me something from the party, Mama?"

"Why should I?" Jacqueline wrapped long white fingers around the boy's pointed chin and squeezed just enough to dimple the flesh. "I hear you bit your tutor."

"He made me angry."

"And what did biting him accomplish? It only made me angry." She shook his head from side to side. "At you."

"No, Mama!"

"Yes, Mama. You must learn control. Lack of it was

your father's greatest fault. It would make me very sad if you to grew up to be like him."

As Jacques had heard all his short life how his mother had removed his father, it was hardly surprising that he paled. "I'm not like him, Mama! I'm not!"

"Good."

He basked in her smile.

"Perhaps I will bring you something from the party."

"Thank you, Mama!"

Watching their embrace, Louise ground her teeth. No one was closer to Jacqueline than Jacques. What a weapon the boy would make against her sister! In her hands he could be a lever to pry Jacqueline out of power and into the grave. But she'd never get her hands on him.

There were watchers in the shadows.

The boy's grandmama, who'd occasionally questioned her daughter's technique, had died under questionable circumstances. Although it was doubtful Jacqueline had actually done away with their mother—and no one, Louise acknowledged privately, actually missed the interfering old harpy—her death had made a convenient lesson on how Jacqueline tolerated no interference of any kind with her son.

Louise scowled. She found the whole thing incredibly frustrating.

"Wouldn't you hate it if your face froze in that expression?" Jacqueline murmured as she passed. "If you're coming with me, I'm leaving now."

* * * * *

"Look at it, Aurek! They must have dozens of lamps in every room!" Dmitri Nuikin steadied himself on the high prow of the canalboat and leaned dangerously far forward. "The reflection looks as though they've scattered jewels on the water!"

"If you're not careful, you'll be in the water with them," Aurek cautioned grimly. "And I doubt you'd survive the experience."

His younger brother snorted derisively and remained where he was. "It'd take more than a swim to kill me. Look at how that boat's lit up! Why don't we have colored lanterns?"

"Because I didn't wish to pay for them."

Theirs wasn't the only craft arriving at the private dock. Most of the party-goers had taken the river road rather than risk the bridges—especially now that cooler weather had made the stench of the water almost bearable. Their boatman jostled for space, was jostled in turn, and when a group of a half-dozen young men and women blithely ordered their larger vessel in between his boat and the dock, he quietly muttered curses.

As one, the six turned and smiled, an impressive array of long yellow teeth flashing in the lamplight. They were dressed alike in the glittering tatters currently fashionable with the young, and all shared a distinct family resemblance. Of the four young men, two were obviously identical twins, impossible to tell apart. One of the young women was dark, the other brilliantly fair. The tallest of the men, none of whom were very tall, shook his head slowly from side to side. "Stupid, stupid, stupid!" he caroled and rested an elaborately shod foot on the gunnel of Aurek's boat.

He was stronger than he looked.

The canalboat rocked under his push. A swell of murky water lapped hungrily up and over the side.

A heartbeat later, Aurek leapt to his feet, one hand preventing his brother from charging forward, the other curved to cup the night air. "Enough!"

The young man glared at him, lip curled. "I'll say

when it's enough, and . . ." He frowned. Survival in
Pont-a-Museau was infinitely more likely if challenges were issued only when the fight could be won.
What he saw in this stranger's face told him three-to-
one odds were not quite good enough. His nose
twitched as though he smelled something unexpected, and with a sharp jerk of his head, he indicated that his companions should disembark.

"But, Yves . . ." protested one of the twins, clutching at his sleeve.

"But nothing," Yves snarled, following them up onto
the dock. While the others started toward the house,
he took a long last look at the stranger. "Muzzle your
boatman," he advised, slapping the words down
between them. "We have very good ears."

"Are you just going to let that insult stand?" Dmitri
demanded, twitching his vest out of his brother's grip
and glaring at the stranger's receding back.

"Try to remember," Aurek murmured by the
younger man's ear, "that it is in our best interests to
get along with these people."

"*Your* best interests." Leaping out onto the dock
before the mooring lines were secure, Dmitri tossed
golden blond hair back out of violet eyes and
scowled. "I don't even want to be here."

Aurek ignored him. What Dmitri did or did not
want had little bearing on the situation. The moment
the boy had attracted Ivana Boritsi's usually fatal
attention, he had no choice but to leave Borca.
When Aurek had informed his sisters he was traveling to Richemulot, they informed him in turn that his
youngest sibling would be accompanying him. He'd
argued against it, but he might as well have saved
his breath. "If he stays, he dies," their eldest sister
told him shortly. "While we're sorry about your loss,
you have no more choice in this than he does."

"I'll have no time to take care of him."

"He's not a child, Aurek. He can take care of himself."

That had yet to be proven to Aurek's satisfaction, but so far, at least, the boy had not gotten in his way.

Eyes narrowed, Aurek turned to the terrified boatman. The man had come very close to involving him in exactly the sort of situation he wanted to avoid. "That was your one chance," he said softly. "You will not cause me another moment of trouble, for any reason."

Expecting to die, the boatman was emboldened by this astonishing show of mercy from a foreign noble. "Th-They'll come after me, sir!"

Aurek allowed himself a small, tight smile as he remembered the dawning realization in the expression of the young stranger who'd confronted them. "No, I don't think so. Not as long as you remain in my employ."

He paused for a moment on the dock and looked back out over the river. The reflection of the house on the water made it seem as if a second party were taking place in the murky depths below. Which, he wondered, is the more dangerous of the two? Catching sight of a wedge-shaped shadow swimming just beneath the surface of the water, he watched the **V** of the creature's passage until it left the light.

* * * * *

A glass of pale wine in one hand, Aurek circled the ballroom, watching, listening, learning the patterns of Pont-a-Museau. These were the aristocrats of the city, those fortunate few with power or position or merely the right connections.

He had been given a letter of introduction to Joelle Milette, the evening's hostess, by one of the travelers he'd questioned. The letter had gained him a brief meeting with her, which had in turn brought an invitation to this, the first party of the autumn Season. That the invitation had been offered with an obvious ulterior motive was unimportant. In order for his search to proceed smoothly—and the search was all that mattered—it was essential that he convince the Lord of Richemulot to allow him the freedom of the city.

Almost lost in a flurry of shredded silk, Dmitri danced by with a striking young woman who shared a similarity of features with the six youths at the dock. The face turned up to his brother's was pointed in all the same places.

His own face expressionless, Aurek scanned the crowd, noting the evidence of a predominant bloodline. Noting how certain eyes glittered more brightly. Certain smiles showed more teeth. Small, compact bodies made movements so lithe and liquid that those surrounding seemed coarse and ungainly. For those who cared, or dared to look, it became obvious that Pont-a-Museau revolved around this extended family. They laughed at, not with, the other guests . . . laughter that held a feral edge and the intimacy of a secret shared.

Whispered rumors that had reached over the border into Borca were apparently true. Pont-a-Museau was swarming with wererats, and the lycanthropes were quite clearly in control. The other citizens of the city either didn't care or were doing their best to deliberately not see a situation they could do nothing to change. Aurek wondered, not for the first time, if he should warn Dmitri, but decided, yet again, that he should not. His younger brother was handsome, and by all accounts, personable and proficient in a number of physical activities, but Aurek had often suspected he wasn't particularly intelligent. If feigned ignorance of the situation was what it took to survive, Dmitri had best remain ignorant in truth, for his ability to dissemble was nearly nonexistent.

"I love to watch the young folks having a good time," declared a middle-aged man, suddenly standing by Aurek's side. He swung his goblet toward the dance floor, slopping the contents up his sleeve, new stains covering old. "The ladies certainly have noticed that brother of yours." Completely unaware of the astonished distaste directed toward him, he chuckled and set greasy jowls quivering. "That's a lad ripe for adventure. I hope your family doesn't expect you to keep him out of trouble."

"He is not a child," Aurek replied coldly, echoing his sister's words. "He can take care of himself." Stepping fastidiously back, he inclined his head and walked away.

From a table filled with drinking vessels of every shape and size, from squat pewter cups to gleaming crystal flutes, Aurek exchanged his empty glass for a full one and continued pacing around the ballroom. He had no idea what had drawn that disgusting man to his side, but he had every intention of making himself a moving target so that it wouldn't happen again.

He recognized neither the dances nor the music the dancers moved to, but that was hardly surprising as he'd spent most of his life with books and scrolls. The room itself was worthy of attention. Great swaths of gold satin hung in tentlike folds from an immense plaster rose in the center of the ceiling, their ends looped through the gilded arms of grotesque statues that lined the walls. If the fabric had been intended to compress the formidable dimensions of the room, it failed, for there was so much of it, the size of the room had to be acknowledged in order to cope. A closer look determined that the fabric was mildewed, and much of the gilding had flaked off the statues' arms. Tiles were missing from the intricate pattern once laid out in the parquet floor, and those that remained were scuffed and stained. The flocked wall-paper dangled in damp streamers in several places, and it seemed as though something had chewed the carved frame of a huge mirror all along one . . .

Mirror.

Aurek's heart stopped. A wild-haired man stared out at him from behind the refection of his shoulder. Heavy-lidded eyes widened in mock astonishment. Thin lips parted in a burst of manic laughter, but no sound emerged. The wineglass slipped from nerve-less fingers as, sweat beading his forehead, Aurek whirled.

No laughing wizard stood behind him.

Forcing his gaze back to the mirror, he could see only a shaken reflection of himself, his face even paler than usual. His hands curled into fists. "You're dead," he whispered through clenched teeth. "Leave me alone."

When the music stopped and a rising babble of voices indicated that someone of note had arrived, he moved across the dance floor toward the noise, grateful for the distraction. As he walked away from the mirror, the skin crawled between his shoulder blades. Let the dead mock him; he would not turn.

"Aurek, darling, there you are." Joelle Milette appeared out of the crowd, wrapped a hand posses-sively around his elbow, and dragged him forward. "My cousins have arrived, and you have to meet them. Where's that lovely brother of yours? Oh, there he is." Changing course slightly, she snagged Dmitri as well and hurried them both out through a semicircle of guests calling supplicant greetings. "Jacqueline, Louise, these are the two gentlemen I was telling you about: Aurek and Dmitri Nuikin."

Suddenly released, Aurek felt as though he were being offered as part of a buffet. He bowed in the Borcan style, though not quite so elaborately as his brother did beside him, and studied the women who were studying them.

Louise's crimson gown hung in soft folds from rounded shoulders, jeweled combs artfully kept intentionally disheveled hair in place, and the entire effect suggested she'd just emerged from a heated tête-à-tête. Jacqueline made no use of such artifice. Black silk flowed like dark water off the ivory swell of her breasts and pooled into liquid shadow at her feet. An emerald choker the exact color of her eyes encircled her slender throat. The sisters were both beautiful, but Louise used her beauty like a weapon.

Their eyes glittered more brightly. Their smiles showed more teeth. Small, compact bodies made movements so lithe and liquid that those surrounding seemed coarse and ungainly.

There was dried blood caked beneath the nails of Jacqueline's right hand.

Lifting his eyes to hers, Aurek barely managed to contain his response as power recognized power and drove all thoughts of a laughing enemy from his mind.

Jacqueline's nose twitched once; then she smiled as she watched him struggle for control.

"Aurek." Joelle's summons dragged him back to himself. "Jacqueline is the head of the Renier family."

"Yes," he managed to respond. "I can see that."

Confused, Joelle plucked at his sleeve until he took a step back. She smiled ingratiatingly at her cousin. "Aurek and his brother are Borcan nobility."

"How nice," Jacqueline murmured.

"Aurek's quite the scholar," Joelle continued. "He's planning to search all the abandoned buildings in the city for some clue as to who abandoned them."

"With your permission," Aurek added quickly as Jacqueline began to frown. With an effort, he kept his tone casual, making it seem as though he asked a favor of the beautiful woman who ruled only the social calendar of Pont-a-Museau. Greatly daring, he met her gaze again.

She stared at him for a long moment, and while he felt a shadow stroke his soul, he also felt a flash of kinship—gone too quickly to be understood or even to be absolutely certain it had ever existed. Then the emerald eyes hooded, and, heart pounding, Aurek looked away. "I assume you've the permission of the city council." Her tone lightly seasoned the words with contempt. "Our mayor is here tonight, if you haven't."

Aurek had seen the mayor, a powerless man who'd been despondently drunk when he arrived and had been getting drunker as the evening wore on. "I have the permission of the council, mamselle."

"To search all the abandoned buildings," Jacqueline repeated mockingly, and for a moment he was afraid she'd deny him. Prepared to fight for access if he had to, this was not the arena he would have chosen nor, now that he finally knew who could stand in his way, was she the foe. Then she laughed. "How ambitious for a . . . scholar. You *will* let me know if you find anything?"

Aurek bowed, the obeisance not quite submission. "Of course."

* * * * *

"What's going on?" Dmitri demanded as, dismissed, they merged back into the crowd.

"What are you talking about?" Aurek asked absently. Having gained the approval he needed, his thoughts were already preoccupied with sketching out the parameters of his morning search.

"You two—you and Jacqueline Renier—came to some kind of understanding back there, and I was deliberately left out."

"We *two* came to an understanding," Aurek reminded

him. "Not we *three*. What passed between Jacqueline Renier and myself had nothing to do with you."

A muscle jumped in Dmitri's jaw. "You know, you're a real jerk sometimes," he snarled.

"Don't be so childish."

"Childish? That's a good one. Go ahead and keep your little secrets then. I know you didn't want me to come here with you, but you needn't be so obvious about it."

Aurek frowned at his brother's back as he stomped off toward the beverage table. Four older sisters had clearly overindulged the boy.

*   *   *   *   *

"Well, what did you think?"

"What did I think of what?" Jacqueline asked, accepting a drink from a fawning third cousin and then ignoring him.

"Of the Nuikins." Joelle leaned closer and lowered her voice. "Aren't they lovely?"

"Have you taken up procuring, Joelle? How nice you've found something to do that suits you so well."

Joelle pretended not to hear the insult. "I just thought that you could use someone to take your mind off that last unfortunate incident with Henri—" The expression on Jacqueline's face closed Joelle's throat around the second name.

"Incident?" the head of the family said coldly. Resting one hand above the neckline of Joelle's gown, her nails just pricked the skin. "My feelings for Henri Dubois are not to be discussed by you or by anyone else. I thought I made that perfectly clear. If you're having difficulty understanding my wishes . . ."

"No, Jacqueline. I'm sorry, Jacqueline." Joelle's voice trembled as she groveled, and she licked at lips gone dry. "I didn't think. I just wanted to help."

After a long moment, Jacqueline let her hand drop to her side. "Don't do it again. There are limits to what I will accept, even from family."

"No, Jacqueline. I'm sorry, Jacqueline." Wringing her hands, Joelle watched her cousin sweep regally away at the center of an adoring crowd, then took a deep breath and turned to Louise. The benefits would not be as great if Louise took advantage of her discovery, but it seemed a shame to waste such a tasty pair. "What did you think, Louise?"

"I think I'm going to rip out his liver and feed it to him." Skirts swirling around her ankles, Louise stomped across the room.

Joelle dabbed at a drop of blood on her collarbone. "Could be worse," she sighed philosophically. "Could be *my* liver."

* * * * *

Enclosed by her own circle of parasites and postulants, eyes narrowed almost to slits, Louise watched Aurek Nuikin through gaps that opened and closed with the movements of the swirling crowd of dancers. How dared he ignore her! How dared he share whatever it was he shared with her twin and not grant her even the slightest bit of admiration! The boy with his cap of golden hair and violet eyes was better looking, true, but the boy was nothing. Louise had lived in the shadow of power long enough to recognize it in nearly any form, and she recognized it in Aurek Nuikin.

The party whirled about him as though he were an island—solid, gray, and uncompromising. Seen against his quiet reserve, the manic gaiety and pockets of deliberate decadence seemed contrived and brittle. The contrast made him even more desirable. In spite of the streaks of white in his long blond hair, Louise judged his age at no more than thirty-seven or eight. His younger brother had the broader shoulders, the more imposing physique, but Aurek was well built enough.

Not that it mattered.

She wanted him; it was all she could think of. The heat of desire clouded her senses to the exclusion of all else.

And he ignored her!

Her lips curled off her teeth. Bone and muscle writhed within their sheath of silken skin. Hissing softly in irritation, she struggled to banish the red haze from her vision. It took all her strength to fight her way back to control without appearing to be fighting at all.

"Incomparable one, you've gone so pale. Are you ill?"

Louise glared at the young man who'd spoken. He wasn't family, merely the son of a man who imported silks and satins. He wouldn't understand. "Get away from me," she snapped.

Hurt and confused, the rejected gallant found himself gleefully pushed back out of the inner circle by those who retained favor.

The moment she could see clearly again, Louise shoved a babbling cousin aside and began to make her way across the room.

* * * * *

The currents of power in the ballroom had changed since the sisters' arrival. Entirely understandable, all things considered, Aurek allowed. For all his preparation, he'd been taken by surprise when brought face-to-face with the Lord of Richemulot. The information he'd been given, while sufficient for him to draw a number of conclusions about who—or rather what—ruled the domain, had been distinctly incomplete as to gender.

He tracked the larger eddies circling about Jacqueline and watched the cream of Pont-a-Museau society, such as it was, fawn over her in a disgustingly obsequious manner. If her glass was empty, someone filled it. Delicacies of every kind were offered from all sides. Her reaction intrigued him: she stood like the dark eye of an encircling hurricane. It wasn't so much that she accepted the homage as her due as that she seemed completely unaware of it, the way she was consciously unaware of her arms or legs. It astonished him that anyone at the focus of so much intense attention could appear so alone. Nothing touched her.

Do I feel sorry for her? he wondered.

"You don't look as if you're enjoying yourself."

Startled, for he hadn't heard her approach, he looked down into the open invitation on the face of Louise Renier. A dead man would have responded. Fortunately, as acknowledging physical needs during most of Aurek's research could result in an immediate and unpleasant death, he'd long since learned control. "I'm observing the crowds," he told her, to all outward appearances unaffected.

"Really?" The tip of a pointed tongue moistened her smile. "And what exactly are you observing?"

"I doubt you'd be interested."

"Try me." It was very nearly a command.

* * * * *

"Yves! Look!"

Still furious about what had happened at the docks, Yves ignored his cousin's imperious order. "Leave me alone, Chantel, I'm eating."

Snatching the cake from his hand, she spun him around and pointed across the ballroom. "You can stuff your face later. Look at Louise! She's hunting the stranger!"

"So what?" he snarled, turning back to the table and cramming a handful of smoked oysters in his mouth. "If she wants to risk it, it's none of my business. If I could smell the stink of magic on him, she should be able to, and if she can't, who cares?"

Chantel rolled strangely colored eyes under pale brows. Yves ruled their little group because of size and speed—they all bore the scars of unsuccessful challenges—but she was beginning to suspect that, though cunning, he wasn't very smart. "One little sniff of power that none of the rest of us caught and all of a sudden this guy's a mighty wizard." She easily dodged his irritated swing. "You're missing the point: if Louise is hunting the older stranger, he's going to be far too busy to protect the younger one."

Ignoring the oil dribbling down his chin, Yves slowly faced his cousin. "And if Louise is hunting . . ." He worked that information through to its logical conclusion. ". . . we can hunt. But suppose Jacqueline wants him?"

"She doesn't. She doesn't want either of them. I heard her."

Yves's eyes glittered in the lamplight. "Find the others."

* * * * *

Across the ballroom, Louise watched a new pattern swirl past and murmured, "I think I would like to dance."

Aurek inclined his head. "As you wish."

"With you." She swung her hips in toward him. Although he made no apparent effort to avoid her touch, the contact she'd intended never occurred.

"I am very sorry, mamselle, but I do not dance."

* * * * *

Suddenly standing by himself, though there'd been a knot of townspeople around him a moment before, Dmitri scowled suspiciously at Yves as he and his five companions approached. "What do you want?"

"To apologize." Yves swept his arm downward in an elaborate bow, the ragged streamers of multicolored cloth that made up his sleeve dusting the floor. "My behavior at the dock was boorish in the extreme, and I hope you'll allow me to make it up to you." At his gesture, Chantel came forward with a pair of immense silver goblets, tarnish dark in the hollows of the heavy embossing. He took them from her and offered one to Dmitri. "Drink with us, and let's all be friends."

"Friends?"

"Why not?"

Why not indeed. Dmitri hadn't lacked for dancing partners nor, for that matter, invitations to a more intimate dance. That he'd declined all of the latter, having no interest in frenzied fumbling with total strangers, had seemed only to put him in greater demand. Although he never would have admitted it, while he enjoyed being the center of attention, he was lonely. He missed having a group of people his own age he could spend time with.

But friends? With this lot? The toothy one offering the drink had insulted his brother.

Almost as though he'd read Dmitri's mind, Yves murmured, "Your . . . brother, is it? Your brother won't mind."

Dmitri followed the direction of Yves's gaze and saw Aurek by the tall windows that led out to the terrace; Louise Renier was standing so close they were probably breathing the same air. No, Aurek wouldn't care what he did.

Why not be friends with this lot? His fist closed

around the bulky stem of the goblet. They looked as if they knew how to have a good time. Besides, he reasoned, taking a long swallow of the sweet wine, no one else seems to be offering.

* * * * *

Aurek had had a single objective for attending the party: acquiring permission to search the ruins. Had he been willing to leave Dmitri alone in such company, he'd have left immediately upon obtaining it. As he was obliged to stay, he found Louise's attempts to attract him diverting. Well aware that any other man would have begged her to accompany him to a more secluded area after the first few moments of such a lascivious assault, he wondered how long she intended to throw herself at him. It was an interesting problem: how long would the apparently irresistible force continue to waste her time on the immovable object.

As a coquettish movement lifted a silken cluster of curls, he also wondered who'd bitten the chunk out of her ear.

* * * * *

The wine was stronger than what Dmitri had been drinking, thicker, sweeter, and the moment he drained the goblet, one of the identical twins filled it again. "Aubert?"

Lips twitched back off long yellow teeth. "No. I'm Henri, the good-looking one. That ugly thing there is Aubert."

Dmitri blinked at them, trying to clear the fog from his head. "But you look exactly alike."

When they all laughed, he laughed with them.

As Dmitri swayed where he stood, Yves leaned forward and dropped his tone to a conspiratorial whisper. "Are you finding it warm in here?"

"Yes, a little."

"Come on." Yves linked his arm through Dmitri's, easily holding him upright in spite of their difference in size. Indicating that the other five should follow, he steered him around the edge of the dance floor toward the windows. "Lets go outside and get some air."

* * * * *

There was something familiar about Aurek Nuikin. Distracted by desire, Louise couldn't quite put her finger on what it was.

Eyes locked on his face, searching for a response, Louise realized that nothing seemed to be working. She fought the urge to snarl and, instead, wet already moist lips. "You're the first Borcan noble I've ever met."

"I'm afraid we're merely a minor house." And were considered nobility only because Ivana Boritsi, who owned everything in the domain, had created a class suitable for her to socialize with.

"Have you left a wife back in this minor house?" Determined to have him, Louise moved closer, laid her hand lightly on his arm, and was amazed to feel the rigidity of the flesh beneath the cloth.

"My wife is dead."

"I'm so sorry. How long ago did it happen?"

"Not long enough." He plucked her hand off his sleeve. "Your pardon, mamselle."

Louise watched him walk away, too stunned by what had just happened to prevent him. He actually plucked her hand off his sleeve. Did he think he could offer her such an insult and survive it? He was either incredibly stupid or the most arrogant man she'd ever met. She took a step after him and forced herself to stop, nails digging bloody half-moons into her palms as she struggled to control her rage.

No, she told herself, not here. It's too public. It was too likely she'd be interrupted before he really started to pay.

According to the little tête-a-tête he'd had with Jacqueline, Aurek Nuikin intended to spend his time searching the ruins of the city. A great many unpleasant things could happen to a man in an abandoned building, Louise mused darkly, eyes glittering in the lamplight. Especially an abandoned building in Pont-a-Museau.

*   *   *   *   *

Outside on the terrace, the night was darker than Dmitri remembered its being. The wine made the shadows whisper and move in ways shadows were not supposed to. With his left arm tucked in the crook of Yves's elbow, and with Chantel a warm presence at his other side, he staggered over the uneven paving stones toward the river. "Where are we going?"

"For a walk."

"Where are the others?"

"Behind us." Chantel pushed closer, and Dmitri could feel the heat even through his clothing and hers. Her hair gleamed in the lamplight, the flickering flames adding color to the pale blonde curls.

He half-turned, saw a pile of cloth on the path, and thought he saw a humped shadow move toward the river. There could be no mistaking the silhouette. Rat. But far larger than any rat he'd ever seen—and during the short time he'd been in Pont-a-Museau he'd seen some big rats. Before he could say anything, he stumbled. Yves caught him and, laughing, set him back on his feet.

Dmitri searched the limited visibility thrown by a single lamp hanging high on a canted pole. "Where's

Chantel?" He peered around in confusion. One minute she'd been by his side; the next she was gone. "It's not safe for her to wander off. I just saw the biggest rat."

"No."

"Yes."

"Show me."

He turned, but except for Yves, the path was empty. Not only was there no rat, but his new friends had disappeared as well. "Where are the twins? And Annette? And Georges?"

"Annette and Georges are also twins. Henri and Aubert merely work harder at using it for protective camouflage."

"But where are they?"

"Perhaps the rat got them."

It *had* been a very large rat. Dmitri searched the shadows and finally turned back to Yves. "I think we should . . ." he began, but Yves was gone too. "Come on, guys, quit fooling around." The wine had wrapped his head in sticky fog. "Aren't we a little old for hide-and-seek?" When no one answered, he giggled. "Okay, I guess not. I'm it. Ollie, ollie, all in . . ."

Claws scraped against stone, and a large heavy shape brushed up against his legs. He whirled, nearly fell, was pushed from another direction. Whirled, nearly fell, got shoved two steps closer to the river.

*   *   *   *   *

Clasping trembling hands behind his back, Aurek searched the ballroom for his brother. His emotions in turmoil, he was furious at himself for forgetting, even for a moment, the reason he'd come to Pont-a-Museau. How could he have been so distracted? How could he have been so inconstant?

He thought he heard the sound of manic laughter, and he welcomed the welts it left upon his soul.

When he found Dmitri, they were leaving. Let the boy whine and complain, but he had been reminded of his purpose, and he would not lose it again.

"If you're looking for that pretty brother of yours," Joelle told him, swaying into his line of sight and smelling strongly of brandy, "he went outside with my youngest brother and his friends."

Aurek curtly inclined his head, ignored the wanton invitation in her glittering eyes, and made his way toward the terrace windows.

* * * * *

By the time Dmitri worked out he was being herded, it was long past the time when he could do anything about it. One final shove—he flailed his arms searching for something, anything to grab— and the dark water closed over his head.

A half-dozen large, furred bodies slid in after him, their pointed heads and naked tails barely rippling the river. Five were dark enough to blend with the night; the sixth gleamed like a corpse-light in the darkness.

Fear finally began to burn through the numbing effects of the wine. Water-sodden clothes wrapped shroudlike around him, Dmitri struggled toward the surface. A heartbeat after he desperately gulped a lungful of air, claws caught at his vest and playfully yanked him back under.

A powerful kick slammed into his shoulder and set him spinning. He lost all concept of up or down. He had to breathe, but he didn't know which way to go. Sleek bodies brushed by him on either side, squeezing him between them as they passed. Claws raked open chest and back, leaving sizzling lines of pain behind.

He had to breathe.

Had to breathe.

Had to . . .

Then his arm splashed out into the night, and he pushed his head out after it. Gasping and choking, he abandoned pride and screamed for Aurek.

*   *   *   *   *

The elongated shadows of the partygoers through the filth-covered windows a flickering background behind him, Aurek dropped to one knee and scooped a pile of clothing off the path. Everyone in the city below a certain age dressed in the fashionable "rags and tatters," but he'd seen this fabric before. Brows drawn in, he tried to remember.

On the dock. Fluttering from the arm of a young man who bore the distinctive physical features of the Renier bloodline.

"*Aur-ek!*"

Names and terror both carry power. Dmitri's voice tore through the myriad sounds of the night. Heart pounding, Aurek leapt to his feet and raced toward the sound, hands curled into fists and pale hair streaming out behind him like a banner. If Dmitri had been injured in any way . . .

He reached the river's edge in time to see his brother's face break the water's surface, cough, and be pulled under yet again. Dropping to his knees and leaning out as far as he dared, Aurek's desperate reach fell short. As he clutched futilely at a handful of murky water, he felt a coarse pelt pass mockingly under his fingertips.

Humped shapes twisted and played in the area around Dmitri's struggling body. The size of the wererats in comparison to the size of their prey didn't seem to matter. Not only were there six of them, but they swam with an eel-like agility, almost as much at

home in the water as they would be on dry land.
Above pointed muzzles, eyes glittered with the
enjoyment of the game. Claws ripped at Dmitri's
clothing, caressed crimson streamers from his skin,
and every now and then allowed him to breathe lest
their fun be over too soon.

A muscle jumped in Aurek's jaw as he raised both
hands to shoulder height, palms toward the water.
His brother would not die as sport for such as these.
His lips parted, and the air around him became
unnaturally still.

"Enough!"

The power in that single word snapped his mouth
closed. It was not a voice that could be argued with.
Not by him nor, apparently, by those in the river.
Finding Dmitri shoved suddenly within reach, Aurek
hauled him, choking and gasping for breath, up onto
the algae-covered rocks of the riverwall. His clothing
had been ripped into a grotesque parody of fashionable dress, but the wounds below were less serious
than they had at first appeared.

"Has he been bitten?"

Aurek twisted and was not surprised to see Jacqueline Renier advance from the shadows, her expression showing only polite curiosity. As the horrifying
implications of her question sank in, he quickly
examined his brother's injuries more carefully.

"No," he said at last, sitting back on his heels,
relief making him weak. "No bites."

"Good." It was clear from her tone that the word
did not refer to Dmitri's state but was rather a
reprieve pronounced for other listeners.

The river was dark and still. The wererats, if not
gone, were watching silently. Motionless.

"I suggest you take him home," Jacqueline continued, the suggestion manifestly one Aurek was
expected to follow. "He has no doubt drunk a great

deal of filthy water, and those scratches should be cleaned before they infect." She paused, and Aurek found his gaze drawn to hers. Unable to look away, he felt a dark power caress his heart with unforgiving fingers. When she spoke again, he heard the warning behind the words. "It is important that we take care of our families."

Still on his knees beside his brother's trembling body—a position, he realized that also put him on his knees at Jacqueline's feet—Aurek inclined his head. Had he not already been certain of who and what she was, this glimpse of a small fraction of her power would have convinced him.

While she acknowledged his right to take care of his own, she had clearly reminded him that, in turn, she would take care of hers.

As Aurek helped Dmitri stand, she murmured, "You've proven yourself to be a discreet man, and you will, of course, say nothing of what has occurred here."

"My brother should be told . . ."

"Nothing," she repeated, and he had the distinct feeling she'd allowed him as much license as he was likely to get. While he doubted he was in any personal danger—he knew his own abilities too well—he was responsible for more lives than merely his own. He had forgotten that once, and the price had been almost more than heart and mind could bear.

"I will say nothing," he agreed reluctantly, hoping that the semiconscious young man in his arms had been forced to figure it out for himself.

Aurek hadn't intended to return to the party, but the fastest route to the private dock where the canal-boats waited passed through the house. With one arm around Dmitri's waist and the other gripping his right elbow, he half-carried his brother in through the terrace windows, ready to defend him if it became necessary. Fortunately, given Jacqueline Renier's warning, it didn't become necessary.

Dmitri's new playmates were either gone or lying very low.

The festivities had degenerated during the short time Aurek had been outside, and the remaining crowd seemed intent on self-abuse and debauchery. The sight of a young man, stinking of river water and bleeding sluggishly from a number of shallow wounds, appeared to attract no interest. Lips pressed thin in disgust, Aurek could only assume it wasn't that unusual a sight.

* * * * *

With lips curled inhumanly far off her teeth, Louise watched Jacqueline follow Aurek Nuikin in from the terrace. Her anger blinding her to everything outside its narrow focus of insult and betrayal, she ignored Dmitri's presence entirely and saw only that Aurek had declined her company for her sister's.

Seeing them together, a mere body-length apart, she suddenly realized what it was about the man that had seemed so familiar. He reminded her of Jacqueline. Not physically, but they shared an arrogance that suggested, rather than considering the rest of the world beneath them, they didn't consider the rest of the world at all. That apparent similarity with her twin was the last thing Louise needed to fan her rage into white heat.

When Jacqueline, feeling the blind fury lap against her back, turned and smiled with taunting triumph, it nearly shredded away the last of Louise's self-control.

Jacqueline could not be made to pay, so Aurek Nuikin would pay for them both.

He will beg for death before I'm through!

 **TWO**

His sleep disturbed by kaleidoscopic dreams of a laughing ghost, Aurek lay awake and watched the gray light of dawn touch his window. As the pigeons in the eaves announced to the day that they'd survived another night, he gritted his teeth and threw back the bedclothes. If he couldn't sleep, he had plenty to do awake.

The huge, four-poster bed had been one of the few pieces of furniture he'd not gotten rid of. Most of the rest had been eaten away by insects and the damp, but the heavy, near-black wood of the bed had seemed impervious. He'd never seen a bed quite like it. As it reminded him of nothing in his past, he'd taken it for his own use.

Slipping his arms into the sleeves of a blue wool dressing gown, he padded barefoot across the floor—deftly avoiding a rough plank patch filling a hole where the original boards had rotted through. The tiny panes of the window had been leaded together from salvaged pieces of shattered glass. Conscious of how few unbroken windows there were in Pont-a-Museau, Aurek opened it carefully and leaned out to study the city.

Mist clung to the curve of the river in smoky tendrils the gray-green shade of fungus. The air smelled no better than it looked and would, Aurek knew, smell worse as the day warmed. Eyes narrowed, he studied the dirty gray stone of neighboring buildings. If their secrets could have been discovered by force of will alone, his gaze would have stripped the crumbling facades away and exposed their rotting hearts.

Richemulot had appeared in his lifetime. Fifteen years before it had not existed, then suddenly there it was, pressed up against Borca's western border. The cities—Mortigny, St. Ronges, and Pont-a-Museau— had been from the beginning much as they were now, complete with buildings, the buildings themselves complete with the decaying paraphernalia of daily life. To this point, though Aurek had searched every existing record, scholarship had been unable to determine if, for some reason, the buildings had been created in the state they were found, or if the mist had dragged them from another time and place.

The mist.

What it was, why it was, no one knew for certain. In the oldest records out of Barovia, Aurek had seen it described as a preternatural force capable of reasoning and response. More recent research suggested it was nothing more than an ethereal border between planes—dangerous and unpredictable but unable to be influenced by those around it.

Although he had dared much for the sake of knowledge, even Aurek avoided the mist.

He didn't care whether the mist had created the cities of Richemulot or if it had dragged them across the planes. He was interested only in the artifacts that could be gleaned from the ruins.

Artifacts like the green glass bead with the golden fire at its heart. Its power had pulled him, red-eyed and shaking, out of his study to confront the Vistana who wore it hung around his neck. The bead had not been for sale—not for any price. Only a madman—which he wasn't, quite, in spite of grief and guilt—threatened the Vistani. The Vistana had known only that the bead had been found in an abandoned building in Pont-a-Museau.

If there was magic abandoned here . . . His fingers closed on the edge of the windowsill. It wasn't really a question. Staring out at the city, he could feel, very faintly, the places where power lingered. Places the city's scavengers avoided. Today, he would begin his search and, perhaps, soon . . .

"Soon," he repeated aloud. And then again, "Soon."

Closing the window and latching it, he entered what probably had been a sitting room at one time but was now his study. Adjoining his bedchamber, it had a second door opening into the second floor hall. This room also had been scrubbed free of accumulated filth until it gleamed. For lack of a bookcase, the notes and papers he'd brought from Borca were stacked on a corner of the large, somewhat worm-eaten, desk.

Although the shutters were closed, a soft light filled the room, its source an alcove cut into an inside wall. The light appeared to have no origin—neither candle nor lamp. It brightened imperceptibly as Aurek slowly approached.

In the alcove was a wooden pedestal, so classically pure in design it appeared to have been grown rather than carved. Centered on the pedestal, bathed in gentle light, stood an exquisitely perfect porcelain statue of a woman. Though she stood barely eight inches high, the clothing that identified her as a member of the Borcan upper class was complete down to the impossibly tiny stitches on her embroidered sleeves. Her back was slightly arched, and her perfectly detailed hands were raised, as though to block a blow. Her face looked up through the shield of her hands, twisted into an expression of utter horror. Except for the horror, she would have been beautiful.

Head bowed, Aurek stood motionless before the alcove. A vein pulsed in his temple as he concentrated with all his power, all his heart, on the tiny figure.

Then his shoulders sagged, and a strangled cry of despair escaped. He could feel the spirit trapped within the statue but, try as he might, he couldn't reach it. Had never been able to reach it.

"It's a new day, Natalia." With a trembling finger, he reached out and tenderly stroked the statue's auburn hair. "Perhaps it will be the day we've been waiting for. I have permission to search," he continued, clasping his hands behind his back as though afraid of what they'd do if free. "The Lord of Richemulot is a woman—well, technically not a woman, but a female—less predictable than the Lady Ivana and probably more dangerous because of that. We . . ." He paused, strangely reluctant to tell the wife he loved so desperately that he and Jacqueline Renier had touched, if only for an instant, beneath the other's surface.

"I don't know why she hides what she is," he said instead. "Her family is so strong here it couldn't possibly make any difference. But then, her kind enjoy dark and labyrinthine games, so perhaps that's sufficient explanation. I'm sure it amuses them to mingle with the citizens of the cities."

That the citizens worked so hard at remaining unaware, he strongly suspected came in a large part from instincts of self-preservation and in a small part from plain and simple denial. The evidence was plentiful if any of them chose to heed it.

"I believe she recognized what I am in much the same way as I recognized her—power calling to power. . . ." His voice trailed off as he remembered another time power had called to power and his beloved Natalia had paid the price of the visit. Finally he regained control and continued. "She as much as promised me that if I leave her family alone, she will leave mine alone. I think we're safe here." He had never worried about safety before, had taken it for granted . . . before.

He half-turned as he heard a door open back in his bedchamber and the floor protesting under a familiar heavy tread. "It's time for me to go, Lia." Swallowing his grief, he cupped both hands around the statue without actually touching it. "I love you," he whispered through the constriction in his throat. "I promise you, I'll find a way."

Face twisted with painful memories, he returned to his bedchamber, pulling the study door closed softly behind him.

Edik, his servant, had come and gone, leaving a pitcher of steaming water on the shaving table. Feeling as though at any moment misery and guilt could tear him apart, Aurek fought for balance as he filled a bowl and reached for his razor.

When he looked into his shaving mirror, his hand froze, the blade cold against the skin of his throat. The laughing face of the wild-haired man filled the glass. His lips writhed with the force of his amusement, and under heavy lids, his eyes, locked on Aurek's, were dark with gleeful hate.

A muscle jumped in Aurek's jaw. Though the man in the mirror was eight months dead—his name unknown, his body food for worms—this was no true ghost. If it were, it would have long since been banished. But Aurek took little comfort in knowing that he haunted himself with a phantom called up out of his own pain and, even knowing its origins, he couldn't help responding.

After setting the razor down with studied care lest he be tempted to use it, he found his voice and cried, "Why bother taunting me? My victory has never been anything but ash in my mouth!"

To your victory! jeered the apparition.

Self-abuse or not, this was more than Aurek could bear. Shrieking in rage, he flung the mirror against the far wall where it smashed into a hundred pieces.

Edik, a carafe of coffee dwarfed by his huge hand, stood in the open door and shook his head at the broken glass. "Break a mirror, break your luck," he intoned portentously, sucking air through his teeth.

"Luck?" As his pride, wearing a dead man's face, mocked him from every piece of silvered glass, Aurek laughed bitterly.

* * * * *

Awakened by the sun shining through the tattered velvet curtains, Louise stretched, freed herself from a shredded tangle of bedclothes, and climbed out of bed. Although she hadn't fallen asleep until nearly dawn, she wasn't the least bit tired. Nearly a hundred carpets of every imaginable pattern and hue, scattered ankle-deep on the floor, provided her a cushioned path from the enormous canopied bed to a tarnished, gilt-framed mirror that took up almost one entire wall.

Pivoting naked in front of the glass, Louise smiled at her reflection, well satisfied with what she saw. The few scars left behind by family arguments she hadn't won in the first few seconds were all positioned where fashionable clothing easily covered them. "Aurek Nuikin is a fool," she murmured, her hands dancing lightly over alabaster skin. "Don't you agree, Geraud?"

The young man lying facedown on the bed made no reply.

Her smile widened as she turned and patted him gently on one bare buttock. He was in no small way responsible for her mood this morning. When she'd brought him home from the party, still blindly furious at the scholar and her sister, he'd done everything he could to make her feel better. Pitifully grateful to be noticed after her earlier dismissal, he'd been attentive and adoring and . . . athletic. Unfortunately, he hadn't survived the experience.

"Geraud?" Louise reached over and drew a fingernail down the sole of his bare foot. The skin parted, but Geraud remained perfectly still. "No matter; just checking."

The servants would know what to do with the body when they found it. It wouldn't be the first slipped into the dark depths of the river to add its soupçon of rot to the muck and decay. It wouldn't be the last.

"It probably won't be the last today." Sliding the crimson silk robe up over her shoulders, Louise exchanged a glance of malicious anticipation with her reflection. "If Aurek Nuikin intends to wander in deserted buildings, he'd best take care. After all, a great many unpleasant things could happen to a poor helpless scholar intent on research." The tip of her tongue slid along the full curve of her lower lip. "A great many unpleasant things," she repeated.

* * * * *

Aurek stood silently in the doorway and watched with a worried frown as Dmitri, his body nearly doubled over in pain, vomited bile into a chipped porcelain bowl. When he finally fell back against the pillows, dripping sweat, hands feebly clutching at the tangled bedclothes, Aurek stepped into the room.

"Are you all right?" he asked, crossing to the bed.

Dmitri stared up at his brother in disbelief, bloodshot eyes squinted nearly closed in spite of the diffused light coming through the drawn curtains. "Oh, I'm just fine," he mumbled. "Just fine."

Brow creased, Aurek laid an inquiring hand on Dmitri's brow only to have it abruptly shaken off. He sighed and clasped his hands behind his back instead. "What do you remember about last night?"

"I remember your being a patronizing . . ."

"No. What do you remember about your . . . adventure?"

"Adventure?" Dmitri laughed humorlessly. "I got drunk and fell in the river."

"That's all you remember?"

"Well, I think there was something in the water with me, but that's hardly surprising. There're probably as many things living in that cesspool as in the city." Misinterpreting his brother's expression, he flushed and added, "Look, it's no big deal—you dragged me out and I'm grateful, but I bet it happens all the time."

"Yes." Aurek nodded grimly. "Very likely."

"What's that supposed to mean?"

"Only that you're probably correct: what happened to you very likely happens all the time." Could he only count on the younger man's discretion, he'd tell him the truth—whether Jacqueline Renier wanted it told or not. Unfortunately, the odds of Dmitri opening his mouth at an inopportune time were too great.

So, my brother tells me you're a wererat.

He could just hear Dmitri announcing all he knew and ruining everything. He must be permitted to search the ruins of Pont-a-Museau. Nothing could interfere with that. Nothing.

"You needn't look so superior," Dmitri muttered defensively into the silence. "I'm sure you've had a few too many on occasion."

Aurek shook his head. "I've never seen the point in

either losing control and making a fool of myself or
in making myself violently ill."

"Oh, right. I forgot. You're a . . . a thing of virtue.
What's that?" he demanded as Edik replaced the
porcelain bowl on the bedside table with a heavy
clay mug.

"A purgative, young sir."

"Another one?"

"It is very important that we are certain you have
flushed all the river poisons from your system."
Wrapping his huge hand around the mug, he lifted it
to Dmitri's mouth, the other hand supporting the
younger man's head in such a way that he had no
choice but to drink.

Dmitri pushed at Edik's arms with the same effect
a kitten would have in attempting to uproot a tree.
Coughing and sputtering, he swallowed.

"I hate you," he muttered melodramatically when
Edik finally moved the cup away. Glaring up at his
brother he added, "And I hate you, too."

"I disinfected all his scratches, sir," Edik told
Aurek placidly, setting the mug back on the table.
"While the water was undeniably filthy, his wounds
were not deep, and I have done what I can to see that
he takes no permanent damage."

"Thank you, Edik." That his servant—his *faithful*
servant for all it sounded so cliché—had effortlessly
taken responsibility for Dmitri lifted a load from
Aurek's mind. He wished only that there were as
easy an answer to the problem of Jacqueline Renier's
young relatives. While he knew very little about their
kind, what he'd learned was not encouraging. He
doubted very much that Dmitri had seen the last of
them, and while their games were not likely to be
fatal, thanks to the Lord of Richemulot's warning,
neither would they be pleasant.

"People," he said at last, falling into the lecturing

tone Natalia had tried unsuccessfully to break him of, "are not always what they appear to be. You're in a new place where the rules might not be what you're used to. Think twice before you believe someone is a friend."

"Like you care," Dmitri scoffed, closing his eyes. "Go away before I puke again."

"I just want you to be careful. . . ."

"And I just want you to leave." His throat convulsed, and he grimaced as he swallowed. "I'm not kidding about the puking."

* * * * *

Closing the door to Dmitri's bedchamber softly behind him, Aurek wearily reflected that, at least for the morning, he'd know exactly where his brother was. He didn't understand why the boy was always so angry, why their meetings always ended—if they didn't begin—with Dmitri snarling and snapping at everything he said. Natalia had understood, but Natalia—his sweet and loving Natalia—was no longer able to explain.

* * * * *

"You're in a good mood this morning."

Louise slid into her seat at the scarred table that nearly filled the morning room, and smiled beatifically at her sister. "Why shouldn't I be?"

"No reason." Jacqueline took a long, slow swallow of coffee and studied Louise over the gilded rim of the cup. While she hadn't yet been to bed, it was obvious that her twin had just risen. "Your fits of pique usually last longer."

Greedily heaping her plate with an assortment of food, Louise shrugged. "I found a diversion."

"How nice. Will he be joining us for . . . breakfast?"

Louise swept a critical gaze over the full platters, a laden fork halfway to her mouth. "I don't think that's necessary. There's plenty here now."

*   *   *   *   *

The burly servant carrying the body out of the west wing heard the twins' shared laughter and suppressed a shudder. As bad as it could be at the Chateau when they fought, it was worse still when they got along.

*   *   *   *   *

The house, or what remained of it, was on the east shore of Souris Island. Only the third story, gray-green lichens flaking off its blackened stonework, showed over the almost leafless branches of the thorn trees. Aurek scanned the empty windows and picked a careful path toward the door through what had once been an attractive courtyard, years of dead and decaying leaves squelching underfoot.

Braided rope straps cut painfully into his shoulders as his oilskin pack snagged on a six-inch thorn. Muttering under his breath, he reached back and snapped it off the tree.

There was power here. It lay like an oily film over the house and grounds. He could all but taste it in the air.

The remains of the door hung from a single, twisted hinge. He checked that the floor beyond the threshold was solid and stepped onto it without pausing to inspect it for arcane protections. The level of power he could sense deep in the abandoned building was far too slight to be a threat. The danger was greater that the house might collapse around him.

The entryway held only a staircase that rose in a

graceful spiral to the second story. Although it remained essentially in one piece, the stairs had long since rotted past safety. Fortunately, the artifact he searched for was below, not above. Eyes narrowed, senses extended, Aurek moved through the ruins of a formal dining room and out the narrow door the servants had once used to bring food from the kitchens. Stairs to the lower levels would be at the rear of the house.

Webs hung like tattered shrouds from every corner, and he was increasingly conscious of being watched. Breathing shallowly, for every step stirred up noxious clouds of dust and mold, he made his way cautiously to the kitchens.

Large spiders, he thought, ducking under the first intact web he'd seen. A floorboard cracked under his heel, and he flung his weight forward barely in time to prevent breaking through. Fully confident of his ability to deal with anything he might meet, he still had no desire to find himself buried under a ton or two of rubble.

Vines growing over kitchen windows long empty of glass filled the room with flickering shadow.

Something skirted the outer edge of his vision.

Shrugging off his pack, Aurek pulled out a small enclosed lantern and quickly lit it. Insects scurried in the walls all around him, above him, below him—it was impossible to tell where the sounds originated. Holding the lantern over his head, he slowly turned in place. The shadows rearranged themselves but didn't entirely flee.

In the far corner, he found what he was looking for: a flight of stairs, leading down.

The desiccated body of a rat hung wrapped in spider silk in the exact center of the doorway. Its condition seemed to indicate it hadn't been hanging there for very long.

Aurek studied the situation for a moment, then

picked a piece of dry and insect-eaten kindling from a half-empty box by the rusted stove and lit one end in his lantern. When the flames caught, licking hungrily toward his hand, he torched the web.

Almost instantly, a sheet of flame filled the doorway and, just as quickly, it was over. The body of the rat fell smoldering to the floor. Nothing remained of the web save an acrid smell that scraped at the back of his throat. Aurek coughed, sucked another shallow breath through his teeth, and froze in place.

A sound . . . above and behind.

The weight of the spider dropping onto his shoulders flung him to his knees. Biting back an involuntary cry—the last thing he needed was to attract more attention—he rolled, dislodging the huge insect as mandibles clattered like knives beside his ear. Regaining his feet, he whirled and barked out a word that tore into the already abraded surface of his throat, the first three fingers of his left hand extended toward the attacking spider.

The oval body of the insect thumped onto the floor as all eight legs collapsed under a sudden increase in weight. Pedipalps whipping frantically from side to side, it dug pairs of hooked claws into splintering boards and dragged itself forward, its prey reflected in each of the eight gleaming black eyes on the top of its head.

Carefully setting his lantern on a dirt-encrusted sideboard, Aurek flipped the table in the center of the room over onto its side and, bracing his foot against the bottom boards, tried to rip off a heavy, carved leg. Soft and punky from the omnipresent damp, the wood crumbled under the pressure. Instead of pulling the leg from the table, Aurek began to kick pieces of the table off the leg.

Inch by inch, the spider advanced.

Finally holding a reasonably solid club, Aurek turned, took a deep breath, and methodically beat the nearly immobile spider to a pulp—its chitin smashing like an eggshell. When its legs had stopped thrashing and the bloated body was no longer recognizable, he flung his dripping weapon aside, grimacing with disgust. He hated the brutality implicit in killing such a creature, even when he admitted the necessity.

Brushing futilely at the moist stains on his clothing, he retrieved his lantern and started down the stairs, irritated by the delay.

The shadows were thicker on the lower level, the air damper, the floors more thoroughly decayed. Even the spiderwebs appeared to have been long abandoned. Pallid colonies of fungus sprouted in cracks and, in spite of moving with extreme caution, Aurek's foot broke through the floor twice before he crossed the first room. The second time it happened, he pitched backward, arms flailing wildly. Although he managed to keep his grip on the lantern, the flame went out.

Except for a gray rectangle marking the floor at the bottom of the stairs, the darkness around him was absolute. Hair rising off the back of his neck, ears straining to hear anything approach, Aurek fumbled the lantern open, found his focus, and spoke a word of power.

The light, once restored, showed he was still alone but, as he cautiously moved around piles of garbage toward the artifact, he suspected that couldn't last. While the ruins of Pont-a-Museau held nothing he considered an actual threat, there would, no doubt, be a number of minor, annoying battles remaining to interfere with his search.

* * * * *

Up on the floor above, the vines covering the larger of the two kitchen windows parted, and a

pointed, ebony snout poked over the sill and into the
room. Whiskers twitching, it wrinkled at the lingering
smell of burned web and singed fur, then swung
around toward the entrance to the lower level. The
notched right ear flicked forward as it listened to
sounds from below. Long, ivory teeth flashed briefly
in what was surely the equivalent of a satisfied smile
as it withdrew. A moment later, curved claws found a
grip on the ledge, and a sleek, black wererat dropped
into the kitchen, landing almost silently in spite of its
size. Green eyes gleaming, it padded over to the
dead rat on the floor and batted it out of the way.

The remains of the spider held its attention for a
moment longer. It sniffed at the pulped body, ears
flat against its skull; then, rising up on its hind legs, it
stared thoughtfully at the entrance to the stairs.

Smoothing long whiskers back off its face, it
watched as a dozen giant rats swarmed into the
room and disappeared into the shadows.

* * * * *

Aurek swept his gaze over the floor-to-ceiling
shelves and saw, through dirt and decay, what had
once been a magnificent library. That the owner of
the library had chosen a windowless room below
ground level surprised him not at all. Sunlight baked
both parchment and vellum to a brittle fragility,
sucked the moisture from bindings, and faded ink.
For certain kinds of books, books whose contents
were meant to remain in shadow, sunlight was more
dangerous still.

"Aurek! You're going to turn into a mushroom if
you spend all your time sitting here in the dark!"

"I have lamps. . . ."

Natalia laughed and pulled him to his feet. "You
need to get out into the sun and do something."

He stood motionless while the memory passed, afraid to move lest he lose it, for memories were almost all he had left.

Almost.

He cursed the circumstances that had forced him to finally respond to his wife's frequent request that he do something, and he would have cursed himself, except that there seemed to be no point.

And I'm wasting time. The artifact he sought, the artifact that might change his Natalia back to flesh and blood, was in this room. Fortunately, though it may have once held thousands of volumes, the room was nearly empty.

Rust-brown beetles as big around as his thumb scurried out of his way as he systematically searched the shelves, sifting through and ignoring worm-riddled bits of moldering books and scrolls. Once, he might have been interested in these fragmented leavings of another's scholarship, but life no longer allowed him that luxury. Finally, just as he'd begun to fear that only the signature of the artifact had survived and not the artifact itself, he found what he searched for tucked into a corner of a lower shelf, buried under a messy nest of chewed parchment and insect droppings. The slim, leather-bound book, barely as large as his palm, sizzled against his fingertips with a familiar sensation of not-quite-pain.

Resting on one knee, the lantern on the floor beside him, Aurek murmured his wife's name as though it were a talisman and carefully opened the book.

The wards that had protected it for so long against the living had been unable to keep out the damp. Many of the upper pages were stuck together, the ink spread out in patterns only marginally similar to the original handwriting. The last few pages had dissolved entirely and clumped against the back cover in a foul-smelling, gelatinous mass.

But in the middle of the book there were pages that could be read. Aurek's pale eyes burned as he stared down at the most legible of these; as he stared down at the words that might possibly hold the key to unlock Natalia's prison.

He heard the silence first, the sudden and complete absence of the insect noises that had provided a constant background hum since he entered the house.

Lips pressed together in irritation, he quickly pulled out a gray silk bag and slid the slender volume inside. Wrapping the excess fabric firmly around it, he tucked it safely down into a corner of the pack, slipped his arms back through the straps, and rose to his feet. That he'd expected this interruption made it no less annoying.

At least I have the artifact, he thought. As soon as he dealt with whatever was approaching, he'd be able to return to the privacy of his study to find out just exactly what he had.

Holding the lantern at arm's length, he caught sight of a humped shadow just at the periphery of the light. Rats. He'd have been more surprised had he not run into rats in the abandoned houses of Pont-a-Museau, all things considered. He took a step forward, and the light reflected from a multitude of eyes—most a great deal farther from the floor than he'd expected.

Not only rats—giant rats. Anxious to return to his study, he scowled at what had become an unavoidable delay.

Flexing the fingers of his free hand, he contemplated the most effective use of the defense he'd prepared. As the rats were now between him and the only stairs he'd found, fire might be somewhat self-defeating, given that it would cut off his own retreat. However, if giant rats were anything like their smaller cousins, killing a few should scatter the rest. Primar-

ily scavengers, rats tended to prefer survival over
valor and seldom attacked prey that fought back.

Then, just as he was about to speak, the largest rat
he'd ever seen moved to the edge of the light. Noting
the obvious similarities between it and the six that
had attacked Dmitri made Aurek's lip curl. Wererat.
It sat back on glossy black haunches and lifted glittering green eyes to his.

Aurek let his hand fall back to his side, the gesture
he'd been about to make now forgotten. He'd seen
those eyes before, and the notch bitten from the right
ear confirmed his incredulous identification. His skin
crawled, and he stepped back, repelled. It was one
thing to know that a beautiful woman was capable of
changing into an immense rodent and another thing
entirely to be brought face-to-face with the physical
evidence.

Unfortunately, Louise Renier wanted him.

She wanted him today for games entirely different
than those she'd wanted him for last night, but her
expression hadn't changed a great deal. He took a
moment to consider how extraordinary that was,
given the difference in her features. Then, all at
once, he realized he was truly in mortal danger.

Aurek knew hate when he saw it. This wasn't a
chance meeting, paths crossing by accident as both
hunted in an abandoned building. It was personal.
But why? Searching desperately for reason behind
the hate, Aurek finally decided it could only be a
result of rejecting Louise's advances at the party.
Surely she didn't kill every man who turned her
down? Perhaps no one ever had. Or perhaps she did.
Here and now, it didn't much matter.

"It is important that we take care of our families."

Remembering Jacqueline Renier's warning, Aurek
knew that if he saved himself today by injuring her
twin, the promise of Pont-a-Museau, a promise

strengthened by the book in his pack, would be closed to him. He doubted Jacqueline could actually kill him, but she could deny him Richemulot.

He could easily defeat the rats.

He didn't know what to do about Louise Renier.

He had to remain in Pont-a-Museau. The mist had abandoned magic in the ruins, perhaps the magic he was so desperately seeking. Freeing Natalia had become all that he cared about.

He would kill if it became necessary to free his wife. Not killing—and surviving—would be much harder.

"Mamselle," he called, "if I have insulted you in any way, I apologize."

"You don't know how you insulted me?" The voice from beyond the circle of light was incredulous—and faintly sibilant, as though she hadn't bothered to change all the way back to human form.

"I can assume only that my refusal to . . . to . . ." He paused, and tried again. "It's just that I loved my wife so very much. I intended no insult to you."

His only answer was a serrated trill of malicious laughter. Obviously, she didn't care what he'd intended.

As he could discover no way of getting by her without hurting her, and as she wouldn't listen to reason, Aurek reluctantly accepted the only possible solution. He flung himself toward the library's second door—not the one he'd come in through but one that led deeper into the building—and he ran.

* * * * *

Satisfied that Aurek Nuikin had recognized who held his life, Louise dropped to all fours. She was going to take her time with the scholar's death, and she was going to enjoy every moment of it.

She laughed again and changed, woman flowing into rat in a grotesque metamorphosis. She was pleased to see him run. He couldn't win the race, but it would add to the fun she planned to have with him before he died.

* * * * *

The narrow flight of stairs angled steeply down into the cellars. Aurek paused for a heartbeat to check his footing and found the top three treads no longer existed. Heart pounding, he leapt over the hole, felt the fourth splinter under his weight, slammed his shoulder into the damp stone wall, and somehow managed to keep his feet. The rats had gone through the walls and cut him off. He had no choice but to go down.

He hadn't seen Louise Renier again, but he could feel the heat of her hate on his back.

Lantern flickering ominously, the oil nearly spent, he dashed along the heavy beams that were, in places, all that remained of the floor. From the smell rising up through gaping holes outlined in bloated half-circles of fungus, the sewers were directly below.

The wall he soon arrived at was, unfortunately, much more solid than the floor.

Too late, he realized the stairs were the only way in or out, and the stairs had become a seething mass of rats. Cornered, Aurek turned to face them in time to see Louise Renier descend. Flanked by the giant rats she commanded, the wererat started across the room toward him.

If he fought and was destroyed, all was lost.

If he fought and won—and to win he must kill the lord of Richemulot's twin—all was also lost.

Rats were still coming down the stairs, and now they'd begun to climb up from the sewers as well.

Aurek found himself wondering how Louise controlled her lesser cousins, if some sort of telepathy occurred between the wererats and the rest. He had to force his attention back to his own safety. Answers would have to wait. For now, the only question had to be survival.

There was nowhere else to run. The ceilings in the mist-created buildings were high, even deep in the cellars—too high for him to reach the room above. He pressed his shoulder hard against the damp and unyielding stone that held him trapped. If only he knew what was on the other side. . . . But he didn't.

He would have to fight.

All other choices had been taken from him.

He turned to face the wererat, fascinated in spite of himself by the similarities between this animal and the woman who had tried to seduce him less than twenty-four hours before.

Rats continued to pour into the room.

The floor shuddered under their combined weight.

Squealing in fury, a rat dropped onto his shoulder from above. Without thinking, he plucked it off and flung it in the wererat's face.

He missed.

She'd moved, almost too quickly for a human eye to follow, and now she stood less than an arm's length away, gazing up at him, their position a perverted mockery of the way they'd stood at Joelle Milette's party.

Whatever he did, whatever the outcome, Aurek knew it destroyed the chance that Pont-a-Museau represented for Natalia.

*　*　*　*　*

Louise reveled in the despair on the scholar's face. Terror would have been good but, now that she saw it, despair was better. Hissing softly, she began to rise up onto her haunches.

With a screech of tortured timber, the center of the floor collapsed.

Rats fell, squealing, into the sewer. Those near enough to the edges of the hole surged forward, adding their weight to wood already stressed. The collapse spread.

Louise felt the floor beneath her hind feet begin to break away. She whipped her tail forward, found her balance, and lost it again when a giant rat, driven by panic, slammed its weight against her legs.

Shrieking in fury, she plunged, tangled in a mess of rats and splintered wood, into the fetid water below.

Manic rage insisted she deal first with the rat that had caused her to slip. By the time it had been rendered into an unrecognizable mass of blood and bone, everything that was likely to fall had fallen. Chunks of broken wood floated with less savory flotsam and, up above, jagged stumps jutted out mere inches from the walls.

Her anger barely abated by the slaughter of the giant rat, Louise searched for Aurek Nuikin. Had he survived the fall uninjured—that in itself was unlikely considering the splinted wood and rusted spikes now in the water—he couldn't have gone far.

Except that it appeared he had.

Shaking a patina of stinking algae from her fur, she climbed up onto a protruding masonry block and surveyed the sewer. Nothing. Not Nuikin, nor his body, nor even his scent.

Eyes narrowed, she looked up.

The joints between the stones in the cellar walls fitted smoothly together. He could not have clung to safety.

Lips drawn back off her teeth, she began to climb.

No floor remained where he'd been cornered.

Tail lashing the air, she climbed the holes that had once held the stairs and sat at last on the threshold of the floor above. Whiskers twitching, she delicately sniffed the rotting wood and found his scent both over and under hers. Her nose curled as she caught a faint trace of the power that had lingered by the crushed corpse of the spider.

He had gone down into the cellar.

She had followed.

He had, somehow, left.

Claws shredding the wood beneath her, her body lengthened, bone and muscle and ligament stretching to the form between rat and human that, being neither, gave her the most use of both. Staring down into the pit Aurek Nuikin had so impossibly risen out of, she spat and derisively snarled, "Mere ssscholar indeed."

 **THREE**

Aurek pushed his hair back off his face and was astonished to notice his hand trembling. If it hadn't been for the leather loop he'd held in his hand as the floor collapsed and the accompanying spell . . . He sat and stared at his trembling fingers for a moment, then slowly laid the piece of leather on the empty desk in front of him. Fate had intervened back in the cellar of that abandoned house, had cast Louise Renier away without him having to raise a hand. Perhaps that was a good omen. Perhaps it meant he was destined to find the answer he sought in Pont-a-Museau.

Perhaps the answer was in the book he'd risked so much to discover.

His pack rested on the corner of desk, where it had remained since he'd returned to the house nearly an hour before. He could feel the book from where he sat, had been able to feel it while he washed and changed into sweeter-smelling clothes. It wasn't the power of the book he could feel, but the book itself— its potential.

Until he opened it, that potential continued to exist, and with it, hope. While he delayed, he held hope trapped. The moment he knew, hope was gone, and each time he found it again it returned to him less willingly.

But the book might hold the answer, and hope was the price he had to pay.

Wearily, Aurek closed his eyes. When he opened them after pulling a long breath in and pushing it out again, he called himself several kinds of fool. You don't look because you're afraid it might be nothing, and your fear keeps you from possibly discovering the nightmare is finally over.

Hands barely steady, he yanked open the mouth of the pack.

A moment later, the small leather-bound book lay on the gray silk bag in the exact center of his desk. He had removed all surviving wards, checked for more subtle protections, and lifted a small, clear crystal from a rosewood box tucked into a desk drawer. Murmuring under his breath—the words merely needed to be said, it wasn't necessary to say them loudly—he passed the crystal over the book from left to right. Finally, nothing remained to be done save actually folding back the cover.

The first few pages had been marbled, front and back, with dissolved ink. Here and there he could make out what might have been the swoop of a letter and once an entire word could be read intact and out of context. The closer he came to the middle of the book, however, the less extensive the water damage and the more legible the handwriting.

While there was nothing about the writing that resembled his own less than legible style, he saw similarities in the way the unknown writer had used all the available space—pages were filled top and bottom and out to each margin, the waxed thread of the spine sewn as close to the text as possible.

. . . in order to change that which is . . .

His heart began beating with such force that he

thought it might burst through his ribs.

. . . to change that which is . . .

The next few words were damaged but not completely illegible. He found four *p*'s and what he thought was a pair of *s*'s. A combination that might have been *hr* or *br* perhaps even *ak*. His hands were sweating, and he continually wiped them on his thighs lest he mark the pages and cause further damage. Circular letters were the worst for *a*'s and *o*'s were virtually identical.

His eyes burned with fatigue when he finally realized what he'd found.

. . . in order to change that which is copper or brass temporarily to gold, the caster must possess either a citrine, a piece of amber free of flaw, or a tiger's eye no smaller than the smallest nail on the caster's hand.

No need to puzzle out the rest, he knew how it ended.

Hope fled. His spirits fell as far as they had risen. He scanned the rest of the book because it would be foolish not to—and for all that he was, he was not a foolish man—but he knew he'd find nothing he needed. He closed it carefully when he finished, pushed it gently to one side, and slammed both fists down onto the desk.

"My love is snatched from my side and trapped in an existence too horrible to contemplate, and now I am taunted with useless magics! Why do the fates conspire against me?"

Hands clasped behind his neck, he rested his forehead on the desk. He didn't expect the fates to answer; they had spoken when his Natalia had chosen the wrong moment to open his study door.

For her sake, he had to go on.

Straightening, he drew in a long, shuddering breath, wiped the moisture from his eyes, and drew a clean sheet of parchment across the desk. He always preferred to use parchment over paper or vellum; its properties were easier to control than those of the latter, and it absorbed power longer than the former. Dipping a fresh-cut pen into the inkwell, he began meticulously copying the fragments that could still be salvaged from the damaged book.

Outside the study window, the raucous cries of ravens became wild laughter.

Oh, yes, a hated voice murmured in his heart, *start to build your spellbook again. I am dead, but there will always be others. After all, you foolishly believed that you had protections enough the last time. What else that you claim to love can you destroy?*

Crying out in anger and grief, Aurek leapt to his feet, the chair crashing to the floor behind him. The voice—the fiendish, remorseless, loathsome voice was right. He could not, *would* not allow his arrogance to be responsible for yet more pain and suffering.

Snatching up the book and the sheet he'd begun to fill, he raced across the room and, with all his strength—had he used less than all, he didn't think he could have done it—he threw them both on the fire. Then he stood and stared, wide-eyed, unable to believe what he'd just done.

The impact spilled embers and ash out onto the hearth. The parchment caught almost immediately. Pale flames licked cleanly over the lower half of the page, flaring suddenly when they reached the ink. The few words he'd actually copied burned with a fierce white light—hot enough to feel from where he stood—that ignited the book.

The explosion shouldn't have taken him by surprise, but it did. A piece of shattered andiron slammed into his shoulder, spinning him about and dropping him to his knees. He welcomed the pain, accepted it as penance for what he'd nearly begun.

Still on his knees, blood soaking into his shirt and trickling warmly over his chest, he crawled to the pedestal and clasped it in trembling arms. Eyes closed, he laid his cheek against the wood, tears staining the pale grain.

"I will find it, Lia. I promise you, my love, I will find it!"

An observer in the room would have seen, by some appalling trick of the light, the porcelain statue that was Aurek's wife appear to stare down at him in horror.

* * * * *

His cheeks pale and his eyes still slightly blood-shot, Dmitri made his way carefully downstairs, having convinced himself that his measured tread had nothing to do with the weakness in his knees and everything to do with rotten wood found throughout the house. Arriving safely at the bottom, he took a deep breath, twitched his jacket into place, and glanced up to meet Edik's steady stare.

He thought he managed to hide his reaction reasonably well, having jumped back only half a step—a movement that could have any number of explanations. "Have you seen Aurek?" he asked, sounding not quite as nonchalant as he would've liked.

The servant slowly swept his gaze down the length of Dmitri's body and back up again. Dmitri tried not to fidget; to even notice the insolence would give the other man more power than he already had.

"He's in his study," Edik said at last, the undertone in his voice clearly adding, *and you are not to disturb him.*

Dmitri knew the subtext well; he'd heard it all his life. When he was younger, he'd tried to make friends with his brilliant older brother, but whatever went on in the study had always come first. Aurek was not to be disturbed. Aurek had important things to do. Obviously, whatever went on in the study was more important to Aurek than he was. Only during those years when Natalia had been a part of his brother's life had the study door ever opened—and then it had opened for her, not for him. As much as he liked the laughing young woman Aurek had married, that had hurt.

"Are you going out, young master?"

"Yes. I'm going out." And if Edik tried to stop him, they'd soon settle who was master and who servant.

But Edik only looked disapproving and said, "Are you certain you are well enough?"

Stupid old mother hen. "I'm fine."

"Have you told your brother that you are going out?"

"I can hardly tell Aurek anything if he's in his study, now can I?" Grinning triumphantly, he swept past Edik and out the door.

* * * * *

"Yves. Look there."

"Don't poke at me, Chantel." Yves swiped at his face with his sleeve. "I really hate it when you do that."

She poked him again, digging the point of her fingernail viciously into his side. "Then look at who's walking right toward us."

"If I look," he snarled, "will you stop poking me?"

"It's the Nuikin," Georges announced, leaning around the twins in order to see. "He seems to have survived his swim."

Yves half-turned, his neck twisting at an angle no human neck could have sustained, then he picked up a pastry and stared at it thoughtfully. "Chantel, you and Annette go and get him. Bring him here."

"Are you crazy?" Chantel stared across the cluttered café table at him. "After what happened last night?"

"Are you trying to get us in trouble with Herself?" Annette added incredulously.

"The trouble with you lot is, you never think. Point one: Herself is interested in the lad. Point two: he's out without his brother. Point three: something'll chew his face off in less than a week if we just let him wander around the city by himself." Yves flicked a finger into the air to mark each point. "Point four: if we take him under our wing, so to speak, he'll survive and Herself will be happy."

"Point five," Georges muttered around a mouthful of half-chewed food, "when Herself is happy, we're all a lot happier."

"My point exactly." Yves leaned forward and glared at Chantel and Annette. "So, go and get him."

"Why us?"

"Because with you two hanging on his arms, he's not likely to start thinking with what's between his ears."

*　*　*　*　*

Dmitri saw the two young women approaching through the gathering dusk and wondered, briefly, if he should turn around and walk the other way. Then warm, yielding flesh pressed itself up against both sides of his body and it was too late.

"Are you all right?" Chantel asked.

"We were so worried about you," Annette added.

Chantel leaned closer. "You were out too far for us to reach so we ran for help, but when we got back your brother had already rescued you."

"You went away," Dmitri said slowly. His memory of what had happened the night before was foggy, but that, at least, he was fairly certain of. All six of them had gone away and left him alone.

"A stupid joke that almost went terribly wrong," Chantel placed soft fingers against his jaw and turned his face toward her own. "Please say you'll forgive us."

Staring down into her eyes, Dmitri suddenly realized they weren't brown, they were red, and hair he'd seen in candlelight as a pale blonde—paler even than Aurek's—was actually a completely colorless white, as were her brows and lashes. Rising out of memory came an image of a white shape in the water, a white shape that held him as he struggled to reach the surface.

"Please," she repeated, her hand closing like a heated band around his arm.

He had to swallow hard before he could assure them both that they were forgiven. The next thing he knew, they were leading him into an outdoor café built on a landing carved into the side of the riverbank. It was crowded in spite of an autumn chill in the air. Then Yves was standing and clasping his hand, Georges stopped eating long enough to shove food and drink toward him, and the twins were shuffling chairs to make room for him at the table.

A few moments later, after apologies and reassurances had been exchanged all around, Yves asked him if he was attending the evening's party.

"Another party?" Dmitri asked around a mouthful of pastry. He noticed that the waiters were all extremely attentive of his friends, and he very much liked being included in that attention.

"There are always parties at this time of the year in Pont-a-Museau," Chantel told him. "In the summer it's too hot and in the winter it's too cold, so in the spring and fall we make up for lost time. Don't you like to party, Dmitri?"

"Of course I do." He flushed. "But I haven't been invited. . . ."

Yves clapped him on the shoulder just a little too hard. "We just invited you. You'll come with us."

"Aurek . . ."

"You don't have to ask his permission, do you?"

Dmitri bridled. "Of course not."

"Good." With a fastidious thumb and forefinger, Yves pulled Dmitri's brocade vest a little way from his body. "This might be the height of fashion in Borca," he sniffed derisively, "but it doesn't work here. First thing we've got to do is get you some decent clothes."

* * * * *

Cinching a broad cloth-of-gold belt around her narrow waist, Louise preened in front of her mirror. Over the course of the afternoon, as she'd thought about what had happened in the cellar of the abandoned house, her fury had turned to speculation.

A mere scholar could not have avoided the collapse of the cellar floor. A mere scholar would have fallen into the sewer and under her claws and would, at this moment, be providing sustenance for any number of lesser creatures.

Therefore, Aurek Nuikin was not a mere scholar. All the evidence suggested he was something far more—which not only explained his survival in the cellar, but also her twin's interest in him. Jacqueline had always been drawn to power.

It was, in fact, a family weakness.

And it was time for a change of lord in Richemulot.

If Aurek Nuikin was more than he appeared, she had a use for him.

Smiling, she hung gleaming gold balls from each ear, then twitched the shoulders of her gown just a little lower. Until she had more information, she would not approach Nuikin himself—the potential risk was too great, and she was too fond of her skin to risk any of it. Touching her throat lightly with scent, she decided he would have to be reached through those around him.

Right through those around him, if it came to it. Someone else could clean up the mess.

Throwing a gauzy shawl around her shoulders, she hurried out of her suite and nearly ran over her nephew in the hall.

Jacques looked at her critically with emerald eyes irritatingly like his mother's and finally smiled.

"You look very pretty, Tante Louise."

He was obviously sucking up. Louise wondered what he wanted.

"Where are you going?"

"Hunting," she replied with a cold, unencouraging smile.

"May I come?"

"No." She swept the gold-bead-encrusted hem of her skirt around his small body and continued along the corridor.

Right after I remove my sister, she vowed silently, I take care of her brat.

*　*　*　*　*

Occasionally, the fates are willing to cooperate, Louise thought as she watched the golden-haired young man swirl past on the dance floor, his arms around a third—no, fourth—cousin. Dmitri Nuikin was attending the evening's festivities without the protection of his older brother. How nice.

Absently accepting a glass of wine from one of her regular circle—a circle made slightly smaller by the absence of Geraud—Louise noticed Dmitri's new clothes. It appeared, given the familiar appearance of the glittering rags and tatters now fluttering from broad shoulders and smoothly muscled arms, that certain younger members of the family had decided to play with him for a while. The white hair of the girl he danced with was unmistakable: Chantel. And if Chantel was involved, could the rest of her little clique be far away?

She crooked a finger and a portly man, his face gleaming with sweat, leapt forward. "Find Yves Milette," she commanded. "Tell him I want to speak with him."

Nearly babbling in his amazement at being asked to serve, the portly man hurried off, almost knocking over a stout matron in a purple turban who happened to be in his way. He returned a moment later, a sullen Yves in tow.

A curt gesture and the circle faded back, giving Louise and Yves as much privacy as possible. Those who were not able to go far enough, given the press of the crowds, immediately fell into covering conversations with their neighbors. Those who overheard Renier family business seldom profited by it. Or survived it.

"I didn't do anything," Yves announced, scowling.

"Of course you did, you always do, but as it happens, I don't care." Louise smiled poisonously at him. "I want to talk to you about your new little playmate."

"What? Dmitri?" His eyes narrowed. "What about him?"

"I don't want him hurt."

"We weren't going to . . ."

She reached out and lightly closed her hand around his arm. "Don't treat me like a fool, Yves. You wouldn't enjoy the consequences."

Yves swallowed and hastily shook his head. "I'm not. I wouldn't think of it. We just thought that we should protect him, you know, from things, because Jacqueline seemed interested. . . ."

"*I* am interested." Her grip tightened, and the points of her nails pierced his skin through a rent torn in the wide sleeve of his shirt. "I am interested," she repeated, "and that should be all that concerns you now."

"Yes, Louise." He wanted to jerk his arm away, but he knew better. His defiant posture softened to submission. "But I thought, that is, we thought you were interested in the other one."

She shook her head, ebony curls whispering across the back of her neck. "Don't think. You'll live longer."

"Yes, Louise."

"As it happens, I am interested in the other one. I'm interested in *both* of them." The delicate arch of one brow lifted higher. "Do you have a problem with that?"

"No, Louise."

"Good." A final squeeze for emphasis, then she released his arm. "Continue protecting him. He's just the type to attract disaster, and I can't be with him all the time." She bestowed an approving smile on her young cousin. "You may even play with him if you like. I'll ignore the odd scratch or bruise, but I don't want him hurt. Do you understand?"

Yves nodded. "Yes, Louise."

"Bring him to see me a little later. Prime him. I want him . . . malleable before he gets here."

Malleable? He thought of how Chantel and Annette had maneuvered Dmitri into the café without really trying. How the human accepted everything said to him at face value, questioning nothing. "That shouldn't be difficult."

"Good."

Recognizing a dismissal, Yves bowed, thankful to be getting off so lightly, and hurriedly retreated.

* * * * *

"What was all that about?" Chantel demanded as Yves finally threaded his way back through the crowds surrounding the dance floor. Although she tried to sound imperious, her voice squeaked out, tight with worry. Attracting that much attention from either of the Renier sisters was never a good idea and usually not entirely healthy.

Having handed Dmitri over to the fawning care of Joelle when she saw Yves summoned to an audience with Louise, Chantel had joined the protective clump the others had formed in a defensible corner. For the younger members of the family, no longer afforded the neutrality of children but with their positions not yet established within the hierarchy, numbers were their only safety.

Wishing that he were closer to the buffet, Georges took a fortifying swallow of wine.

Yves snorted, snatched the tarnished goblet from his cousin's hand, and downed the contents. "We're not to hurt the little Nuikin," he said, wiping his mouth on the back of his hand. "She wants him."

Georges looked out to where Dmitri was circling the dance floor with Yves's sister. "But I thought she wanted the other one."

"She wants them both." Yves rubbed his arm, wondering how long the memory of her touch would linger. "And we're not to think. She says we'll live longer."

Aubert and Henri wore identical concerned expressions. Considering the source, it was not a threat to be taken lightly.

"What about Herself?" Annette wondered, dark brows drawn into a deep **V** over her nose.

"Jacqueline's not here, and Louise is," Yves reminded them. "And unless Herself gives us a direct order . . ." He didn't have to finish the sentence. Even together, they weren't strong enough to stand up to Louise Renier. Leaning back against the wall, he told them the rest of what Louise had said.

When he finished, Chantel's lips had lifted off her teeth. "I hate being told what to do."

Georges shrugged philosophically. "It sounds as if she's told us to do pretty much what we were going to do anyway."

"It's the principle of the thing," Chantel snarled. "She told us what to do."

Yves laughed humorlessly. "So *you* tell her we won't."

Chantel half-turned, and for one heart-stopping moment her cousins thought she was actually going to confront Louise. Then she sighed and shook her head. "Only Herself can argue with her sister." All at once, she smiled and repeated, "Only Herself."

Yves quickly drank another glass of wine and grumpily contemplated how much Chantel's smile was beginning to look like Louise's.

* * * * *

"She wants to meet me?"

"That's what she said." Yves dug Dmitri in the ribs with his elbow, just a little too hard. "She thinks you're pretty *capiteuse*."

"Capiteuse?" Dmitri frowned. "What does that mean?"

"Hot."

"Me?"

"You."

Dmitri's hands went to where the edge of his vest should be, found only a tattered fringe of fabric, and tugged at that instead. "Actually, your sister introduced me to her last night."

"Well, you obviously made quite the impression." A hand in the small of the back steered Dmitri around a gossiping cluster of fat and prosperous townsmen. "She couldn't take her eyes off you."

"Really?"

"Would I lie to you?"

Dmitri paused. Something in the tone of Yves's voice answered his own question—and the answer was: "Any chance I get." He's your friend, Dmitri reminded himself, and he hasn't lied to you yet. You're doing him an injustice.

"The thing to remember about Cousin Louise," Yves continued as they crossed the last bit of open floor before they reached the outer edge of the circle of fawning admirers surrounding her, "is that she can have any man she wants, and she told me, she wants you."

"Me?"

"You." He shoved Dmitri forward, hard enough to make him stumble. Wouldn't that be funny? he mused. The little Nuikin throwing himself at her feet.

Dmitri took an extra step to keep from falling and suddenly found himself face-to-face with Louise Renier. She's so beautiful. He took another step, Yves forgotten. And she wants me?

Reading his thoughts from his face—as hard as it was to believe, he really seemed to be almost completely without guile—Louise drifted toward him, hands outstretched. "You came," she said softly. "I'm so pleased."

Cheeks flushed, Dmitri took both her hands in his and pressed his lips first against one and then the other. He couldn't remember ever feeling quite so adept. "You have only to command," he murmured, mesmerized by her smile.

* * * * *

Some time later, Chantel and Yves leaned on a worm-eaten banister and stared down into the entry-way as Dmitri laid Louise's gauzy shawl across her shoulders, tucked her hand up in his arm, and led her out of the house.

"That seems to be working out," Yves muttered irritably, picking off pieces of the flaking paint and letting them fall to the tile floor below.

"She sure knows the strings to pull," Chantel agreed, her expression half admiring, half annoyed. "I just hope she remembers that we had him first."

"Oh, definitely," Yves sneered. "I mean, Louise cares so much about what we think. Let him go, Chantel. The best we can hope for now is that she leaves a few leftovers lying around for us."

Chantel straightened. "I don't want Louise Renier's leftovers!"

Rolling his eyes, Yves wondered why the women in the family were all so dangerously extreme.

* * * * *

A candle had been left burning on the hall table. Dmitri threw the trio of bolts that secured the door and gratefully picked it up. He hadn't been looking forward to making his way up steep and not entirely secure stairs in the dark. Limping slightly, he crossed the hall and actually had one foot in the air when Aurek's voice said softly, "Do you know what time it is?"

He turned, careful not to let the candlelight fall too fully in his eyes, and peered through the shadows. Aurek was standing in the doorway to the sitting room, arms folded on his chest, pale hair loose over his shoulders.

"After midnight?" he answered brightly.

"Long after. It's nearly dawn." Aurek stepped away from the wall, expression stern. "Where have you been?"

Dmitri smiled. "I have been to paradise."

"Paradise?"

"That's right." Louise Renier had made him feel as though he were the most important man in the world. He wasn't going to let his brother steal that feeling away. "I was with a beautiful woman." His voice rose and picked up a sardonic tone. "And I was doing things you've only dreamed of."

"Does this woman have a name?" Aurek asked grimly.

Dmitri tossed his head. "A gentleman doesn't kiss and tell."

"A gentleman doesn't brag either," Aurek reminded him.

"I wasn't bragging." But he had to let Aurek know. Had to throw it in his face. "What you think," he said, "doesn't matter, because Louise Renier had no complaints."

Louise Renier. Aurek felt as though he were going to be sick. The thought of his younger brother and that . . . that *thing* was worse than he possibly could have imagined. "Stay away from her." He had to force the warning through the bile in his throat.

There was something in Aurek's voice—something very like revulsion—that Dmitri refused to acknowledge. "Why?" he asked. "Because she's older than I am? If she doesn't consider it, why should you?"

"It's not because she's older." The Lord of Richemulot had said Dmitri was not to be told. And he'd agreed. But that was before . . . "She's dangerous."

"So?" Dmitri tossed his head. "I can handle her."

Aurek gave a sudden, humorless bark of laughter. If Dmitri were told, he would lose Pont-a-Museau. Lose the hope it offered. "You have no idea . . ."

"I think I do."

He would have to be told. This couldn't continue.

Natalia, forgive me. But he snapped his mouth closed when Dmitri continued talking.

"You may be happy worshiping at a shrine to your dead wife," he scoffed, "but some of us prefer women of flesh and blood."

The silence that followed was so complete, Dmitri could hear the candle flame hiss as it devoured the twisted nub of wick, could hear the blood pounding through the throbbing vein in Aurek's temple. He knew he'd gone too far, knew he'd rubbed salt in a wound still open and raw. He didn't know why he'd said it; the anger at this sudden interference after so many years of indifference had risen up and taken over his mouth. He wanted to take it back, but he had no idea how.

And then it didn't matter.

His face twisted in pain, Aurek pushed past him, took the stairs two at a time, and disappeared into the darkness above. A moment later, Dmitri heard the door to his study open and close.

"Fine," he snarled, wishing he could go outside and come in again and do it all over. "Don't let me apologize. See if I care."

*   *   *   *   *

"Has he found anything?" Louise asked, running her ankle along Dmitri's calf under the cover of the table. "I mean, he's out rummaging through abandoned buildings, all day, every day. He must've found *something*."

Distracted by the heated contact, it took Dmitri a moment to find his voice. "I don't think he's found anything," he said hoarsely. "He wouldn't tell me, anyway."

"Why not? Is he afraid you'll steal his secrets?"

"Secrets?" Dmitri shook his head. "He doesn't

have any secrets."

Louise moistened her lips. "All men have secrets."

Tugging at the black cravat spilling out from under the points of his collar, Dmitri had to look away. He swept his gaze over the other patrons of the tiny café and noticed—without really understanding—that they were all carefully directing their attention away from the shadowy corner where he sat with Louise. Her hand closed around his wrist almost uncomfortably tight as she repeated her belief that all men had secrets.

"Not Aurek."

"What, no hidden necromancy in the dark of the moon?"

Dmitri laughed, careful to make sure his companion knew he wasn't laughing at her. For such a beautiful woman, she was very insecure—and quick to anger because of it. Yves had told him that he'd been lucky to have lost only a small bit of skin where it wouldn't show. "All Aurek's interested in is cramming more useless bits of information into his head. He's a scholar. He's always got ink on his fingers from copying and annotating, and he never actually does anything but make notes."

"Are you sure?"

"Positive." But under the glittering compulsion of her eyes, he told her everything he knew about Aurek's life. He discovered he didn't know much. In Borca, Aurek had lived in the country, while Dmitri had spent most of his time at the family's townhouse. Now, Dmitri spent most of his days asleep and his nights partying with either his friends or Louise. He often saw a light beneath the study door, but he seldom saw his brother.

"I wonder . . ." Louise flicked her nails against the empty oyster shells piled on a tray between them. ". . . how his wife died."

Dmitri shrugged. "A thief got into Aurek's study, maybe a wizard, I don't know. No one ever tells me anything," he added, his tone sulky, remembering how he'd paced up and down the garden paths for what seemed like hours, waiting for Natalia to return with his brother. Finally, he'd gotten fed up, certain Aurek was refusing to leave his precious studies, and had ridden back to town. He found out what had happened the next day, when Edik sent a message to his sisters. "Natalia walked in on the fight, and her body was destroyed. Aurek won't talk about it."

Her smile made him feel short of breath. "Then he does have a secret, doesn't he?"

* * * * *

Dmitri paused outside the dining room door and smoothed his vest. Knowing Aurek didn't care for them, he'd given up Pont-a-Museau styles for the evening. He didn't know why he should feel like an intruder in what was, after all, his own home, but he did. If Louise hadn't wanted to know the answer so badly, he doubted he'd have found the courage to go in.

Which is ridiculous, he told himself, opening the door. What's he going to do? Spill ink on me?

Aurek, sitting at the far end of a long table, looked up in surprise when Dmitri entered, but said nothing.

The silence lengthened, thickened, and Dmitri's voice when he finally spoke sounded unnaturally shrill. "I thought I'd eat at home this evening."

Reaching behind him for the bellpull, Aurek said only, "I'll have Edik set another place."

Dmitri took a deep breath and sat carefully down on one of the less rickety chairs. His brother was obviously going to make this as hard on him as possible. Smug and sanctimonious, I should've known. He watched Edik put down cutlery and china—none of the pieces matched—and waited until the servant left the room before asking, "So, uh, how goes the search?"

"It goes."

"Have you found what you're searching for?" Dmitri helped himself to some of the turtle soup steaming in a white tureen in the center of the table.

"No."

"Just what are you searching for Aurek? You've never said."

"Knowledge."

"Of what?" He threw down his spoon. "I mean, there's a lot of stuff out there that it's not healthy to know about, and if you're looking for something that could put you, or me, in danger, then I think I've got a right to be told."

Aurek stared out at him from under pale brows. "You," he said emphatically, "have put yourself in more danger than I ever could."

"Oh, it's that again, is it?" Dmitri shoved his chair back from the table and stood. Though Dmitri was about to slam out of the room, something in the set of his brother's shoulders stopped him. Never a large man, for all his height, Aurek had lost weight over the last few days, and it almost seemed possible to see grief scraping him thinner moment by moment. Impulsively, Dmitri reached out and touched him lightly on the back of one hand. "I'm sorry about what I said," he murmured. "I never meant to hurt you."

Turning his hand, Aurek grasped his brother's fingers for a moment, then gestured at his chair. "Your soup's getting cold."

They ate in an easier silence than had been between them for some time.

Edik had brought in the pudding when Dmitri decided he might as well ask. "Aurek, what really happened that afternoon in your study? How did Natalia die?"

How did Natalia die? Aurek stared blindly down the table, not seeing the dishes, the candles, anything in his line of sight. Blood roared in his ears. How did Natalia die?

"Aurek?"

Dmitri's voice faded. The dining room faded. Pont-a-Museau faded.

He was back in his study, sleeves rolled up, contentedly copying the contents of a battered scroll onto a new parchment page. Drawing in a deep breath, he smiled at the dusty scent of leather-bound books. Heavily laden shelves surrounded him on all four sides, leaving only enough space for a narrow door and a small window—and he had the window only because Natalia insisted he couldn't spend all his time sitting in the dark.

"Sunlight," he'd told her, "is bad for books."

"Lack of it will turn you into a mushroom." She'd gone up on her toes to kiss him and murmur against his mouth, "Do it for me?"

And so he had a window because, when it came right down to it, he could deny her nothing—especially not when she asked for so little.

"I could give you the world. . . ."

Her smile held all the world in it. "Give me your heart."

Separate from the other books, resting on a simple wooden pedestal, was his pride and joy. He could feel the power pulsing from it even from where he sat. It almost felt as though it had a life of its own. In its pages, carefully sewn to a red leather binding, were over a hundred spells, each carefully copied from a hundred different sources. Most were minor, practically common knowledge. Some were complex and beautiful and the result of a lifetime spent listening, searching, wanting to know. A few—a few were dark and perilous, and he didn't like to remember what he'd had to do to find them.

The book made his Natalia nervous, but he'd patiently explained how knowledge was the only thing in the world that was pure and untainted, and she'd laughed and believed him when he said there was no danger.

He dipped his quill and enjoyed the way the ink seemed almost to flow into words on its own. When the door opened behind him, he smiled and called out. "It can't possibly have been an hour already, my love. I've barely gotten started."

The blow to the back of his head took him completely by surprise. He grunted in pain, his face slammed down into the desk, and his hand knocked the inkwell flying across the room. Through the oblivion attempting to claim him, he saw a man hurrying toward the pedestal. Wild tufts of gray hair stood out from the intruder's head as he passed his hands rapidly back and forth over the book.

The sudden realization that his protections were failing gave Aurek strength enough to find his voice but, unfortunately, not much more. His attack bounced off the other man, gaining his attention but doing no damage.

"I guess I didn't hit you quite hard enough, did I?" The long, beardless face, the heavy-lidded eyes, the narrow nose and thin-lipped mouth, all belonged to a total stranger. "I abhor violence, but I found it impossible to resist in this instance. You were just so oblivious." One hand dropped into his pocket, and the other rose to shoulder height.

Aurek flung himself to the floor at the last possible instant, feeling the heat of the lightening bolt as it passed. Obviously, the thief had come prepared. Aurek fought to clear the pounding pain from his head as he felt another protection ripped aside.

Rising to his knees, he had time to see a gloved hand gesture in his direction, then he was brutally lifted and thrust back against the shelves, a massive, invisible weight crushing his chest. Gasping for breath, he struggled to remember.

He knew what to do if only he could concentrate, but the need to breathe kept shoving all other concerns aside.

Then the last of the protections fell, and the thief held the book. Laughing maniacally, he held it above his head and danced in place. "Power calls to power," he cried.

"Aurek?" Natalia stepped into the study and stared in confusion at the stranger. "Who are you?"

He smiled at her. "Fate," he said, and cradling the book against his chest, began to mutter quick syllables under his breath.

Aurek recognized the spell, though it was one so unpredictable he'd never dared to use it himself. When the wild-haired thief had gathered power enough to carry him, he'd be gone.

"What are you doing with my husband's book?" Natalia hadn't seen Aurek, pressed up against the wall. Brows pulled down, she advanced on the intruder. "Put it down! Now!"

He ignored her, but then he had to. If his focus wavered for even a moment . . .

All at once, Aurek felt the pressure on his chest ease as the power holding him was drawn away. The next instant, he dropped to his knees, sucking in great lungfuls of air.

He had no time for subtlety. Crawling forward, he scooped up the fallen inkwell and threw the carved stone with all his strength at the intruder's face.

It hit just as Natalia grabbed the arm holding the book.

The explosion lifted Aurek up and smacked him hard against the wall. He heard Natalia scream his name, he heard laughter—no longer merely maniacal but insane—then he heard nothing at all for some time. When he regained consciousness, he was alone in the study except for a corpse with a crushed temple . . . and a tiny porcelain statue—hands lifted in a futile attempt at protection, face twisted in horror—holding the soul of his wife.

Between the red leather covers of the book nothing remained but a fine, gray ash.

He'd told everyone Natalia had died in the attempted robbery. She was so fragile, so incredibly vulnerable; the lie would help to keep her safe.

He had to keep her safe. He had to find a way to free her.

"Aurek?"

Dmitri's voice calling his name pulled him back to the present, and he managed to focus on his brother's concerned face.

"Are you all right?"

He shook his head and reached for his wineglass, his throat too dry for words. With the glass halfway to his mouth, he saw the wild-haired wizard's face suddenly reflected in the liquid.

"Aurek?"

The reflection began to laugh.

"*NO!*" The glass shattered against the far wall, a deep purple stain dribbling down the plaster.

"Aurek! What's wrong?"

Breathing heavily, Aurek flung himself back from the table. "I don't want . . ." He closed his eyes and tried again. "I don't want to talk about it."

 **FOUR**

"So your brother doesn't want to talk about it."
Louise tilted her head and looked up at Dmitri from
under thick black lashes. "Doesn't he trust you?"

"It's not that."

"Then what is it?"

Unable to remain still, Dmitri leapt up off the garden bench and began to pace, his path delineated by
the spill of light that shone through the windows of
the house and turned the shadows of the dancers
inside into contorted silhouettes. "He just doesn't
want to talk to me about Natalia's death because it
still upsets him so much."

"Oh."

He recognized the tone. "You don't think that's the
reason, do you?"

"He's your brother." She stretched out a leg and
admired the way the moonlight shimmered in the
blue silk draped over her calf. "If you think that's the
reason . . ."

"What do you think?"

Alabaster shoulders lifted and fell in a graceful
shrug. "It doesn't matter."

"It does." He dropped to his knees by her side and

captured one of her hands in both of his. "Your opinion," he told her earnestly, "means more to me than life itself."

Carefully hidden in an overgrown tangle that was once a shrubbery, a white wererat rolled its eyes in disgust and mimed throwing up. The little Nuikin had a talent for saying the most nauseating things.

"It occurs to me . . ." Louise traced the line of his jaw with a fingernail, not quite hard enough to hurt. ". . . that a scholar would be more interested in sharing his discoveries. Spreading knowledge as it were. Teaching."

"Well, he's always been . . ."

"Secretive?"

Golden brows dipped down. He'd been about to say "private" but, staring into the emerald depths of Louise's eyes, secretive suddenly seemed the better word.

"He's definitely more than he appears," she mused, tapping her lower lip. "But the question is, how much more?"

"Why do you care?" Dmitri asked cautiously. He was ready to apologize in case he'd offended, but Louise's continuing interest in his brother had begun to bother him. Aurek this and Aurek that—"Why can't you be more like him?" "Why can't you be less like him?"—he'd heard nothing but Aurek from his sisters all his life. Louise was supposed to be interested in him, not in Aurek.

Louise heard the jealousy in his voice and hid a smile. "He frightens me," she said.

From the shrubbery, the white wererat stared at her cousin with openmouthed admiration. The little Nuikin didn't stand a chance.

"He spoke to me at Joelle's party," Louise continued, her hands clutching Dmitri's in heated entreaty. "And there's a taint of . . ." Her grip tightened, and she delivered her final pronouncement with no trace of self-consciousness. ". . . wizardry about him."

* * * * *

It wasn't until he stepped out over the ruins of the door that Aurek realized the hour had grown so late. The sun had obviously set some time before, and evening had nearly been overtaken by night. He shrugged his pack higher on his shoulders and carefully made his way down the crumbling townhouse stairs. There were families—or at the very least, people—living in the houses on either side, but the building he'd searched was empty. All the buildings he searched were empty. Apparently, the traces of power that drew him kept others away.

"Have you found anything of interest?" inquired a silken voice from the shadows.

His heart beating a little faster, Aurek turned and waited as Jacqueline Renier approached. She burned in the dusk like a black flame, and he wondered how many moths had scorched their wings flying too close. "I would have informed you if I had," he told her flatly, keeping any and all reaction completely hidden.

"Good. I appreciate a man who remembers his commitments." Falling into step beside him, she shot him an enigmatic look from under thick lashes. "But after all this time, you must have found something?"

"Little things," he admitted. "Broken things." Her silence seemed to pull a further explanation from him. "Today, I found a mirror." Whole, it would have been used for simple scrying. "Or, if you prefer, I found pieces of a mirror."

"Which you left where they were."

"I have no interest in mirrors." His lips pressed to a thin line, he waited for her to ask him where his interests lay.

But after a long pause, all she said was, "I can see that. You're growing a beard."

Aurek felt as though something had just slipped through his fingers, but he had no idea what it might have been. Until this moment, he'd had no doubt that Jacqueline Renier would take full advantage of any opening he might give her.

They walked together in an almost companionable silence and once, when a number of paving stones had disappeared from their path, leaving a rough and shallow hole, Aurek held out his arm, forgetting for that instant just who exactly he was with. Jacqueline looked down at the bend of his elbow in some astonishment, then, with a gurgle of laughter, allowed him to help her over the break.

At the bridge to Lacheur Island, she stopped, and he realized that she wasn't going to accompany him across. "You're a fascinating man, Aurek Nuikin, and not much fascinates me anymore." Her manner bordered on friendly as she extended her gloved hand.

He took it, and lightly brushed his lips over the knuckles. *Get your sister away from my brother.* The words hung in the back of his throat, but something stopped him from voicing them. The last thing he wanted to do was direct Jacqueline's attention to Dmitri. He found himself saying instead, "I was wondering, who took that piece out of Louise's ear?"

"I did." Jacqueline smiled at the memory. It wasn't a pleasant smile. "An uncle once said he couldn't tell us apart. Now he can."

She withdrew her hand, half turned, and murmured, "I hear that your wife is dead. How sad." When he made no reply, she added, "I'm sure you did all you could to prevent such an unfortunate . . . accident."

Natalia. He closed his eyes for an instant to deal with the sudden overwhelming feeling of guilt, and when he opened them again, Jacqueline was an impossible distance away. He watched, almost mesmerized, until her slim, black-clad figure blended with the shadows. "It is dangerous to walk alone at night in Pont-a-Museau," he said softly, but he meant the warning for the people of the city, not for Jacqueline Renier.

*   *   *   *   *

Hidden behind a faded but clean curtain, Dmitri peered out at the esplanade bordering the river in front of their house and tried unsuccessfully not to fidget. Its foundation undermined by the water, a considerable chunk of paving by the dock had collapsed, leaving a hole too wide to jump and impossible to avoid. There had been a rough plank bridge laid over it, but Dmitri had removed the boards earlier in the afternoon while Edik was busy in the kitchen.

Now, he waited for Aurek. He hated waiting, and he wasn't good at it.

When Aurek reached the hole, he'd have two choices: either do something wizardlike to get over it, or go a very long way around—not a pleasant prospect given the time and the reputation of the city.

It was almost full dark, the sky the deep sapphire that colored the moments between evening and night. It was also hours later than Aurek usually returned and, in spite of himself, Dmitri began to worry. Although the musicians did their nightly best to drown them out and everyone else seemed happy to ignore them, he was sure he'd heard screams rising like an incriminating counterpoint behind more than one evening's merrymaking.

Concern warring with irritation, he'd just decided to take a lantern out searching when he saw Aurek approaching, his pale hair ghostly in the shadows. Relief that the test would soon be complete overwhelmed any other emotions.

"Finally," he muttered, drawing back a little from

the window. "Now, we'll see."

The hole was a black pit in the gray stone. Aurek stopped on the far side, looked around for the boards, and threw up his hands in patent exasperation. He didn't seem surprised the bridge was missing, but then scavenging was Pont-a-Museau's leading industry.

"He's thinking about how late it's getting," Dmitri told himself as Aurek glanced at the sky. "And he's working out how far he'll have to walk if he goes around."

Dmitri planned to run out with the planks if Aurek decided to go around; he wanted to test his brother, not risk getting him killed. He didn't have a good explanation of why he'd removed the boards in the first place, but as Aurek never listened to him anyway, he supposed that didn't matter.

He shifted his weight from foot to foot as Aurek studied the pit and then methodically scanned the area. "He's checking to see that he's unobserved."

Apparently satisfied, Aurek slid his right hand into the pocket of his jacket and brought it out with something—it didn't look like a ring, but Dmitri was too far away to be sure—around his thumb. With the hand held parallel to the ground, he floated over the hole.

Dmitri felt his jaw drop.

*　*　*　*　*

"You were right."

Louise tousled a golden curl. "Of course I was. I always am. What was I right about this time?"

"Aurek. He's a wizard. And he never told me." Staring just past her, his eyes unfocused, Dmitri recounted the result of his little test.

"Floated across?" She pouted. "Is that all?"

"Isn't that enough?" he asked bitterly, refusing to

meet her gaze. His sisters probably knew and had never seen fit to tell him either. Edik knew, of course; Edik knew everything. He wondered how many other people had been let in on the secret while he'd maliciously been kept ignorant.

Laying her palm flat against his chest, Louise could feel his heart beating, young and strong and hers. "You're upset because he doesn't trust you."

"I'm upset because he's my brother, and I don't know anything about him." Which was true as far as it went. It just didn't go far enough. He'd spent his whole life trying to measure up to Aurek, and now he'd found out he never could.

"You don't know *enough* about him anyway," Louise conceded, frowning slightly. "Come walk with me; I always plan better when I'm moving."

"But I thought we . . ."

She pressed a finger against his lips. "Don't think."

* * * * *

When they paused on the bridge joining Isle Delanuit—whether the Renier Chateau had given its name to the island or the island to the Chateau was not entirely clear—to Craindre Island, Dmitri pointed up into the sky. Although the air held a chill that foreshadowed winter, the sky was clear, and the stars seemed close enough to touch. "Do you know what they call that constellation in Borca?"

Louise pressed her cheek into his shoulder, willing, for the moment, to allow him to instruct her. "No, what?"

"We call it the Broken Heart."

She tugged him into motion again. "I don't believe in broken hearts."

He smiled adoringly down at her, his eyes adapted enough to the darkness to see the pale beauty of her face. "Then you'll never break mine."

Under the bridge, clinging easily to the rough stonework, the white wererat followed, shaking its head. *She won't break your heart, you idiot. She'll rip it out and eat it.*

"I think," Louise murmured as they started along one of the city's many riverside esplanades, "that your little test was just a bit too simple. It isn't enough to know that your brother is a wizard; we need to know how much of a wizard he is."

By now, Dmitri knew better than to ask her why. "I guess I could find out," he offered doubtfully.

"How? He won't tell you anything; we've already established that." She felt his arm grow rigid under her fingers and tightened her grip, pleased with his anger. "No, my sweet, you've done enough. Leave this to me."

"But if he frightens you . . ."

Although her eyes glittered in anticipation, she managed to keep the sarcasm from her voice. "We should face our fears, don't you think?"

"No. I don't think," he continued quickly as he felt her tense, "because you don't want me to." Her smile was all the reward he could have desired.

"It would help if we knew what he was searching for."

"Knowledge." Dmitri tried not to grind his teeth at the memory of Aurek's sanctimonious one-word reply. "That's what he said when I asked him but, as you pointed out, I know he's not telling the truth."

Louise ignored him. "What would a wizard be searching abandoned buildings for?" she mused, chewing on her lower lip.

"Abandoned wizardry?" The look she turned on him stopped him in his tracks, the soles of his boots slapping down hard against the pavement. "What? What did I say?"

"Exactly the right thing."

Surprised by her response, he beamed. "So you're pleased?"

She gave his arm a squeeze and turned him back toward the Renier estate. "Very pleased."

Her words were a promise, and Dmitri felt his pulse quicken.

While they walked, Louise made gleeful plans. If Aurek Nuikin was searching for magical items in the abandoned buildings of Pont-a-Museau, she'd just see to it that he found a few and, if he survived the finding, she'd know for sure if she could use him.

At the bridge, Dmitri shook his head and looked out over the city. Lights were burning in a number of windows and, though he couldn't see it, he knew the party they'd left earlier was still going on—would be going on until dawn. "I don't understand why everyone says this city is so dangerous. Standing here, with you, I feel perfectly safe."

He jumped as a half-starved alley cat slunk out of the shadows, and then he laughed at his reaction. "Mind you, that's not to say that some of the stories I've heard haven't made an impression."

Scrawny body low to the ground, scarred ears flat against a triangular head, tail lashing the night, the cat glared up at Louise and hissed.

Louise glanced down over one slender shoulder and hissed back.

The cat leapt into the air, tripped over its own hind legs, and fled in terror.

*   *   *   *   *

The sewer system that ran under Pont-a-Museau was a mist-created marvel. The stone tunnels spread under all of the islands and both shores of the mainland. The occasional collapsed ceiling notwithstanding, it was possible to use them in combination with the river and the canals to get anywhere in the city.

The extended Renier family spent as much time in the sewers as they did anywhere. The other inhabitants of the city did what they could to avoid spending any time in the sewers at all. Those townspeople who entered seldom did so under their own power and never survived the experience.

Staying well back and in deepest shadow, the white wererat followed its ebony counterpart through the sewers. Although Louise had not brought Dmitri under the city with her, Chantel was still curious about where her cousin was going. Overhead, in the most decayed of the buildings, lived the most desperate of the refugees who had come to Pont-a-Museau. While the entire family tended to treat the area as a private hunting preserve, none of them were in the habit of visiting it with a couple dozen common rats in tow.

And the squeakers were obviously under Louise's command. Safe behind a buttress, Chantel smoothed back her whiskers and watched as Louise changed into her intermediate form. The older wererat studied the ceiling for a moment, nodded in satisfaction, and began to move a spill of rock away from an old, rusty iron door.

Chantel barely managed to close her teeth on a surprised gasp that surely would have given her away and very likely gotten her killed. She wouldn't!

The deep catacombs that ran under the sewers were out of bounds to the younger members of the family. Not because Jacqueline objected to losing relatives—Chantel had heard her say that at the rate certain people reproduced, she welcomed a good culling now and then to keep the numbers in line—but because winning a battle with even an immature wererat made the goblins cocky and annoying. As a

result, all but a few secret entrances to the deep catacombs had been closed and locked.

And were supposed to remain that way.

But there was Louise taking a large iron key from
the pouch she wore strapped to her chest and
unlocking the door. Chantel frowned. Louise had to
know the entrances that remained open, so what
was she doing?

Abused metal shrieked.

Chantel leapt back and clapped her front paws
over sensitive ears. A moment later, when she dared
to look again, she saw the last of the rats disappear
into the dark opening. She waited a moment longer,
decided Louise must have already descended and,
whiskers twitching, cautiously approached the door.

Standing on the ledge, she listened to the last of
the rats move down the stairs, put a front leg over
the threshold, and changed her mind. More important than what Louise was doing in the catacombs
was her manner of entry. The closed doors were not
supposed to be opened. After grooming accumulated muck from ivory flanks, Chantel started back
toward the center of town. Knowledge, delivered to
the right person, was power.

* * * * *

Louise ignored the goblin-sign. The smart ones
would avoid her; the stupid ones, she'd kill. Almost
covering the ceiling, huge, spreading patches of
phosphorescent lichens glistened with a pale green
luminescence just barely sufficient for wererat vision.
As inadequate as they were, she was glad of them—a
lantern would've meant a two-legged form, and two
legs were not enough security given the fine patina of
slime that made the footing less than stable.

Dragging the rats behind her by force of will, she

hurried along the narrow ledge that ran just above the murky water on both sides of the catacombs. At one point, where a section of the ledge had crumbled— the stone looking almost as though it had been eaten away—she leapt the gap with care. Jacqueline might know everything that hunted this deep below the city, but no one else did.

Feeling ill-used, she smacked one of the rats with her tail, knocking it off the ledge. It surfaced, squeaked once, and suddenly disappeared, leaving only a pattern of ripples behind.

Louise moved a little faster, even though she realized that whatever was in the water had to stay there. Had the creature been able to hunt on land, the goblins wouldn't have infested the catacombs in such numbers. And if my dear sister knows what's down here, she has no right to keep that kind of information to herself. I could get hurt. But does she care? No.

She was still silently complaining when the ledge widened out to become a deep landing at the foot of a broad flight of shallow stairs. The walls at bottom bore the crumbling remains of a number of fanciful creatures carved into the yellow-gray stone, and glyphs covered the huge blocks that delineated the doorway.

Settling herself in a spot where she could watch both the doorway and the catacombs—and as far from the door as possible—Louise sent the rats up the stairs. It took nearly total concentration to force them over the threshold, and one died on the topmost step—too terrified to obey but not strong enough to resist.

Not even for control of Richemulot would she cross through that doorway herself. She'd discovered this place years before when the goblin she'd been hunting ran in panic up the stairs and was thrown, broken and bleeding, back down, its body stinking of magic. Returning involved all the personal risk she was willing to take. The power oozing down the stairs sizzled over her skin and made her fur stand on end.

The rats had been ordered to bring her the most powerful magical item they could carry. She only hoped she'd sent enough so that one, at least, would survive.

As the last rat disappeared over the threshold, the sound of a battle began inside the room.

Rats screamed.

Three heartbeats later, a hideous laugh dragged razor-edged fingers along her spine. Although the sound had been muffled by stone and distance, Louise had to consciously force herself not to turn and flee. Trembling, she groomed and regroomed the same spot on her haunch, the air filling with ebony hair as fear made her shed.

By the time silence fell, she'd regained most of her equilibrium and had begun to grow impatient. She could hear movement out in the catacombs as the goblins realized they had company and drew closer to check it out. They didn't especially worry her, but their unseen presence was an irritant. Grinding her teeth, she wished one of them would do something stupid so she could use up some of the extra energy that kept her shifting in place.

Finally a single, wounded rat emerged carrying a gold amulet on a chain. Louise waited while it made its painful way down the stairs, its labored breathing nearly drowning out the slither and clunk of its dragging prize. When at last it reached the bottom, she rushed forward, snatched up the amulet, and hastily scurried away.

The metal disc felt warm and greasy to the touch. Rubbing it between clawed fingers, Louise squinted at the raised inscription, but the words meant nothing to her. As long as they mean something to Aurek

Nuikin . . . And they would. She could smell the hot scent of magic even over the stink of the catacombs.

Tucking the heavy artifact into her pack, she waited a moment longer in case one of the other rats had survived. The more she had to tempt Aurek Nuikin down into the catacombs with, the better. The hackles lifted off the back of her neck as the sound of something much larger than a rat slowly approached the glyphed doorway. Dropping onto all fours, she spun around and sped toward the entrance to the upper levels.

Behind her, the wounded rat struggled to keep up, blood bubbling from mouth and nose with every panicked breath.

The shadows took on distinct goblin shapes.

Before Louise had gone very far, the unmistakable sound of a morning star connecting with a small furred body echoed through the catacombs.

"Overkill," she snarled derisively, leapt the gap, and hurried home to plan.

* * * * *

"Why," Jacqueline wondered, picking a chunk of meat off a plate, discarding it, and choosing another, "are you telling me this?"

"Don't you want to know that Louise has opened one of the locked doors into the catacombs?"

Jacqueline stared at her young relative. She chewed and swallowed, then said, "What makes you think I didn't know?"

"Did you?" Chantel asked pointedly.

"That, my dear, is none of your business. Now, answer my question: why are you telling me?"

"I can't get Dmitri Nuikin away from Louise, but you can."

Not for a moment did Jacqueline assume Chantel

was trying to save Dmitri for altruistic reasons; obviously, she wanted him for herself. The girl's ambition amused her. "I thought I made it quite clear that night by the river that he is under my protection."

"I'm not going to hurt him, but he was my . . ." Suddenly remembering there was safety in numbers, Chantel corrected herself. "*Our* toy first."

"True enough. But why should I help you get him back?"

"I've given you information. . . ."

"Exactly. You've given me information, therefore you no longer have anything to trade." She brushed a strand of hair back off her face. "I might also point out that my sister probably knows you've been following her. You're white. You don't exactly . . . blend."

"I've been white all my life," Chantel protested indignantly.

Jacqueline ceased to be amused. "And if you want to be white for much longer you won't ever take that tone with me again."

Realizing that she'd overstepped the bounds, and well aware of the usual result, Chantel twitched and stammered, "I-I'm sorry, Jacqueline."

The head of the family bared her teeth in an expression that did not even approximate a smile. "Get out," she said.

Chantel ran.

* * * * *

That evening, stepping into the gazebo where a canalboat waited, Louise nearly leapt out of her skin when Jacqueline appeared suddenly out of the shadows. Furious that not only had she reacted, but that her sister had seen the reaction—that smug self-satisfied smile could refer to nothing else—

Louise gathered up the fringed ends of her shawl and refused to speak first.

Jacqueline stepped closer and, still smiling, announced, "I hear you were in the lower tunnels this afternoon."

Louise waited, but her twin said nothing more. Obviously Jacqueline didn't know about the amulet, now wrapped in bloodstained silk and safely tucked away, or she'd have mentioned it. She'd never been able to resist showing off just how much she knew, flaunting her power. Apparently, Louise thought with no small satisfaction, she doesn't know everything and is not as powerful as she thinks. Cradling that small, secret pleasure, half-tempted to tell the story she'd spent the evening fabricating, Louise murmured, "What if I was?"

"Nothing. Just be careful." Jacqueline's tone was edged with less-than-gentle sarcasm. "I'd hate for anything to happen to you."

"Unless you did it yourself," Louise amended silently at her sister's departing back.

*   *   *   *   *

"No." His brother's expression convincing him he'd been, perhaps, a bit abrupt, Aurek added, "I don't care for parties and see no reason to attend. You, of course, may go or not, as you wish."

Dmitri caught at Aurek's sleeve as he pushed past, not even noticing the resultant glare as his mind searched furiously for a way to persuade his brother that tonight's event was one he shouldn't miss. Louise had been very explicit about her expectations. "They've, uh, been asking about you."

Pale brows rose. "Who have?"

Who indeed. "Well, you know . . ."

"No. I don't." Aurek impatiently tapped the fingers

of his free hand against the bottom curve of the ban-
nister. "If I did, I wouldn't have asked."

Biting back his rising anger at Aurek's patronizing
tone, Dmitri snapped, "The Reniers. That is, not the
whole family but enough of them." He saw he'd
made an impression and hurriedly continued. "I
think they may be getting, well, insulted that you've,
you know, been ignoring them."

"I haven't been ignoring them!"

Dmitri shrugged. "It looks that way, doesn't it? You
never go anywhere they are."

He seems pleased with himself, Aurek thought. I
assume he got the reaction he wanted. Aurek set
aside his annoyance, uncertain if it was directed at
his brother or himself, and tried to consider Dmitri's
words objectively. While he couldn't swear that none
of the Renier family had seen him—there were
enough common rats in the buildings he searched
without assuming that the noises he heard were anything more—he had seen only Louise and Jacqueline since the party where he'd first met them. And
the second meeting with Louise could hardly have
been called a social occasion.

If other members of the family felt they'd been
insulted by his absence, they could easily interfere
with his search. That must not be allowed to happen.

"Very well," he sighed, deploring the waste of his
time. "I'll go."

"Great." Dmitri released him. "Now, about your
clothes . . ."

Aurek shook his head. "If you're suggesting I go out
looking like a ragbag, think again." He lifted the small
candelabra off the table at the bottom of the stairs and
started toward the second floor, the three candles
making his shadow dance against wallpaper Edik had
glued piece by tattered piece back into place. "I have
no wish to look like anything but what I am."

I have no wish to look like anything but what I am, Dmitri mocked silently. "And what is it you are?"

Aurek paused, turned, and stared down at his brother in confusion. "What are you talking about?"

"Don't you have something you'd like to tell me?"

"Only what I've already told you: stop seeing Louise Renier."

Dmitri's eyes flashed; he'd given Aurek a chance and had it thrown right back in his face. "You," he snarled, "have no right to try to run my life."

To his surprise, Aurek merely stared at him a moment longer, his expression above the beard soft and sad. He sighed again then said, as he continued climbing, "No. I don't."

* * * * *

"This is so lame," Yves muttered. "The same people, the same music, the same stupid plots and counterplots." He threw both arms open wide and scowled at the dance floor where couples whirled carefully around each other, the family members a little more graceful maneuvering and a little more brutal on impact. "We dance, we drink, we eat; nothing ever changes."

"Food's better," Georges pointed out, mouth full.

Yves flicked a piece of cake onto the floor. "So what? That's just because Jules Ebert is sucking up."

Ebert's family had started as scavengers and risen in a generation and a half to control all of the grain that came into the city. Those who wanted breads of any kind had to deal with Jules Ebert. This was his first attempt to buy his way into the privileged upper classes, and he was spending most of his time sweating in fearful anticipation. A chance to gorge at another's expense was enough for most of the Reniers, but social success required either Jacqueline or Louise—neither of whom had so far put in an appearance.

Georges swallowed and pointed. "Looks like the little Nuikin dragged his big brother along."

"And it looks like Chantel's attached herself to the little Nuikin," Yves growled. "She's going to get her tail ripped off if she isn't careful."

Georges shrugged. "Louise said we could play with him when she didn't want him, and she isn't . . . Hey!" He clamped his palm against bleeding scratches on one cheek and glared at his cousin.

Yves lifted his upper lip off his teeth. "Who said I was talking about Louise?"

"You're jealous!"

Realizing he'd given away far more than he'd intended to, Yves crammed a cake into his mouth and muttered around it, "Who said I was talking about me?"

Ignoring the blood dripping onto his tattered collar, Georges allowed Yves the point and continued eating. If Yves wanted Chantel, that was no business of his. If Chantel wanted the little Nuikin, that was no business of his either. Of the two ways to survive in the family, aggression or invisibility, he chose the latter, and he worked very hard at staying out of those corners where he'd have no choice but to fight.

I will grow old, he thought with smug satisfaction, keeping one eye out for Annette and the twins and the other on Yves just in case his temper flared again. The family had an overabundance of power seekers, but faithful lieutenants were much harder to find.

* * * * *

Across the room, a sudden burst of wild laughter spun Aurek around to find the source. A portly matron stared at him in some astonishment and dragged her laughing beau to a more private area.

Fighting to keep his hands from trembling, Aurek took a long swallow of wine—white wine that held no reflection. In every chuckle, every giggle, every snicker throughout the house, he could hear echos of the wizard who had destroyed his life. Faith had turned to ash again and again as the ruins of the city yielded nothing, and he feared that by holding so tightly to the small amount of hope remaining, he'd begun to let go of sanity.

He was lost outside the safety of his study or the parameters of his search. Dancers swirled by, random shapes and colors assaulting the rigid self-control he struggled to maintain. The music struck his ears as a cacophony of individual notes without tune or pattern. It had been a mistake to come.

But would it have been a greater mistake to annoy the Reniers of Richemulot further?

Searching for a little quiet and a chance to pull himself together, Aurek made his way to the card-room. Although the noise levels were just as high, at least no one was laughing. He watched Laurent Haurie blatantly cheat while sycophantic members of the merchant class marveled at his luck and praised his ability. Married to Antionette Renier, the elder and seldom seen sister of Jacqueline and Louise, Laurent obviously took as much advantage of the relationship as he could. Aurek couldn't see a blood member of the family bothering to cheat at cards. Not only would every one of them expect to win, but they'd expect the other players to take care of it.

Eyes glittering in the lamplight, Laurent threw down his final grubby cardboard rectangle. "I win again," he crowed. "Once more, the imperial suite."

The emperor on the face of the card began to laugh maniacally, his wild hair all but burying the seven pointed crown.

"No!"

In the sudden silence, the dance music spilled loudly into the room.

Laurent stood, mouth twisted unpleasantly, and slowly turned. "Are you suggesting I didn't win?" he snarled.

Aurek reached out and touched the card, now merely a badly painted portrait of an emperor no one knew. He had seen . . .

What had he seen?

"I'm talking to you, Borcan."

Finally focusing on Laurent's face, some hint of the danger he was in penetrated Aurek's panic. This man had actually married one of the Reniers. Married a wererat. The concept made him feel ill. "I'm sorry, were you talking to me?"

"Are you deaf as well as stupid? You challenged my win."

"No. I didn't. Of course you won." Bowing quickly, Aurek hurried from the room.

When Laurent merely watched him go, no one else tried to stop him. "Pet of my sister-in-law's," he said sitting down, as though that were explanation enough.

Which it was.

* * * * *

"It's nice to see you again, Aurek. You look terrible."

He hadn't seen Louise approach, and he jerked back a step, nearly stumbling over a heavy wood and leather chair.

Hiding her smile, she waited until he steadied himself before continuing. "I'm glad you're here tonight because I have something for you. A cousin of mine heard you were searching for magical artifacts in the ruins." A raised hand, jeweled rings flashing on three of four fingers, cut off the protest she could see rising in his eyes. "Who knows how he heard? People will gossip. Anyway, he gave me something to give to you. Says he found it under the city in some sort of ruined workshop."

"Why did he give it to you?" Aurek asked, his voice hoarse as he fought to force the past back where it belonged.

Louise smiled, showing teeth. "I expect it's because your brother and I are such friends." She reached into the heavy folds of her skirt and pulled out an untidy package.

Desperately trying to regain the equilibrium he'd lost in the cardroom, Aurek shook his head.

"You don't want it?" A slender finger flicked back a fold of bloodstained silk. "Are you sure?"

Aurek stared down at the flash of gold, his eyes widening as the power of the amulet, no longer blocked by the silk, began to seep out into the room. "He found this under the city?" Almost of its own volition, his hand stretched out toward the amulet. Hope rose unbidden.

"That's what I said. But if you don't want it, I have better things to do than stand around offering it to you all evening." With a twist of her wrist, she rewrapped the fabric and began to put the amulet away.

"No." Aurek nearly snatched it off her palm. He swallowed once, hard, as his fist enfolded it, then, obviously no longer even aware of her, whispered, "Thank you. Thank you very much." And nearly ran from the room.

"Well, I guess it was enough after all." Louise looked around for someone to celebrate with, and her gaze fell on Jules Ebert who stood some distance away, staring at her in rapt adoration. She liked that in a man. Crossing to his side, she linked her arm in his while he was still trying to stammer out his appreciation. "Let's go for a walk on the terrace," she suggested, her tone making her meaning plain.

When she was finished, she left the body where it fell.

* * * * *

Dmitri bounded over to her side as she returned to the party. "You came!"

"Of course I did." She was in a mood to be generous so she ignored the implied accusation.

"I brought Aurek." He glanced around, looking for his brother. It shouldn't have been hard to find him, as both Nuikins were taller and blonder than nearly everyone else in the room. "I don't know where he's gone."

Louise tucked her hand in the crook of his elbow and steered him toward the tables laden with food. "I expect he went home."

"Home?"

"That's right. After I spoke with him, I saw him practically run from the room." She smiled up into Dmitri's puzzled frown and twisted the knife. "Looks like he's forgotten all about you."

* * * * *

"Should I go back for the young master, sir?"

One foot already on the dock, Aurek stared back at the boatman in confusion. "What?"

"The young master, he's still at the party. Should I go back for him, sir?"

"Yes. Whatever." It didn't matter; nothing mattered except the amulet he clutched in his fist. Terrified of losing the chance it represented, he hadn't opened his hand since he'd closed it. He raced up the dock, across the esplanade, and into the house. Grabbing up the candles waiting at the foot of the stairs, he took the steps three at a time, pounded down the second floor hallway, and entered his study.

Gasping for breath, he closed the door and almost reverently spread his fingers. "It's a key, Lia. A key to unlock a book such as I once owned. And the one who created it had power, my love." His gaze gently stroked the statue of his wife. "Enough power to have commanded the spell we need. When I find the workshop, and I unlock the book, perhaps . . . perhaps I can finally free you."

The words on the disc said merely "I AM THE WAY." They were an automatic result of turning the amulet into a key; when the spell was cast, the words appeared. But until he found the book, Aurek had no use for the spell that unlocked it and, in order to find the book, he needed only the physical existence of the amulet itself.

A workshop containing an item of such power, even if the amulet was all the workshop contained, had to be shielded, or he would have found it himself. But now, now he had a guide.

Ignoring the hot path of tears running over both cheeks and into his beard, Aurek crossed to his desk and carefully laid out a map of the city. It wasn't a very good map, but it showed all sixteen islands and both shores and it would be enough to serve his immediate needs.

Slipping the chain over the index finger of his left hand, he stretched the hand out over the map, the disc dangling below. "Where did you come from?" he murmured. "You must show me where."

The amulet began to swing, slowly at first, then faster and faster, across the map one way and then the other, its path growing more chaotic with every pass.

"Show me!" Aurek barked.

A spark of pure power raced down the chain and

exploded against the parchment. The amulet stopped, stretched out to the right, the chain stiff, the angle defying gravity. The air stank of sulphur.

A hole had been burned into the map directly below the point where the amulet hung motionless. The east bank. The area they called the Narrows. Not a pleasant area but then, so little of Pont-a-Museau was. Once in the Narrows, Aurek had no doubt the amulet would lead him to the workshop. Power called to power.

And in the workshop . . .

He looked over at his wife, touched the faint glimmer of her life, and his face twisted with new hope. Every moment of her suffering ate into his soul. "Oh, Lia. Oh, my dear one, this could be our salvation."

 **FIVE**

The houses in the Narrows were originally much the same as the houses in many other parts of Pont-a-Museau. Once, in another time and another place, they had been tall and elegant, their four stories faced with pale gray stone, the lintels over doors and windows carved with fanciful plants and animals. Wrought-iron balconies had extended out from the base of floor-to-ceiling windows, railings cleverly sculpted to look like trailing vines.

But in the Narrows—thus named because it ran along the east side of the narrowest river channel, not, as some thought, because the forest pressed so close against it—most of the facing stones had fallen to lie shattered on the broken pavement in front of those few buildings that remained standing. The carvings had been all but obliterated by mold and lichens and other, even less savory, growths. Windows were gaping holes into darkness, and the bravest, or most desperate, of the scavengers had long since removed every scrap of iron.

A number of the exterior walls had crumbled completely, and even buildings with all four walls intact leaned dangerously far off rotting foundations.

As Aurek's canalboat approached the narrow entrance of what had once been a private slip, he squinted against the rain gusting into his face and tried to work out exactly where the amulet was leading him. He didn't feel the icy water running under his collar and down his back. He didn't hear the boatman softly cursing as he maneuvered around a bloated and unrecognizable body snagged by a mat of floating garbage. He didn't see the desolation or the danger.

Blinded by hope and pride combined, he leapt up onto the dock's one remaining beam and, without turning, told the boatman to wait.

"No, sir, I won't."

Oblivious to the slick and treacherous footing, Aurek whirled around, such blatant insubordination reaching him the way nothing else had been able to.

"You won't?" he repeated, barely believing what he'd heard.

"No, sir." The boatman was respectful, but adamant. "There's things in these here ruins, sir, worser than what you'll find in the rest of the city. If I stays tied up here, there'll be nothing left of me, or me boat, when you gets back."

"Then anchor out in the channel," Aurek commanded. He didn't have time for this.

The boatman shook his head, collected rainwater spraying off the greasy brim of his hat, obviously more afraid of what lurked in the Narrows than he was of Aurek. "Even if the weather permitted, which it don't, sir, it ain't no safer out there." Gnarled hands clasped over the handle of his oar, he gathered his courage and looked his employer in the eye. "You gots power, sir, or them young bloods from way back would've taken care of me before now, but you're not going to be here, so neither am I. What I will do is go out to the main channel and come back. As long as I keep movin' I guess I should be safe enough."

"I don't know how long this is going to take me," Aurek warned him.

The boatman shrugged. "Then I guess I'll keep coming back till you do."

Aurek stared at him for a long moment, trying to force his mind to work on something, anything besides the amulet and the hope it represented. There was obvious merit in what had been suggested: a live boatman returning for him was infinitely preferable to a dead one waiting. "All right," he agreed abruptly, "but be here when I return."

"You can count on it, sir." Leaning his weight on the oar, he backed the boat out into the current and allowed the prow to sweep around to the north. "Two things, sir!" His voice battered through the noise of wind and rain like a club. "Don't be caught here after dark, and you'll be a sight safer if you keeps movin'!"

Watching him row away, Aurek was touched by an instant of dread, and he felt, for that instant, more alone than he'd ever been in his life.

"Which is ridiculous," he told himself, making his way to the relatively solid ground of the esplanade. "I'm no more alone now than I have been during any search."

Except he'd never searched in the Narrows. His voice hung in the air like an intruder, and he decided it might be a good idea not to speak aloud. Slipping a hand into his pocket, he pulled out the amulet and, as rain added new stains to the silk, carefully unwrapped it.

* * * * *

Deep in the Narrows, three heads lifted on dried and desiccated necks. Three faces, identical in death as they'd never been in life, turned toward the river. Years ago, they'd been set to guard the contents of a wizard's workshop. With no concept of time, they neither knew, nor cared, how long ago that order had been given.

Something had been stolen.

They would get it back.

But the outside was too big, too open, too confusing. They lost contact with the stolen object. Regained contact. Lost it again. Gray light had come. And falling water. Unable to reason, or even truly think, they knew only three things:

They were to guard the contents of the workshop.

Something had been stolen.

They had to get it back.

Then, suddenly, they made contact once again.

Unable to do anything but smile, as their lips had long since shriveled back into interchangeable rictus grins, they shuffled toward the river.

*   *   *   *   *

Tucking the damp silk back into his pocket, Aurek hung the amulet's chain over the index finger of his left hand, looped it once for security, and let the disc swing free. It spun in place for a moment, then slowly began to inscribe an arc on the air. At the apex of its swing, it stopped.

East. Wiping the rain from his eyes, Aurek moved away from the river, following the tug of power against his hand. The cracked and uneven paving stones were slippery, and every step brought with it the potential for a fall. He wanted to run, to leap, to shout, but he allowed caution to rule and walked in careful silence.

East. Then slightly north. Rounding a blind corner, he found the amulet pointed directly at a pile of rubble, all that remained of a once-grand house, its rain-slicked stone too high and too unstable to climb. Aurek fingered the leather loop in his pocket but left it where it was. With no idea of what he'd face upon finding the workshop, spending unnecessary power could be more than foolish—it could be suicidal. Before he wasted what could not easily be replaced, he'd search for another way around.

The way he found was not one he would've taken under other circumstances. The cavity was dank and dark, and the entry barely broader than his shoulders but, when he knelt to peer into it, he was sure he could see gray daylight in the distance—on the other side of the rubble.

Carefully rewrapping the amulet, he shoved it to the bottom of an inside pocket and wriggled feetfirst into the opening.

* * * * *

They lost it again.

Their purposeful advance turned to an aimless wandering as bedraggled ravens watched in beady-eyed amusement from the shelter of shattered casements.

In the hollow breast of what had once been a powerful and feared man, a red heat began to burn. Too many years had passed, forgotten in the catacombs, for him to recognize anger now that it had returned to him, but he welcomed the warmth that burned away the confusion.

He reached out and grabbed the unyielding flesh of his companions' arms, yanking them to a halt by his side.

They would wait and, when they could feel their master's stolen property, they would move quickly. He would not allow it to disappear again.

*   *   *   *   *

His heel compressed something soft against the slippery surface of the rubble, and Aurek nearly lost his balance as he dropped to more-or-less solid ground. He straightened in almost full darkness, as what little daylight there was seemed unwilling to enter with him. Using the sound of his entrance to define the dimensions of the room, he determined it was larger than he'd thought from outside, the gray light of his exit was farther away, and he wasn't alone.

He could hear something breathing, noisily sucking moist air in and just as noisily blowing it out through phlegm-encrusted passageways. There might have been more than one something, but the noise he heard was too diffuse to tell for sure. Prepared to defend himself, he decided that light would probably be his most potent weapon.

Slipping his hand into the pocket of his coat—the items it held would be less than useless tucked safely away in his pack—he rummaged among the possibilities until his fingers touched an oilcloth-wrapped lump about the size of his thumb. Drawing it out, he quickly unwrapped it to expose a whitish, waxy substance glowing faintly in the dark. Although the spell he was about to evoke was extraordinarily simple, finding phosphorous in large enough pieces to make using it worthwhile was not. Under normal circumstances, lanterns made much more sense, used no power, and were infinitely easier to replace. Today, however, he wanted his hands free.

At any other time he'd have drawn in a deep breath to help his focus, but the stench surrounding him made shallow breathing much healthier—even the thought of a deep breath turned his stomach. Holding the phosphorous on his left palm, he closed his fingers around it, spoke the necessary words of command, and threw it into the air. The speck of light whirled about his head and divided into eighteen specks that grew brighter with every revolution. On Aurek's command the eighteen became six, then three globes of light, each the size of a man's fist.

"Spread," he said curtly. Each globe moved about three feet away, one in front, two behind in a triangular pattern. In their clear white light Aurek finally saw where he stood.

Before the house had collapsed, the area had likely been part of an attached coachhouse; now it was a long, narrow cavern. Rising just barely higher than his head, the ceiling looked ready to collapse at any moment. Moisture glistened on the rubble, collecting on low points and dripping into foul puddles. The stink rose from piles of rotting garbage and excrement and was strong enough, in such close quarters, to make his eyes water.

Edik is going to have a fit about the condition of my boots, he found himself thinking as he took a cautious step forward. He could still hear the moist and labored breathing, but had no better idea of where it came from than he'd had while in the dark.

Then one of the larger piles of garbage moved. Something whimpered as it squinted at him through red-rimmed, rheumy eyes. It had been human once. Perhaps it still was, under a looser definition of human than Aurek used. A second pile of garbage lifted up to the light a face covered in oozing scabs. A third scuttled back into the shadows.

The other residents of the city named these pitiful refugees the lost ones. They were the people who had seen one too many horrors. Had fought one too many battles. Had been forced to endure more pain than they were able. Had finally surrendered to horror, to defeat, to pain. Lost ones.

They were well named, Aurek acknowledged as he walked carefully among them. They cowered as he passed, but that could have as easily been from the unaccustomed light as from any threat he presented. They'd gone far beyond caring for their own safety; all that remained was the lowest, most bestial level of survival. They lived, but that was all. The worst of it was, when he forced himself to look closer, he could see the atrocities that had driven them to surrender lurking behind the blank despair in their eyes. Because they'd stopped just short of death, they hadn't found the forgetfulness they sought.

One of them sucked something dark in between cracked and bleeding lips and began to chew. Aurek gave thanks he hadn't seen what it actually was.

Once these people had lives, loved ones.

Natalia . . .

She had brought light and love and laughter into his life, and all three had been taken from him as she had been, trapped with her. If he couldn't save her, could he, even he, fall this far?

His mouth went dry, and he began to shake, fighting a wave of despair that threatened to drag him under and throw him up as wreckage on a not-so-distant shore. He would save her! He would! This was not his future!

Gradually, he fought his way back to calm and found himself with one hand up on the damp lip of the exit hole with no memory of how he'd crossed to it. I *will* save you, Natalia, he promised, as he had a thousand times before. I will *never* surrender. He took a deep, steadying breath of the cleaner air pouring in from outside and silently cursed his imagination. He was an intelligent man, a strong man, yes, even a powerful man. He would never come to this.

His lip curled in disgust—at the weakness of others, at his own momentary lapse—he started to climb out into the rain. A noise behind him made him turn, unable to deny curiosity. The third of the lost ones, the one who had originally moved away from the light, crept toward him on hands and knees. The tangled remains of blonde braids and a face clear of beard suggested it had once been a woman, though its condition destroyed any claim to gender and it could have as easily been a beardless boy. When it felt Aurek's gaze upon it, it lifted its own sunken eyes to his face and stretched out a filthy, almost skeletal hand.

Save me.

He could hear it as clearly as if the words had been spoken aloud.

A moment later, the hand fell and eyes stared at nothing, said nothing, wanted nothing.

Aurek climbed out into a garbage-strewn cul-de-sac, dimmed his lights, put the wrapped phosphorus back into his pocket, and threw up until his stomach twisted painfully around nothing.

"But, Aurek, you could do so much with the power you have." Natalia's voice rang in memory.

"I'm a scholar, Lia. Try to understand."

She'd put her hands on her hips and sighed. *"Actually doing something will make you no less a scholar."*

I'm doing something now, Lia, but I can't save everyone who needs saving.

Aurek spat and straightened. With trembling fingers, he pulled out the amulet and followed it farther to the east.

Although he tried to turn his thoughts in other directions, they kept returning to the lost ones. Burying his emotional response in scholarship, he tried to work out how something so uncaring of personal safety could possibly survive in such a hostile environment. The Narrows were reputed to hold packs of wild dogs as well as wandering undead, giant spiders, a variety of snakes, and the ubiquitous rats—sewer and otherwise. The lost ones would be easy prey.

Unable to find an answer, he decided that the dominant predator of Pont-a-Museau would consider them poor sport—wererats liked to have more fun with their food.

Wererats. He wiped the rain out of his eyes and found himself about to consider Louise Renier and his brother for the first time without rage or disgust. What, besides the obvious, did she want with Dmitri? Or was that all she wanted? Perhaps she had no interest beyond the physical. Wererats were, after all, in the habit of concerning themselves with self-indulgence and little else. If that was the case, Dmitri was in no real physical danger until she tired of him.

But other dangers . . .

Aurek shook his head, rainwater spraying off the ends of his hair. His warnings had gone unheeded. What was he supposed to do? Keep his brother locked in the house while he searched the ruins for a magic to free his Natalia? He would not sacrifice his wife to Dmitri's stubbornness.

"If he still doesn't see what Louise Renier is," Aurek muttered to a cold autumn wind, wondering how anyone could be so willfully blind, "then perhaps his naiveté is protection enough."

The chain tugged at his finger, and he followed the pull down a narrow alley between two buildings still miraculously intact. Stepping over the gnawed bones of a cat, he considered recalling his lights, then decided not to waste the power. Except for the three lost ones—who were definitely no threat—he'd seen none of the creatures supposedly so prevalent in the Narrows. Granted, a number of the hunters were nocturnal but a few were not, and the appearance of prey should have brought them out. Perhaps the rain kept them from hunting; it was certainly unpleasant enough.

Shoulders hunched against the wet, Aurek picked his path with care. His map of the city had indicated there were underground canals cutting through the area, and he had no desire to find himself suddenly swimming. As his eyes grew accustomed to the lack of light between the buildings, he saw that the amulet seemed to be glowing faintly.

He wasn't surprised, given the power it held and its current proximity to the place it had been found.

"A cousin of mine heard you were searching for magical artifacts in the ruins. . . . He gave me something to give to you. Says he found it under the city in some sort of ruined workshop."

"Why did he give it to you?"

"I expect it's because your brother and I are such friends."

Why are you giving it to me?

He hadn't asked her that and, all at once, he realized he should have. Why would Louise Renier give him anything? Certainly not merely because a cousin had asked her to. She'd hated him even before the cellar had collapsed beneath her, and he couldn't see how being thrown into the sewers could've changed her opinion.

Why hadn't he asked her?

Why hadn't he seen anything unusual in her even speaking with him?

Because he'd been thrown off-balance by what had happened in the cardroom. Because once he'd seen the amulet, he could think of nothing else.

Aurek stopped where he was and stared at the surrounding shadows. He was very likely walking into a trap.

Louise Renier had lied to him: that was a given. Her feelings about him aside, he doubted she was capable of telling the truth. But, in all his long years of study, Aurek had never heard of a true lycanthrope being a wizard, nor could he imagine a wererat, for all they were probably the most intelligent of the creatures, having the necessary discipline to study the art.

For all the lies that had come with it, the amulet was real. It had been created by a powerful wizard, and wizards had workshops. Even now the amulet was drawing him toward the place it had been found. He had to follow it. Whatever the risk, he couldn't chance missing the one opportunity he might have to return his Natalia to life.

"And surely," he allowed, as the amulet led him deeper into the alley, "I can overcome any trap devised by a wererat." If he had no answers, he, at least, had faith in his own abilities.

The alley continued, offensive to both eye and nose, for another thirty feet, then opened out into a ruined courtyard. Aurek stepped out from between the buildings, relieved at being away from their oppressive bulk even though he now had no protection from the nearly opaque sheets of rain. He had no idea he was no longer alone until a gray hand wrapped around the amulet and yanked the chain from his finger, ripping off skin and the fingernail with it.

Aurek's jaw dropped, but no sound emerged. He had nothing to fuel a scream; the sudden pain had forced all the air from his lungs. He struggled to fill them, injured hand cradled against his chest. Then he realized . . .

. . . he'd lost the amulet!

*   *   *   *   *

That which had been lost, was found. With it clutched in the more functional of his hands, he led the other two back toward the entrance to the catacombs. The living thing he'd retrieved it from was not their concern.

*   *   *   *   *

Handkerchief wrapped awkwardly around his bleeding finger, Aurek followed the power signature of the amulet just as he'd followed the power signatures of a dozen pieces of junk he'd found abandoned in Pont-a-Museau. He squinted through the storm's sudden fury, saw three shadows rounding a distant corner, and pounded after them as fast as he was able.

Splashing through the gutter, he slipped on a cracked paving stone. Without thinking, he threw out a hand to catch himself and slammed his injured finger into the ground. This time, though he had breath enough to scream, he didn't have the energy to waste.

He had to get the amulet back; without it he'd never find the shielded workshop.

Lunging around the corner, he could barely make out his quarry crossing a flooded street.

There was something about the way they were moving. . . . The more analytical part of his brain worried at it while the rest concerned itself solely with recovering Natalia's best chance.

He caught up to them as they passed under a narrow portico. Out of the obscuring storm, there could be no mistaking what they were.

Undead.

Zombies.

His studies having made him familiar with the theory of necromancy, it never occurred to Aurek that he should be afraid. He could, if he so desired, create similar creatures. Better creatures, he observed disdainfully, noting how every step seemed likely to shake the trio apart. Under tattered clothing, gray skin had cracked in a number of places like badly tanned leather. He could see the amulet swinging from a rotting hand, but two of the zombies were between him and the artifact. Rage propelling him over the last few feet, he grabbed the closest arm and threw the zombie out of his way . . .

. . . *intended* to throw the zombie out of his way. The arm ripped right off the shoulder, ball and socket separating with a brittle cracking sound. Beetles that had been living in the joint scurried away from the sudden wet. Aurek stared down at what he held, noted how his fingers made no impression on the woodlike flesh and, with a grimace of disgust, flung the arm away.

The remaining arm caught him a glancing blow on the side of the head. Ears ringing, Aurek staggered back, tripped, and fell under a second swing that would have opened his throat had it connected.

I haven't time for this!

He kicked out and, off-balance, the one-armed zombie stumbled back against its companions. The staggering dance that resulted as the three tried to keep their footing would have been funny under other circumstances. As it was, Aurek used the time to collect his scattered thoughts.

Unlike Dmitri, who'd wasted countless hours practicing with an ugly assortment of weapons, he was no fighter. It was obvious that in order to get to the zombie with the amulet, he'd have to fight the other two. Their apparently fragile condition aside, Aurek doubted he'd win and, even if by some wild chance he did, during the time it would take him to destroy the first two, piece by piece, the third zombie could easily disappear with the amulet. Once the amulet was in the workshop, he'd never find it through the protective shielding. If he couldn't find the amulet, he couldn't find the workshop.

He couldn't risk it. He had to settle things definitively before that could happen.

As a scholar, he'd had little use for the more aggressive spells, but he was glad now that he'd taken the time to study them—both in Borca and early this morning when he'd prepared weapons for the day's search through the Narrows. Rolling the tiny ball of sulphur and bat guano against the palm of his right hand, he found his focus, pointed, and shouted out the range.

He hadn't expected them to burn with such violence.

Perhaps the blood, added inadvertently to the spell, gave it extra power. Perhaps the three had been undead for so long the years had sucked all moisture from their bodies, leaving them tinder-dry. When the fireball exploded, all three zombies were instantly consumed. The rain hissed as it hit but had no effect on the roaring ball of flame.

On his knees, Aurek shielded his face with his arm. The wet cloth steamed. He could feel his forehead tightening from the heat.

One heartbeat. Two. Then it was over.

Aurek staggered to his feet, coughing and choking. His throat burned from the heated air he'd inhaled; his head pounded from the unanticipated power surge; tears poured down his cheeks as his body attempted to clear the acrid smoke from his eyes.

The heat had been so intense that the stones in front of him—pavement, building, and portico—were white, not black. All three bodies had been so completely consumed not even ash remained.

But where was the amulet?

Barely noticing that the rain had once again

become a constant, soaking drizzle, he circled the parameter of the fireball, desperately looking for a glint of gold. It took all his strength to wait, but the stones were still too hot to walk on. Not until the rain began to make a darker pattern against the blasted white did he step forward. He could feel the results of the fireball through the soles of his boots, but he couldn't hold back any longer.

Where was the amulet? Had the zombie carrying it thrown it aside at the last minute?

Palms clapped to his throbbing temples, Aurek reached out and searched, power to power.

Down?

How could it . . .

His gaze dropped to the crack between the pavement and the building. A howl began to build in the back of his throat as he threw himself to his knees, ignoring the pain as the stone scorched his seeking hand. A faint residue of gold remained on the crumbling marble edge of the crack. He picked at it, unable to make the hole any larger, unwilling to acknowledge the horrendous result of his attack. Unable to ignore it.

The heat of the fireball had melted the soft metal, and the molten gold had poured through the crack in the stone sheath that enclosed the city. In a thousand places a strong kick would've opened up a way to retrieve it. In a thousand places . . . but not this one. Aurek flung himself against it, but blood and bone lost the battle to stone. He could sense where the gold had gone, knew it still held power enough to lead him to the workshop, but try as he might, he couldn't reach it.

The pain in his hand became nothing to the pain in his heart as a howl of despair clawed its way free.

*   *   *   *   *

The bloodscent had drawn the hunters from their dens. The sound of despair quickened their pace.

* * * * *

Louise listened, head cocked, as the goblin she'd been hunting scurried down a narrow side passage it obviously believed too small for her to negotiate. Idiot, she thought. They never seemed to learn that size could be misleading, and the family could maneuver through areas too small for goblins. Of course goblins, she added silently, are notoriously thickheaded.

As she was hunting for fun, she allowed her prey to gain a little distance while she groomed a flank and wondered what was taking Aurek Nuikin so long. Although she'd slept earlier, she didn't enjoy being up in the day, nor did she enjoy being kept waiting; both made her irritable and difficult to get along with.

If the delay was a result of something as simple as an inability to find the entrance to the catacombs, Aurek obviously wasn't powerful enough to be of any use to her. If the delay meant that he'd run into an inhabitant in the Narrows he couldn't handle, the same conclusion applied. If he was just taking his time, he was extremely fortunate that she needed to test him or, when he finally appeared, the guardian in the workshop would be the least of his worries.

She'd wait for him until she finished with the goblin. If he hadn't appeared by then, he'd better be dead in the Narrows—or he was going to wish he were.

* * * * *

Mangy fur plastered to near-skeletal bodies, the pack of feral dogs followed the bloodscent to the

edge of the portico. In the Narrows they were as
often prey as predator and so approached with caution. Although the rain had washed away the smoke,
hackles rose at the lingering scent of power.

Had it not been for the blood drawing them forward . . .

*   *   *   *   *

On his knees, his body curled around his misery,
Aurek rocked back and forth, unable to go on. To
have come so close and then have hope snatched
away by cruel fate—to have himself destroyed his
love's best chance. The reason he so prided himself
upon had melted in the conflagration with the
amulet, had, like the golden artifact, dribbled away
and left nothing behind but empty hopelessness.

The pack leader, its hide an intricate pattern of
scars, snarled as it attacked, hunger finally overwhelming fear.

Instinct flung Aurek's arm up over his throat. Teeth
closed around wet oilskin and the heavy sweater
beneath it rather than soft flesh. The weight of the
dog threw him back against the building, and the
pack could come at him from only three sides.
Clothing intended as protection against the cold and
damp delayed the inevitable as Aurek's world collapsed to tooth and claw.

He kicked out. An animal yelped. Another instantly
replaced it.

All at once he realized he didn't want to die. Not
here. Not like this. Not ripped apart by wild dogs like
some common wanderer too weak to go on.

With a sudden surge of strength, he slammed the
dog gnawing at his right arm against the wall, loos-
ening its hold. As satisfying as it was to hear it yelp
and feel it fall away, brute force could not be the

answer. There were too many for his meager fighting skills. The pack leader's teeth pressed dull points of pain into his forearm—the animal either too stupid or too hungry to release its initial hold—and another dog tore at the coat by his elbow. Once the protection of the thick oilskin was gone . . .

Thrusting his good hand into his pocket, shoulder raised to protect his face, he frantically searched for an answer. It would have to be fast, and it would have to be easy, for focus would be more difficult to achieve than usual.

His fingers passed over the wrapped lump of phosphorous, a tangle of copper wire, a piece of thick chalk, a leather loop, a small silk bag filled with fine sand. . . . Of course! It was the first spell he'd ever learned and, while he hadn't used it in some years, he knew it so well he doubted he'd get it wrong even with something trying to eat his arm.

Hot breath washed against the side of his head.

He jerked back in time to save most of his ear.

Working his thumb through the drawstring of the silk bag, he spilled the contents awkwardly into his palm. Some of the sand fell to the bottom of his pocket, but he thought he still had enough. Rolling to the left, using his weight to dislodge a dog worrying at his buckskins, he yanked his hand free and threw the sand into the air. Praying it would cover a wide enough area, he clutched at the minimal focus he needed and shouted out the simple one-word component of the spell: "Sleep."

He could hear the rain again.

Prying the jaws of the pack leader loose, for it hung on even in its sleep, Aurek got slowly, painfully, to his feet. Five dogs lay breathing heavily on the pavement around him, and one small bitch was backing warily away—lip curled off her teeth but self-preservation overwhelming hunger.

Swiping at the blood dribbling down from his torn ear and soaking into his collar, Aurek waved his injured hand in her direction. "Go," he panted, "away."

She growled. When he took a step toward her, she backed out into the rain and disappeared around a pillar of the portico.

Leaning, exhausted, against the wall, he bound his finger more thoroughly but, as he could do nothing about it, he ignored the damage done to his ear. The pain of the bite, compared to the pain of having a fingernail ripped out, was nothing. With luck, Edik would get a chance to clean it before infection set in. His arm felt badly bruised but, though there were tooth marks indenting the sleeve, the fabric had held.

"Now what?" he asked himself. Logic suggested that if he intended to continue searching in the Narrows, he kill the dogs while they slept; mercy would only result in further attacks. Unfortunately for logic, as interbred and vicious as they were, they were still dogs, and Aurek couldn't do it. Not in cold blood.

"So that's that." He would use the remaining daylight, such as it was, to concentrate on finding the workshop. While it wouldn't be easy without the amulet to guide him . . .

It'll be impossible, a hateful voice scoffed gleefully in his head.

Aurek set his teeth and pretended not to have heard. If he couldn't find the workshop, perhaps he could find the shielding. The power required to hide the amulet should surely leave some signature of its own. He would quarter the Narrows until he found it.

Disregarding the protests of abused muscles, he straightened, then paused. He'd used the only fireball he'd prepared. Would it be wiser to return home and rearm himself in case there were more of undead wandering about?

Except the zombies he'd destroyed weren't merely wandering. They'd snatched the amulet from him, and then headed purposefully away. Almost as if they were returning it to someone.

Aurek's heart began to pound. Could they be returning it to the workshop? A workshop that might not, after all, be abandoned? Was that the trap Louise Renier had set? Was he to walk blindly in and come face-to-face with disaster?

The trio of zombies were ancient, dried and desiccated. If they'd been created by the wizard who'd created the amulet, then the wizard couldn't possibly still be alive. Actually, Aurek could think of a number of ways the wizard could have survived—none he'd have tried himself, but as he already seemed to be dealing with a necromancer, he couldn't rule them out.

"But that's not important." He sagged back against the wall, unwilling to use energy on standing that he might use on reasoning. If the wizard was alive—or at least living—he'd deal with that in its own time. His immediate problem remained finding the workshop.

His studies had indicated that zombies were often used as guards. They were cheap to sustain and, though not very bright, they followed simple orders to the letter. If the zombies he'd destroyed had been left to guard the workshop and its contents, it would explain why they'd been interested only in the amulet.

Unless another wizard had sensed the artifact once it had been taken out from the shielding and sent the zombies after it.

Aurek sighed. There was a simple way to find out. If the same wizard who had created the amulet also created the zombies, the power signature would show it. The power signature of the amulet had been burned into his brain by a delirious hope but unfortunately, the zombies had been merely burned. Not enough ash remained for him to use in even the simplest of identification spells.

All at once, he threw back his head and laughed. The conscious feral dog, who'd been creeping closer to her pack, leapt back into the shadows. Blood and bruises forgotten, Aurek ran out into the rain.

He found what he was looking for halfway up a pile of crumbling masonry. The arm he'd torn from the zombie lay palm-up, unable to turn over, gray fingers flexing uselessly in the air. Holding it carefully just above the elbow, Aurek concentrated.

The amulet and the zombies had been created by the same power source.

Smiling broadly, though it hurt his face, Aurek laid the arm carefully on the pavement and stomped it into little pieces. A disgruntled beetle, narrowly avoiding oblivion, scurried for safety under a block of stone. Scooping up a finger bone, Aurek pulled three hairs from the crown of his head and rapidly braided them into a slender thong. Dmitri had been whining at him to get his hair cut, complaining that long hair was no longer in fashion for men. Good thing he hadn't listened.

Then he cast the same spell on the bone as he'd cast on the amulet.

It spun in place then slowly rose to point northeast.

Exactly the direction in which the zombies had been traveling.

*   *   *   *   *

As the human strode away, the raven watched from its perch on the roof of the portico. Too wise to get involved with wizards, it had come, as its kind always did, to feed on the carrion that remained after battle. That this battle had left not exactly carrion behind mattered not in the slightest.

The dogs were sleeping, not dead.

The dogs were helpless. That was all that was important to the raven.

It launched itself into a swooping dive and landed by the head of a heavy-boned mutt of dubious parentage. A bit of a snob, like most of its kind, the raven cocked its glossy black head but decided a meal was a meal. It hopped up onto a scarred shoulder and aimed its beak at the rounded promise of an eye.

A heartbeat later, it was dead.

Not long after, all that remained were a few feathers and a pleasantly full dog who had a long scratch and sat down out of the rain to wait for the rest of her pack to wake.

 **SIX**

The pull on the finger bone was now straight down, the thong of braided hairs stretched taut, the loop beginning to dimple the skin of his finger.

Aurek scowled at the cobblestones, but they were solid enough that even the rain ran off them toward the gutter in the center of the street. He turned, slowly, and looked up at the semicircle of town-houses leaning drunkenly toward what once had been a private park.

Below the houses were cellars, and below the cellars—as he had so nearly discovered firsthand—were sewers, and somewhere down below the Narrows was the workshop he needed to find.

Slipping the finger bone into his pocket, he looked at the nearest house. Once, its tiny below-street-level courtyard had provided an entrance to the kitchens for servants and tradespeople. Now that approach was blocked by rubble and provided no entry at all. He'd have to go in the front door—or more specifically, through the gaping hole where the front door had been—and hopefully find a functional set of stairs.

The edges of the front steps had been broken off, as though something heavy had bounced down them. Aurek studied the leering gargoyle that remained tucked under the eaves of the house, decided it likely would not fall in the next few moments, and hurried as quickly as the slick, uneven footing allowed up to the entrance. Once inside, out of the rain, on what appeared to be a reasonably solid floor, he took a moment to braid his hair. Wincing as he dragged it across his injured ear, he managed to get it more or less neatly back and out of his way. The last thing he needed was a hank of wet, bloody hair obscuring his vision.

The entrance hall evoked a not entirely pleasant sensation of dèjá vu, as it was nearly identical to the house he currently lived in. The moldings, the paneling, even the black roses on the wallpaper were the same, only in a much more advanced state of decay. Rodent droppings were everywhere, and a hole the size of his fist had been gnawed through the wainscoting.

Rats ruled the Narrows after dark.

Although disconcerting, the similarities had one obvious advantage: he knew where everything was. The stairs down to the kitchens should be just behind the dining room.

Stepping over the dining room threshold, his foot continued to drop after it should've touched the floor. Aurek bit off a yell, grabbed for something—anything—to stop his fall, and ended up angled over a pit of indeterminate depth, clutching a heavy wooden door. Below him, he could see nothing but darkness within the missing circle of floor.

The one hinge remaining attached to the doorframe began to pull loose.

If he could get his right hand into his pocket and the leather loop . . .

. . . but that would entail supporting his entire weight on his injured hand. He couldn't risk it. He would have to save himself the hard way. Inch by torturous inch he crept back, barely daring to breathe until both feet were planted firmly on solid wood.

"I'm an idiot," he muttered, pulling out the phosphorous. "Saving power will do me little good if I splatter my brains over some long abandoned wine cellar."

A moment later, the clean white light of the three globes illuminating the gutted interior of the house with depressing clarity, he successfully made his way around the damaged piece of floor and found the stairs leading down to the kitchens. Two of the risers had rotted out and collapsed under the weight of the treads but, surprisingly, he'd seen worse in other parts of the city.

The air in the kitchen tasted of rust and other, less savory things. Fungus grew in a thick, oblong pile along the base of one wall, but Aurek had no interest in what lay rotting beneath it. He had to go deeper still.

Constructed of stone, the stairs to the cellars had survived remarkably intact. Keeping a wary eye out for webs, Aurek began a careful descent. About halfway to the bottom, he paused. A trail of slime, glistening in the wizard-light, began at a rat hole gnawed through the outer wall, slid down each subsequent step, and continued across the cellar floor to a closed door at the back of the subterranean room. After thoroughly inspecting the ceiling, Aurek followed the trail, crouching to study the passage under the door. By reading the pattern of the slime, he was fairly certain the creature secreting it had spread out enough to move through a space no more than an inch high.

"Fascinating." Shaking his head in amazement, he straightened. "I thought they were extinct," he told the silence. There'd been no reported attacks by black puddings in decades. In fact, a number of the younger scholars and adventurers he'd been in contact with had expressed scornful doubts that such a creature ever existed. Once he freed Natalia, there were obviously a number of things worth studying in the ruins of Pont-a-Museau. For now, however, he needed to head toward the front of the house, toward the street. The opportunities for scholarship lurking behind that door would have to wait.

Bringing out the zombie's finger bone, he followed its pull to an open trapdoor beside a pile of decaying furniture, crushed and broken fungus clearly indicating it had recently been moved. It makes sense, Aurek mused, relieved he wouldn't have to dig his way through the foundations of the house. The zombies could no more walk through stone than he could. In order to follow the amulet out of the sewers, they needed to find an actual exit.

A rattling noise behind him spun Aurek around, thumbs together, fingers spread, trying desperately to remember the words of his last truly offensive spell.

In the far corner, a pile of human bones stirred. A kneecap, pale green with mold, rolled off the top of the pile and bounced to a halt some three feet away. Eyes squinted nearly shut in the unaccustomed light, a rat heaved itself up and out of its nest, glared at Aurek, and disappeared through a crack in the wall.

Aurek let his hands fall back to his sides. Rats, he thought, releasing a breath he couldn't remember holding. I can cope with rats, but I'm not sure I'm up to another encounter with the undead.

Well aware that one rat could easily mean hundreds more lurking in the shadows, and that number could more than make up for lack of size, he sent one of his three lights through the trapdoor so he could see his way. Rusty steel rungs had been set into the damp stone of the sewer wall. In spite of the rust, they seemed solid.

Seemed solid.

There was only one way to be certain.

Sitting on the edge of the hole, Aurek felt for the first rung with the toe of his boot. As much as caution seemed to be called for, he had to move quickly. He'd seen nothing waiting for him below, but that could as easily mean he'd seen nothing as that there was nothing there to see. While he climbed to the lower level, he'd be as vulnerable as he'd been at any time since he'd entered the Narrows.

His mind focused on freeing Natalia—leaving no room for fear—he trusted his weight to the ancient ladder. It protested but held. The curve of the sewer wall forced him to descend at an awkward angle, pack dragging at his shoulders, sharp flakes of rust chewing into his palms. It wasn't a pleasant climb, but as he'd foolishly forgotten to bring a rope, he was glad to be making it. The ledge running just below the widest point of the curve was slick when he finally reached it, and the stink coming up from the brown, turgid water nearly made him sick.

The bone continued to drag at his finger.

Apparently the sewers of Pont-a-Museau had more than one level.

He took one last look up at the circle of darkness that marked the open trapdoor in the arc of the ceiling—locking its location in memory, for to be lost in these sewers was to die in these sewers—then began to search for the way down. It was a surprisingly short search.

The zombies had left ajar the steel door leading to the catacombs.

A closer examination determined that the surrounding piles of rubble had not been pushed aside by the opening door. They'd been removed, one at a time, from in front of the threshold. Someone had gone down into the lower levels shortly before the zombies had come up.

The cousin Louise Renier claimed had found the artifact?

Perhaps.

It wasn't important.

Finding the workshop was important. Freeing Natalia was important. The rest he'd deal with as circumstances forced him to. Not before.

Although the zombies had nearly taken it from him with the amulet, he held on tightly to a strong belief in his ability to deal with anything.

* * * * *

Louise Renier lifted her head, her ears pricked forward as she heard the sound of booted feet against stone. The tread was too heavy to be that of another goblin, and none of the family ever descended into the catacombs in skin form. It had to be Aurek Nuikin.

And it's certainly about time, she snarled to herself.

The goblin, bleeding from a number of not-quite-fatal wounds, struggled weakly under her front paws. Adjusting her grip, Louise considered what she should do with it. In spite of what it obviously feared, she wasn't going to eat it. Although her twin insisted goblins were an acquired taste, she found them bitter and containing far more gristle than should be anatomically possible. Old boots were less chewy and significantly tastier.

The footsteps came cautiously closer.

Louise shrugged furred shoulders, braced her haunches against the wall, and rolled the goblin off

the ledge into the water. Its remaining eye opened
wide with terror and, had it not earlier lost its tongue,
it would have screamed. It gurgled once and sank
without a trace. Just before she tucked herself away
out of sight, Louise batted its tongue in after it.

*   *   *   *   *

Aurek followed the pull of the zombie bone along
the narrow ledge, the trio of lights maintaining their
distance around his head. After he passed, the
lichen—obviously phosphorescent—glowed with a
greater intensity. Unfortunately, the effect created
new shadows rather than banishing the old ones.

With every sense warning him he wasn't alone and
suggesting greater speed, he continued to move
methodically forward. He had every confidence he
could survive an attack, regardless of type or direction, but doubted he'd last a heartbeat if he slipped
and fell into the water.

His caution was justified when he reached the
place where the ledge had crumbled. Looking like
nothing so much as if a large bite had been taken out
of the stone—a resemblance Aurek sincerely hoped
was coincidence—the ledge tapered inward to the
curve of the wall, disappeared completely for a full
twelve inches, then tapered out again.

Not trusting masonry clearly older than the rest of
the city, he decided not to creep out onto the damaged stone even though a good eighteen inches
remained, wide enough to hold him before the ledge
disappeared. He'd jump over the damaged areas—
from solid stone to solid stone. Or what he assumed
was solid stone.

Scuffing his boots, clearing the place he'd launch
himself from, he reasoned that if he kept his feet
apart and his weight on the forward foot, he'd slide

along the ledge rather than across it when he landed.

The quiet sound of water lapping against the gap nearly stopped his heart. As far as he could tell, these lower sewers had no currents. What, then, had moved the water?

Drawing in several deep breaths, his nose having become nearly numb to the stench, he shook himself loose and got ready. He couldn't hesitate. It would have to be one smooth, powerful movement.

"One, two," he murmured; then he stopped and shook his head. "I'm an idiot," he told the catacombs at large, slipped his hand into his pocket and his thumb into the leather loop.

Up above, tucked into the arc of the vaulted ceiling, a foul smelling mist—its stink lost in a hundred other putrescent odors—drifted along the dripping stones. Although its edges were translucent and marked by eddies as air currents lightly touched its diaphanous perimeter, the center seemed, at times, almost opaque.

Aurek, now across the gap and back on his own two feet, never even noticed the mist as he paused to identify a series of scratches in the wall at about waist level. Goblin. He didn't know what the marks meant, but they could've been directions, warnings, or love letters for all he cared.

With a contemptuous smile, he kept walking. Goblins were unworthy of his attention unless they were waving short swords in his path—and barely worthy of it even then.

* * * * *

Can you possibly be as good as you think you are? Louise wondered from her hiding place, the contemptuous smile irritating her more than she'd thought possible. Or are you merely too arrogantly stupid to be afraid? Had it been Dmitri she watched, she would have assumed the latter but, though Aurek Nuikin and his younger brother were similar in a great many ways, this was not necessarily one of them. Aurek had years of living Dmitri didn't have. Aurek had confirmed power Dmitri didn't have. And if he was as good as he seemed to think he was, Aurek would have uses Dmitri didn't have.

* * * * *

When the ledge spread out onto a broad platform, two body lengths wide and at least twice that long, Aurek felt the hair lift off the back of his neck. This close, he could sense the power trickling through the ancient shields.

"This is it, Natalia," he whispered. "I know it is."

Slowly, he crossed to the foot of the stairs. The ruined carvings almost seemed to writhe in the multiple shadows thrown by the wizard-lights. Holding out his hand, he watched the zombie bone rise until it angled against gravity and pointed directly up the stairs.

Moistening his lips, he put the bone away; he wouldn't need it anymore. The longer he stood at the bottom of the stairs, strangely reluctant to begin the climb, the more the emissions spreading down from the archway made his skin crawl. It felt as if a thousand ants scurried about beneath his clothes.

All his instincts screamed, "Evil! Evil! Evil!"

How could he find his Natalia's freedom in such a place? But how could he run away without being certain? Without, at least, discovering the full extent of the knowledge behind the shields? Hidden knowledge was wasted knowledge.

"There are no evil spells," he reminded himself sternly. "Only spells put to evil uses."

Manic laughter drew his gaze down to a scummy puddle filling a shallow depression worn into the stone just past the lowest step. A wild-haired man stared up at him from under heavy lids, thin lips twisted into a sneer. *You're a fool, Nuikin. You were a fool then, and you're a fool now.*

Teeth gritted so tightly that the pull of muscles along his jaw broke open the scab barely formed over his torn ear, Aurek stomped the puddle into a hundred scattered water droplets, each with its own laughing image. Resisting the urge to burn them all to faceless steam, Aurek began to purposefully climb the stairs.

The laughter followed him.

I don't really hear it. It's all in my head. I don't really hear it. He's dead. Repeating that mantra over and over, Aurek climbed a little faster, miserably aware that he couldn't out-climb memory.

At the top of the stairs he paused, a little out of breath, and studied the arched doorway. Grotesque faces stared back at him from the stone. Some were meant to be men, and some were meant to be beasts, but the sculptor had captured on each of them an expression of utter terror. The unknown artist's skill was so great that rather than feel sympathy for such torment, the observer felt caught up in their horror. Aurek couldn't stop himself from glancing back over his shoulder, as if to see what they were watching for.

For a moment, he thought . . . but no. There was, as he knew there would be, nothing behind him.

* * * * *

Louise darted back behind the curve of a buttress, wondering what could possibly have caused Aurek Nuikin to turn around at the exact moment she stood exposed on the ledge. She didn't think he saw her—his circle of light spread barely to the bottom of the stairs and humans had notoriously limited vision—but her heart pounded in her chest. Sitting back on her haunches, she groomed her whiskers with quick, jerky motions.

She was too close to success to spook him now. She couldn't take the chance, not when in another moment she'd know.

And if he was as powerful as she suspected? What a weapon he'd be to wield against her twin!

* * * * *

On either side of the archway, facing each other across five and a half feet of open space, was a slit about three inches high and twelve inches long cut into the stone. Checking for traps, and not finding any, Aurek curiously approached the slit on the left.

His initial impression was incorrect: the slit hadn't been cut into the stone, the pale gray blocks had been laid to form it. Beckoning a light closer, Aurek peered into the cavity. He could see nothing but the identical stones of the back wall; if anything lay abandoned on the floor, the angle was too steep for him to see it. Not until he crossed over to the right did he discover what the cavities had been used for.

Finger bones, their ends cracked and shattered from trying dig a way to freedom, lay on the bottom of the slit, time having long since turned tendons and ligaments to dust.

As he could feel no power gathered specifically around either cavity, Aurek could only assume that there had been no magical purpose in bricking these two people in alive. They weren't guardians, and they were far too enclosed to have been an effective deterrent. Without the chance that had left the finger bones in sight, there would have been no way of knowing the cavities ever had been occupied. Had they been enemies? Slaves bought especially for the purpose? Had the ancient wizard gathered power from their terror and their lingering deaths? Had he taken pleasure in their dying? Had he put them there merely because he enjoyed causing pain?

Aurek hated unanswered questions. The search for solutions had driven him all his adult life. Unfortunately, he searched for a specific solution now and had no time to waste on uncovering general knowledge.

But after his Natalia was freed and he could approach scholarship once again not in necessity but in joy . . . He made a silent promise to the two and, heart pounding with near-painful anticipation, turned to face the entrance to the workshop.

There was no actual door, just the archway opening into the room, but light stopped at the inner edge of the arch, as though the shield protecting the workshop and its contents from discovery kept it from entering. If I have to remove the shield, Aurek mused, fingers splayed out but not quite touching the perimeter of the light, I won't be entering the workshop today.

But the shield wasn't a physical barrier and should have no effect on the physical plane.

Should have no effect.

Although the shield and his lights were the only spells Aurek could sense running, the shield itself would prevent him from sensing power use within its borders. He had no way of knowing what he'd step into. But it would take time and energy he didn't want to expend to lower the shield.

Why should his Natalia have to wait any longer?

He rolled the piece of zombie bone between his fingers. He'd already destroyed the workshop's guardians, and he could surely defeat anything that remained. He had, during the course of his life, learned more than most men would ever know.

Caution or cowardice; he would not force his Natalia to wait for her freedom.

Squaring his shoulders, he stepped through the shield.

* * * * *

Yes!

Louise crept closer, her ebony fur making her a large, rat-shaped shadow in the near darkness. There was nothing to do now but watch and wait and dream of the day when she would be Lord of Richemulot.

Overhead, the patch of mist drifted closer as though it, too, watched and waited.

* * * * *

Aurek stood perfectly still, the archway a blank sheet of opaque nothing at his back. In front of him were cases upon cases of books and scrolls. More lay scattered over a massive table, its surface scarred with a hundred ancient experiments. Metal cylinders, glassware of all descriptions, and squat clay jars sealed with stoppers of cork and wax jostled for room with pieces of bone, half a dozen whole skulls of various species, horns and claws and teeth. What had once been a human brain lay like a gigantic shriveled prune on a silver tray. A cabinet, six feet high by three feet wide by two feet deep, held a multitude of tiny drawers, each meticulously labeled in a language Aurek couldn't read.

Yet.

In the far corner, a horsehide chair and worn

ottoman sat in a cluster of tall iron candlesticks. A thick book bound in pale leather and a pair of round spectacles rested on the small table drawn close to the chair.

The dust, which should have lain over everything like a translucent gray blanket, had been disturbed in a number of places. Red-brown stains were splattered over many of the nearer scrolls, and the drying body of half a rat still held a scrap of vellum in its teeth.

Perhaps Louise's cousin used them to run interference when he retrieved the amulet, Aurek mused. With the rats keeping the zombies occupied, it would be easy enough to go quickly in and out again.

Trembling in reaction, Aurek reminded himself to breathe and moved forward, stepping over the body of a dead rat without even noticing it. He understood now why his own book had drawn the attention it had. He could no more walk away from this room than he could voluntarily stop his heart from beating. Such a huge amount of knowledge gathered in one place! Eyes wide, he lightly caressed one of the scrolls. Time had left them dry and brittle, but the preservation spells had held, and even the most delicate could still be read.

The spell he needed was here. He'd grown so attuned to it over the course of his desperate search that he could feel its presence without having to do anything but stand and stare.

Slowly he turned toward the book by the chair. He would undoubtedly already know a sizable proportion of the spells it contained—the spells that every wizard learned in common before scholarship turned to a specific path—but even if the book held only the one spell he had yet to learn, it was worth everything he'd gone through to find it.

* * * * *

In an alcove, a six-foot nightmare of bone straight-ened. A horned skull turned on a human spine over the shoulder bones of a bear. Dried blood flaked out of joints and crevices as it flexed clawed hands. Empty sockets stared at the intruder's back.

*   *   *   *   *

Thrown sideways, bruised and bleeding from a shallow gash on one arm, Aurek slammed into the cabinet and dropped to the floor—the remains of half a rat squashing under one knee. Scrabbling to his feet, he stared in horror at the creature that had attacked him. The zombies were not the only guardians the ancient wizard had left behind.

Nor, it appeared, were they the most dangerous.

Whatever it was, it wasn't merely undead, for no living creature had ever worn flesh around that mis-matched collection of bones. Diving under the mas-sive table, hearing claws rip into the wood above him, Aurek searched his memory for some clue as to the horror's identity.

It would have to be a necromantic spell. . . .

And then his blood chilled as he realized what it had to be: a bone golem. Created from the previ-ously animated bones of skeletal undead. No more intelligent than other golems, but strong, and virtu-ally indestructible. Worse still, the physical attacks were not the greatest danger he faced—the laughter of a bone golem could kill, and usually did.

*   *   *   *   *

It'll laugh soon. Head cocked, listening to the sound of battle, Louise backed away. She'd never been closer than the bottom of the stairs, but she knew what guarded the workshop. Although the family traditionally had nothing to do with wizards or wizardry, they were adept at recognizing an opportunity for personal advancement and, after the first time Louise had heard the bone golem laugh, she'd made a point of learning what it was and how it might be used against Jacqueline.

She had a number of such opportunities cached throughout Richemulot, just waiting for the fates to provide her with the final piece she needed to set them in motion—and lo, the fates had provided Aurek Nuikin.

The simple scholar he claimed to be would stand no chance in a confrontation with her sister. A journeyman wizard would die only a little less slowly. But if Aurek Nuikin had power enough to defeat the bone golem, he would have power enough to be an effective weapon against Jacqueline.

If the bone golem killed him, it proved he wasn't strong enough for her purpose.

And it was all at minimal risk to her.

*   *   *   *   *

He had to defeat it before it laughed. Knowing what it was and what it could do would provide some small protection but not, Aurek feared, enough. Fire would destroy it, but fire would also destroy the rest of the workshop. If the golem burned with even half the intensity of the zombies, it would ignite every combustible object in the room.

A trio of ivory claws scored the heavy leather of Aurk's boot, ripping away its protection. Another in the same place would tear off his foot.

Even if he had wanted to run, to abandon the book that held Natalia's freedom, he couldn't. The golem paced between him and the door.

All at once, the table's protection was thrown

aside as the golem finally figured out how to reach him. Aurek dove and rolled and felt his shoulders nearly yanked from their sockets as his pack was torn away. He screamed as claws gouged searing lines of pain into his back. Shredded, his clothing hung off his shoulders in a grim mockery of the fashionable dress of Pont-a-Museau.

Gasping for breath, he struggled to his knees, expecting another attack. When he turned, he saw the golem lift its horned head and its jaw begin to open.

All golems were susceptible to dispelling magic, but only if the wizard executing it was as powerful as the wizard who had originally created the creature. If it turned out he wasn't powerful enough, he'd have spent all he had for nothing and leave himself defenseless.

But I haven't much choice.

It was either take the chance or die for certain when it laughed.

Lifting trembling hands to shoulder height, Aurek clung to what little focus he could find and shouted out the words of the spell, fighting not only the power that animated the golem but his own pain and exhaustion. Sweat ran hot, then cold, down his sides under the ruin of his clothes. His vision turned yellow, then orange; then black spots crept around the edges of his sight.

His abused lungs screamed for air.

The torn muscles across his back began to jump, each involuntary motion sending new agony to distract him.

He wasn't . . . going to be . . . strong enough.

He could taste failure like rusty iron in his mouth.

Then, one bone at a time, the golem collapsed.

Panting, Aurek collapsed as well, barely managing to keep his face from smacking into the stone floor. At that moment, he wanted nothing more than to lie there for an eternity or two until the world stopped spinning around inside his head. But it wasn't over yet.

He couldn't stand; his body refused to hold him, so he crawled to where the horned skull crowned a pile of bone. He had to be sure that it was truly, finallydestroyed.

Passing his uninjured hand over the pile, he found a shaky focus and tried to detect any remaining trace of magic. For one horrifying moment, he thought he could feel an aura of power clinging to the bones, then they shuddered and, as time caught up with them, crumbled to dust.

Aurek knelt where he was, counting his own heartbeats to convince himself he still lived. Overhead, the three globes of light became six smaller globes, then eighteen specks, then nothing at all. Caught in a darkness so complete it was like being wrapped in fold after fold of black velvet, Aurek did the only thing he could think of.

He laughed.

*   *   *   *   *

Laughter. Touched with hysteria, but human laughter nonetheless. It sounded good after all the screaming that had been going on. Louise smiled and groomed her whiskers. She had her weapon, and she had Dmitri who would teach her how to use it. Soon, she would be second-best no longer; she would be Lord of Richemulot.

And Jacqueline would be dead.

*   *   *   *   *

It took him half a lifetime to find his pack and another lifetime for his shaking hands to tumble out the tinderbox, strike a spark, and get the lantern lit.

He had nothing left. No hidden strengths. No reserves. Nothing. But he was still alive, and the way to Natalia's freedom lay clear.

Dragging the pack, pushing the lantern across the floor in front of him, Aurek crawled to the chair and somehow managed to pull himself up into it. When his torn back hit the horsehide, he sucked air through his teeth and jerked forward. No. It wasn't time to relax. Not yet.

He rummaged in the bottom of the pack and fumbled out the package of food Edik had insisted he take. It was only cold meat and a biscuit with a small flask of water, but as any apprentice wizard soon learned, power used had to be replaced; it didn't miraculously reappear. As he chewed and swallowed, Aurek tried to hold a vision of the food spreading throughout his body, replenishing his strength. By the time he finished, he could sit without swaying, but nothing else had changed.

It wasn't important. He had the book.

He was reaching for it when his gaze fell upon a circular indentation in the cover.

The amulet had been a key, but the amulet no longer existed. The book would be protected—by more subtle protections than zombie guards and bone golems. He couldn't feel the protections, not in his current condition, but they were surely there.

Slowly, he drew his hands back.

In time, he would be able to open the book. He'd opened a number over the years of his scholarship and had no doubt that this one would succumb to careful, painstaking research as all the others had. In time. But not now. Not when he had no idea of what he faced. Even touching the book, unprotected by the amulet, could destroy it, or him, and he couldn't take that chance.

Nor could he wait in the workshop until he regained

his power. If the wizard who created the bone
golem—and who very likely had been destroyed by
the pact made with the Dark Powers in order to do
it—had left any lesser precautions, he'd be helpless
to deal with them. To have prevailed so far and then
fall before a minor spell would be bitter irony indeed.
His death would doom Natalia, regardless of how
close to success he was at the time.

He had to live for her.

Picking up the lantern, but leaving the pack with
its broken straps behind, he staggered to the archway and out onto the stairs. Somehow, he reached
the bottom without falling.

On the landing, he turned and stared up at the
dark entrance to the workshop. He should feel triumphant, but staying on his feet in spite of exhaustion
and pain took all the strength he had. "I will come
back," he promised, clutching the stones for support. "My redemption is here, and I will claim it."

* * * * *

From the shadows, Louise watched Aurek Nuikin
stagger forward and decided that if her weapon was
going to make it out of the catacombs in one piece,
he needed help. Bone and muscle stretching and
changing, she sat back on her haunches and then
continued rising up until she stood on two feet,
furred but vaguely human.

The flickering flame of his small lantern made it
easy for her to stay close by his back and remain
unnoticed. She matched her footfalls to his, though
she suspected he wouldn't have heard her had she
blown a trumpet by his ear. Her nose twitched continually at the bloodscent rising up off the wounds on
his back, on his hand, and on his head, the rich,
meaty smell enveloping him. When her stomach

growled, she began to wish that she'd eaten the goblin regardless of the taste.

This wizard is much too valuable to be wasted as a snack, she reminded herself, swallowing a mouthful of saliva.

Although drawn by the bloodscent, the goblins stayed back. She could hear them, smell them. Once or twice she even saw a stealthy shape leap back into a side tunnel. They wouldn't approach as long as she remained on guard and, as it was in her best interests for Aurek Nuikin to arrive home safely and regain the full use of his not inconsiderable powers, she wasn't going anywhere.

Unnoticed by them both, the foul-smelling mist drifted up the stairs and into the workshop. A moment later, an ebony wererat, identical in every way to Louise Renier except that both its ears were whole, appeared in the doorway and stared thoughtfully down the catacombs.

* * * * *

At the gap in the ledge, Aurek sagged against the damp stone of the catacomb walls and weakly shook his head. He had no power to use the leather loop and no strength to jump. The gap had looked less treacherous when he'd crossed it on his way in.

It's no wider than it was. If I inch forward along the broken edge, I can step over. A bit of stone crumbled under his boot and plopped down into the water.

He got one foot across, looked down, and froze. It must've been a trick of the lantern light, but it looked as though the ripples from the stone had turned. As he watched, a ripple rolled under his spread legs and lapped against the wall.

And then another.

And then another.

And then a ripple that by rights should be called a wave.

Aurek couldn't move. Couldn't get his other leg across to save his life. He stood, stretched over the gap, as a second wave joined the first.

Something pushed him hard from behind.

He catapulted forward, slipped, went down on one knee, and barely managed to keep his hold on the lantern. He wanted to scream but suspected that attracting more attention would not be a survivable idea. His heart pounding so loudly he thought he could hear it echoing through the tunnels, he dragged himself back onto his feet and forced himself to keep going. He didn't turn around to see what had saved his life—a small, barely functioning part of his brain insisted he didn't want to know.

* * * * *

At dusk, it stopped raining—good news and bad news combined. The good news: the end of icy water running down collars and up cuffs. The bad news: it was dusk. In a very short time, it would be dark.

The boatman peered anxiously into the Narrows, where shadows lengthened and hunters stirred. Calling himself several kinds of fool, he decided to wait just a few minutes longer. The next time he moved out into the river, he wouldn't be coming back.

* * * * *

When he stumbled down the steps of the townhouse and into the pallid light of early evening, Aurek dropped the lantern and let it shatter on the cobblestones. He no longer had the strength to carry it. He was beginning to doubt he had strength enough to make it to the river.

Staring around him, searching for the route he had
to take, he tried to remember climbing back up the
rusted ladder and couldn't. Likewise, his journey
through the townhouse was a kaleidoscope of
images, cohesion shattered by pain and exhaustion.

The river was . . .

The river was . . .

He didn't know where the river was.

The scrape of claws against stone drew his head
around. Fifteen or twenty rats, their humped bodies
low to the ground, came out of the ruined park.
Another half dozen had followed him out of the townhouse.

Whatever direction he went, staying where he was
was not a good idea.

As it grew darker, more and more rats came out of
the shadows. They never quite cornered him—there
always seemed to be a path he could take—but
Aurek knew that wouldn't last.

He also knew the rats were not the only hunters in
the Narrows.

So close, Lia. I'm so close. I can't, I *won't* die
before I free you.

He fell once, the impact with the cobblestones
surging through him like a red wave. His individual
wounds no longer hurt, but that was only because
his entire body had become pain. Somehow, before
the first rats reached him, he lurched to his feet and
kept going. He had finally found the spell to free his
Natalia.

Aurek clung to that for strength and refused to
think of the second trip that would have to be made
back into the catacombs in order to retrieve it.

When, as the last of the day was failing, he reached
the river, he gave thanks to the fates who'd guided
him and reeled toward the dock.

The boat . . .

. . . was there.
He was . . .
. . . safe.

*   *   *   *   *

The long braid of silver-blond hair was unmistakable, even if the one who wore it looked little like the gentleman who'd left him in the morning. His boat braced against the remains of the dock, the boatman couldn't stop a horrified exclamation as his employer pitched face first into the bilges, and he saw the full extent of the damage.

He bit off his initial impulse to ask if the man was all right—it seemed a fool question under the circumstances—and bent his back to the oar. The best thing he could do for them both was to get his employer home.

As the blunt nose of the canalboat swung into the current, he thought he saw, just for an instant, a black rat larger than any he'd ever seen silhouetted on the shore. An instant later it was gone, and as he rowed, he worked very hard at forgetting he'd ever seen it.

It was much, much safer that way.

 **SEVEN**

The boatman tied up in front of his employer's house and wondered, brow furrowed, how best to get the injured man to safety. Had their sizes been reversed, perhaps he could have carried him over the esplanade and up the stairs into the house. But as it was, he doubted he could even lift his tall employer onto dry land. Unfortunately, given the bloodscent hanging over him, leaving the injured man in the boat while he went for help wouldn't answer. Coming out of the Narrows, he'd had to ship his oar and use his gaff when something had tried to climb over the side. It had been too dark to see what it was but, given the feeding frenzy he'd heard when it fell back into the water, it hadn't been alone.

Hollering to attract attention could easily do more harm than good, given the type of attention likely to be attracted after dark in Pont-a-Museau.

He prodded his employer in the thigh with the toe of his boot. "Sir? Can you stand?"

Apparently not. The harsh rasp of labored breathing was all that indicated the man was still alive.

Maybe he'll die, and I can just dump the body. The boatman sighed. The longer he hung on to this cargo, the greater the risk to himself. Besides, he'd gotten him this far. It had become, though he wasn't in the habit of using the phrase, a matter of honor.

He trimmed the stern lantern until the flame shone clear and bright, then picked a careful path to the bow, trying not to step on sprawling bits of Aurek Nuikin. When the bow light also burned as brightly as possible, shoving the shadows out another few feet from the boat, he leapt up onto the shore and ran for the house.

Carriage lamps burned on either side of the door, and he noted with astonishment that the brass knocker had actually been recently polished. The only things that usually gleamed so in Pont-a-Museau were eyes in the night. The third time he slammed the knocker down, the door swung open, and he found himself staring up into the broad features of a yellow-haired servant.

"I gots your master in the boat," he said abruptly. "He's hurt."

The manservant asked no questions, merely ran for the river. By the time the boatman arrived on his much shorter legs, the other man had leapt down into the boat. It rocked wildly with the sudden addition of his weight, and a rat scrambled from its perch on Aurek's thigh to the gunnels. A hand shot out, there was a crack of breaking bone, and the limp body of the rodent flew through the air, silhouetted for an instant in the bow light.

"How did this happen?" the manservant demanded, his Borcan accent nearly obscuring the words as he carefully gathered his master up in his arms.

Still on shore, the boatman shrugged, the gesture unseen but apparent in his voice. "He came outta the Narrows like that. I don't know how it happened." He would not mention the giant ebony rat. He tried not even to think of it. Braced for the accusations that would surely come, the servant's next question took him totally by surprise.

"Do you need refuge for the night?" the servant asked as he stood up, his master's body resting across his broad shoulders like an elongated lamb.

The boatman stared at the larger man, amazed he'd even thought to ask under the circumstances. "N-No," he stammered when he found his voice again. "I can make it home."

"Good. Return with the daylight, and you will be well rewarded for this."

"Yeah. Yeah, I will." He wiped his hands on dirty trousers. "Do you, uh, need help?"

"Thank you, no. I can manage."

The boatman watched their progress to the house, uncertain if he was merely curious or if he actually intended to help should they be attacked. His gaze kept returning to the swaying blond line of Aurek Nuikin's braid, its gentle back and forth motion sketching an almost hypnotic pattern across the night. It flared then disappeared in the general illumination as they reached the circle of light around the door.

Then the door closed.

The boatman jerked at the sound, suddenly realizing he was alone in the night. Breathing a fervent prayer to whatever benevolent gods might be listening, he cast off and stroked strongly for home. In order to return in the morning for his reward—and, though his lack of doubt surprised him a little, he believed the reward would be given as promised—he had to survive the night.

* * * * *

Buttoning his beribboned vest, Dmitri walked out onto the second floor landing and frowned down into the entryway. "Who's banging on the door at this hour, Edi—*Zima veter!*" Astonishment jerked out the Borcan exclamation, though upon crossing the border Aurek had self-righteously insisted for fluency's sake they not speak their native language. Dmitri threw himself down the stairs, touching maybe one in three. "What happened to my brother?"

"The boatman says he came out of the Narrows in this condition."

"The boatman?" Dmitri frowned, trying to place the man and finally touching a dim recollection of a shadowy, faceless figure standing at the stern of the canalboat. "And you believed him?" He tried to push past, but Edik left him no room. "Get out of my way, and I'll deal with this boatman. We'll see what he knows."

"Had he injured the master, he would not have been so stupid as to bring the body home." Edik shifted Aurek's limp weight across his shoulders. His face wore no more expression than usual, but the edge in his voice betrayed a certain amount of inner agitation. "I will continue straight to his bedchamber."

"You can't carry him upstairs like that."

Edik set one foot carefully on the first step. "I believe there is room, sir."

"No!" Dmitri grabbed his sleeve. "I mean, you can't carry him like *that!*" His emphasis laid indignation over horror that his brother should come home in such condition, to be draped like a slaughtered stag across Edik's broad shoulders.

"If I do not carry him like this," Edik said, continuing to climb, his sturdy linen sleeve pulling out of Dmitri's grasp, "I cannot carry him at all. If you will note, sir, his back has been laid open and cannot be touched."

Dmitri spread his hands, unable to argue but needing to rail at something. "Well, yeah, but . . ."

"If you could keep the master's skull from impacting with the wall, sir."

"I can do that!" He leapt forward and gently cupped one palm over Aurek's head, knuckles brushing the flocked black roses in the wallpaper. Unfortunately, this brought him distressingly close to the three slashes across his brother's back—their edges drying, their centers still seeping blood. Every movement cracked open the few scabs that had formed. "He looks . . ." Dmitri swallowed and tried again. "He looks as if he's been attacked by a big animal of some kind."

"Yes, sir."

"But what kind? That's the question."

Edik carefully maneuvered down the second floor hall, his steps becoming more and more deliberate as his burden grew heavier. "I suggest you ask your lady friend, sir."

"My lady friend?" Dmitri ducked past Aurek's head and opened the bedchamber door. "What are you implying, Edik? Why would Louise know anything about this?"

"Servants hear things, sir. And I have heard that both the *sestra* Renier know everything that occurs in the city." He stopped, knees pressed against the side of the huge bed. "If you could take the master's feet, sir."

Together they slid Aurek facedown onto the bed.

"Should we send one of house servants for a doctor?" Dmitri asked as Edik deftly peeled the shredded clothing from his brother's torso. He vaguely thought that with Aurek injured, he should be taking over, making the decisions, but he couldn't seem to concentrate.

"No." Edik's contempt of the local practitioners rang clear in that single syllable. "I will take care of the master, as I always have."

"But . . ." Then he remembered some of the stories he'd heard about what happened around the sickbeds of Pont-a-Museau.

". . . *so while the learned doctor is pouring medi-
cines past this poor sot's teeth,*" Georges laughed,
the fingers of one hand playing negligently with a
strand of his sister's hair, "*the rats in the mattress
have eaten off the toes and are working their way up
to the ankles. The idiot couldn't see the blood
through a pile of filthy blankets, and he thought all
the twitching had to do with his useless potions.*"

Most were probably exaggerations, some outright
lies, but if any were true, then the loyal Edik's care
would be infinitely preferable. "What can I do to
help?"

Edik stared at him for a long moment, and Dmitri
found himself feeling somehow wanting—as if the servant's steady gaze saw into his heart and didn't much
like what it saw. He began to bridle. "Look, Aurek and
I might not always get along, but he's my brother."

Meeting his gaze, Edik weighed the emphasis,
then nodded and said, "If you would go for the
brandy, sir, while I get boiling water and clean
cloths."

Outside in the hallway, Dmitri had to lean for a
moment against the wall. All he could see was his
brother's pale and bloodstained body lying still and
helpless on the bed. Aurek had never been much of
a fighter—their sisters had often remarked on it. So
what if he was a wizard? He'd still spent most of his
life with his nose in a book. What kind of training was
that for a fight? He had no business going into the
Narrows by himself. If he'd taken me with him, I
could've protected him.

He doesn't want you with him, murmured a voice
in his head, a voice that took on the tones and
cadences of Louise Renier's. *He never even told you
he was a wizard. He's been lying to you all along.*

He's still my brother, Dmitri thought as his hands

curled into fists. And for the first time in my life, he needs me.

* * * * *

Aurek woke to pain—searing lines of it across his back, a hot ache in one hand, and dull throbbing over most of the rest of his body. He thought for one terrifying moment he was still in the workshop, that he had to move, to dive out of the way or the bone golem would tear him apart. He jerked, rolled onto his side, felt the rough familiarity of the blanket beneath him, and realized where he was.

Home. He'd made it home.

"Natalia . . ."

His news—his glorious, magnificent news—couldn't wait. Teeth clenched, he slid his lower body off the bed and allowed his knees to drop to the floor. He tried to rise, fell back; tried to rise, succeeded. With his left hand leaving bloody handprints against the wall, he staggered into his study one pain-filled step at a time. When he arrived at the alcove holding his Natalia, his naked torso dripped sweat the color of cheap red wine.

"I found it, Lia," he gasped. "I found your freedom." He drew in a deep breath, ignoring the way it burned in his throat. "There's a workshop in the catacombs, and a book, and the spell we need is in that book. I hadn't strength enough to open it but I will, Lia, my love, my life. We are so close. I promise you, so close . . ."

The fine hairs on the back of his neck—or, at least, those few not stuck down in a gory mat—lifted. Slowly, Aurek turned to see Dmitri standing little more than an arm's length away. "What are you doing in here?" he demanded.

"The door was open," Dmitri began, but Aurek cut him off.

"I told you never to come in here!" As he swayed, the bloody braid swept across his chest, leaving a pinkish red smear. "Never!"

Dmitri fought against his immediate, defensive reaction. His brother was injured. Hurting. He didn't know what he was saying. Gesturing toward the adjoining bedchamber with the bottle of brandy, he murmured, "You shouldn't be out of bed."

"I should be exactly where I am!" Eyes rolling, voice sharp, Aurek felt as though he were on the edge of a precipice. For Natalia's sake, he had to stop himself from toppling over. "I have work to do. Important work. Get out! Leave us alone!"

"Us?" Dmitri glanced around the study. "There's no one in here but you and I."

"Natalia . . ."

"Is dead! She died over a year ago! Her body was completely destroyed!" Concern and irritation combined to override sense. Dmitri strode across the room and snatched up the figurine before Aurek could stop him. "This," he declared, waving it in the air, "is a piece of morbid statuary. It's not your wife!"

Moving faster than his wounds should've allowed, Aurek grabbed the figurine. Eyes blazing, he straightened to his full height and, in his rage, towered over Dmitri. "Get out!"

Raising the bottle of brandy like a shield, Dmitri stepped back and shook his head in hurt disbelief. "You-you need help."

"Get! Out!" Each word was a separate, barely controlled explosion of rage.

Dmitri stared at his brother, saw nothing in his expression that acknowledged either him or their relationship in any way, turned on his heel, and nearly ran from the study. By the time he met Edik in the bedchamber, his hurt confusion had merged with the emotions of a lifetime of injustice, of not ever being quite good enough, and turned to anger. "Apparently," he informed the frowning servant bitterly, "I am of less importance to my brother than a bad depiction of his dead wife."

"Young sir . . ."

"Forget it." Throwing the bottle on the bed, Dmitri stomped out of the room. "You're on your own. If he dies, don't imagine I'll care."

* * * * *

Slumped on the plank floor of the study, Natalia cradled protectively on his lap, Aurek jerked as the bedchamber door slammed. He had the strangest feeling that he'd just pushed his younger brother across a bridge into a dark and violent place—that he'd made a very grave mistake. His thoughts spun round and round and round.

"Too tired," he murmured to the auburn braids wrapped around the top of his wife's porcelain head. "And too close to success. I'll deal with him when you are free, my love." With his right thumb, he rubbed at a drop of blood rolling down the full folds of her skirts. No matter how much he rubbed, he couldn't seem to rub it off.

"Once you are free," he repeated, wondering how one drop of blood could spread so far, "I'll make everything right with Dmitri. I promise."

* * * * *

"You're looking very cheerful tonight."

Louise draped an artistically disheveled curl over the notch in her ear and smiled at her sister's reflection in the mirror. "I guess I am pretty cheerful tonight at that."

"Any particular reason?"

Skirts swirling, Louise spun around on the leather
stool and faced Jacqueline. "It's a pretty wonderful
world."

"Isn't it," Jacqueline agreed dryly. "You were out
all day in it; you couldn't have gotten much sleep."

"I'm fine." Does she suspect? Pulse beating a little
faster, Louise studied her sister's face but saw only
ennui and no sign of suspicion. "But thank you for
your concern. I take it you're not going to be attending the evening's festivities?"

Jacqueline glanced down at the loose robe she
wore and then at Louise's gilded finery. One angled
brow angled higher. "No," she said, "I won't. I'll be
having a private party of my own."

Pursing glistening lips, Louise looked arch. "Anyone I know?"

"I haven't decided yet." The Lord of Richemulot
turned out of the doorway, throwing a disinterested,
"Have a good time," back over a slender shoulder.

Louise slipped a golden bangle over her wrist and
began to hum. She had a weapon to use against her
sister—sooner or later she'd discover the best way to
use it—and now she'd just been handed the one
thing she needed to make her evening perfect. There
would be no Jacqueline at the party to take the shine
off the evening. No Jacqueline to outshine her.

*   *   *   *   *

"Stop eating the candles, Georges, you look
ridiculous!"

"No one noticed," Georges murmured around a
mouthful of beeswax.

"*I* noticed!" Snatching the taper from his cousin's
hand, Yves savagely threw it into a corner. When a
townsman turned to protest the violent appearance
of a half-eaten candle in the midst of his conversa-

tion, Yves bared his teeth, and the man hastily changed his mind.

Georges hunched his shoulders and slid farther down the wall. "I've seen you gnaw on a candle or two," he protested sullenly.

"Not in a drawing room, not in skin form, and so what?" The last three words carried a ring of challenge.

Resigned to the inevitable, Georges straightened.

"Stop it, both of you," Chantel snapped, stepping between them. "If you want to fight, at least find something less childish to fight over." If she'd intended to say anything else, it was forgotten as a sudden commotion drew everyone's attention to the entrance.

"She's got that razored look tonight," Yves muttered, thinking that the blast of cold air accompanying Cousin Louise into the room had little to do with the falling temperatures outside. He could see the emerald glitter in her eyes from where he stood, and that meant someone was in a lot of trouble. Considering their last conversation, he only hoped it wasn't him.

Chantel took a step forward, breasts heaving under the thin silk of her gown. "I'd like to notch her other ear," she growled.

"Are you out of your mind?" Yves deftly placed himself in Chantel's line of sight. "If you want to die young, you go right ahead and challenge her, but don't do it when we're around. She'll never believe we had nothing to do with it, and I, at least, have no intention of dying with you."

Chantel scowled up at him, her eyes within their fringe of pale lashes appearing even redder than usual. "Move."

He ignored the command. "You can't still be annoyed about the little Nuikin?"

"She took control of him weeks ago," Georges added.

"So?" Her tone made it quite clear she was, indeed, still annoyed.

Yves jerked his head at his cousin, and they each clamped a hand around one of Chantel's slender arms and began to lead her toward the ballroom at the back of the house, where they could reinforce their numbers with Annette and the twins and, if nothing else, the music would make it harder to be overheard.

"I wonder why females are so competitive," Georges mused.

"Go chew on a candle," Chantel snarled.

* * * * *

Tossing his coat and hat to a footman in faded, mismatched livery, Dmitri jerked at a tangle in one of his streaming ribbons and yanked the ribbon right off the shoulder of his vest. Snarling a curse, he threw the narrow satin streamer aside and stomped toward the sound of conversation. Yves and the others would probably be in the ballroom, but the last thing he felt like doing was dancing.

A number of faces turned his way when he entered the drawing room but, all at once, their welcoming expressions seemed false. He'd been attending their parties, fêtes, balls, for weeks now, but he didn't really know any of them. They don't really care that I'm here, he muttered to himself as he scowled his way past a number of cheerful greetings.

As it happened, he was right, but there wasn't a person in the room who could afford to ignore Louise Renier's current favorite.

He got himself a glass of punch, downed it, and got another, even though it tasted as if its principle ingredient was a close cousin to turpentine.

Too close to the fire and this stuff'll ignite, he thought woozily. Contrary to popular opinion, it tasted no better by the bottom of his third glass. His tongue didn't feel numb; it felt flayed.

The end of the room holding the grated fireplace was too hot. The far end, too cold. Between, there were too many people he didn't like, most of whom smelled sweaty and unwashed under a masking splash of cheap scent. Just for a moment he saw the rags and tatters not as fashion but as decay; saw the crumbling plaster, the moldy corners, the filthy floor. He rubbed watering eyes, shook his head, and it became just another townhouse in Pont-a-Museau.

He was thinking about moving on into the card-room, if only because Aurek despised gambling, when he heard the unmistakable trill of Louise's laughter.

At least she'd be glad to see him.

"I have heard that both the sestra *Renier know everything that occurs in the city."*

Savagely repressing the memory, he made his way toward the ballroom. He would not have Edik's suspicions—a servant's suspicions—taint what he had with Louise. Louise was all he had left.

Her smile when she saw him was everything he could have asked for. *You are important to me,* it said. *Now that you are here, the night is complete.*

In its light, Dmitri dropped to one knee, athletically graceful in spite of the punch he'd imbibed, and raised her fingers to the soft caress of his lips.

"You look unhappy," Louise murmured, false sympathy masking pleased satisfaction. Unhappy young men were so much easier to manipulate. She drew him to his feet and tucked his hand into the heated crook of her elbow. "Lets find someplace quiet," her voice rose slightly, "and private, to talk."

Her circle of sycophants, who had reluctantly dropped back when Dmitri approached, took their dismissal with ill-grace. One elderly swain went so far as to voice a faint protest. Human ears might have missed it; Louise's did not. She turned just enough to sweep the edge of her glittering gaze over the offender; then she permitted Dmitri to lead her from the ballroom. Behind them, the man who'd spoken stood alone, as though the others were afraid his fate might be contagious.

* * * * *

"Now then . . ." In a small room on the second floor, Louise sank down on a red velvet sofa and pulled Dmitri down beside her. "Tell me what's wrong. It hurts me to see you so unhappy."

Dmitri shrugged, suddenly uncertain how much of what had occurred between himself and his brother he should tell her. *"Servants hear things, sir. And I have heard that both the* sestra *Renier know everything that occurs in the city."* He couldn't seem to get past the combination of Aurek's wounds and Edik's words. He opened his mouth to ask her if she knew what had torn up his brother's back and closed it again, lost in the depths of her eyes.

This is ridiculous. Look at her. He drank in her delicate beauty, blinded, as he was meant to be, by the surface luster. She could no more know what attacked Aurek than she could've struck the blow herself.

"Dmitri . . ."

He jerked as she called his name.

". . . let me help."

"Yes."

* * * * *

A short while later, Louise stroked Dmitri's hair back off his face and smiled triumphantly—not bothering to mask her expression, for the besotted young fool she planned to make such lovely use of was sitting on the floor with his head resting on her knee.

So her wizard had a figurine of his dear, departed wife that he deeply loved. Loved to the point of stupidity from the sound of it—even accounting for her informant's bias. *What would he do if he lost that little statue?* she wondered. *Fall apart? How nice. And what would he be willing to do for the person who could put him back together? Almost anything, I expect. How pathetic.*

Should Aurek Nuikin prove to be not quite so pathetic as she anticipated, she would still come out ahead. The loss of the statue would, at the very least, make Aurek unhappy, and unhappy young men—she gave Dmitri's golden curls a vicious, triumphant little tug—were so much easier to manipulate.

"I feel like dancing," she said suddenly. "Dmitri, take me back to the ballroom."

Confused by the abrupt change of subject, Dmitri scrambled to his feet and held out his hand. "But what about Aurek?"

Wrapping her fingers around his, Louise allowed him to pull her to her feet. "Aurek clearly doesn't care about you," she said, the words sticky with sincerity. "You've got to stop caring so much about him. You'll only keep getting hurt, and that hurts me." She caught his gaze and held it. "You don't want to hurt me, do you?"

"No." Lost in the emerald depths of her eyes, that was the one thing he was sure of. "I'd do anything to keep you from being hurt."

"I know you would." Louise pressed the warm length of her body against him for a moment and rested her head on the broad strength of his shoulder. Her voice quavered slightly. "I know I can depend on you." She felt him tremble and hid a toothy smile against his vest. At that instant, he would have done anything for her—all she had to do was ask. Letting the instant go—there'd be plenty more where it came from—she pulled back.

"Take me down to the ballroom," she declared, "and we'll dance all over Aurek's inflated opinion of his own importance."

Dmitri blinked as the room spun a half turn to the right. The taste of the punch clung like an oily film to the inside of his mouth. "Aurek's not here, Louise. He's injured, remember."

"It was a metaphor, my blond darling." She reached up and patted his cheek a little harder than was absolutely necessary. "Just take me dancing."

*   *   *   *   *

Swirling around the floor in Dmitri's arms, other dancers moving carefully from their path, Louise couldn't remember when she'd had a better evening. Her plans were falling into place, her dancing partner was tall and beautiful and nowhere near smart enough to survive the relationship, and, best of all, she stood second to no one. Without Jacqueline, she was the center of everyone's attention.

And someday soon, it'll be like this all the time. Eyes half closed, she built a pleasant fantasy of her life as Lord of Richemulot. Jacqueline allowed the townspeople too much autonomy and the younger members of the family too much room for ambition—that would most definitely change. The silly masquerade; a pretense of humanity because of a hunted past? As much as Louise hated to admit it, Jacqueline was right; it was amusing to watch the clever ones deny the evidence, and there was nothing funnier than the look on the face of the more irritating social climbers when they found themselves at the estate for an evening's private entertainment.

When I am lord, I shall "entertain" more often.

"Mamselle Jacqueline! So glad you could attend!" Their host's shrill voice cut through the music and conversation and shredded Louise's pleasant evening. As the intricate movement of the dance spun her toward the door, she could feel the focused attention of both family and townspeople slipping away.

Jacqueline stood just inside the ballroom, already at the center of an obsequious crowd. She caught Louise's eye as her twin danced past and smiled.

She's here just to irritate me. Louise was as certain of it as if Jacqueline had admitted it aloud. *How dare she! She said she wasn't coming!*

"You're frowning. Was it something I did?"

Louise jerked. She'd forgotten all about Dmitri. "No," she spat through clenched teeth. "Nothing you did. I wasn't expecting my sister is all."

Dmitri looked a little confused. "But she's always there. I can't remember being at a party without her. Ow! Louise, your nails . . ."

While her mouth voiced insincere apologies about the crimson half-moons soaking up through the slashed sleeves of Dmitri's shirt, Louise considered what he'd said. To her deep disgust, he was right. Nothing happened in the city without Jacqueline. The realization left a bitter taste in her mouth.

However, a great deal was about to happen without her. When Aurek Nuikin was back on his feet and ripe for manipulation, Jacqueline would have to be temporarily removed from Pont-a-Museau.

And then they'd bring her home just long enough to make her removal permanent.

* * * * *

"Young sir, the master wishes to see you."

Dmitri snorted and tossed his hair back off his face. "Well, I don't want to see him." When Edik continued to block the top of the stairs, he scowled and folded his arms across his chest. "What?"

"It has been nearly a week."

"This may surprise you, but I know what day it is. Now, get out of my way."

Edik shook his head. "The master wishes to see you."

"I heard you the first time." Dmitri squared his shoulders, realizing all at once that he was as tall as Aurek's servant and nearly as broad. "And I don't want to see him." He smiled as he realized that Edik understood the subtext. "If you were planning to drag me into his bedchamber, I'd just like to see you try it."

Silently, Edik moved from the top of the stairs, disapproval radiating off him in heated waves.

Flushed with triumph, Dmitri descended to the entrance hall and out onto the front steps, where he paused in the circle of lamplight to pull on his gloves. *So Aurek wants to talk to me, does he. Probably wants to make another sanctimonious announcement.* He tugged the gray kid smooth over the backs of his hands and murmured aloud, "Lets see how *he* likes being ignored."

* * * * *

"So . . ." Aubert—at least Dmitri thought it was Aubert, though the twins went out of their way to make identification difficult—tipped his chair back on two legs and tossed a splintered chicken bone onto the platter in the center of the table. "How's your brother?"

Before Dmitri could answer, Yves hooked a foot around his cousin's chair and sent him crashing to the floor. Although the other patrons in the café kept a politic silence and their eyes locked on their food, the members of the family made plenty of noise without them.

"What did you do that for?" Aubert demanded when the peals of laughter had subsided enough for him to be heard.

"You were being a bore," Yves told him. "Dmitri doesn't want to talk about his brother. His brother is . . ."

"*Morne?*" Georges interjected around a mouthful of food.

"*Fatigant?*" Annette offered, smiling across the table at Dmitri.

"*Hors de propos?*"

"*Contrariant?*"

"All of the above," Yves declared, lifting his glass so that the dark wine gleamed in the lamplight. "And as Dmitri here is none of the above, why would he want to talk about his dull, tedious, irrelevant, and vexacious brother?"

"He wouldn't," Dmitri agreed, laughing, lifting his own glass in answer.

Georges swallowed and stood, swaying slightly. "A toast to our friend Dmitri. Pont-a-Museau wouldn't be the same without him."

Dmitri colored as they drank, his fair skin a deep crimson with pleasure and his eyes overbright from all the wine already drunk. This was the acceptance he'd searched for all his life. When they finished, he toasted new friends; Henri toasted family—a designation, he pointed out carefully, that excluded Dmitri's brother but included Cousin Louise—and Yves called for more wine.

Empty bottles and empty platters were already piled high on their customary table.

"I don't understand how you all can stay so thin," Dmitri marveled as Aubert, or maybe Henri, topped up his glass. "If I ate like you do, I'd be the size of a horse."

"Horse is good," Georges muttered. "In a sausage with a little red sauce . . ." Annette elbowed him in the ribs, and he began to hiccup.

Dmitri laughed with the others. In the early days, he'd tried to share the costs of the massive meals but had been told that the Renier family had made arrangements with the cafés. As discussing money was distinctly not done among the upper classes, he'd never asked what those arrangements were.

Businesses that dared to charge the family didn't remain in business for long. However, as Pont-a-Museau society followed the Reniers' lead, the cafés they frequented stood to make a profit in spite of the freeloaders' appetites. Unfortunately, younger members of the family found it amusing to randomly announce that everyone in the establishment was, for the evening, their guest, leaving the owners to reflect that alive and bankrupt was infinitely preferable to the alternative.

Leaning back in his chair—though carefully keeping all four legs on the ground lest he repeat Aubert's tumble—Dmitri reflected that he'd never had better friends. They'd accepted him into their circle as though he were one of them. And they were certainly a lot more fun than the friends he'd left behind in Borca—even young Borcans had a certain solid respectability completely lacking in this group.

Completely lacking, he reaffirmed, hastily averting his eyes from the twins and Annette. Although he tried, he couldn't quite get used to such blatant sensuality. Casting about for something else to look at, his gaze fell on Chantel, moodily rolling a walnut between two pale fingers. "You're very quiet."

She shrugged.

"She's jealous of all the time you spend with Cousin Louise," Yves mocked, leaning forward.

"Are you?" When she only shrugged again, Dmitri laid a hand on her arm. "Please don't be. Louise is very, very special to me, but I don't want to lose our friendship."

Chantel sighed, unable to decide whether she was more irritated by his blindness or amazed by it. Naiveté was not something she'd had any experience with—family members exhibiting such a fatal flaw were weeded out very young. "I don't want to lose you either," she replied at last. That the admission was the truth—if slightly skewed—leant a certain amount of sincerity to her voice.

Dmitri smiled and lifted the back of her hand to his lips. "Good. Now if you'll excuse me . . ."

Twisting her hand, Chantel grabbed his and hung on. "Where are you going?"

Yves laughed as Dmitri blushed. "He wants to see a man about a waterworks, Chantel."

"Oh." She released him and watched him weave across the crowded room. Her knuckles whitened and the walnut cracked, spraying bits of shell across the table. "I wonder what would happen if I told him Louise was only using him to get to his brother."

"Louise would kill you."

"What do you think she's up to?"

"Who? Louise? What difference does it make? If you find out, she'll kill you."

"Only if she knows I know."

"She'd know." That was a given he shouldn't have had to remind her of. Yves leaned forward and lifted her chin on the tip of one finger. "And I'd miss you when you were dead."

Chantel snatched her head away from his touch, then whipped it forward and closed her teeth, through flesh to the bone.

Yves screamed as she released him, and for the first time that night, Chantel smiled.

* * * * *

The cool night air cleared Dmitri's head, and he barely swayed as he walked across the inner yard to the privies. A lot of men didn't bother, just stood clear of the back door and let it go. Even drunk, Dmitri couldn't do that. He'd tried one night when Yves and he had left the café together, but his sisters' opinion of such behavior kept ringing in his head and, in spite of the other man's scornful laughter, he'd continued to the row of latrines. Besides, the latrines smelled marginally better than the yard.

A few moments later, while readjusting his clothing, he heard running footsteps in the alley on the other side of the stone wall the privies were built against. The staccato sound held a certain desperate rhythm. A moment after silence fell, a hoarse, terrified scream lifted the hair off the back of Dmitri's neck and slammed his heart up against his ribs.

He charged out into the yard, saw no gate or door through the wall, and leapt for the iron spikes set into the top of the stonework. Muscles straining, pitted metal digging into his palms, he heaved himself up onto the broad top and, body twisted around the spikes, squinted down into the alley.

Although the moon was only a quarter full, there were clouds enough to spread the pale silver light. Dmitri could just make out a thin and ragged man trying frantically but unsuccessfully to scrabble over the wall at the end of the alley. Three, no four shadows were moving slowly, deliberately toward him. At first he thought they were dogs, but the hump-backed silhouettes were unmistakable. They were the biggest rats Dmitri had ever seen. They had no need to hurry; it was obvious their prey would be unable to escape.

Apparently well aware of this, the ragged man redoubled his futile efforts and screamed again.

Eyes widening in anticipation of the fight, Dmitri inched forward and clapped a hand to his hip—grabbing only air. Swords were considered unfashionable in Pont-a-Museau. With his sword, even at four-to-one odds, he wouldn't have hesitated for a heartbeat. Without his sword . . .

The first rat rose onto its haunches and almost delicately closed its teeth around a flailing arm. Even over the screaming, Dmitri heard bones crunch. A second wedge-shaped head darted forward at a scrawny calf and pulled back, jaw moving up and down. The rats were eating the man alive.

His leap from the top of the wall took Dmitri halfway back across the enclosed yard. Without his sword, he'd have to get help. Pushing his way through the crowded cafe, he grabbed Georges by the shoulder and tried to drag him from his chair. "Come on!"

Georges scowled and lithely twisted free, smacking away an opportunistic hand making a foray at his plate. "Why? Have you lost something?"

"There's a man in the alley being eaten by rats!"

The café had fallen silent, and the final word filled the room.

Rats.

Yves's edged laughter seemed to rebound off of every staring patron. "Busy night for it," he snarled, waving a finger wrapped in a bloodstained handkerchief.

Confused, Dmitri clung to the one thing he knew.

"We've got to help him!"

"Why?"

"Because . . ." Wide-eyed, Dmitri stared around the table, unable to believe the response. Or more specifically, the lack of one. "Because there're four rats as big as dogs eating a man alive out there, and we can't just let it happen!"

"It's already happened," Annette told him calmly, leaning forward and untucking a fold of his vest from the waist of his trousers. "Unless he was hugely fat."

"No, no he was skinny but . . ."

"Rats are quick eaters." Georges managed to kick both of the twins as they started to snicker. "Four of them will be finished by now."

"But . . ."

"Trust us," Chantel said with a smile that reminded Dmitri uncomfortably of Louise. "We know."

He scanned the features of his friends and saw a feral similarity on all six faces. They were obviously not going to help. He turned to survey the café. Conversations hurriedly started up again as everyone ignored him. No one, not even the servers, met his gaze.

Fists opening and closing at his sides, he took a step forward and then stepped back. He couldn't win on his own. Not without a weapon. He was certain of that. His shoulders slumped. "It's already over?"

"They'll be gnawing on his bones by now." For emphasis, Georges cracked a pork rib and noisily sucked the marrow out.

"You wanted to be the white knight, didn't you?" Yves's eyes glittered mockingly. "Riding to the rescue?"

Surprised by the cruelty in Yves's voice, Dmitri shrugged. "I just thought I should do something," he muttered.

"En garde, rodent!" Aubert flourished a baguette

at his twin, who recoiled in feigned terror. Around and around the table they went, Aubert shouting lofty epigrams, Henri squeaking, their nearest neighbors hastily snatching to safety possessions in danger of being trampled. The chase ended when Henri suddenly turned, grabbed the baguette, and broke it over his brother's head, yelling, "Rats win!" At which point they collapsed into their chairs, howling with laughter.

As he took his seat, Dmitri joined in the hilarity because it had been pretty funny. While he'd been outside, Yves had apparently cut a finger, so that explained his mood. Of course Chantel's smile was like Louise's; they were cousins. There was a simple explanation for everything.

With no idea of how simple the explanation was, he drank until he killed the memory of the screaming, thanking all the gods that he hadn't seen the man's face.

 **EIGHT**

Louise tucked a silken curl back into place and stared thoughtfully at the mirror, ignoring the places where the silvering had flaked off the back, creating what appeared to be decaying patches in her reflection. According to her faithful and aching-to-be-needed Dmitri, Aurek Nuikin would be well enough to leave the house within the next few days. She had no doubt that the moment he was able, he'd head straight for the catacombs and the abandoned workshop—which was good, for it meant he'd be out of the house and away from his study for a sufficient amount of time.

This trip, he could make on his own. A wizard powerful enough to destroy a bone golem, and who'd no doubt be picking up still more power from the abandoned workshop, hardly needed her protection against a few insignificant goblins.

She had other plans—lovely, labyrinthine, dark, and twisty plans. But before she could put those plans into motion, she'd have to get rid of Jacqueline.

Get rid of Jacqueline. She repeated the words silently to herself as she stood and swept out of the dressing room set aside by the evening's host for her private use. It gnawed at her that there was a slightly larger one for her twin. Her frown parted the crowds as she descended the stairs and reentered the crowded drawing room.

It wasn't hard to find a messenger. There were always social climbers at these affairs who wanted so desperately to get ahead that they'd do nearly anything without a thought for the consequences.

*　*　*　*　*

The front gate of Chateau Delanuit was half open. Guy Muridae stepped under the arch and felt as though he were stepping from evening into night. Shadows that merely slanted through the rest of the city gathered together here and presented a dark and united front. He kept his eyes locked on the pale gray light spilling in from the courtyard and walked as fast as he could without actually running.

Under his best jacket and vest, sweat plastered his shirt to his sides. He nervously brushed a lock of brown hair back off the damp curve of his forehead. His footsteps echoed off the surrounding walls of the gatehouse, and he found himself carefully setting each foot down on the cobblestones so as to make the least amount of noise.

You're being an idiot, he told himself, holding, like a talisman, the memory of Louise Renier's promise. Twitching his cravat straight, he stepped out into the courtyard, blinking a little in his sudden return to the late afternoon light.

The vast open courtyard was overgrown and ill tended. Guy was surprised, actually, at how ill tended it was. The Reniers were at the top of the Pont-a-Museau social hierarchy; surely they could afford caretakers? His gaze skipped from cracked and broken cobblestones to stone tubs holding small

ornamental trees he was sure were long dead, to a
tangle of leafless vine nearly burying a three-tiered
fountain—where it stopped.

Something stared back at him from the top tier.

Then it was gone.

He wiped his palms on the thighs of his pan-
taloons. It was probably nothing more than a rat.
There were rats all over Pont-a-Museau—why not
here? Taking his cue from the stratum of society he
longed to be fully accepted into, he'd learned to
ignore them. Mostly.

Being out in the open helped.

The stone arch over the front door echoed the arch
of the gate, and the door itself echoed the squalor of
the courtyard. The black paint not actually peeling
off the wood had cracked into a thousand pieces like
a mudflat in the heat. The massive brass knocker had
been etched with a pattern once, but too much of it
had corroded away for him to recognize what it had
been. The sound it made was surprisingly mellow.

"I have come with a personal message for Jacqueline Renier," he informed the elderly servant who
dragged open the door, her scowl somewhat deflat-
ing his lofty tone. "My card," he said grandly, handing it to her.

She stared at the small pasteboard rectangle held
in a three-fingered hand, and then at him. After a
moment, the scowl smoothed out into a near total
lack of expression. "Follow me, Monsieur Muridae. I
will take you to the mamselle."

The decay so obvious in the courtyard was not as
evident in the house. Or perhaps the house was just
too overwhelming for a visitor to notice the decay.
Following the servant across the great hall, Guy
stared at the oak roundels in the ceiling, at the
curved molding around the paneling, at the stained
glass in the windows turned to glorious color by the

last rays of the setting sun. They went through a door, dwarfed by the sixteen-foot walls, and passed a second servant in the hall.

He had much the same expression, or lack of it, as the first.

These were people, Guy realized, who didn't see what they weren't supposed to see. *I wonder how I could train my servants to be this discreet.* Although his entire staff currently consisted of a cook-housekeeper, he had big plans—big plans that this visit would help him accomplish.

"Wait here, Monsieur."

He waited, crushing his gloves in first one hand and then the other as his escort disappeared behind a baize-green door. Although he was alone in the corridor, he felt as though he were being watched. *Which is ridiculous,* he told himself. He wished only that the protest sounded more convincing.

A few moments later, the elderly servant returned and ushered him into the Chateau's library.

Jacqueline Renier sat in a crimson, wingback chair as though she sat on a throne. At a ball, any ball, she shone like a diamond, brilliant and cold. Here in her own home, she was the most beautiful woman Guy had ever seen and, for no reason he was consciously aware of, he felt a return of the terror he'd felt crossing through the dark under the gatehouse.

"Mamselle." He bowed gracefully, knowing how crucial it was he make a good impression.

"You have a personal message for me?"

"I do, mamselle."

"From whom?"

"I beg your pardon, but I swore not to reveal that."

Red lips drew back off ivory teeth. "Swore to whom?"

His heart pounding harder, faster, Guy spread his arms. "Mamselle," he said chidingly. When she smiled, he remembered that Jacqueline Renier was a widow and wondered if she'd ever considered remarriage. Now that would definitely make his fortune.

"And your message?"

"I was to tell you only that Henri Dubois has been seen in Mortigny." He heard her sharp intake of breath and saw her fingers tighten on the brocade-covered arms of her chair.

"And what," she asked after a moment, her voice sounding as though it had traveled from far away, "is there in this message for you?"

Guy bowed again. "Only the honor of doing you a favor."

"This is news my sister desperately wants to hear." Louise leaned a little closer to him, wrapping him in the heat of her body. *"If you bring it to her, she'll be so grateful she'll see to it that your social standing in Pont-a-Museau is assured."*

Swallowing hard, Guy tried to force his brain to function. *"Why don't you tell her yourself?"*

"You know how it is with sisters." She drew her fingernail lightly down the line of his jaw. *"This man came between us and . . ."*

"Say no more." As a man of the world, he completely understood.

"The honor of doing me a favor? That's all?"

He smiled charmingly. "To have the most beautiful woman in Pont-a-Museau in my debt? I think that's enough."

"Yes, I think you're right."

Her smile reminded him very much of her sister's—but that was hardly surprising as they were twins. When she stood and began to walk toward him, all he could think was that, since they were alone, she was about to show him just how grateful she was. *This is incredible. All I really needed was her public approval.*

It was his last thought.

"I dislike being in debt," Jacqueline told him, wiping bloody fingers on the full skirts of her dress. Stepping over the body, she walked quickly back to her private apartments through a Chateau suddenly crowded with memories of Henri Dubois. . . .

His dark hair had come free of the ribbon that usually held it confined at the nape of his neck, and he shoved it out of his way as he scanned the shadows. Clinging to the wall where it met the ceiling in the far corner of the bedchamber, Jacqueline reveled in the play of muscle beneath the thin cotton of his shirt and drank in his scent.

Henri Dubois, a human as unscrupulous as he was beautiful, had been willing to play lovers' games as long as he thought he'd been making the rules. He was charming, funny, and smarter than he looked. He was able to enjoy life in a way she'd never realized a human could, and he made her feel as though anything were possible.

Of course, she hadn't intended to fall in love with him. Didn't even know how it had happened. She knew when though. He'd walked into the room and smiled down at her, dark eyes twinkling, his hand wrapped warmly around hers, his expression an invitation. She'd felt her heart race, her breath catch in her throat . . . and her body begin to change.

To her fury, she hadn't been able to control the metamorphosis. Even as she came to know her heart, her body betrayed her. His look of admiration had turned to loathing as her clothing sagged and slid off sloping shoulders, her muzzle formed, ebony fur covered her body, and her naked tail curled around elongated, clawed feet. Not full rat, but the intermediate form that was, if anything, worse, for there were reminders enough of the human form within it.

She could see him remembering how he'd shared

a bed with this creature. Her heart breaking at his expression, she stretched out a front hand/paw and called his name. He backed up two paces, turned and ran.

That she could not, *would* not allow.

The Lord of Richemulot did not love and lose.

Except for this time. Repelled by what she truly was, Henri Dubois wanted nothing more to do with her. Anyone else who offered such an insult she would have killed, but her love for him had become his shield. Which left her only one choice.

She'd tracked him to this house, to this room and, when he came close enough, she would have him. If he would not be her mate, he would become a wererat and her slave. One way or another, he'd be hers.

He knew she was there.

"Jacqueline, I'm warning you!"

She couldn't help it: she laughed. He was warning *her?* His arrogant belief that he was the center of the universe was one of the things she loved best about him.

Henri whirled to face the sound, a long dagger suddenly in one hand.

He dared? He dared to draw a blade on her? She stared at him in disbelief. Love or not, this had gone quite far enough. Scurrying rapidly along the wall, Jacqueline flung herself at his head, one hand/paw going around his throat, the other effortlessly smacking the dagger away. When he hit the floor, she straddled his chest and sank her teeth into the fleshy part of his shoulder.

His scream had as much to do with his sudden realization of what she was attempting as with the pain. She bit him again and again, careful to make no single bite fatal. Licking his blood from her muzzle, she prayed to the dark gods.

When he lay limp and barely breathing, she car-

ried him back to the Chateau and her bed, and she
waited. For nothing. Perhaps his disgust of her rat-
woman form gave him strength, but his body fought
the lycanthropy infection. His skin burned; he lay for
three days drenched in sweat and blood, muscles
knotted, spine arched, fingers curled into fists.

And he won.

He would not be changed.

Furious, Jacqueline smashed furniture, gouged
holes in wood and plaster, destroyed her bedchamber and everything in it but Henri Dubois. When it
seemed that even he was in danger, she gained control enough to leave, lest she hurt him in her rage.

The townspeople of Pont-a-Museau still refused to
speak of that night.

That was the last time she saw him.

When she returned to the Chateau, he was gone.
No one saw him leave, though he must've had help.
Nor could she find him, though he should not have
been able to remain hidden from her.

Perhaps he'd been praying to the dark gods as
well. . . .

Dropping to her knees, Jacqueline pulled a bloodstained shirt from an oak trunk at the foot of her bed
and held it to her cheek. Even the lingering scent of
his blood and sweat was enough to twitch bone and
muscle beneath her skin.

Henri Dubois, her one true love, had been seen in
Mortigny. How could she be expected to stay away?
It might be true.

*   *   *   *   *

"Will you be back soon, Mama?"

Jacqueline took her son's mournful face between
both her hands and dropped a kiss on his forehead.
"Soon," she promised. "Remember, you are the man

of the house while I am gone."

"Aren't I the man of the house while you are here?" Jacques asked, brows drawn down in confusion.

"It doesn't mean the same thing when I am here." Her tone warned him not to contradict her again.

"Yes, Mama." With all the seriousness of a child of ten, he helped her into the boat. "You're going to be all by yourself. Won't you be lonely?"

Jacqueline glanced south, up the Musarde River toward Mortigny, and murmured softly. "I hope not." Then she turned and stared at Louise, the deep green of her cloak making her eyes appear more jade than emerald, but just as hard. "If anything happens to my son, I will hold you personally responsible."

"What could happen?" Louise closed one hand around her nephew's slender shoulder. "Jacques and I will manage together just fine. You've gone away a hundred times before; this isn't any different."

"No. It isn't." She stared at her sister for a moment longer, then finally took her place and indicated that the pilot could cast off. As the boat pulled away from the landing, she called, "I don't know when I'll be back."

Well aware that she was being warned, that her sister had actually reminded her that she could be back at any time, Louise smiled. Based on the most insubstantial of rumors, Jacqueline would tear Mortigny apart to find Dubois; she wouldn't be back anytime soon. "Take all the time you need."

* * * * *

"That's all?" Lucien Renier cocked his head and studied Louise suspiciously. "We wait until the human leaves, break into his house, and steal a little statue of his dead wife?"

Louise nodded. "That's all."

"If it's so simple, why don't you do it yourself?" his twin, Jean, demanded belligerently.

"Perhaps I will. I merely thought you might enjoy the opportunity to get back in my good graces after that disgusting exhibition at Tante Marguerite's party." Over steepled fingers, she smiled at her cousins. During an argument, one of them had been overenthusiastic with his gestures and had spilled a cup of punch in her lap. They'd spent the last week blaming each other for the accident and expecting to die. Which made them perfect candidates to break into a wizard's study, given that she had no intention of risking her own fair skin. Neither did she intend to tell them they were breaking into a *wizard's* study. "But if you don't want to make up . . ."

"We do, Louise." When Jean remained quiet, Lucien kicked him hard in the ankle.

"Yeah," he muttered. "Yeah, we do."

"Good." Her smile sliced a few pieces off each of them. "You can keep anything else you find, just bring that statue to me."

Lucien reached under his cravat and scratched at a partially healed scar along his collarbone. "What if someone gets in our way?"

Louise shook her head and wondered for a moment if there was a direct correlation between the intelligence of the females in the family and the stupidity of the males. "Don't touch Aurek Nuikin," she said with emphasis. "Kill anyone else you like."

"Anyone else?" Jean looked more cheerful. "Now that's more like it!"

*   *   *   *   *

Amusing himself by pulling the wings off a pigeon, Lucien nearly fell from the roof when Jean yanked on his tail. Claws scrabbling for purchase on the lichen-encrusted slate, he whirled around and smacked his brother in the head with the bleeding carcass, snarling, "Keep your hands to yourself or lose them."

Rubbing an ear thick with old scars, Jean silently pointed down toward the entrance to the house.

Aurek Nuikin and the big, blond servant stood at the bottom of the steps.

* * * * *

"Sir, please, just a few more days to regain your strength." In his attempt to keep his master alive, Edik had switched back to his native tongue. The Borcan words had a desperate urgency he couldn't give to another language.

Every movement carefully planned to cause the least pain to healing tissue, Aurek shook his head. "No, Edik." Without thinking, he answered in Borcan as well. "I've wasted too much time as it is."

"Then take the young master with you."

Aurek stared at his servant for a moment in astonishment. "Dmitri?" he said at last. "Take Dmitri? He hasn't even spoken to me since . . ."—the day I found my redemption and Natalia's freedom—". . . the day I returned from the Narrows."

* * * * *

"What are they saying?" Jean hissed, picking gory feathers from his fur. "They're not making any sense."

Lucien's ears flicked forward. "That's because they're speaking another language, you idiot. Now shut up."

* * * * *

"If you would explain to him, explain everything to him, I think he would listen." Edik spread his hands. "The young master has his pride, sir. Just as you do. He knows you are keeping things from him."

"I kept nothing from Natalia, and look where it got her. I will not be responsible for disaster happening to my brother as well. The less his life touches mine, the better for him." His expression darkened. "Especially considering the company he's been keeping of late."

"Sir, I . . ."

"Enough." Aurek chopped at the air. "You presume upon long service."

Edik inclined his head. When he raised it again, it wore the slightly blank expression of a well-trained servant. "The boat has arrived," he said.

Aurek turned eagerly toward the river, took a step toward the boat, toward the Narrows, toward the workshop, then stopped and, with an effort, turned to face Edik once again. "Dmitri is safest if he lives his own life, but I do appreciate your concern—for us both." He didn't wait for a reply; the pull of the workshop was too strong. Moving as quickly as healing muscles allowed, he ran for the boat, and a moment later stood in the bow, leaning upriver as though to speed it on with his body.

Behind his back, the boatman lifted a hand to Edik, who raised one in return. He stood on the step and watched until the boat and his master passed under the South Lacheur bridge; then, shaking his head, he went inside.

A bloody feather fell unnoticed as he closed the door.

* * * * *

In full rat form, Jean climbed down the tower wall, pried open the window, and climbed inside. As his tail disappeared over the crumbling stone of the window ledge, Lucien leaned forward, ears cocked. If the window were trapped, he reasoned, better Jean discover it. A moment later, when there were no sounds at all from the tower room, he followed, grumpily reflecting that only fools and humans were up at this hour.

Jean sat on his haunches in the middle of the room, head back, whiskers twitching. "Smells like magic," he hissed, changing just enough for speech.

"Of course it does, you fool." Lucien changed as well, quickly combing the fur on his shoulders down into place with his claws. "This Nuikin's been searching for magic stuff in the city. You never pay attention."

"I don't like magic. It makes me itch." Jean began to scratch vigorously. "Louise never said there'd be magic."

"You think she tells us everything? Think again, Brother. Let's get the statue and get out of here."

With his muzzle, Jean pointed to the figurine on the pedestal. "You think that's it?"

Lucien's only answer was a muttered, "Idiot," as he crossed over to the alcove. Dropping down onto his haunches, he studied the area with eyes and nose. He could see no traps, smell no traps, and that usually meant there were no traps, as humans seldom were devious enough to fool the members of the family. *Most* members, he corrected shooting a glance at his twin.

"What are you waiting for?" Jean demanded. "I'm hungry. Let's go." He reached past his brother's shoulder, but Lucien snarled and batted his hand/paw aside.

"I'll take that—" The instant his fingers touched the porcelain, he knew he'd made a mistake. Few things move faster than a terrified wererat, and Lucien snatched his hand away with all the speed his terror lent him.

Too late.

The room whirled and dissolved around him, walls melting into windows, melting into doors, melting into the ceiling, melting into the floor. He tried to scream, but something held his throat in an iron grip, and no sound emerged.

When the room stopped spinning, he saw he was no longer in the human's study, but crouched at the end of a narrow corridor. Corpse-gray walls stretched up on three sides of him as high as he could see. Claws extended, he leapt for the wall to his right but slid back, unable to gain any sort of purchase. He tried again. And again. And again.

Finally he stopped, gasping for breath, and took another look around.

The wall at the end of the cul-de-sac seemed a lighter gray than those on either side. When he pressed his hand/paw against it, he felt it give, though his claws continued to make no impression. Frowning, he stepped back and suddenly realized that something was pressing on the wall from the other side. Strange shapes bulged toward him, moving from place to place as though they were testing the strength of the barrier.

If whatever lurked on the other side of the wall got through, he was dead.

He didn't know how he knew that, but Lucien had never been so sure of anything in his entire life. Changing to full ratform, he turned and ran.

After about twenty feet, he came to a T-junction— nearly invisible in the gray-on-gray corridor—and without slowing, threw himself to the right. As he cleared the corner, he heard something tear behind him. The wall? He ran faster.

When the corridor turned left, he turned with it, then left again, then right. Another dead end. He threw himself at the wall, and felt something throw itself at the other side. The impact knocked him backward. As he hit the ground, he rolled and raced back the way he'd come.

Whatever they were, there was more than one of them.

He didn't think he could cross the mouth of the original corridor, but he found he had no choice—he had no idea of where the original corridor was. Everything looked the same, and nothing carried a scent. He couldn't backtrack because he couldn't find his own trail.

He ran back through the turns he remembered, raced down a long, straight section and, claws scrabbling for purchase, turned right. Left. Another T-junction. Right. Dead end. He didn't wait to see if his presence caused a third attempt to breach the walls. Back past the junction. Right around two corners, three, four, five, shorter stretches of corridor turning tighter and tighter . . .

. . . to a fourth dead end.

By the time he found where he'd made his mistake, Lucien knew they were in the maze with him.

Around another tight turn to a another junction. Left. Left. His breath tore at his throat. He couldn't hear them over the sound his own heartbeat, but he knew they followed close behind. One turn back. Maybe two. If he stopped—if he paused—if he hesitated—they'd have him.

Only his fear kept him moving. Exhaustion dropped his tail to the floor. It dragged, slowing him further. If I change . . . But he couldn't change on the run, and he couldn't stop running.

The center . . . If I can make it to the center . . .

Left and left and left again.

They were gaining on him. He could feel their hot breath on his back, their claws reaching out to rend and tear. But he could also feel how close he was!

Drawing strength from reserves he didn't know he had, he put on one final burst of speed and left the gray walls behind.

Unfortunately, he also left the gray floor behind.

He screamed as he fell, a long, drawn-out, horror-stricken sound caught halfway between a human cry and a rat's squeal. It went on, and on, and on.

They were waiting at the bottom.

* * * * *

Jean watched as his brother thrashed about on the plank floor of Aurek Nuikin's study—legs pedaling the air as though he were running full-out; eyes wide, staring at nothing Jean could see.

He was afraid to touch him and equally afraid to leave.

The room stank of magic.

When Lucien began to pant, Jean shrank back.

When he opened his mouth and screamed—first in terror and then in such agony that there could be nothing left of living but pain, Jean dove out the open window, scurried down the dead ivy clinging to the tower wall, and raced away.

Whatever had Lucien was not getting him.

* * * * *

Edik threw open the study door and stared down at the largest dead rat he'd ever seen.

Shifting his grip on the axe he carried, he quietly closed the door and scanned the room. Where there was one, there could be more.

Not until he was certain he was alone did he actually study the grotesque corpse.

He'd been in the basement kitchen, trying futilely to instill a basic concept of cleanliness into the house servants, when the young man hired to keep the floors scrubbed had stumbled into the room, frightened out of his wits. Pale and shaking, he'd stammered out that he'd heard something scream in the master's study.

Edik had snatched up the axe and leapt up the stairs. He'd heard the house servants bolt the kitchen door behind him, but he'd deal with their cowardice later.

Right now, there was the rat.

Brow furrowed, Edik studied the body for a moment. Given its position at the foot of the pedestal, he had a good idea of what had killed it—the master would not have left the porcelain statue unprotected. Why a wererat wanted the figurine of the late mistress was no concern of his. His problem was one of logistics.

Dumping the body in the river as it was could quite possibly cause nasty repercussions if he was seen— unlike the young master, he'd listened to the house servants' lurid stories of what lurked in the sewers and shadows of Pont-a-Museau, added them to personal observation, and drawn his own conclusions.

He measured the thickness of muscle and joint, then changed his mind. Chopping the body into unrecognizable pieces seemed just a bit extreme and would be more than a bit messy. Setting the axe aside, he left and returned with a worn blanket, a large piece of rusted angle-iron, and some rope. After wrapping rat and iron together, he bent and heaved the weighted corpse up onto his shoulders. This wouldn't be the first large, unidentifiable bundle to be slipped into the river, nor, Edik was certain, would it be the last.

He was actually more concerned about getting the urine stain off the floor and its acrid odor out of the room.

*   *   *   *   *

The path through the Narrows, through the sewers, through the catacombs to the landing at the foot of the stairs had been etched in his mind. Aurek couldn't have forgotten it even if he'd wanted to. All the long days and nights he'd lain trapped in his bed by slowly healing injuries, he'd dreamed of returning.

This time, nothing would get in his way. He'd use the skills he'd honed through years of scholarship and open the book. He'd find the spell. His Natalia would be free.

And he would be redeemed.

The scrape of steel on stone jerked him out of pleasant memories—his Natalia waiting for him when he emerged from long hours of study, with a smile and meal and strong hands to work the tension from his shoulders—and back to the grim reality of the catacombs. The goblin sign he'd noted on his previous visit quite likely explained the sounds he heard, but analysis indicated that this part of the catacombs had to be on the outermost edge of their territory. Two or three sentries were the most he could expect to run into. He wasn't particularly worried. While goblins weren't very bright, neither were they very brave, and his trio of wizard lights made clear the power they'd be dealing with should they attack.

In fact, as goblins were predominantly subterranean creatures, the light alone should be enough to keep them away.

Then he realized the sounds were flanking him.

He stopped and listened, a hand braced against the damp stone to steady himself. Another scrape of steel on stone before him, as though a weapon brushed against the curving wall, and the creak of leather armor behind. They were close enough that, had the catacombs themselves not smelled so foul, he very likely could've caught a distinctive whiff of goblin.

Just at the edge of his light, he could see the break in the ledge—the place where the stone had crumbled and the murky water lapped hungrily against the wall. A shadow lurked on the far side. Aurek saw no glint of light on weapons, but then, goblins weren't known for spit and polish. Jaw set, he readied a spell. The one behind him, he could ignore, but the one in front stood between him and the workshop, thus between him and the spellbook, and he had no intention of allowing Natalia's freedom to be delayed.

At the edge of the break he paused and, to his astonishment, the goblin stepped forward to the opposite edge. Yellow eyes squinted nearly shut in a dull orange face, the creature lifted its stained morning star and barked an obvious challenge.

Aurek stared at it in disbelief. Although goblins were not his area of expertise, this one seemed to be acting distinctly strange. He had no way of telling exactly how old it was, but it seemed young. And large. If goblins were usually under four feet, this one stood considerably above average.

As the creature repeated its challenge, tone blatantly mocking, Aurek chewed at the puzzle.

Goblins lived in a tribal society, the strongest ruling the rest. In order for a young goblin male to challenge the chief, it had to fight a number of smaller battles and establish itself in the pecking order. If a young, strong goblin wanted to skip a few fights on its way to the top, one way would be to challenge and defeat an enemy considered unbeatable.

Like a wizard crossing the perimeter of the territory.

Of course, Aurek thought, it would've made a lot more sense had it attacked me on my way out the last time. He didn't remember much of his trip back to the river, but he doubted he could've defended

himself against strong language, let alone a determined goblin. But then, he'd already established that
the creatures were not very smart. The sentries had
probably reported his presence, and his young chal-
lenger had been hanging around ever since, hoping
he'd return.

Aurek raised his hands, thumbs together, and
spread his fingers.

The sheet of flame not only ignited the goblin, but
swept it off the ledge and into the water. With a sizzle
and a cloud of putrid steam, the fire went out. Its
face and hands a mass of cracking blisters, the goblin bobbed to the surface, screamed once, and disappeared.

Nothing living sank that fast on its own.

Aurek tried to back up and found his shoulder
blades already pressed hard against the wall—which
was when the second goblin shoved a spear handle
between his legs and tipped him off the ledge.

It seemed to take forever to hit the water, and then
it wrapped around him like a liquid shroud, surprisingly warm. Fighting panic, he let himself sink, shoving his left hand toward his pocket, ignoring the pain
when his injured finger caught on wet fabric. He
wasn't a fighter. He had only one chance.

GET OUT OF THE WATER! The words echoed
against the inside of his skull. He couldn't die. Not
here. Not so close to redemption, so close to freeing
his Natalia! He would not fail her again!

Whatever was in the water seemed momentarily
preoccupied with the goblin. Aurek thanked the gods
for that moment. His lungs began to burn. He sank
lower. Began, finally, to rise. Kicked toward the surface now that he knew where it was. Felt something
long and sinuous brush against him. Again. Finally
shoved his thumb through the leather loop.

It was an easy spell, one he used frequently. Why

couldn't he remember it now?

The top of his head broke the surface.

Something wrapped around his leg.

He shot upward. His head, shoulders, chest . . .

The thing was obviously unused to meals that pulled back.

. . . hips, legs . . .

Still fighting to hold his focus, Aurek looked down. Two loops of gray-green tentacle were wrapped around his right ankle. The spell pulled him in one direction; then muscles bunched under mucus-covered skin, and the tentacle pulled in the other. Aurek's knee popped, but he managed to hold on to his concentration. I will not fail her again!

The air became the deciding factor. Whatever the tentacle was attached to, it seemed to lose much of its elasticity out of the water. When it could stretch no farther, it let go. Aurek snapped upward and cracked his head against the arched ceiling. Stars exploding behind his eyes, he momentarily lost control of the spell, dropping down nearly his own body length before he managed to rise again.

Close to six feet of tentacle whipped back and forth in the air and, though it might have been the bump on the head causing him to imagine things, Aurek thought it seemed confused as it slipped back beneath the murky surface of the water. He doubted that its prey had ever left the water in such a way before—or that its prey had ever left the water at all.

Not until he was safely back on the ledge, eyes burning, nose running, gasping for breath, did he remember the second goblin. It seemed to be nowhere around.

It might have decided it won the moment Aurek hit the water.

It might have taken one look at that tentacle and run for its life.

Aurek didn't care. Leaning heavily against the wall, he staggered to the landing in front of the workshop and took a quick inventory. There was a goose egg rising on the crown of his head, but the skin hadn't broken and, as near as he could tell, his skull hadn't cracked. His right knee and ankle throbbed but appeared to have taken no serious damage. The scab had come off the injured nail bed on his left hand, and he'd have to assume the area was infected. Fortunately, the water seemed not to have soaked through his clothing and the bandages on his back, though the wounds were throbbing in time to his heartbeat. He'd best have Edik clean those wounds as well. His nose continued to run, and his beard stank, but against all odds, he was alive.

He made it to the stairs before his legs gave out, and he collapsed, shaking, onto the third step. He was alive. But it had been very, very close.

"I'll tell you one thing, Natalia," he murmured when the reaction seemed to have finally run its course, "I'm taking that book out of here and back to my own study to work on it. I can't go through this every time I need to use it."

All at once, he realized why Edik had thought Dmitri might prove useful to him. While the boy wasn't very bright, he was undeniably athletic. This was exactly the kind of leaping about he'd enjoy. "More fool him." For a brief moment, Aurek considered sharing the burden he carried. Then he tossed the thought aside. The fault was his; the burden was his. His alone.

Drawing in a long breath, no longer able to smell either himself or the catacombs, he got slowly to his feet and limped up the stairs. There seemed to be more of them than there'd been before. By the time he reached the top step, he was breathing as heavily as if he'd climbed a mountain.

"Too much time spent with books," he gasped, leaning forward with both hands on his knees. "Too much time at a desk." When he straightened, he frowned.

The shielding remained in place behind the carved archway, but something had changed. It took him a long moment to realize what it was. No power leaked through the shield spell. He began to stiffen; then, all at once, his shoulders sagged, and he shook his head in relief.

Of course there's no power leakage, you fool, the bone golem's been destroyed, and it was the only active spell running. Rolling his eyes at his willingness to immediately believe the worst, he stepped through the shield.

There was nothing left but ash.

No table. No shelves. No chair. No book.

Everything had been destroyed.

He felt as though he were looking at the room from a very long way away, insulated by the enormity of the loss. He swayed, looked down, and saw the goblin footprints patterned in the ash.

"I did this."

His voice echoed in the empty space.

"I destroyed the guardian. I opened the way."

The weight of that realization settled on his shoulders and drove him to his knees. He had little control over the motion and no control at all over the scream of denial when it finally broke loose.

As his pain bounced off the stone, the dead wizard's delight bounced about within his skull, the mocking laughter chipping pieces from his sanity with every pass.

NINE

". . . touched it, and he jumped away. Then he fell down, and he changed, and he started, well, running."

Louise lifted an ebony brow, distinctly unimpressed by the stammered story. "Running? I thought you said you left Lucien's body in the study. He couldn't have run far."

"He wasn't really *running*." Jean paced jerkily back and forth across the room, his face twitching as though it wore the whiskers that went with his other form. "He was lying there, thrashing, but his legs were moving as if he were running. You know, the way they move when you're dreaming."

"Yes. I know." More significantly, she was beginning to understand what must have happened to poor, unfortunate Lucien. She'd expected traps, which was why she hadn't gone personally. Obviously, there'd been a trap set on the figurine itself. Triggered by touch, the results seemed to indicate that it threw the intruder—in this case Lucien—back into his own head and killed him there. Certainly not beyond the powers of a man who'd defeated a bone golem.

Wrapping a curl around one finger, Louise decided Jean would have to remain ignorant of her theory. He'd likely be quite angry if he ever found out that she'd known that Aurek Nuikin was so powerful a wizard. "Then what happened?"

"Then he screamed, and I left."

She sighed and shook her head. The family believed strongly in discretion over valor. "So you don't actually know that he's dead."

"He's dead." Arms wrapped tightly around his body, Jean seemed to fold in on himself as he remembered his brother's screams. "He has to be dead."

"Well," Louise murmured thoughtfully, "he certainly is by now. Those screams must've attracted some small amount of attention, and I doubt very much that whoever found him bundled him off to a healer."

"The point is, he's dead," Jean growled. "Aurek Nuikin killed my brother."

"Carelessness killed your brother," Louise snapped, hearing the challenge and having no intention of allowing it to stand.

"It happened in Nuikin's house, and he's going to pay."

As he stomped past her, she grabbed his arm and yanked him to a halt, her nails digging into the soft skin of his inner wrist. "Aurek Nuikin is *mine*. Don't touch him."

"I thought you claimed the other one."

"They're both mine."

"No." He shook his head, thin lips pulled back off yellow teeth. "You've claimed the younger one. You can't have them both."

Arguing would make him angry—Louise could see that in his eyes—and if he were angry enough, he might be willing to fight her for the right to kill Aurek

Nuikin. She didn't want to fight him. Fights within the family tended to leave scars on the winner as well as the loser—her free hand dropped to trace the silk that covered the twisted red lines gouged across her hip. Intimidation was infinitely more attractive, even though the words tasted of gall and caught in her throat. "They're both under Jacqueline's protection."

Her sister's name had the desired effect: aggression became confusion. "But if she wants them, how can you have claimed them?"

"She doesn't want to play with them, and I have no intention of hurting them." At least not until what Jacqueline wanted was no longer a factor. Abruptly, she let him go.

Glaring at her sullenly, he licked at the small puncture wounds she'd made in his wrist. If Jacqueline was interested in the humans, then all other interests were subverted by hers. "Someone has to pay for my brother," he whined. "Someone has to pay for Lucien's life."

"Are you suggesting *I* pay?" Snarling, lips pulled right off her teeth, Louise surged up off of the chaise and backhanded her cousin hard enough to knock him to the floor.

Jean scrambled to his feet, took one look at her expression, and ran.

Louise smiled as the door slammed behind him. "As Grandpapa always told us, the best defense is an ambush." It was a useful lesson. Jacqueline had applied it to their grandfather, and now Louise was about to apply it to Jacqueline.

Humming a popular dance tune, she lowered herself back onto the chaise and arranged her skirts around her ankles. Obviously this figurine was very important to the wizard. She was even more strongly convinced that it remained her best bit of leverage.

"Perhaps now that the danger has been defined,"

she said thoughtfully to herself, "and the parameters for safety have been established, I'd best become more personally involved."

*   *   *   *   *

Shaking his head, the boatman watched Aurek stagger across the esplanade and up the front stairs of the townhouse. Something bad, something very bad, had happened in the Narrows. He didn't know what, and his employer wasn't talking, but the man he'd let off in the early morning was not the same man he'd picked up in the late afternoon.

Sometime during the day, Aurek Nuikin had been broken and just barely put back together again. The boatman had never considered himself an imaginative man—imagination was usually a liability in Pont-a-Museau—but it seemed to him that the wrong word would shatter his employer into a thousand pieces. He could almost see the cracks.

"I guess book learnin's no protection after all," he muttered, pushing out into the river and turning his boat toward home.

*   *   *   *   *

The door opened as Aurek reached it, and he stumbled into the entryway, only Edik's hastily outstretched arm keeping him from falling on his face. Fingers tight around the servant's arm, Aurek looked wildly about and muttered, "Can't you hear him? He hasn't stopped laughing since I entered the workshop. He laughs and laughs and laughs and . . ."

"Master!" Edik's voice cut off the flow of words. "There is no one laughing."

Aurek sighed and pushed himself erect. "He's laughing. And why shouldn't he be? There's nothing left in the workshop; all of it was destroyed. No book. No spell. No freedom. No redemption. I wanted to die when I saw it, Edik. I wanted to die, but I can't. I can't give up, because my Natalia is trapped in horror and I am responsible. I'm as trapped as she is, and I only hope her horror is less than mine." All at once, he clapped his hands over his ears. "I could go on if only he'd stop laughing!"

Edik closed his hands around Aurek's wrists and pulled them away. He could see the challenge in other man's eyes, and he ignored it. "You need food, master. And rest. But first, you need a bath."

With no denial to fight, the laughter dimmed. Aurek drew in a long, slow breath and savored the absolute normalcy of Edik's words. "A bath," he agreed weakly. "Yes." Ever since he'd seen the destruction of the workshop, he'd felt as though he were falling. Finally someone had thrown him a line. He was still in a pit, dark and grim and echoing with malicious glee, but at least he wasn't falling anymore.

He allowed Edik to help him up the stairs, strip off his sodden, stinking clothes, and wrap him in a robe. He watched dully through the open door of his bedchamber as the house servants filled the hip bath, and he sank into the hot, scented water with something very like relief. As Edik cleaned old wounds and investigated new bruises, Aurek drifted, obeying instructions—"Lean forward, sir." "If I could see your finger, sir." "Please, sir, close your eyes while I rinse your hair."—but refusing to think. To remember.

But eventually he was clean and dry and fed, and it was time to face his failure once again. As though it had been waiting for his return, fully aware that there could be no real escape, the laughter grew louder.

"Master?"

One hand already on the study door, he was

stopped by Edik's voice.

"There's something you should know."

The laughter reached a crescendo.

*   *   *   *   *

Struggling to control his rage, Aurek reached out and gently touched the imprisoned spark of Natalia's life. It felt no different than it ever had, no different than it had the day he'd crawled across his study floor and clasped the figurine in both shaking hands. He had to assume that the day's events had left her safe and unharmed. He had to assume that, because if even for an instant he thought differently, he'd lose his final grip on sanity.

Opening his eyes, he traced the perimeter of the maze spell with trembling fingers, smoothing over the disruption the wererat's death had made in the pattern.

Not until he had fully reassured himself that his Natalia's protections were unbreachable did he turn to Edik.

"Why—" he began, then repeated it a little more loudly as the mocking laughter threatened to drown out his voice. "Why didn't you tell me about this the instant I entered the house?"

Edik considered his answer for a moment, and when he spoke, the words emerged with the conviction of truth. "I believed it would drive you mad."

Aurek wet his lips and forced his rage to give way to reason. "You were probably right." He ground the admission out through clenched teeth. Had Edik told him about Natalia's danger immediately upon his return, he'd still be falling into that black pit. But, while he acknowledged the need to take care of himself before he could hope to take care of his beloved wife, he didn't have to like it. He wanted to destroy something, he needed to destroy something, and Edik was all there was to destroy. "Get out," he growled, pounding his fists into his thighs. "Do not return until I send for you."

"But . . ."

"I said GET OUT!"

When the red cleared from his vision, Aurek was alone with the trapped spirit in the study. He had never kept anything from her, and he couldn't start now. He was all she had. Sinking down to the floor at the foot of her pedestal, he stared up at her with tears in his eyes. The laughter found his tears amusing.

"I went back to the Narrows today, Lia . . ."

When he finished, he asked for her forgiveness, much as he had a thousand times before. She stared at him in mute horror, unable to forgive.

"There's a chance," he said quickly, almost babbling in his need for absolution, "a very small chance that the book survived, that it was taken from the workshop before the place burned. A wizard's spellbook is a powerful artifact. . . ." His voice trailed off as he realized what he was saying, and he closed his eyes. Moisture trickled down each cheek and into his beard. He had no need to tell Natalia about the attractions of a wizard's spellbook.

The explosion lifted him up and smacked him hard against the wall. He heard Natalia scream his name, he heard laughter—no longer merely maniacal, but insane—then he heard nothing at all for some time. When he regained consciousness, he was alone in the study except for a corpse with a crushed temple and a tiny porcelain statue of his wife, her hands lifted in a futile attempt at protection, her face twisted in horror.

Between the red leather covers of the book nothing remained but a fine gray ash.

When Aurek opened his eyes his beard was wet,

and he could still hear the laughter. He brushed his hair back off his face with shaking hands. "No. The shield spell, I forgot the shield spell. Only another wizard could have removed the book through the shield and have it survive the passage, and I am the only wizard in Pont-a-Museau.

"The book has been destroyed."

And with it hope?

He felt the pit open beneath his feet, and he longed to let it swallow him. He was so tired. But if he surrendered hope, he surrendered Natalia and, while life remained, that he could not do.

The mad wizard in his head stopped laughing long enough to point out, *That's guilt, you fool, not hope!* but Aurek ignored him.

"I found the spell once, Lia. I can find it again."

*   *   *   *   *

"Phew! What stinks?" Shrugging his multi-caped greatcoat up onto his shoulders, Dmitri waved a hand in front of his nose. "You haven't been swimming in the sewers, have you, Edik?"

"No, sir, I have not."

Dmitri's eyes widened as he recognized the clothing held between the servant's thumb and forefinger. "Hey, that's Aurek's. Don't tell me *he* went swimming in the sewers?"

"Very well, sir."

As Edik passed, Dmitri took a closer look. "It looks as though he went for a roll in a fireplace after he got out of the water. What's going on?"

"I can't say, sir."

"Of course you can't," Dmitri agreed bitterly. "You can't, and he won't. I suppose he's locked himself in his precious study with his precious little statue doing some precious studying of whatever precious bit of crap he dragged out of the sewer or the fire this afternoon."

"No, sir. Your brother went to retrieve something today, something very important, and he found it had been destroyed."

"He told you that?"

"Yes, sir."

"Oh, that just figures." Dmitri spat out the words. "He'll tell you—a servant—but he won't tell me—his brother. Well, he can just keep his lousy little secrets." His lip curled up into a sneer he'd learned from Yves. "I stopped caring weeks ago. He can't shut me out if I don't want in!"

Edik winced as Dmitri slammed the door behind him, the draft blowing out three of the five candles illuminating the entry hall. He supposed he should have anticipated the young master's reaction. The situation had deteriorated too far for the knowledge that a servant knew more than he did about his brother's pain to cause anything but anger.

Anger being a young man's way of expressing fear. Fear of yet another rejection. Fear of not measuring up. Fear of never being thought necessary.

Perhaps he should've spoken sooner. Or not at all.

* * * * *

"I'm not sure I should give you my hand." Louise peered at Dmitri through lush lashes, her fingers held back just out of his reach. "You look as though you'd like to bite it off."

"Not your hand!" Dmitri objected vehemently, capturing it and covering the back with heated and enthusiastic kisses. "I worship this hand. I adore this hand. This is the hand of the most beautiful woman in the world, to whom I have lost my heart."

"Yes, yes." With a toss of her head Louise dismissed

his continuing vows of infatuation. While approving of
the content, she was beginning to find the boy's
extreme moods a tad tedious. "Whose hand would
you like to devour then?"

"My arrogant brother's!"

"Of course." Lowering herself gracefully to the settee, she patted the red velvet cushions beside her.
"Sit down and tell me all about it."

"All about it? That's just it." He sat where she indicated and turned an indignant face to hers. "I don't
know anything about it because Aurek doesn't see fit
to tell me. Edik knows what's going on. Edik can go
into Aurek's precious study. But not me!"

"Who," Louise asked, "is Edik?"

"Aurek's servant. Been with him for years."

Louise frowned. She supposed that the servants at
the Chateau had names, but even those who'd survived with the family for years had never presumed
to burden her with them.

"Take today," Dmitri went on, pleased by his companion's interest and completely unaware she
expected to hear about Lucien's untimely death. "He
went out as he always does, looking for magical
junk, and something went really wrong. He ended up
in the sewers, and then went rolling through ashes,
and it turns out that something really important he
went to get was destroyed. But did he tell me, his
brother, all this? No. He told a servant. I'm not good
enough for him."

"Ashes?"

"Yeah, there was ash smeared all over his clothes."

"Did this . . . Edik, did he tell you what had been
destroyed?"

"No." His voice rose. "Nobody tells me anything!"

"Don't shout." She laid a finger against his mouth.
He began to nibble on it, then up her arm, then
across her shoulder to her lips. Distracted by her

thoughts, she responded absently. Had the workshop been destroyed? It certainly sounded as if it had. While continuing the estrangement between Dmitri and his brother was still her best path, it did leave holes in the information she received. Curiosity finally got the better of her, and she pushed Dmitri aside.

Surprised to find himself suddenly thrown into the far corner of the settee, Dmitri pulled himself back into a sitting position and stared at Louise in astonishment. "What's wrong?"

"Nothing's wrong." Rising, she smiled down at him. "I just remembered I had plans for this evening. Can you show yourself out?"

"Louise . . ." Mouth open, he watched her leave the library, certain of only one thing—stopping her would not be a good idea. "Oh, plans for this evening," he repeated in hurt disbelief. Snatching up hat, gloves, and coat, he headed despondently for the door. "I'm sure."

As he crossed in front of a crimson, wingback chair, he stepped on a large, dark stain in the carpet that squelched under his boot. The smell rising up from it was vaguely familiar, sweetish and not entirely unpleasant. On any other evening, he'd have mentioned the wet area to someone, but tonight he didn't see why he should.

Because he never looked behind him, he never saw that the single footprint he left was a sticky red-brown.

* * * * *

Safely hidden in the shadows, Jean Renier watched Dmitri Nuikin leave the Chateau and scuff his way toward the northeast bridge. It seemed that cousin Louise was finished with him early tonight. Ears pricked forward, eyes glittering in the starlight, the wererat followed close behind, disdainful of human senses. Good. He'll have more time for me.

Aurek Nuikin had killed his brother. So he would kill the brother of Aurek Nuikin.

All afternoon, his fear of Louise had fought with his growing rage over Lucien's death. It wasn't right that a human should kill a member of the family. He gnawed at the problem, chewing it over from every angle, and he finally came up with a solution he felt even Lucien would've been proud of.

Jacqueline would be angry when she discovered a member of the family had been killed—her protection would not extend to cover the killer. She would, as head of the family, want revenge. But Jacqueline was in Mortigny; no one knew when she'd be back, so he'd take revenge for her. Then he'd run to Jacqueline's side, and she'd protect him from Louise.

Tail tucked tight to his body for warmth, he crept closer. He would do it on the bridge, attacking from behind, throw the body in the water, and be safe with the Lord of Richemulot before the scavengers finished eating.

*   *   *   *   *

His mood black, Dmitri raised the collar of his greatcoat and stepped out onto the bridge. While Aurek's preference for a servant's company over his own hadn't surprised him, Louise's sudden departure had. He'd thought he was important to her. Obviously, he'd been wrong.

"No one in this entire city cares if I live or die," he muttered dramatically, cresting the slight arc and staring down at the esplanade on Craindre Island. Although it was nearly full dark and a chill wind swept down the river from the north, he could see clumps of people moving about under the lamps.

Back in Borca, the middle and lower classes would be readying for bed, but in Pont-a-Museau the shops and cafés opened late and stayed open into the night. The family preferred it that way.

* * * * *

"Isn't that the little Nuikin?"

"Where?"

"There. On the bridge."

Chantel peered along the path of Henri's—suddenly unsure, she checked the scent—no, Aubert's pointing finger. "I wonder what's wrong?"

"Now, why do you think something's wrong?" Yves asked with exaggerated concern. "Surely even you can't read his expression from here."

"Just look at him!" Chantel snapped, becoming increasingly tired of Yves's attitude. "He's walking as if he just lost his best friend."

"Perhaps Cousin Louise kicked him out," Georges offered.

Yves shook his head at the sudden light in Chantel's eyes. "Don't get your hopes up," he said sarcastically. "Even if she has kicked him out, that wouldn't necessarily mean she's finished with him."

"She's toying with him." Annette slid her hands into the velvet muff hanging around her neck and cocked her head appreciatively in Dmitri's direction. "Toying with him like a rat with a bug."

"And here's poor Chantel"—Yves took Annette's arm and rubbed his cheek over the top of her head. "—still stupidly hoping to toy with him herself."

Slowly, Chantel turned. "Who did you just call stupid?"

Annette prudently disentangled herself from Yves's caresses. He'd used her as a shield before when he wanted to get a rise out of Chantel, but not this time.

Her gaze drawn past Chantel's shoulder, she frowned. "There's someone on the bridge behind the little Nuikin. Family . . . Not Cousin Louise. It's a male and he's hunting!"

Yves snorted. "Don't be ridiculous. Louise has claimed him and no one in the family, except possibly you," he directed pointedly at Chantel, "would be stupidly suicidal enough to challenge that."

"Not everyone in the family is as terrified of Louise as you are," Chantel snarled.

Georges stepped cautiously between them. When they fought, the whole group took sides, and he still had a half-healed bite on his leg from the last time. "You've both forgotten that Herself is protecting him."

"Jacqueline isn't here!" Chantel pushed by him, shoving him so hard he slammed into Yves, who jerked aside and let him crash to the cobblestones. Skirts whipping around her ankles, Chantel raced for the bridge.

"You don't actually think she'd ever challenge Louise over the little Nuikin, do you?" Henri asked as Georges picked himself up.

Yves snorted again. "Don't ask me. I stay well out of anything the women in this family are doing."

"Very wise," Annette murmured quietly.

*   *   *   *   *

Dmitri jerked back as Chantel seemingly appeared out of nowhere at his side. "Where did you come from?"

"Down there." Her other hand tucked snugly into the crook of his elbow, she pointed to the esplanade. "I didn't exactly sneak up on you, but I guess you were thinking about other things."

"Yeah," he muttered despondently, "I guess I was."

"Were you on your way to join us?"

He shrugged. "I didn't even know you were there."

"Oh."

Her tone of hurt disappointment was so obvious it cut through his own misery. "I'm sorry, Chantel. But I wouldn't be very good company even if I did join you."

"Please. It's like something's missing now when you're not there." Pressed close to his side, she smiled hopefully up at him, wondering if she were laying it on just a bit thick.

Apparently not.

Well, at least someone wanted him. He smiled back at her. "I didn't really have anything else to do."

As they started to walk toward the others, Chantel turned her head and showed her teeth at the humped shadow nearly on Dmitri's heels.

*   *   *   *   *

Although Chantel's warning was clear, Jean did not consider Chantel herself a threat. She was young; he could beat her easily, especially now, when layers of fashionable clothing would hinder her change. But because she was young, she still kept a group of friends close about her, and he had no intention of finding himself in the midst of six-to-one odds.

With an answering, silent snarl, he slunk away.

There would be other times.

*   *   *   *   *

"Well, now the evening is complete."

Dmitri bowed elegantly at Yves's welcome. Yves had never figured out whether Dmitri was too stupid to recognize sarcasm or too polite to resond. Perhaps it was a human thing; by family standards, humans were irritatingly nice to each other far too much of the time.

With Chantel staying possessively close to Dmitri's side, the seven of them wandered down the esplanade, window shopping and loudly discussing which café they'd honor with their presence, the earlier argument forgotten in the certain knowledge there'd soon be another to take its place. Passing a display of fall fruit outside a small mercer's establishment, Henri snatched up an apple, tossed it to his twin, and grabbed another one for himself. Georges, protesting both his exclusion and his hunger, took two just as the mercer burst out of his shop, a hefty switch swinging from one hand, his face twisted with rage.

"I'll stop you stealing from me you miserable little . . ." His sudden stop and abrupt change of expression brought laughter from the group.

"Miserable little what?" Yves asked, eyes glittering in the spill of light from the shop.

Ruddy checks pale, the heavyset man—large enough to make two of any of them save Dmitri— backed up a step. "I—I didn't know," he stammered.

"Let's hope not." Plucking the switch from between trembling fingers, Yves swung it lazily through the air. "He thinks we're stealing his apples."

"Who, *us?*" Georges protested through a mouthful of fruit.

Henri threw his half-eaten apple aside and grabbed another. "I've never heard anything so . . ."

"Slanderous?" Aubert suggested, mirroring his twin's action.

"Dangerous," Annette corrected, lips lifting into a curve only a fool would mistake for a smile.

Chantel stepped forward, and with one dainty foot kicked away the support under a corner of the display. Fruit tumbled to the cobblestones as the stand collapsed, red and gold and green apples rolling and bouncing down the esplanade. The other people on the street worked very hard at not seeing what was going on.

The mercer's gaze slipped past Yves to rest on Dmitri, who scowled and booted an apple into the river. The older man closed his eyes for an instant, as if in pain, then returned his gaze to Yves. "I thought you were thieves," he said with quiet despair.

He jerked back as Yves started to laugh, and barely stopped himself from jerking again when Yves grabbed a fold of his cheek and pinched it, hard, saying with poisonous sweetness, "You were wrong."

Georges picked up two more apples as they left, and Henri laughed so hard he cried as they continued down the esplanade. "Did you see his face?" he kept repeating, though he knew all of them had. "When Yves handed back the switch, I thought he was going to piss himself." Aubert rolled his eyes. For the moment, it became relatively easy to tell the twins apart.

Dmitri shared in the laughter as he'd shared in the power, resenting the mercer's silent plea. These were his friends.

*   *   *   *   *

Ash. Louise crouched just inside the door to the workshop and stared at the destruction. Whatever had been in the room had burned so hot that nothing had been left behind but ash.

She sat back on her haunches and groomed her whiskers while she thought. Under her theory that a distressed wizard was easier to control, this could only strengthen her position. Whatever Aurek Nuikin had found here had clearly been very important to him. And now he'd lost it.

How nice. Pity I didn't think of torching it myself.

As she turned to go, she paused and lifted her muzzle toward the ceiling. Just for an instant, she thought she'd caught—and lost—a familiar scent.

Rising, and continuing to rise as she changed, she stood and took another look around. Finally, she shook her head, turned back to rat form, and left the workshop.

The place stank of the catacombs, of goblins, of the fire; anything else she imagined she smelled was just that, imagination.

Or possibly, she admitted, irritably shaking ash from a hind foot, paranoia.

*   *   *   *   *

Emerald eyes watched Aurek leave the house just after dawn. His movements exhibited a certain quiet desperation Louise hadn't noticed in them before. He walked like a man determined not to let the world see he was in pain.

And not succeeding. How nice.

She assumed he was off on yet another search for magical artifacts—a scholar looking for scholarship. Actually, his reason for being out of the house was unimportant. It only mattered that he was gone.

Assuming that the windows of the study were now warded, she ignored the scent trail Jean and Lucien had left and moved down the wall on the north side of the building, claws easily finding purchase between the pale stones. Tail balancing the weight of her body, she crouched on an impossibly narrow ledge, muzzle wrinkled as she checked the scent wafting through the closed shutters of the room she planned to enter.

Satisfied, she took a slender dagger from the harness strapped across her chest—a belt was less than

useless as full rat form had nothing that could be
called a waist—and slid it through the crack between
the shutters, silently lifting the catch. As she'd
expected, the shutters opened noiselessly on oiled
hinges. The big blond servant would've seen to that.
Anyone who washed the steps of a house in Pont-a-
Museau had a fetish for cleanliness and would never
allow the hinges in the occupied rooms to squeak.

She slipped into the room, latching the shutters
closed behind her, and rose up on two legs. Her ears
pricked forward at the sound of heavy, regular
breathing, and she glanced toward the bed.

Golden curls tousled on the pillow, one muscular
arm outside the quilts, Dmitri was asleep and likely
to remain so. After all, he'd had a late night. Louise
wasn't sure she approved of him enjoying himself
without her, but as his night of revelry now served
her purpose, she supposed she'd let it go. This time.

Servants, doing whatever it was that servants did
in the rooms below, would not be surprised to hear
movement in this room or coming out of it. Although
more than willing to kill if it became necessary, or
even possible, Louise believed strongly in minimiz-
ing personal risk.

The hall was empty, and she sped along it to
where Aurek Nuikin's scent was the strongest. The
first door she opened led to his bedchamber, the second to his study. There were no wards on the inner
door—but then, she asked herself as she rose again
to two legs, why should there be?

The stink of Lucien's terror and death still hung in
the room, overlaid by the smell of strong soap and
magic. All four were strongest in front of the alcove
containing the pedestal that held the figurine.

Squatting beyond the edge of the magical perimeter, Louise shook her head. If Lucien had been paying
attention, he wouldn't have died. The boundary was

so obvious to wererat senses that there might as well be a sign that said: This far and no farther. Of course, if she'd warned the brothers of what to expect, Lucien wouldn't have died.

Her lips curled in silent laughter. She was neither her cousin's keeper nor responsible for his being such an idiot. Fortunately, he died before he could breed.

Tail twitching, she studied the figurine. Why, she wondered, would a human commission a portrait of a supposed loved one in such a position? While she personally appreciated the expression of horror, she couldn't see how Aurek would. Her eyesight, much better than a human's, noted the perfection of each tiny feature. It was amazing, and far too perfect. Aurek's wife seemed frozen in time, as though the right word would allow her to complete her warding motion, to voice her scream.

Louise frowned. There were no answers here, only more questions. The ebony fur between her eyes still creased, she turned her attention to the desk.

Few members of the family bothered to learn to read, but Marie Renier had insisted that all of her children acquire the skill. "Knowledge can be a powerful weapon," she'd been fond of saying. Louise acknowledged that her mother had been right, though perhaps unwise in thus arming her offspring. She wasn't certain which of her siblings had poisoned dear Mama and planted the list of ingredients in the kitchen, but she rather suspected it was a parting gift from Raul before he left for Barovia. Poison was a coward's way, and Raul had always been a foppish coward, even by family standards. Besides, he'd always hated the cook, who'd been messily slaughtered upon discovery of the list—a list that the cook, of course, had been unable to read.

The rest of the family blamed Jacqueline, and Jacqueline had been quite willing to allow them their mistaken suspicions.

Fanning through Aurek's papers, Louise found the handwriting barely legible and many of the notations completely incomprehensible. One word, however, appeared over and over, often heavily underlined, sometimes the only word on the page. Polymorph.

To change one thing into something else.

Slowly, Louise turned to face the alcove once again.

The figurine was too perfect.

Louise smiled. She'd believed that acquiring the statue of Aurek Nuikin's much beloved and dearly departed wife would help her manipulate him. She'd been right . . . almost.

Once she had the statue, if she said jump, Aurek Nuikin would ask how high on the way up, because his much beloved wife had not actually departed. She'd merely gone through a somewhat precipitous change of life.

As the study's windows had not been warded to keep something in, Louise took the more direct route out of the building. Enthralled by her discovery, caught up in new plans, she didn't notice Jean crouched in the shadows on a neighboring roof.

Neither of them noticed the white wererat watching them both.

*   *   *   *   *

Heavy gray clouds buried the sunset in gloom. Dmitri scowled up at the western sky and shoved his hands into his gloves. The weather exactly matched his mood.

He contemplated not showing up at Chateau Delanuit, though he was expected. If Louise had better things to do than be with him, then he had better things to do than to be with her. Except that he didn't. When he was with her, he felt ten feet tall and invincible, able to slay monsters at her command. He felt necessary.

Usually.

Last night had been the exception.

The single exception.

"So I'll give her another chance." Having made his decision, he set off, with a lighter heart, toward the nearest bridge. There was one thing that growing up with four older sisters had taught him: women occasionally behaved in inexplicable ways.

"Dmitri!"

He turned at Chantel's call and waited while the whole group of them caught up.

"We're all going to dinner before we make an appearance at Laurent and Antionette's boring little affair," Yves told him when they were close enough. "Come along."

"I can't. Not tonight." He spread his hands and shrugged apologetically. "Louise is expecting me at the Chateau."

Yves shot a quick, warning look at Chantel, but she only said, "Then we can all walk together as far as the second bridge."

Dmitri smiled down at her. "I'd be honored." He offered her his arm.

Although overcast and likely to rain, the evening was the warmest the city had seen in some weeks. The more popular promenades were crowded with the fashionable and those hoping to be seen as fashionable. Nodding to family and ignoring or recognizing the townspeople as whim took them, Dmitri and his six friends crossed the first bridge and started down a shadowed and nearly deserted street—the buildings a dark wall to their left, the river a darker barrier to their right.

When an elderly man approached, Yves murmured, "Let's have some fun."

Uncertain of what was about to happen, but willing to be a part of it, needing to belong, Dmitri watched his companions spread out across the street, leaving only a narrow path between Annette and the river.

Shuffling along, the weight of his clothing appearing to be almost too much for him, the old man eyed the only route allowed him if he intended to pass, and sighed audibly. With a weary shake of his head, he turned and headed back the way he'd come, unwilling to play the game.

Dmitri heard Yves snarl and, though no word had been actually spoken, the six surged forward as one and cut off the old man's retreat. They'd moved impossibly quickly, and while Dmitri hurried to join the circle, Yves's voice lifted in exaggerated surprise.

"You weren't avoiding us, were you, old man?"

"I'm tired. I wants ta go home." He was a laborer by his accent and still more irritated than frightened.

"No one was stopping you from going home," Yves pointed with poisonous reason. "You haven't answered my question. Were you avoiding us?"

The man's head sank lower between the rough edges of his upturned collar. "What if I was?"

"Then you owe us an apology."

"I owes you an apology?"

"That's right. One for each of us."

He sighed again and Dmitri, filling the space between Chantel and Georges, could smell the ale on his breath. The man's mouth opened, but whatever he'd intended to say got lost in his astonished glance at Dmitri's face. "What're you doin' here?" he demanded. "You don'ts belong with these vermin!"

The six exchanged pointed smiles.

They gave him a moment to realize his mistake, a moment for the dawning horror to blanch the color from his cheeks; then, in a sudden swirl of movement, they were standing on the river's edge, and the old man was in the water.

He surfaced, lank hair plastered against his scalp, arms thrashing as he fought the pull of his clothing. His terrified gaze locked on Dmitri. "Help me . . ." He didn't have breath enough to scream it.

Feeling as though he were caught in some kind of horrible dream, Dmitri stepped forward, only to find Chantel blocking his way.

"He called us *vermin*," she reminded him, her voice and manner more like Louise's than they'd ever been. "Vermin. Are we to ignore such an insult?"

"No, but . . ."

"Oh, look, he's almost made it back to shore." Georges dropped to one knee, reached out over the dark water, and grabbed the pale wrist below the desperately grasping hand. A gentle shove put the shore out of reach once again.

"Please . . ." Voice and thrashing both had grown weaker.

Dmitri stared down at the pale face in the water. It was a joke. Surely they weren't going to let the man drown. But when he lifted his eyes to the semicircle of fashionably dressed young people avidly watching a man die, he knew it was no joke.

"Are you one of us, or not?" Yves asked quietly.

One of them or not? He felt more like the man in the river, darkness closing over his head, knowing he was dying and knowing he could fight all he wanted but there was nothing he could do to prevent it. And more terrifying still, he had thrown himself from the shore. Then all at once, it wasn't fancy, it was memory. He could feel the river greedily dragging him down.

He fought his way free and swallowed his fear before it could show.

Was he one of them or not? And if not, where did he belong?

He closed his eyes and made no answer at all.

Which was answer enough.

He couldn't just stand there with his eyes closed, so he stared across the river at the lights in the distance and tried to remember the last time he'd seen the day; the last time he hadn't returned home at dawn, slept until late afternoon, and emerged at dusk.

"Shouldn't have called us vermin," Yves declared cheerfully, when all sounds of thrashing had stopped.

During the answering murmur of agreement, Dmitri drew in a deep breath, let it out slowly, and looked at his friends. They didn't look any different. The old man shouldn't have called them vermin, he told himself. He was a common laborer; they're members of the leading family of Pont-a-Museau. How could they ignore an insult like that?

They couldn't.

Obviously, they couldn't.

But he didn't join in their laughter as they walked with him to the second bridge—the bridge leading to Isle Delanuit and Louise—and he stood watching them until they disappeared around a corner, heading for their favorite café.

He walked slowly to the crest of the bridge and stopped again, his attention captured by a shadow drifting by in the water below. A body? Perhaps. Not the old man, the current would've taken him the other way, but there were plenty of bodies in the river. Everyone complained about it. No one seemed to worry about adding one more.

Turning back the way he'd come, Dmitri thought about going home. He wanted to talk to Aurek. Aurek always knew the answers and was more than willing to tell his younger brother what to do—usually it was the most irritating thing about him, but tonight it would be a comfort.

And then, almost as though the gods had read the

desire of his heart, he saw a familiar silhouette making its way along the lower esplanade. There could be no mistaking either the breadth of Aurek's shoulders or the silver line of his braid. Before Dmitri could move to join him, Aurek looked up.

Too far away to read his brother's expression, Dmitri saw the shoulders slump and Aurek turn abruptly into the dark mouth of an alley. He waited, but no one emerged.

He saw me. I know he saw. His chest felt as though there were iron bands wrapped tight around it. It was just like when he was a kid with four older sisters who made a pet of him and one older brother he desperately wanted to be close to. An older brother who never had time for him.

It wasn't just the difference in their ages, Dmitri had realized when he reached his teens; it was because he wasn't smart enough. What difference did it make if he could run faster or fight better than all the other boys his age? Aurek was a scholar, and it was clear that scholarship was all that mattered to him.

Dmitri had finally stopped trying when Aurek had turned away from the awkward words of sympathy he'd offered at Natalia's death. She'd almost been his friend—would have been, he was sure, had she lived—but his grief and his pain had meant nothing to Aurek.

Not a thing either of them had been able to say—and Dmitri had said plenty—had prevented their sisters from sending them together to Richemulot. Although as Ivana Boritsi's attraction had grown more marked, he'd recognized the need to leave Borca and welcomed the chance for adventure, the last thing he'd wanted was Aurek's company.

"You haven't a choice and neither does he." All four sisters had made that clear. "Perhaps as two adults you can be friends."

There didn't seem to be a chance of that happening now.

He'd been shut out of Aurek's plans and discovered he'd been lied to all his life—Aurek was more than a mere scholar.

And now it was painfully obvious: he was still the younger brother Aurek had no time for.

Brushing the back of one hand over his cheeks, scrubbing away angry tears, Dmitri squared his shoulders and turned toward the black bulk of the Renier estate.

* * * * *

Aurek sagged against a building and wondered if Dmitri would come after him. He was too exhausted, too ashamed of his failure, to endure his brother's anger.

There'd been nothing but angry accusations between them since Dmitri had begun to keep company with Louise Renier.

Perhaps Edik was right. Perhaps he should tell Dmitri the truth—not the truth about the wererats, for with the loss of the workshop he still needed Jacqueline Renier's permission to search in Richemulot—but the truth about himself.

Laughing bitterly, he pushed himself erect and continued toward home. He wouldn't have the faintest idea of where to start. Shall I burden him with the disaster I've made of my life? Can I trust him not to share the details with his new friends?

Natalia had believed in the boy, but could he entrust her fragile existence to someone who could, even in ignorance, share the bed of Louise Renier?

He couldn't risk it.

 **TEN**

Vermin indeed. Trust the young to want immediate gratification. They should have made the old man suffer for that insult, toyed with him, killed him more slowly. Forced him to watch them devour his steaming entrails . . .

"Louise?" Dmitri captured one of her hands in his, frowning as he noticed how warm her skin was and how damp her palm. "Are you all right?"

"I'm sorry." She forced a smile—he need never know she forced it through irritation rather than some gentler emotion—and truthfully explained, "I just can't help thinking about that old man."

"Maybe I shouldn't have told you."

"No, I want you to tell me everything. We should have no secrets between us, and this is something that affected you deeply." Leaning forward, she touched him lightly on the cheek with her free hand. "I want to be there for your pain."

Missing the double meaning, as he was intended to, Dmitri sighed. "I'm glad somebody does."

"Aurek! I can't believe anyone would treat a brother in such a way! Turning his back on you! Reniers would never turn their backs on family!"

Watching him wince as her words deliberately rubbed salt in his wounds, she reflected that, among her family, a turned back usually ended up wearing a dagger embedded hilt-deep. "How I hate to see a family torn apart like this."

"It's not my doing," Dmitri murmured, sliding off the chaise to the library floor and resting his head on her knee.

"I know, dear one. It's him. It's all him." Her voice wrapped him in sympathy and warm concern. "He treats you as if you were nothing."

"Nothing," Dmitri agreed mournfully. "He thinks more of that figurine of his wife than he does of me."

The figurine. The hand that had been reaching down to stroke Dmitri's hair lifted to rub at Louise's cheek, though there were no whiskers there to groom. She'd forgotten something, something important about that figurine. She could feel the heat of his sigh against her leg.

"If he had to choose between us, I sure wouldn't be his first choice. Remember how I told you I picked it up once and he practically threw me out of the house?"

"How could I forget him hurting you like that?" He picked it up! And if he did it once, she thought gleefully, he can do it again. Her brow wrinkled slightly. It seemed very likely that Dmitri's blood relationship with Aurek neutralized the effects of the protection spell. Or perhaps the spell just wasn't in place at the time. She considered the possibility and decided that it didn't matter. If Dmitri couldn't get her the figurine, then he'd die in the attempt—catering to his constant juvenile self-pity and the perpetual need to shore up his tender male ego was becoming just a tad tedious.

"I know how you can force Aurek to pay attention to you," she murmured. "Take the little statue of his wife away from him and refuse to give it back until he listens to your concerns."

Dmitri twisted around so that he could look up at her adoringly, his chin pillowed on the arm he rested on her knee. "It's a wonderful idea," he said regretfully, "but you've forgotten that Aurek's a wizard. If I take away the figurine of Natalia, he'll just take it back."

Eyes glittering in the flickering light of the library fire, Louise smiled. "Not if you bring it to me."

*   *   *   *   *

Dmitri had come in, as usual, long after Aurek had gone to bed and would, so close to dawn, still be asleep. Aurek paused in the hall outside his brother's room, one hand on the latch. A restless night, twisting and turning in tangled bedclothes, had brought with it the realization that he owed Dmitri an apology. To have turned away from him so obviously had offered him a grievous insult.

After a moment spent listening to the prodding of his guilt, he sighed quietly and shook his head.

Dragged out of a sound sleep, Dmitri would be sullen and resentful, in no mood to listen to anything he had to say.

I'll wait, Aurek decided, shrugging his pack up onto his shoulders as he continued down the hall, ignoring, as best he could, the mocking laughter that accompanied him. There'll be time enough to speak with him tonight.

*   *   *   *   *

Dmitri heard Aurek leave his room, heard him come down the hall, boot soles slapping against the uncarpeted floor, then, to his amazement, he heard him stop right in front of the bedroom door.

Ear pressed against the wood, Dmitri froze, barely

daring to breathe. What does he think he's doing? Sluggishly—for he'd gotten very little sleep in the short while he'd been home—he tried to come up with a plausible reason that would explain his being up and fully dressed should his brother open the door. To his relief, Aurek started moving again.

He listened as Aurek descended the stairs, then waited, heart pounding uncomfortably hard, until he heard the faint but unmistakable sound of the front door closing.

Slipping quietly from his room, avoiding the loudest of the creaking floorboards in the hall, he made his way to Aurek's study. Outside the door he paused, his hand on the latch, voices out of the past ringing in his ears.

Old voices.

"No, Dmitri, don't go in there."

"You must never bother your brother when he's in his study."

"The master is in his study and does not wish to be disturbed."

And a more recent one.

"I told you to never come in here!"

"I have work to do. Important work. Get out! Leave us alone!"

"Get out!"

"Get! Out!"

Jaw set, teeth gritted, he opened the door.

Aurek's study was just a room with a desk, some shelves, and a pedestal in an alcove. Dmitri hadn't really taken the time to look around at it during his single visit—at first he'd been too worried about his brother, and then he'd been too mad at him—but his imagination had filled a wizard's sanctuary with the strange and the bizarre. His imagination had gotten it pretty much completely wrong. There were scorch marks on the floor by the fireplace as though something burning had fallen out past the edge of the stone hearth, desk and shelves were piled high with notes in Aurek's illegible handwriting, ruined pens and uncut quills were scattered randomly about, and a large map of the city had been pegged to one wall and covered in strange notations, but there was no indication that the usual occupant of the room was a wizard.

No newt eyes. No frog toes. No bat wool. No dog tongues. Only the light over the figurine, light that had, as far as Dmitri could determine, no source.

The Natalia he remembered had not been beautiful like Louise was beautiful; she was softer, gentler, kinder. She always seemed to understand what he meant, and though she laughed frequently, she never once laughed at him. Aurek had adored her, and if she'd had a fault at all in Dmitri's eyes it was in the way she'd hung on Aurek's every word as though it were holy writ.

"Just what his overblown ego needed," Dmitri muttered, looking down at the statue. "Another woman telling him how smart he was." Their sisters had always been very vocal about that. "Frankly, I'm amazed he got his nose out of a book long enough to get married, let alone stay married for three years."

As far as he was concerned, Natalia was the best thing that had ever happened to his brother. While she was alive, Aurek had been almost human.

Lightly stroking the figurine's upraised arm, he shook his head. "I wonder why he had this commissioned in such a stupid pose." Maybe, if Louise's plan worked and he and Aurek actually held a conversation, he could ask. In the meantime . . .

He scooped up the statue and wrapped it carefully in a silk scarf, then a piece of sheepskin, then he tucked it into the bottom of a small leather pouch. Louise's instructions had been explicit: "Do everything you must to see that it isn't damaged in any way.

We want only to get his attention; we don't want him to turn whatever powers he might have against us."

"I'm his brother," Dmitri had reminded her.

"And he's already made it clear that he thinks more of the figurine than he does of you."

An inarguable observation.

Back in his own room, Dmitri shrugged into his greatcoat and set the pouch on top of the clothing he'd packed into a small carpetbag. Louise wanted him to stay at the Chateau until he and Aurek straightened things out between them. Considering how Aurek would likely react to the loss of the statue, Dmitri figured that his absence from the house would be a definite plus on the survival side of the ledger.

He stretched out his hand toward his sword, hanging over the bed on two pegs, and let it fall again. Swords were not a part of fashionable dress in Pont-a-Museau. He hadn't worn his since he'd arrived. At the door, he turned and shrugged ruefully before recrossing the room, taking down the sword, and buckling it on. It looked ludicrous against the full skirts of his greatcoat, so he removed it and put it back on beneath the coat. It wasn't a special weapon by any means. It wasn't even an expensive weapon, but it was his, and he wasn't going to leave it here for Aurek to destroy in a fit of petty revenge.

* * * * *

Jean roused as the front door slammed a second time, and he poked his muzzle over the edge of the roof. The brother of the human who'd killed his brother was leaving the house. Alone.

The wererat snarled softly as his prey moved toward the river. A boat would delay the hunt yet again, as it had when the young idiot left the Chateau by way of the gazebo just before dawn.

* * * * *

Dmitri scanned the narrow channel of the river flowing turgidly past the house, but there were no boats close enough to hail. Shifting his carpetbag into his left hand and shooting a nervous glance back at the curtained windows, he started toward the nearest bridge.

"I guess it won't hurt to walk," he told a disinterested pigeon as it strutted from his path. "Maybe a little fresh air will make up for the lack of sleep."

* * * * *

The prey was walking. Jean scrambled over the rooftop and down a drainpipe, eyes slitted nearly closed against the early morning light. There would be no white-haired girl arriving to save the prey this time; the family went abroad by day only when it had plans for mayhem the night could not fulfill.

* * * * *

I've never seen this place so dead. Dmitri paused on the arc of the bridge and stared upriver and down, looking for some sign that he wasn't the only living creature awake in the city. A sudden bang whipped him around only to see the tiny figure of a servant struggling to close an upper shutter blown back by the wind. He watched until the . . . Man? Woman? At this distance he couldn't be sure. . . . until the servant succeeded, then started walking again, feeling reassured.

The black slate roof of the Renier estate was visible over similar rooftops on Craindre Island. Dmitri stared at the rutted path cutting through the ruins in the center of the island and then at the safer, longer road that led around to the northeast bridge.

He'd just borrowed his brother's most prized possession, and all at once, taking the shorter route to
safety made a great deal of sense. He'd never have
dared cut across the island at night but, in the pale
light of day, it seemed foolish to trade a possible risk
for a probable one.

The path quickly left inhabited buildings behind.
As alert as very little sleep and his recent lifestyle
allowed, Dmitri followed it through a gap in a crumbling wall and into what had once been the extensive
grounds of a city estate. Not nearly as large as the
Chateau Delanuit, there was still an impressive
amount of land involved, considering that Pont-a-
Museau had been built on an archipelago where land
had been at a premium from the very beginning.

In the years since the estate had been inhabited,
the trees had grown up and created a small forest in
the center of the island. Although the deadfall had
been cleared away, no one apparently wanted to
spend time enough in the trees' midst to actually cut
any of them down. There were no stumps and no sign
of axe or saw. The bare branches of the deciduous
trees clutched at the sky like greedy fingers, and the
evergreens held pockets of shadow, deep and black.
The air smelled of mold and fungus and decay.

Dmitri's heart leapt into his throat as three crows
exploded into sudden flight, screaming insults. Forcing a shaky laugh, he watched them, silhouetted
against the sky, until he lost them in the pattern of
branches. Then, shaking his head at his overreac-
tion, he continued toward Chateau Delanuit.

He took two steps, boots making no sound against
the thick mat of fallen, rotting leaves; then he
stopped, as it occurred to him to wonder what had
spooked the crows.

*   *   *   *   *

In any and all of their three forms, wererats preferred to attack from the rear—though they seldom wasted their efforts on a quick kill. In full rat form, they used their speed and their razor-sharp teeth to dart in and, with a sideswipe of their wedge-shaped heads, hamstring their opponents. A man or woman lying screaming on the ground, unable to stand, became little threat and could provide hours of enjoyable terror.

Jean had fully intended to take Dmitri down the way he had so many others. He'd pictured it over and over in his head as he'd followed the human's trail. He planned to make the dying last as long as possible, and he meant to enjoy every moment of it.

Unfortunately, when it came time to actually attack the brother of the man who'd killed his brother, his fury became more than he could control, and he launched himself, shrieking with fury, at the back of the human's neck.

* * * * *

The sudden weight flung Dmitri flat on his face, pain searing through one shoulder. He could feel coarse whiskers crushed against his ear, hot, fetid breath against his cheek, and claws ripping apart the protective layers of his clothing. Both arms were beneath him. Somehow he managed to get his palms flat against the ground. Using all his strength, he shoved himself up into the air, and then, muscles popping, he turned over backward. For a moment, he held whatever creature that had attacked him pinned.

An instant later, he leapt to his feet, leaving the greatcoat behind. As the creature fought its way free of the heavy folds of cloth, Dmitir drew his sword and threw the scabbard to one side.

The rat facing him was as large as the four he'd

seen that night in the alley, the four who'd eaten that poor man alive. But that man had been unarmed and outnumbered. Dmitri smiled. He was neither.

"En garde, rodent!" He couldn't remember which of his friends had laughingly made the comment, but it seemed apt.

Snarling with rage, the giant rat glared up at him with glittering ebony eyes, naked tail lashing the air.

Trying to ignore the burning ache in his left shoulder, Dmitri flicked his sword tip just before the pointed muzzle. "Or are you afraid?"

The human was actually taunting him. Him. Jean Renier. Humans did not speak so to members of the family.

When the next attack came, Dmitri was almost ready for it. The rat moved fast—faster than should've been possible. Dmitri grunted as a claw ripped through his buckskins and into his thigh, but twisted his leg away before much damage could be done. His own blow went wide. The rat was not where he expected it to be. It was almost as though the creature were thinking.

They circled, facing each other again. Dmitri set his jaw and prepared to fight for his life.

He added a number of new scars to the patchwork parting the dull brown fur that covered the huge rodent's body, but twist and feint and thrust as he might, he couldn't get in a killing blow.

On the other hand, he was still alive.

The claws ripped at him every time they passed—front claws, back claws, he could seldom tell which. His clothing was in ribbons, but unless he died from the slow loss of blood, the rat had been as unable as he to make a fatal strike.

The fight had moved them out from under the trees and up against the ruined walls of the old building. This gave the more agile rat a decided advantage.

To his horror, Dmitri began to realize that he couldn't win. That all he did was postpone the inevitable. That this was the time and place of his death. A sword stroke faltered. He stumbled, nearly fell, the knowledge dragging at him.

Jean saw the realization of death in the eyes of his prey but didn't have the energy left to enjoy it. He was hurt, bleeding from a number of wounds, none alone worse than any he'd survived in the past, but together they sapped his strength. Had the human continued to believe he had a chance, he might have had.

In a moment, he'd have the human down and then he'd feed. That would make him feel much better.

Breathing heavily, the taste of iron in his mouth, Dmitri stumbled backward, lifted his sword in a last-minute parry, and slammed the side of the blade against the rat's head. It was a lucky blow, but he doubted it had been hard enough to do any major damage.

Ears ringing, Jean staggered sideways, felt a block of stone tip beneath his paws and, before he could stop himself, he plummeted into one of the ruined cellars. Twisting in the air, trying to get his feet under him, he braced himself for an impact that never came.

When he realized what he'd landed in, he began to shriek.

Supporting himself on his sword, Dmitri made his way to the edge of the pit. About ten feet down, he could see the body of the giant rat, thrashing about in midair.

Then he saw the spiderweb. It shimmered like gossamer in the shadowed light, each strand at least as big around as his thumb. The rat had landed almost right in the middle of the circular pattern.

The panicked shrieking drove spikes of pain into Dmitri's skull, and he began to turn away. When the rat began to change, he froze in astonishment. Bones lengthened, muscles flattened, the muzzle became less pronounced, front paws became almost hands, back paws almost feet; only the fur and tail and wounds remained the same.

"Wererat," Dmitri gasped, trying to remember to breathe.

"Help me, human! Help me!"

Dmitri's eyes widened in disbelief. "Help you? You tried to kill me!"

"You tried to kill me!"

That was true enough, and he was so tired it very nearly made sense. He hesitated, almost considering it.

Then the spider crept down from the shadows to claim its meal. The bloated gray sac of its body was as large as the wererat's head. Each of the eight legs that stepped from strand to strand with obscenely delicate precision was longer than one of Dmitri's arms. As it began to methodically wrap the screaming wererat in loops of sticky white webbing, Dmitri backed away, swallowing bile.

He wouldn't, *couldn't* face such a horror. If it were a friend, or family member . . . Then he'd help, he told himself, trying unsuccessfully to ignore the continuing cries for assistance. But not for the sake of a wererat that had tried to kill him.

Bloody sword waving at the air before him, Dmitri stumbled back to the carpetbag, grabbed it, and moved as quickly as he could toward the other side of the island and the bridge to the Renier estate. When the wererat's screams grew louder, he moved faster.

The only things that would be attracted to such a sound in Pont-a-Museau were scavengers.

He killed four rats of normal size before he reached the far side of the overgrown estate. Whether they were drawn by the fading cries of the dying wererat or by the scent of his blood, Dmitri neither knew nor

cared. He would survive to get to Louise; he concentrated on that and let the rest go.

A fifth rat attacked as he staggered out onto the
deserted esplanade. He crushed its skull beneath his
boot heel. A sixth he skewered on the point of his
sword and flung off the bridge. The streets remained
empty. Those few who were up and about worked
very hard at not seeing his bloody, sword-waving figure pass. The citizens of Pont-a-Museau were
experts in the art of turning a blind eye.

Eventually, staggering and retching, he reached
the Chateau. It took the last of his strength to lift the
corroded brass knocker and let it fall against the
door. When—after hours or minutes, he was no
longer able to tell the difference—a servant cautiously pulled open the door, Dmitri gasped out,
"Louise . . ." and fell flat on his face, the carpetbag
clutched protectively in the crook of one arm.

The elderly woman stared down at him, her face
impassive. After a moment, she stepped back and
said, "I'll tell the mamselle you've arrived," as
though bleeding young men collapsed on the threshold too frequently for her to summon a less phleg-
matic reaction.

* * * * *

Her mood sunny, Louise stood in the doorway of
the guest room and watched one of the younger,
more expendable servants wiping the blood from
Dmitri's torso. The water in the chipped enamel bowl
on the bedside table had turned a pale crimson that
grew darker every time the cloth was rinsed.

Louise's nose twitched. Not all the blood belonged
to Dmitri, and she could only assume that, as the
little Nuiken had made it to the Chateau, Jean was
dead. No great loss, she mused. Although humans

killing family was not to be tolerated, since Jean had ignored her direct order to do nothing, it could, under the circumstances, be ignored.

"Was he bitten?"

The servant's back hunched as though expecting a blow, her cheeks pale beneath two barely healed lacerations. "Yes, mistress. There, on the shoulder."

Leaning forward, Louise examined the puncture. Surrounded by purpling flesh, it looked as if her cousin's teeth had gone cleanly in, then cleanly out again, with no tearing. "It must have been an interesting fight." She almost wished she'd seen it, males whacking at each other could be so . . . stimulating.

She pursed her lips and considered the possibilities. There was a chance Dmitri would be infected with a lesser form of lycanthropy, becoming, for all intents and purposes, Jean's wererat slave. But Jean was dead. My slave then. That could be inconvenient. Although she had the little statue of Aurek Nuikin's wife safe in her bedchamber, new plans would have to be devised if Dmitri became a wererat. What a selfish little human he'd turned out to be.

"Let me know if there are any . . . changes."

"Yes, mistress. And if he dies?"

Her palm smacked against the back of the servant's head. "Don't be a bigger fool than you have to be. If he dies, dispose of the body."

*　*　*　*　*

Shoulders hunched against the cold of early evening, Aurek saw neither the boat nor the river it traveled on. His eyes were locked on a private vision of the workshop and the book that held the spell to free his Natalia. The book he'd lost. The peals of malicious laughter in his head rose and fell with the motion of the waves.

Had the day given him any encouragement at all, he thought he might be able to quiet the laughter, but he'd spent futile hours searching an abandoned building and found only a preservation spell set into the stones of a room that had once been the wine cellar.

Nothing for his Natalia. Nothing at all.

He jerked as the boat careened into the dock and pulled himself slowly up onto the repaired stone wall, not even hearing the boatman's offer of help. Another day, another failure.

But you're still trying, consoled a little voice, barely able to make itself heard over the laughter.

Trying doesn't matter, he told it. Only succeeding. And my Natalia is still trapped.

"Will you be wantin' me tamorra, sir?" the boatman called out.

Aurek forced himself to turn. "Tomorrow and every day after that," he said wearily, no longer clinging to hope as much as clutching at habit.

With his pack dragging at his shoulders, weighing more empty than it would full, he made his way across the esplanade to the house. Edik opened the door and stood backlit by the candles in the entry hall as Aurek heaved himself up the steps.

"Mamselle Louise Renier has sent around a note, sir." The servant proffered a thick, cream-colored sheet of paper, folded twice and sealed with crimson wax, as Aurek pushed past. "The messenger indicated it was of some urgency."

"I don't care." Without even looking at it, Aurek plucked the paper from Edik's grasp, crumpled it, and threw it aside. Halfway up the stairs, he remembered his morning's resolution and paused. "Is Dmitri in?"

"No, sir."

"Well, when you see him next, escort him to my study. I want to speak with him."

"Yes, sir." Eyes narrowed in worried disapproval, Edik watched until his master disappeared into the shadows of the upper hall, then he bent and picked up the crumpled message. Whether Aurek Nuikin deigned to read it or not, the entryway was not the place for garbage.

A sudden desperate howl snapped Edik erect so quickly he nearly threw out his back. The next instant, he was pounding up the stairs, paper still clutched in one hand.

* * * * *

She was gone.

Gone!

His Natalia was gone.

With trembling fingers, Aurek caressed the empty air above the pedestal. Gone? How could she be gone, and the protective spells not breached? It was impossible. Gasping for breath, as though he'd just been dealt a mortal blow, he tried to work out what could have happened and kept returning to the one thing he knew for certain—it was impossible. No one could get safely through the defensive spells.

No one.

No one except he, himself, had so much as touched the figurine of his precious Natalia since she'd been so horribly transformed.

And then he had a sudden vision of Dmitri lifting the figurine and shaking it at him.

Dmitri?

Could Dmitri have betrayed him so?

"Edik!"

"Here, sir."

Aurek's heart leapt into his throat as the servant's quiet answer sounded directly behind him. He spun around and grabbed the other man's sleeve. "The note from the Renier . . ."

Brow furrowed, Edik handed it over, his gaze flicking between the empty pedestal and his master.

The top of the page had been dated that afternoon. The handwriting was bold and dark, each letter traced heavily by a hand that seldom held a quill.

My dear M. Nuikin, it read. *An item you value has recently come into my possession. Please call on me at your earliest convenience to discuss its return.* The looping stylized signature took up the bottom half of the page. *Louise Renier.*

*   *   *   *   *

"Is he still alive?"

"Yes, mistress."

Ducking under a dust-laden fringe of dangling cobwebs, Louise entered the room, lips pursed in a moue of distaste. "Has there been any sign of change?"

"No, mistress." The young woman prudently backed away from the bed as Louise approached.

His breathing moist and ragged, Dmitri lay beneath a moth-eaten blanket, fitfully tossing his head from side to side, his face flushed, golden curls plastered to his skull. Angry red flesh surrounded the bite on his shoulder, scarlet lines spreading out from it into his chest and back. In comparison, the rest of his wounds, claw marks all, appeared to be minor and painless.

"Could still go either way," Louise muttered, wrinkling her nose at the scent of sweat and blood.

"He's very strong, mistress."

The wererat's laughter all but echoed in the nearly empty room. "Oh, yes, strong like an ox, smart like an ox cart."

On the bed, Dmitri jerked toward the sound. "Lou . . . ise."

Tentatively, the servant glanced from the injured young man to her mistress. Having miraculously survived the violence after Henri Dubois had escaped Jacqueline and the Chateau, she knew that wererats were capable of love—or a wererat variation of love. If she'd expected a softening of Louise Renier's expression, she was doomed to disappointment. Brows drawn in, eyes narrowed, her mistress looked, at best, calculating.

"At least he's calling for me rather than for his brother. I can use that." Tapping long, curved nails against her thigh, Louise frowned, weighing her options. If the impossible chanced to happen—and the impossible had happened before in Richemulot— and her darling sister defeated Aurek Nuikin, she would need Dmitri as an excuse for Nuikin's behavior: *When Dmitri moved into the Chateau, Nuikin went crazy. He swore revenge on the whole family. I'm only glad that you were ready for him.*

Presenting Dmitri essentially unharmed would add a certain verisimilitude—after all, Jacqueline had told her not to harm Dmitri, and she hadn't. Jean had. And Jean, who had disregarded Jacqueline's instructions to the family, was dead. Jacqueline would be happy about that. And with Jean dead, no one need ever know what had happened to Lucien.

Louise glanced derisively down at her wounded gallant. It would easy enough to convince Dmitri, weakened as he was, of any story she chose to tell him. For that matter, it was easy enough to convince Dmitri of almost anything, even when he was in perfect health.

"All right," she declared abruptly. "I've decided. Do everything you can to keep him alive."

As her mistress left the room, the servant returned to the bedside, shoulders slumped and feet dragging. Now that she'd been ordered to keep the young man alive, it would become her fault if he died. Her hand

rose to lightly touch the double scar slashed into her
cheek. If the young man died, her punishment would
go far beyond mere disfigurement.

*   *   *   *   *

"Mistress, there is a man named Aurek Nuikin
here to see you."

Louise glanced back over her shoulder at the
closed door hiding Aurek Nuikin's younger brother
and smiled broadly, exposing a great many pointed
teeth. "Light the candles in the library and offer him
something to drink. I'll be down in a moment."

*   *   *   *   *

Fighting the urge to tear through the Chateau, fire-
balling everyone and everything in his path until his
Natalia was safely returned, Aurek followed the bent
and shadowed form of the elderly servant into the
library. He stood, arms folded, and watched through
narrowed eyes as she took her single candle and lit a
number of candles scattered about the room.

As the sweet scent of the warming beeswax began
to replace the dry and dusty odor of neglect, she
nodded once in his general direction and left the
room through a narrow door opposite the one they'd
entered by.

Louise Renier, Aurek surmised, would grant him
an audience when she was good and ready, not an
instant before. Fine. He could wait. He wasn't leaving
until he spoke with her, and he wasn't leaving without the figurine of his wife.

Even under the most extreme of circumstances,
which these undoubtedly were, Aurek was incapable
of standing in a library and not examining the books.
Holding a branched candelabra in one hand, he

approached the shelves. The books, like most everything else in Pont-a-Museau, were falling apart. Mold
and mildew made titles difficult to read, and when he
pulled out a volume for a closer inspection, the pages
fluttered to the carpet in amber-colored flakes well
mixed with dried insect parts and rodent droppings.

Few of the books were in any better condition.
Some were worse. Most had probably not been
touched since the night the mist-created city had
appeared.

This too, they should be made to answer for, he
snarled silently as he set the empty cover back in its
place.

A small stack of more recent publications caught
his eye, and he crossed the room to take a closer
look. Not only were these half-dozen, clothbound
books still readable, but one had been published
since his arrival in Pont-a-Museau.

"Centuries of scholarship rots away," he muttered
in disgust, glaring at a lurid woodcut depicting
something vaguely female wrapped in a long black
cloak indulging in a close embrace with an attractive
young man, "but *The Dead Travel Fast, a Romance
from Beyond the Grave* is not only in perfect condition, but well read!"

"I read it twice the week it came out."

Aurek whirled about to discover that Louise Renier
had seated herself in a thronelike wingback chair
and was regarding him with interest. He hadn't even
heard her enter the room.

"I so enjoy a good romance," she continued, as
though there were nothing of more import occurring
than an unexpected social call. "Girl gets boy; boy
dies tragically; boy becomes girl's zombie slave."
She pressed one hand dramatically against her
chest. "I just love a happy ending."

"Where is she?" Aurek growled, his left hand

curled into a fist, his right rising to gesture.

Louise basked in the heat of his anger, so much more potent than his brother's fits of pique. "Don't you know, wizard?"

Silver-blond brows drew together into a sharp **V**. "Why do you call me that?"

"Call you what? Wizard?" Her laughter had edges that could flay skin, and her eyes glittered in the candlelight. "You know what I am. I know what you are. Lets not play this game any longer, especially not when I've gone to so much trouble to set up a new one." She leaned slightly forward in the chair. "So, if you want to know where your beloved is, wizard, all you have to do is sense the waning struggles of her poor trapped life." When he jerked toward her, she shook a finger at him. "Not if you want her back. The poor little woman is in a very fragile state right now."

Teeth clenched, Aurek stopped himself from advancing farther. Forcing himself to calm, he stretched out his senses until he brushed against the butterfly flutter of Natalia's life.

Watching some of the tension leave his shoulders, Louise smiled triumphantly. Aurek Nuikin had just confirmed that the figurine was exactly what she'd assumed it to be—and therefore infinitely more precious than a mere representation of a lost love. While he wasn't as stupid as his brother, he was no harder to manipulate than the rest of his sex. "Now that you've determined she's safe, perhaps we can discuss the terms of her return."

"No terms, wererat." His voice sounded hoarse, as though it scraped across ground glass. "You will return my wife to me, and I will not destroy you. If you do not return her, I *will* destroy you. You can count on it."

"Not me. My sister."

He blinked, confused. "Your what?"

"My sister, Jacqueline. You will destroy her, wizard, or I will destroy your wife."

Aurek laughed humorlessly. "What is to stop me from killing you right now, between one lie and the next, and ripping this festering dungheap apart until I find her?"

"Two small things. The first"—she flicked a slender finger into the air—"if I am hurt in any way, my servants will smash the figurine not even knowing that they kill the poor, helpless Madame Nuikin. The second"—a second finger rose—"I have your brother. Again, if I am hurt in any way, he will die." She smiled up at him, her expression poisonously sweet. "Personally, I much prefer that Jacqueline die instead, and you, wizard, are my only hope of achieving that goal."

"Too cowardly to face her yourself?" If he could goad her into an attack, he might be able to hold her life for Natalia's and Dmitri's.

Louise refused to be insulted. "Too smart. Especially when I have you. You proved down in the catacombs that you're powerful enough to stand a very good chance of success." Buffing curved nails against a silken fold of her full skirt, she added, "You will take all the risk, and I will have an excellent story prepared should you fail. I can't lose, and you have only one chance to win."

The catacombs. Now he knew why she'd given him the amulet. It had all been part of an elaborate test! His fist closed again around the tiny lump of bat guano in his pocket. He somehow managed to force his voice around the rage that locked his muscles and sat like burning coal in his throat. "You set me up, and then you burned the workshop!"

"Actually, no, I didn't."

"Liar!"

Her lips lifted off her teeth. "Don't push me,

human. Remember, I hold all the high cards in this game. If I wanted to, I could merely tell my darling sister that you killed Lucien. Jacqueline doesn't like it when someone outside the family thins our ranks."

It was a fight to think, a fight to do anything but react. "Lucien died in my study?"

"That's right."

Jacqueline had warned him that the family was not to be harmed.

Louise had wanted him all along, Aurek realized. Had seen only a weapon she could use to gain power. Her interest in Dmitri had been nothing more than a way to get to him. "How did you persuade Dmitri to go along with this? Did you convince him that you loved him?"

"I didn't have to." She leaned back in the chair, steepling her fingers together. "I merely convinced him that you didn't."

Aurek felt as though he'd just been clubbed with a blunt object. "I . . ."

"Didn't have time for him. Didn't want him around. Thought he was stupid," Louise finished. "He wasn't necessary to you; he was necessary to me. You didn't want him, so now he's mine. If you destroy my sister, maybe I'll give him back.

"The last ball of the season is always held here, at the Chateau," she continued. "I guarantee that Jacqueline will be in attendance. You will use your power to hold her completely immobile but unharmed. Once I'm certain she can't fight back, I'll kill her myself. Once she's dead, you and yours are free to go. You have my word on it."

"Your word?" He stared at her in astonishment. "How can I trust your word?"

This time her laughter held honest amusement layered in smug self-satisfaction. "You don't have any choice, do you?"

ELEVEN

"Louise has Dmitri at the Chateau."

"So?" Yves crossed his bare feet at the ankles and flung a dart into the opposite wall, skewering a roach. A random scattering of stained holes indicated this wasn't the first roach so skewered. "You know what they say; when Herself's away, the rats will play." He snickered appreciatively at his own poetic wit.

"This has nothing to do with Jacqueline." Stuffing her gloves into her high-crowned fur hat, Chantel threw the hat down onto the table and began unwrapping the many folds of her scarf. "He went in there three days ago and hasn't come out. Louise is doing this to keep him away from me."

Wearing a totally unbelievable expression of weary concern, Yves sighed in exasperation. "If, my sweet cousin, I could just make two points before you get yourself in any deeper. One, everything in Richemulot has to do with Jacqueline, and you'd best not forget that. Two, Louise couldn't care less about you. She wants the little Nuikin for her own reasons. Don't you remember what she told me?" He rubbed at the memory of her grip on his arm. "Let it go, Chantel."

"We're going hunting in a little while," Georges

offered from his place by the parlor fire. He rolled a candle like a baton between his fingers. "Do you want to come?"

"Don't be an idiot," Chantel snapped. She threw her coat over the end of a chaise and stomped up the stairs, the sole of each boot slapping viciously against the boards.

"You figure she'll change and go hang around the Chateau? Try to figure out what's going on?" Georges asked.

"Of course she will," Yves told him petulantly. "And when Louise finds her, she'll get herself killed." Before his companion could jump to the totally erroneous conclusion that he was worried about Chantel, he added, "And I'll likely get blamed because Louise gave me the warning to pass on, and then I'll get killed."

"Maybe you should do something to stop her."

"Stop who? Louise?"

Georges rolled his eyes. "Chantel."

"Stop her how?" Yves snorted. "Kill her myself?"

"No. Just tell Herself everything that's going on."

"Oh, that's a great idea, Georges." His voice dripped sarcasm. "But Herself isn't in the city, and we don't know where she is."

"It's simple."

"You're simple."

Having long since learned to ignore anything that didn't draw blood, Georges continued. "She's got to be staying with family, so we'll send a message to my sister in Mortigny, and Marri will pass it on."

Yves's brows drew together as he considered it, making his nose appear even more sharply pointed. Weighing his options, he flung a dart at a whiskered face peering out of a hole gnawed in the baseboard near the stairs. "You mean rat out Louise to her own twin sister?"

"Yeah."

"I like it."

Georges preened, then jerked aside as his cousin's last dart thudded into the mantel a whisker's width from his head.

"Georges, how many times do I have to tell you? Don't eat the candles!"

*   *   *   *   *

Her face arranged into an approximation of concern, Louise perched on the edge of the bed. "Dmitri? Can you hear me?"

He dragged his tongue over cracked and bleeding lips. "Where am I?"

"You're in the Chateau." She motioned the servant forward and watched while Dmitri gulped down a mug of water. "How are you feeling?"

"Weak." His brows drew in. "There was a fight. . . ."

"Yes."

As he remembered, his voice grew stronger. "I fought a . . . wererat. It fell into a spiderweb. Giant spider—" Then his eyes widened in sudden horror and he jerked up, clutching at Louise's arm. "It bit me, Louise! The wererat bit me!"

"It's all right." She peeled off his sweaty fingers and pushed him back against the pillows with more distaste than care. "It's been three days. If you were going to change, you'd have done it by now."

"Then I'm safe?"

Louise smiled. "Of course you are." When he sighed and relaxed, she added a silent, you fool.

"The figurine?"

"It's safe too."

"Aurek?"

She ducked her head, unable to keep the triumph from her eyes, masking it with a thick fringe of ebony lash. "He came by the first night you were here."

Dmitri swallowed and tried to look as though her answer meant nothing to him.

". . . but he didn't want to see you."

"Oh." His voice sounded absurdly young in contrast to the golden stubble on his chin and the broad muscles bare above the sheet.

"I told him that if he didn't talk to you, we wouldn't give him back the little statue of his wife. He threatened me."

"He *what?*"

"Threatened me," she repeated, enjoying the effect her words were having, "with dire and fell magics if I didn't turn over the statue immediately. I refused, of course."

Snatching up her hand, Dmitri pressed his lips against it. "Oh, my brave, brave darling. But . . ." As Dmitri thought about what she'd told him, his grip slackened, and Louise pulled her hand free. "Why would he threaten you?" It made no sense, and even through the fog of pain and fear and Louise, he knew his brother well enough to realize that. "I'm the one who stole it."

"He still considers you of no account." The sudden hurt that rose in his eyes was all she could have wished for. "I'm afraid he blames the whole thing on me."

"On you?"

"Yes."

"And I am of no account?"

"The figurine matters more to him." In the silence that followed, she could almost hear his resolve harden.

Dmitri's eyes narrowed, and a muscle jumped in his jaw, his expression, though he had no way of knowing it, identical to the one his brother had worn when he'd challenged Louise in the library. "Then he means nothing to me. We'll send his precious figurine back to him in pieces!"

"Remember, he's a wizard."

"I'm not afraid of Aurek!"

Louise didn't doubt that for a moment—he didn't have the brains to be afraid—but his staggering off and challenging his brother was not in her best interests. "But you're still so weak," she murmured. "I don't think we should enrage your brother further until you're strong enough to protect me." When he seemed to be about to protest, she added, "Remember that I was the one he threatened."

Instantly contrite, Dmitri reached for her hand, but she deftly kept him from capturing it without appearing to have moved at all. "You're right. I'm so sorry. I'd never do anything to place you in danger. We won't confront Aurek until I can protect you."

"Thank you." When he blinked a little at the sarcasm shading her tone, she stood and smiled down at him, washing his unease away in a look of pure adoration as false as it was fulsome. "Rest. Get your strength back. I'll come to see you later."

Out in the hall, she barely managed to keep her laughter in check until she was out of earshot. Tying the Nuikin brothers in knots was more fun than she'd had in years. That their torment would end with her sister's death only made it better.

*   *   *   *   *

"What are you doing?"

Chantel whirled around and nearly fell from her perch at the base of one of the Chateau's chimneys. Her claws scrabbled for purchase on the wet slate, and she somehow managed to keep from pitching over the edge.

Framed in one of the attic's tiny dormers, Jacques frowned down at her. "You're Chantel, aren't you? Mama says she's surprised you've lived so long.

'Cause you're white," he added in case she needed an explanation of his mama's pronouncement. "Does Tante Louise know you're on the roof?"

Her footing secure, Chantel quickly changed enough for speech. "No. I'm—I'm watching her for your mother."

Jacques frowned, his expression so like Jacqueline's that Chantel found herself trembling. "I don't believe you," he said. "I'm going to tell Tante Louise you're here."

"No!"

He paused, head cocked. "Why not?"

Desperately, Chantel searched for a reason. Threats wouldn't work; Jacques knew himself to be inviolate. Then she remembered what she'd been like at his age. "How would you like to get your Tante Louise into a lot of trouble?"

"A lot of trouble?" His eyes brightened at the thought. "With Mama?"

"Your tante is up to something with that human she has—"

"He was bit but he didn't change."

"Bit?" Chantel felt her hackles rise. "Who bit him?" she demanded, tail lashing from side to side.

Jacques shrugged. "I dunno. Wasn't me." He studied her with sharp curiosity as though trying to fathom just why it was grown-ups did what they did. "Did you want to bite him?"

"No. Yes." She snarled. "I don't know. Do you know what room he's in?"

"Yes. But they'll see you if you try to get to it."

The attic window appeared to be unguarded by anyone but the boy. "I could get in through there."

"No." His mouth set in an obstinate line. "I don't want you to. And if you try, I'll tell on you. I want to get Tante Louise in trouble. Me. Not you. I'll talk to the human, and then I'll talk to you. No one ever comes up here but me, so you can meet me here tomorrow night." With that, he slammed the shutters closed.

Changing back to full rat form, Chantel leapt forward and sank her claws into the wood.

"If you come in, I'll tell." The boy's piping voice carried easily through the barrier.

Teeth bared, she sank back onto her haunches. If he told Louise he'd seen her skulking about on the roof, Louise would kill her—or have her killed, it amounted to the same thing. She had no choice but to return the next night and hope she could convince Jacques to take her to Dmitri. Or at the very least, tell her where he was. If she knew for certain what room he was in, she'd risk moving down off the roof, but she couldn't risk searching randomly from window to window—her white fur would shine like a beacon against the dark face of the Chateau.

* * * * *

Jacques paused in the hall outside the human's room, suddenly realizing Chantel hadn't told him just what his aunt was up to with the human. Tante Louise did a great many things with humans that he wasn't supposed to know about, but it never made his mama angry. His nose wrinkled. Except, he amended silently, for the time she'd forgotten about one, and the pieces had stunk up the whole trophy room.

Shrugging narrow shoulders, he pushed open the door. It didn't really matter. If he couldn't get Tante Louise in trouble with Mama, he could definitely get Chantel in trouble with Tante Louise. Maybe, he thought cheerfully, I can get this human in trouble with someone, too.

A trio of candles burned on the small table by the bed, and the servant his mama had marked slumped, exhausted, in a chair. Her head jerked up as he entered.

"Get out," he said shortly.

She glanced at the bed, opened her mouth to protest, sighed, and left the room. Jacques could hear her waiting in the corridor outside but he decided, with all the magnanimity of a privileged child, that he could allow that. Even regular humans couldn't hear much, and the servants at the Chateau learned to hear less.

He stared at the sleeping human for a moment, noting with ghoulish curiosity the scabbed bite on his shoulder, then poked him hard in the ribs with a skinny finger.

Dmitri jerked awake, glancing wildly about him.

"Hello. Who are you?"

Heart pounding, Dmitri stared at the boy beside his bed. "D-Dmitri Nuikin," he stammered.

"I'm Jacques Renier. My mama is Jacqueline Renier."

"Yes." The glossy ebony cap of hair, emerald eyes, and pointed features were almost exact replicas of his mother's—barely even allowing for age and sex.

Jacques frowned. "What do you mean, yes?"

Beginning to recover from his sudden awakening, Dmitri found an explanation. "I mean, you look very much like her."

"I do?"

The boy seemed so pleased, Dmitri smiled. "Yes, you do."

"She's the most beautiful, the most wonderful person in the world!"

Dmitri's smile broadened. While he personally considered Louise Renier to be the more beautiful of the twins—to be, in fact, the most beautiful, the most wonderful person in the world!—he certainly wasn't going to argue with a boy's opinion of his mother. "Yes," he said. "She is."

"I like you." Jacques made himself at home on the

bed at Dmitri's feet. "What are you doing in my mama's house?"

"Well, your Aunt Louise and I . . . I mean, that is . . ." He felt his cheeks grow hot and his ears burn. "I had a fight with my brother."

Jacques shook his head. "That's not the real reason."

"I did have a fight with my brother."

"Okay." His tone suggested he'd allow the fantasy for the moment. "Who bit you?"

"A wererat."

"I know. Which one?"

"There's more than one?"

"Of course there's . . ." Then, just in time, he stopped himself. His mama had said never to tell the humans anything they hadn't already worked out for themselves, and this human obviously hadn't worked out anything. The idiot, he added silently. ". . . always more than one." That seemed safe enough.

A sudden scrabbling in the wainscotting jerked Dmitri around. "What was that?"

"Rat."

"You have rats in your house?"

Jacques shrugged. "Everybody has rats in their house."

"Can you see my sword?"

"You have a sword?" The boy's eyes widened. He dove off the bed and did a whirlwind search of the room. "There's no sword here," he concluded at last, voice and expression an accusation.

"I had a sword when I got here."

"Maybe Tante Louise took it away. I'll go look for it for you."

"Why would Louise take away my sword?"

Jacques paused at the door and turned around to face the bed again, one eyebrow cocked. "You're not very old are you?"

"I'm twenty," Dmitri told him, confused.

"Uh-huh. I'm ten."

As the door closed behind him, Dmitri had the strangest feeling the boy knew something he didn't. Something he didn't, but should.

* * * * *

"Sir, please, you must eat."

"Go away."

"You have barely eaten or slept since you returned from that house, sir. You will be able to help neither of them if you fall ill."

With ink-stained fingers, Aurek pushed a strand of filthy hair back off his face. "I have much work to do and little time to do it in. Leave me alone."

"Sir . . ."

"Edik." He lifted bloodshot eyes off the parchment sheets spread across the desk and turned just enough to see the bulky shape of his servant outlined in the door to the bedchamber. "I said, leave me alone."

Edik's sigh said enough to fill volumes. After a pregnant pause, he bowed and retreated. Aurek knew he wouldn't go far, but distance was unimportant as long as he went. He'd rarely had to raise his voice to Edik, unlike Dmitri . . .

Dmitri.

How could he have done such a thing? How could he have given Natalia to that contemptuous vermin?

The quill in his right hand bent and finally snapped as his fingers curled into fists. Irritably throwing the ruined pen onto the floor, Aurek's gaze ended up, as it always did, on the alcove and the empty pedestal.

How could Dmitri have done such a thing?

Well, he didn't know what he was doing, did he? chortled the hateful voice in his head. *You never saw fit to tell him about the results of your arrogance. You were the great scholar, and knowledge was your power. You were too blind to see that knowledge is powerful only when you use it. Your arrogance, your blindness, trapped your precious Natalia.*

Aurek ground his knuckles against his temples. "Shut up," he snarled.

You know, you might get further if you asked yourself why he took the little lady. Maybe he was trying to get your attention. Maybe he had something to say to you, and it was the only way he could get you to listen. The voice twisted itself into an edged parody of concern. *Now, why would he think that, I wonder?*

"You know nothing about this," Aurek ground out through clenched teeth. "Nothing!"

The laughter swelled until it beat against the inside of his skull, pounding and pounding and pounding as though it were determined to break free. *You blind and arrogant fool! I know everything you know!*

"You know NOTHING!"

"Sir?"

"Go away, Edik!" With trembling fingers, Aurek dipped a fresh quill into the dish of ink and began to write. Once he'd had a hundred spells at his command, a hundred spells collected and bound into a single volume. Some were so simple they barely needed to be written down. Some were so complicated they barely could be written down. Some were original. Some variations. He'd studied them all—studied them, learned them, inscribed them, and gone on. He'd almost never used them, unless it became necessary to clarify the details of a gesture or a material component. He thought of himself as a scholar, not a wizard.

"A scholar." His own bitter laughter joined the echoes in his head. A wizard would have thought first of the power he'd collected and protect it. He'd thought only of his scholarship, and it had destroyed his life.

He stared down at the words he'd written, pushed the parchment aside, and began again. Once he'd had a hundred spells. He didn't have them now. He needed to re-create, out of memory, a spell to hold a wererat captive, a spell to hold Jacqueline Renier. He had to be a wizard now, or his Natalia would die.

And your brother? How fortunate that you warned him of what he was getting into. If I'd blithely allowed my brother to become involved in a wererat power struggle, I'd be feeling pretty guilty right about now.

Calling up his last reserves of strength, Aurek pushed the voice to the back of his mind and buried it under memory. Dmitri had been lost—tragically and irrevocably lost—when he'd given Louise Nuikin what she wanted. No matter what the wererat said, he doubted his brother had lived even a moment after handing over the figurine.

"How did you persuade Dmitri to go along with this? Did you convince him that you loved him?"

"I didn't have to. I merely convinced him that you didn't."

Just as his Lia had, Dmitri had paid for his blind arrogance. But there was still a chance to save Natalia, and grief would have to wait. As Aurek worked, he could still hear faint reverberations of the laughter, but he'd grown almost used to that.

The lamp on the corner of the desk sputtered. Shadows danced manically about the room. Snorting impatiently, Aurek reached out and turned up the wick. He didn't have time to tend to insignificant details, but when the flame leapt up in answer to his touch, he stared at it, suddenly mesmerized by the light.

"Something to burn the darkness away," he murmured, leaning wearily toward it.

Then, in its white depths, he saw a familiar face under a wild shock of gray hair. Pale eyes gleamed under heavy lids, and thin lips stretched into a cruel smile.

"NO!"

The lamp's clay bowl smashed against the mantel, burning oil spilling down over the brick, and across the hearth. Flames danced out onto the wooden floor, and the planks began to smolder.

That's it, laughed the hateful voice. *Burn the darkness away.*

Aurek sighed and stretched out his hands to the blaze. He was just too tired to do anything about it. And the warmth felt so good.

Then he jerked back as a man-shaped shadow leapt into the room, viciously slamming a folded blanket down on the fire. A moment later, he could smell burning wool and feel large hands close around his upper arms. The smoke made it hard to see and caused his eyes to water so badly tears ran freely down both cheeks.

"Edik?"

"I'm here, sir. The fire's out. Come, I have a bath drawn for you and a light supper prepared, and then you'll sleep for a while."

He allowed himself to be lifted to his feet and led from the study. He didn't have the strength to protest. "Edik?"

"Yes, sir?"

"I never meant to hurt him. I never meant to hurt either of them."

"Master Dmitri made his own choices, sir. You are not solely responsible for his fate."

"And hers?"

When Edik made no reply, Aurek listened to the laughter instead.

*   *   *   *   *

"Jacqueline?" Marri Renier advanced timidly into
the drawing room holding a folded piece of paper in
front of her like a shield. Why the head of the family
had decided to stay with her, she had no idea, but it
made her very nervous. Scarred in a sibling battle
she'd barely won, she'd moved to Mortigny to live a
quiet life away from family power struggles and,
while she appreciated the honor of having Jacqueline
in her house, she didn't appreciate the undercurrent
of terror that came with her. These last few weeks as
Jacqueline had searched for the human, Henri
Dubois, Mortigny had not been a pleasant place—
though that had actually been kind of fun. "Jacqueline, this just arrived from Pont-a-Museau."

When Jacqueline stretched out an imperious
hand, Marri dropped the paper into it and scuttled
away to stand by the door, curiosity keeping her in
the room.

Ignoring her cousin, Jacqueline glanced down at
the wax seal. She didn't recognize which of the com-
mercial scriveners the seal belonged to but, if she
correctly interpreted the bloody claw prints scratched
on the paper beside it, whoever had sent the message
had also taken care it would never be repeated. The
family put little trust in promises of confidentiality.

She cracked the seal and moved closer to the
candles on the mantel as she unfolded the single
sheet. After a moment, she began to laugh.

"What is it?" Marri asked, encouraged by Jacqueline's amusement.

"You can always count on family," Jacqueline told
her, still chuckling as she dropped into a wingback
chair. "If they find a chance to stab someone in the
back, they'll jump at the opportunity. And if they
don't find a chance, they'll create one. It's so nice to

see my trust was not misplaced."

"You were expecting this note?"

"I was expecting *a* note. If not this one, then another." Black silk rustled as a rat crept out from under Jacqueline's skirts and climbed up to perch on the arm of the chair. Her expression hardened as she lightly stroked the top of its head with one finger. "Bring me paper, pen, and ink," she said. "I think I'll let my dear sister know when she can expect me to arrive home."

*   *   *   *   *

"Jacqueline will be back early on the day of the ball. I knew she wouldn't miss an opportunity to be the center of attention." Louise looked up from the letter on her lap and studied Aurek Nuikin, the minimal candles burning in the Chateau library sufficient for were-sight. His pale blond hair had been pulled back into a dull and dirty tail, and his beard appeared to have turned more gray than gold. Ink stains made black blemishes over both hands. His eyes were bloodshot. "Frankly, you look terrible. Are you certain you'll be able to fulfill your part of the bargain?"

"And if I'm not able?"

Louise smiled unpleasantly, the civilized, conversational tone falling from her voice. "Then I'll think you're not trying. Perhaps I should send you bits of your brother as incentive. It's amazing how many bits a strong young man can lose and still live." Reading his thoughts from his expression, her smile broadened. "You think I've already killed him, don't you? Perhaps I'll send you a bit to prove I haven't."

Hope rose unbidden, and with it, a warning. "If Dmitri is harmed . . ."

"You'll do what I ask anyway—you know it, I know it, and I assume your wife, if she knows anything at

all in that exquisite little prison of hers, knows it too."
Leaning back in the chair, Louise crossed her legs,
silk skirts whispering secrets. "You know what you
have to do and when, so I don't think it's necessary
for us to meet again."

Aurek's eyes narrowed. "It wasn't necessary for us
to meet tonight."

"Not necessary, no. But I do so enjoy having a
powerful wizard at my beck and call." She dropped
her chin and peered flirtatiously up at him through
her lashes. "Or do you think it's unladylike for me to
gloat?"

A muscle jumped in his jaw as Aurek spun on one
heel and stomped toward the door. With his hand
against the worm-eaten wood, he paused and half
turned. "Your sister has no doubt been told of your
comings and goings and of your guests."

"I know." Louise stood, and her fingertips brushed
over the notch in her ear. "But what can they tell her?
That young Dmitri has moved into the guest cham-
bers, and his older brother has come to the Chateau
to try to convince him to come home? I doubt very
much that she'll care. While distraught relatives
aren't exactly frequent visitors to the Chateau, neither
are they unheard of. As long as you both remain
unhurt, I have done nothing for her to complain of.
Had she objections to my relationship with your
brother, she'd have voiced them when it began." She
took a step toward him and, though she didn't actually change, her features suddenly appeared sharper,
more menacing. "And if you decide to tell her what's
going on, I guarantee I'll know about it, and your family will become significantly smaller."

"I'm not a fool," Aurek growled.

"Not a fool?" she repeated, with a serrated laugh.
"Only a fool would have allowed his relationship with
his brother to have deteriorated to the point where

that brother became a threat. Especially when that poor, sweet brother so desperately wanted to be friends." Watching her accusation cut into his heart, she twisted the knife. "I used the tool you forged for me, wizard."

He stared bleakly at her for a long moment, then bowed his head and left the room.

*   *   *   *   *

"I found your sword."

Dmitri jerked out of a light doze and stared in confusion at the slight figure silhouetted in candlelight beside the bed. "Jacques?"

"Of course," the boy replied impatiently. "And I said, I found your sword."

"My sword?" Dmitri pushed himself up so that he reclined against the pillows in a half-sitting position. "You found my sword," he repeated. "Thank you. Where was it?"

"In the trophy room." Responding to the unaffected enthusiasm in Dmitri's smile, the boy's mouth curved tentatively in return. "It didn't have a scabbard though. And it's pretty dirty." He reached down, grabbed the leather-wrapped hilt in both hands, and heaved the heavy blade up onto the bed. Bits of dried blood flaked off onto the coverlet. "Have you killed many people with it?"

"Only one." Dmitri's expression sobered. "A man insulted one of my sisters, and I fought a duel with him."

Jacques eyes gleamed. "Was it exciting?"

"Very exciting." The smile flashed again as he remembered, then faded as he remembered further. The man's family—more embarrassed by Dmitri's relative youth than outraged by the actual death— had been about to declare *cmepte chorosh*, death debt, when Aurek had suddenly appeared, and the extended feud had not occurred. He had no idea of what Aurek had done, but their sisters had insisted he'd saved Dmitri's life.

He was probably more worried about his stupid studies being disturbed by my funeral, Dmitri told himself bitterly, since he didn't think I was worth even a quick two words of explanation. Now that he knew Aurek was a wizard, it explained a lot.

"What are you thinking about?" Jacques demanded, unused to being ignored.

"My brother."

"You have a brother and a sister?"

"I have four sisters."

Jacques sighed, thin shoulders lifting and falling melodramatically. "I have only me."

"You must have lots of cousins," Dmitri offered. It seemed a fair guess as nearly everyone he met professed to be one of the Renier family.

"It's not the same as having a brother." His nose wrinkled as he pointed at the sword. "That's wererat blood. You didn't kill a wererat did you?"

"It attacked me—" Dmitri began, but the boy cut him off.

"Mama is not going to like that. She says . . ." He paused and rearranged what his mama said so that he wasn't giving anything away. "She says only wererats can kill wererats."

The child looked so serious and disapproving that Dmitri found himself protesting. "I didn't exactly kill it. We fought, and it fell into a giant spider's web."

"So the spider killed him?"

"I didn't actually see . . ." The wererat's screams rose up for a moment in memory. "Yes."

"That's all right then." He climbed up onto the end of the bed, folded his legs, and declared, "I like you. There are too many women around here."

Dmitri grinned and scratched at the bristles on his chin. Four older sisters gave him a good idea of what life must be like for Jacques. "You can come and visit me anytime. I'd be glad of the company." He glanced toward the lines of night visible through the closed shutters. "But isn't this a little late? Shouldn't you be in bed?"

"No!"

The boy looked so scornful, Dmitri had to hide a laugh in a fit of coughing.

Jacques studied the human thoughtfully and wondered if he'd tell him what Tante Louise was up to. Probably not. No one ever told him anything. Chantel wouldn't tell him either, even though he'd met her every evening at the attic window. Actually, he rather suspected from the frantic way she was acting that Chantel didn't know either, and she desperately wanted to. Maybe the human—Dmitri—would tell Chantel. She was older. Although not, Jacques amended silently, as much as she thought she was. If he brought Chantel here, he could listen from the next room—there were holes that went almost all the way through the wall. And then I'd know something that no one would know that I knew. He frowned as he worked through the tangles. I'm sure I could use that against someone. His mama always said that knowledge was power. She would be so proud of him.

"Do you know my cousin Chantel?"

Surreptitiously rubbing at his stained blade with a corner of the coverlet, Dmitri started guiltily. "Yes. I do. She's a . . . friend."

"Would you like me to bring her to see you?"

"Could you?" His voice sounded a little wistful. Although Louise came by as often as she could, none of his new friends had come to see him, and he'd been feeling forgotten about and sorry for himself.

" 'Course I could. Or I wouldn't have asked."

The corners of Dmitri's mouth twitched at the indignant answer. "Then yes, I'd like to see her."

Jacques nodded solemnly. "Then I'll bring her."

"Jacques! What are you doing in here?"

Jacques threw himself off the bed, whirling around to face the door in the same motion. "Tante Louise!"

Eyes narrowed dangerously, Louise advanced into the room. "I asked you a question, Jacques."

"I was visiting Dmitri." He sidestepped out of her direct path. "I brought him his sword."

"His what?" Surprise stopped Louise in her tracks.

"My sword," Dmitri put in from the bed. "Please don't be angry with the boy," he pleaded, sounding not a lot older than Jacques. "I asked him to bring it."

The boy? Jacques shot an indignant glare at the bed. How dare the human refer to him in such a way!

"I'm not angry with him." Louise stepped forward again, the hem of her skirt marked with the dust of her passage through the east wing. She smiled down at her nephew and then extended the smile to include Dmitri. "I just don't want him to tire you."

"He isn't." Dmitri returned her smile with such infatuation that Jacques thought he was going to be sick. The human had no idea Tante Louise was lying. Of course she's very good at it, he reminded himself, remembering how she'd fooled even him once or twice. When he was much younger, of course.

"Nevertheless," Louise went on, lowering herself gracefully to the edge of the bed and resting one long-fingered hand on Dmitri's bare shoulder, "I think he's stayed long enough." She glanced down at the sword with distaste and added, "Quite long enough. Jacques, go back to your rooms."

He didn't like her tone. "Mama . . ."

"Your mother isn't here now." Very slowly, Louise turned her head around to face him. When she lifted her lips off her teeth, it looked nothing like a smile. "I am."

The boy's lower lip went out, but he'd been trained both to recognize power when he saw it and to survive it. He nodded curtly to his aunt and headed for the door.

His movement distracted Dmitri, who'd been staring at the angle of Louise's head. Surely it was impossible to turn one's head so far around? He leaned past her. "Thanks again for my sword, Jacques. And the company."

Still a little piqued about being called a boy, Jacques shrugged. "Yeah, all right," he muttered and pulled the door closed behind him.

Tante Louise was right; his mama wasn't here, so he'd have to deal with her himself. He had only a vague understanding of just how, exactly, grown-ups worked, but it seemed to him that Tante Louise wouldn't much like it if Chantel, who seemed just as possessive as his aunt, came to visit Dmitri.

Smiling in pleased anticipation, Jacques headed for his nightly rendezvous at the attic window.

* * * * *

"You're messing my hair." Louise pulled back out of the heated embrace, one hand rising to fold an errant strand back over her notched ear, the other gripping Dmitri's wrist.

"Sorry." He grinned foolishly up at her. "You make me forget everything. You make me believe there's nothing I can't do."

"Well, you can't mess up my hair." She laid his captured hand on his chest and sat back. "And, no matter how good you feel, you're still wounded, and you should be resting."

"I am resting."

"You shouldn't have had Jacques bring you your sword. If you open that shoulder wound again . . ."

"I'll bleed." He laid his hand on her arm, took a moment to marvel at the play of warm flesh under his fingers, and added brightly, "I'm fine. Really."

"Good." She sighed and refused to meet his eyes.

Dmitri frowned and, placing a finger on her chin, turned her head to face him. "What's wrong?"

When this is over, if you're still alive, you're going to lose that finger, she thought, arranging her features into broad concern. "Aurek was here again. Making threats."

"Threatening you?" He sat up, groping for the hilt of his sword, eyes blazing. "That's it. That does it. I'm going to do something about this right now!"

"Do what?"

"Something."

Telling herself sternly not to laugh, Louise widened her eyes and stood, backing away from the bed. This was as good an opportunity as any to see just how recovered her guest was—while she still had time to do something about it. "Dmitri, you can't. You'll get hurt."

"I can't just lie here and do nothing." He swung his legs over the side of the bed and lurched up onto his feet. Linen drawers covered enough for modesty, so he concentrated on finding his balance. Toes splayed against the worn carpeting, he walked from the bed to the door to the bed to the door to the bed, swaying only a very little. Jaw set, he lifted the sword and swung it dramatically over his head. "I can protect you, and I will protect you. Even from my thrice-damned brother."

* * * * *

"Tante Louise comes and sees him all the time." Out of the corner of his eye, Jacques watched Chantel's tail snap from side to side. The fur had lifted off her spine, and her ears were laid back flat against her skull. Every time he mentioned his Tante Louise and Dmitri's being together, she got more and more upset. So he mentioned it as often as he could.

Chantel'd had to change from full rat form in order to lie to the questions Jacques threw at her as they made their way to the east wing. Although she carried a dusty, moth-eaten robe they'd found in one of the attic's trunks, she maintained the intermediate half-human, half-rat form for the trip through the halls of the Chateau. Should they, by chance, run into Louise, she wanted as much mobility as possible, as well as the use of tooth and claw.

"You know, I think Dmitri really likes her," Jacques continued with studied disinterest.

"What do you know about it!" Chantel hissed.

"Nothing much." He stepped back and waved at a half open door. "This is his room." Head cocked, he added, "Sounds like she's in there now."

He was just a little too innocent. Chantel slowly turned and stared at him, sensing a trap. He met her gaze fearlessly, secure in the knowledge that the rest of the family held his mama in terror and awe and would never, because of that, lay a finger on him.

She stepped back, away from the door, poised for flight.

"Dmitri! Put the sword down!"

Louise's shrill command rising out of the murmur of voices jerked Chantel around. The robe fell forgotten to the floor. Two steps forward, and Chantel could peer through the wedge-shaped opening and into the room. She blinked, half blind in the sudden light—her eyes had always been more sensitive than the rest of the family's. With tears marking the fur on her cheeks, she strained to see exactly what was happening.

Dmitri stood with his back toward her, facing the just barely visible figure of Louise. Chantel could smell his sweat, his blood, his exhaustion. As she watched, he swung the bright line of a sword around his head.

He was defending himself against Louise!

He was hers!

Louise would not have him!

Bone and muscle moved beneath fur. In full rat form, shrieking with rage, Chantel launched herself into the air.

*   *   *   *   *

Growing increasingly irritated with the stubbornness of human males, Louise opened her mouth to tell Dmitri for the last time to stop swinging the sword around before he cut off one of his own ears. She'd managed to get out the first letter of his name when a shrieking white fury flung itself into the room.

Dmitri, reacting to the sudden terror on Louise's face, whirled around, dropped to one knee, and thrust upward with the sword, locking his arms.

The steel point drove deep into Chantel's belly just below the sternum. The force of her leap dragged the blade the length of her body, spilling blood and intestines down over Dmitri's head and shoulders. Her shriek changed timbre, from rage to pain, and she crashed to the floor.

His grip on the sword pulled him over, and Dmitri found himself under a thrashing body, twisting frantically to keep claws from ripping open his bare chest. As he struggled to free himself, he worked the sword in deeper. All he could see was bloodstained fur; all he could smell was the stench of ruptured bowel; all he could hear was his own fear roaring in his ears. Finally, just as he thought the creature would never die, it jerked once and was still.

*   *   *   *   *

Eyes wide, Jacques watched his aunt step away
from Chantel's body, breathing heavily and inspecting her hands for bloodstains. The snapping of
Chantel's neck at the end had been a bit of an anti-
climax—Tante Louise must've wanted to keep Dmitri
from getting in trouble with his Mama—but the whole
sword thing had been terrific!

I'm going to learn how to do that! I'll make the
human teach me!

Jacques bounced a little in his excitement, then
froze as a glittering jade-green gaze turned toward
the door. When she finally looked away after what
seemed like hours, he crept quietly down the hall,
breaking into a run only when he'd safely cleared the
first corner.

*   *   *   *   *

She would take care of Jacques after she took care
of his mother. For now, the boy was unimportant.
Drawing in several deep, slow breaths, Louise fought
to control her rage. How dared Chantel attack her in
her own house! Had Dmitri not reacted so quickly, the
incredible audacity of the attack might have worked!

Dmitri . . .

Her rage dissipated in the possibilities raised by
Dmitri's unexpected talents. Even injured and surprised, his skill with a blade was nothing short of
amazing. She could use that, oh, yes, she could.

"Louise?"

As he pushed aside Chantel's limp body, Louise
rearranged her features into something approximat-
ing shock. "Dmitri! Are you all right?"

"I'm fine." He gained his feet, staggered, and
would have fallen had he not used the dripping

sword to prop himself up. "Are *you* all right?"

"Thanks to you, she never touched me." She threw herself into his arms, careful not to knock him over, glorying in the smell of death that hung around him. "You saved my life!" That, at least, was the complete truth, and her sincerity, undeniable.

"I would die for you," he murmured ardently into her hair.

"Not now." She caught him as he swayed and steered him toward the bed. "You've got to lie down. You're hurt again."

He stared stupidly down at the red streaks on his torso, suddenly more tired than he could remember ever being, then his gaze slid sideways to the body of the giant rat. Something was wrong, but he couldn't seem to figure out what it was. Blood matted the white fur, and one dark red eye stared sightlessly at the ceiling. He had the strangest feeling he'd seen that eye before. "Not mine; the blood's not mine."

"Good." Prying the sword out of his grip, she let it fall to the floor and pushed him down onto the mattress. "Rest, my love. You need your strength." When he opened his mouth to protest, she added. "*I* need your strength." He smiled up at her, and she was suddenly reminded of a puppy she'd drowned as a girl. It had looked up at her much the same way just before she shoved it underwater. Turning to hide her smile, she waved a hand at the congealing body in the center of the room. "I'll send servants in to bathe you and to remove that."

* * * * *

"You want me to poison him, mistress?" The old man's grip tightened on the bowl of warm water he carried in both hands, and he looked vaguely pleased to have been asked.

"I don't care what you call it," Louise snapped. Servants came to the Chateau for two reasons—they wanted to know that humped shapes of tooth and claw would never climb through their windows at night, or they needed a sanctuary and therefore placed what skills they had at the service of the house. This servant had arrived just in front of an angry lynch mob. "Just don't kill him, and remember that I need him up and functional the night of the ball. I don't want him wandering around before then." She stepped aside as a pair of burly servants carried out the stained carpet with Chantel's body wrapped inside. "At the very least," she added dryly, "he's inconveniently messy."

"Yes, mistress." His eyes tracked the dripping bundle as it was carried down the hall. "What if he asks about . . . that?"

Louise showed her teeth. "Isn't it terrible how giant rats can get into even the best houses?"

"Yes, mistress."

Turning over the new pieces of the plan, examining each for flaws she couldn't find, Louise followed Chantel's body as far as the central hall.

"Dump it in the usual place, mistress?"

"Of course. Use extra weights—she's family."

It had been some time since one of the younger members of the family had tried to kill her and, upon reflection, Louise felt almost sorry for the girl. Given time and patience, Chantel might have amounted to something, but she'd made her power play with the lack of subtlety so prevalent in the young, and she'd died learning the one lesson that would have ensured her survival:

Never do your own dirty work.

TWELVE

"I hear we have a visitor at the Chateau."

Louise lifted an ebony brow. "Do you have a problem with that?"

"Should I?" Jacqueline finished removing her gloves and stared levelly at her twin. "I also hear that Lucien and Jean and Chantel are dead."

The brow lowered, and the other joined it as Louise frowned. Although it wasn't surprising that Jacqueline, as Lord of Richemulot, knew of the deaths in the family, there were few things she hated more than her sister's little displays of power. "Lucien killed himself," she said tersely. "Jean fell into a spiderweb. Chantel attacked me, and I broke her neck."

"Lucien killed himself?"

If the trap on the figurine had thrown him back into his own mind and killed him there, then, technically, Lucien had killed himself. "Yes."

"Why?"

"How should I know?"

Jacqueline smiled. "Indeed. How should you know?" Lifting her skirts in one hand, she started up the stairs to the west wing.

"And was your trip a success?" Louise asked,

falling into step beside her.

"No." Jacqueline's tone gave clear warning that she would not expand on her answer.

Louise hid a satisfied smile at the thought of Jacqueline chasing phantom rumors of Henri Dubois and finding only greater heartache and pain. "I'm so sorry."

Jacqueline paused at the door to her suite and glanced over at her sister. "Don't be a hypocrite, Louise," she said wearily, one hand resting on the latch. "It doesn't suit you."

"It doesn't?" Louise stared at her in such astonishment that Jacqueline had to laugh.

"You're right; I'm wrong. Hypocrisy suits you very well."

Louise returned her smile, feeling fonder of her sister at that moment than she had in some time. "Sleep well, Jacqueline. I'll see you this evening."

When I'll kill you, she added silently as the door closed between them.

* * * * *

"Mama?"

Jacqueline set her hairbrush down and turned to face her son. "Were you given permission to come in here?" she asked sternly.

His face fell. "No, Mama."

"We'll excuse it this once." She opened her arms, and he ran into her embrace. "Did you miss me?"

"Oh, yes, Mama!"

"Were you a good boy while I was gone?" When he paused before answering, she held him out at arm's length. "Well?"

"What exactly would you call good?" he wondered, looking worried.

Jacqueline laughed. "Let's make it simpler then. Did you break any of Mama's rules?" He looked so relieved that she laughed again and swept him into another hug, muffling his answering, "No, Mama." against her breast.

When she released him, he brushed a shock of dark hair back off his face and gazed up at her seriously. "Mama, I have things to tell you."

"Not now, Jacques. I've been traveling all night, and I'm very tired."

"But, Mama," he protested as she stood, "Chantel is dead."

"I know."

His face fell. "Oh."

Jacqueline placed one finger under her son's chin and tilted his head up until she stared into his eyes. "I *always* know, Jacques. Never forget that."

"No, Mama." He sighed deeply. "I mean yes, Mama."

She smiled down at him. He looked so much like her and so little like his father, he was easy to love. "Later, I'll want to hear everything you know."

His face brightened. "I was taking her to see Dmitri when it happened."

"Jacques, I said later. It's nearly dawn, and I need to sleep. I expect that the ball tonight will be very tiring."

"Yes, Mama. Sleep well, Mama."

She watched him dance out of the room, waited until she heard the outer door close behind him, and made her way to the bed. "I always know," she repeated as she slid between perfumed sheets, wondering why Louise hadn't bothered to lie about the recent and frequent visits death had made to the family. Perhaps it was because she knew a lie would be discovered. "Or perhaps she's smarter than I give her credit for."

* * * * *

Pont-a-Museau's best musicians arrived at dusk and began setting up in the gallery that stretched across one end of the Chateau's ballroom. As the sound of strings being carefully tuned floated out from behind the pillars, servants bustled about tending to last-minute details. All three of the massive chandeliers held new candles of hard white beeswax, bleached for purity and guaranteed with the candlemaker's life not to drip on the dancers below. Piles of wood had been stacked ready in both fireplaces behind iron screens designed to protect against accidental immolation. Purposeful immolation was another problem altogether. Not a crack, not a smut marred the tall windows that glittered along the length of the south wall, and if there were dark stains that would not come out of the hardwood floor, they, too, had been polished until they gleamed.

Outside, the night was clear and cold with the promise of the coming winter in the bite of the wind. The moon, burnished bronze, hung low in the east, and as the sky darkened, a thousand stars, bright enough to draw blood, appeared to join it. The river ran fast and high, and on its banks society prepared for the last entertainment of the season.

* * * * *

"Did you sleep well?"

"I always do." Jacqueline rose, steaming, from the bath and slid her arms into the offered robe. "But I doubt you came here so early to ask me that. What do you want, Louise?"

"I had an idea that might make tonight's party more . . . interesting."

"Interesting." Jacqueline repeated both the word and the emphasis as she walked into her bedchamber. "In what way?"

Louise swept her arm toward her sister's bed, where a crimson silk gown lay spread out over the coverlet. "I thought you might wear this tonight."

"I always wear black."

"I know. And so does everyone else." Her eyes glittered in the candlelight as she leaned toward her twin. "I'll be wearing a dress exactly like this—I had the seamstress make two, then I killed her. Half our guests will be in a panic trying to figure out which of us is which, and the family will be going crazy trying to figure out what we're up to."

Jacqueline glanced up at her sister and frowned. It had been a very long time since they'd played the games so favored by the identical twins in the family, games where a case of mistaken identity could easily conclude with death or dismemberment. "We're not as identical as we used to be," she pointed out.

Forcing her hand away from the notch in her ear, Louise shrugged. That one visible scar had complicated this part of the plan. Without it, it would've been enough for her to wear black as well. With it, she'd needed Jacqueline's cooperation. "If we wore our hair the same way . . ."

"It's a childish idea, Louise. Childish and mean." Jacqueline crossed to the bed and held the dress up against her. The demi-train spilled, like fresh blood, over her bare feet. She smiled. "I like it."

* * * * *

In the east wing of the Chateau, Dmitri stared, perplexed, at the evening clothes laid out on his bed. "These are mine."

"Of course they are."

He adjusted the towel wrapped around his waist. "But I left them at the townhouse."

"I had them sent for."

"But Aurek . . ."

"One of my servants got them from one of your servants. Aurek wasn't involved. I told you, you mean nothing to him now." Louise laid her fingers on his bare shoulder just to feel the muscle shiver at her touch. "You saved my life. It was the least I could do."

He shook his head; golden curls still damp from the bath tumbled down into his eyes. "I still can't believe that a giant rat came right into the house," he declared. "Right into the room!"

"It was young. The young seldom take the time to think things through."

"Young?" Frowning slightly, he turned to face her. "How could you tell? Are the adults so much larger?" The white rat had been the largest he'd ever seen— except, of course, for the wererat he'd fought in the ruins. His frown deepened, and he felt himself totter on the edge of an important discovery. He remembered how he'd looked down at the body and thought that something was wrong. "Louise, could that white rat . . . I mean, is it possible it was a wererat?"

"I didn't come here to talk about that rat!" Louise snapped. When he recoiled slightly at her anger, she grabbed at her control and stared up into guileless violet eyes with as much false concern as she could muster. "I'm so worried about you. I need to know how you feel. Are you sure you're well enough to come downstairs? If anything should happen to you . . ." Her voice trailed off as though she were already anticipating the loss.

Reassured, Dmitri lightly stroked the velvet curve of her cheek with the backs of two fingers. He wanted to sweep her up into his arms, but he sensed she wouldn't welcome the move. She was so small and delicate that sometimes he felt like a clumsy giant beside her. "I'm fine," he told her softly. "It was the strangest thing, but after days of not knowing up from down, I woke this morning almost clearheaded, and as the day's gone on, I've regained more and more of my strength. It's almost as though I'm intended to be at your side tonight."

"Almost as though," Louise repeated. The low doses of poison appeared to have worked perfectly. She turned away from him and forced a catch into her voice. "You know that Aurek is going to be there?"

"No. I didn't know that."

Giving thanks that he couldn't see her face, she smiled, enjoying his pain. "Jacqueline insisted he be invited." One finger traced the tin edge of the hip bath set up before the fire. "I'm afraid."

"Don't be." He took a step toward her. "I won't let him hurt you."

"He's so powerful."

"I'm not afraid."

She shook her head, ebony curls dancing across the back of her neck. "He's your brother. If it came to a choice between us . . ."

"Louise."

She allowed her name to pull her around. Dmitri's expression of besotted gallantry was all she could have hoped for, even though it made her slightly nauseated.

"Haven't I already chosen?" he asked. "You have my heart in your hands."

His heart in her hands. She relished the sight of it, dripping and bloody, impaled on her claws, then reluctantly banished the vision as she pulled an ancient dagger from the folds of her skirt. "This is for you."

"But I have a blade."

"Not like this one. This dagger has been enchanted to cut through any magical defense. It's one of the ancient artifacts of my house."

His eyes widened with awe as he stared down at the scuffed leather scabbard and the protruding wirewrapped hilt. "And you want me to have it?"

"If your brother attacks, this might be the only thing that can save me." She lifted his hand and laid the dagger across the palm, folding his fingers tightly around it. "I not only trust you with this family treasure, I trust you with my life."

His left knee hit the floor, and he pressed her hand against his lips, murmuring, "I will not fail you."

She lightly stroked his curls with her free hand. "I know."

A few moments later, outside in the dusty corridor that stretched the length of the east wing, Louise beckoned the servant who had been tending Dmitri for the last few days. "You stopped giving him whatever-it-was last night?"

"Yes, mistress."

"Before he goes downstairs, bring him a little more in a glass of wine. He's too clearheaded. I want him reacting, not thinking."

"It will be a difficult dosage, mistress, to affect the brain and not the body."

"Can you do it?" Her claws dimpled the flesh of his throat.

He started to nod and thought better of it. "Yes, mistress."

Humming a popular dance tune to herself, Louise hurried to her suite to dress. The dagger, while undeniably old, was neither a family heirloom nor enchanted. It was, however, very sharp. Although her fettered wizard would no doubt have defenses up, he wouldn't be expecting an attack from his brother. If Dmitri could be convinced to attack—convinced that Aurek had attacked her and not Jacqueline—he just might get through and rid her of a powerful and dangerous enemy. If he didn't, and was killed in the attempt, she would instead be rid of an increasingly tiresome and no longer necessary young fool.

"I can't lose."

* * * * *

A short distance away, in the bedchamber of his townhouse, Aurek twitched the sleeves of his dark gray evening jacket into place over pale gray silk cuffs. He had bathed and dressed and could delay the moment no longer. Walking slowly into his study, he stared for a long minute at the single parchment sheet that lay in the center of the desk. Filled top to bottom, left to right with his untidy scrawl, it was the only solution he'd been able to devise, and he had no idea if it would be enough. On the desk beside the spell were two small metal rods. They'd been, before he removed both head and point, nails he'd had Edik pull from a loose board.

Two rods.

Two rods would hold both the Renier sisters, but at only half the strength of holding Jacqueline alone. He hesitated, listened to the laughter, and slid only a single rod into his pocket. He couldn't risk it. Not when Natalia could be so easily destroyed.

Closing his eyes for a moment, he wished that there were another way. He couldn't trust Louise Renier, but he had to believe that she would return his wife and brother unharmed. To not believe—that way lay madness.

When he opened his eyes, he was facing the alcove and the empty pedestal. Heart heavy, he stepped toward it and dropped to his knees, resting his forehead against the fluted wood. There were a hundred things he wanted to say—a thousand things, perhaps—but he needed to say them to Natalia, to laughing, loving flesh and blood, not to the figurine where his pride had trapped her, not to empty space.

Finally, he stood; he had no reason to stay and every reason to leave. It was time.

Behind him, in the empty room, a clear white light continued to burn in the alcove.

*   *   *   *   *

Edik, waiting by the front door, noted the set of his master's shoulders, the almost fatalistic light in the pale eyes, and knew without being told that everything would be risked tonight. Worry masked behind efficiency, he bowed and said, "The boat is already at the slip, sir."

"I won't be taking the boat." Aurek pulled his braid free and shrugged his greatcoat up onto his shoulders. "I'm walking."

"Sir?" Both Edik's brows rose, the closest he came to astonishment.

"I want to be alone."

"But, sir, to be alone at night in Pont-a-Museau . . ."

"Is dangerous?" Accepting the offered hat and gloves, Aurek joined in, for a moment, with the laughter in his head. He was still chuckling quietly as he went out the door and down the stairs into the darkness.

*   *   *   *   *

Most of those who traveled to Chateau Delanuit that night traveled by water. The advancing season had driven away the last lingering stink of rot, and though a tracery of frost along the shoreline made heavy wraps a necessity, the trip had become as pleasant as it ever got.

"Hey! What's that?" Georges leaned out dangerously far over the bow of the boat and shaded his eyes from the lantern light. "There's something in the water at the base of the bridge."

"So what?" Yves muttered from his place near the stern. He'd sunk so far into the folds of his greatcoat that only his eyes and nose were visible between the upswept points of his collar. "There's always something in the water."

"Yeah, but this is big." Still hanging out over the
bow, Georges turned his head farther than was
humanly possible and looked back over his shoulder. "And it's white."

As Yves surged to his feet, the boatman croaked a
warning and leaned hard on his oar. Yves ignored
him. Shoving past Annette, he pushed Henri into his
brother's lap—the twins were individuals tonight, for
Henri still bled sluggishly from a gash along his
jaw—and leapt up on the seat beside Georges.
"Where?"

"There. By the center pillar."

Something white and large bobbed up and down in
the icy water, rubbing against the filthy stone, caught
at the point where the current divided and passed to
either side of the center support.

"Boatman, take us there."

The boatman knew better than to protest. There
was a small chance he could keep the boat from
being caught in the eddies under the bridge and cap-
sizing, and no chance at all of surviving an argument. Muscles straining, he guided the boat out of
the safe channel and let the current aim it right at the
bridge. At the last moment, he grabbed as much
water as he could and swept the oar around, turning
the boat across the current and bringing it to a gentle
stop up against the pillar, the floating white shape
squashing slightly between wood and stone. Heart in
his throat, he started to breathe again.

Yves stared over the side for a moment.

"Well?" Aubert demanded.

"It's Chantel."

"Dead?"

"No, you idiot," Yves snarled, "she's just gone in
for a swim before the river freezes. Of course she's
dead!"

"Who did it?" Georges asked, feeling that the question was more expected than necessary.

Yves rolled his eyes. "Who do you think?"

As one, the five turned toward Isle Delanuit and the Chateau—tonight so brilliantly lit that it chased the night away from its walls. They all knew where Chantel had been going, and why.

"The little Nuikin?" Annette wondered aloud.

"Against Chantel? Don't be ridiculous."

"Lou—" Henri choked as his twin drove an elbow into his stomach and, with a jerk of his head at the boatman, hissed, "Family business, you fool."

"What are we going to do about it?" Georges wondered as Yves returned to his seat and motioned for the boatman to continue their journey.

Yves stared at him in some surprise. "Do? Are you out of your mind? We're not going to *do* anything." He paused and swept a warning glance over his remaining cousins, one by one. "The river's gotten a little cold for swimming, don't you think?"

Annette and the twins nodded. Georges shook his head. "I still think we should do something."

"We are going to do something," Yves told him. "We're going to be smart enough to survive." But he locked his gaze on the river as Chantel's body, pushed back into the current by their visit, continued on its final journey through Pont-a-Museau, and his lips were drawn up off the ivory gleam of his teeth.

He'd expected it to happen but, now that it had, he found he didn't like it much.

*   *   *   *   *

Jacques started as Tante Louise swept out of his mother's suite and started again when he realized it wasn't his aunt. "Mama?"

She turned and ebony brows rose. "Were you

surprised to see me, Jacques?"

"No, Mama, it's just you never . . . I mean . . ." He swallowed. "You always wear black, Mama."

"Did you think I was your Tante Louise?"

"Only for a moment, Mama."

"And what made you change your mind?"

The question had an edge he recognized. "You're much more beautiful than Tante Louise."

Jacqueline smiled and bent to kiss his cheek. "Thank you, my darling. If you don't bother the musicians, you may watch for a while from the gallery."

"Thank you, Mama."

It wasn't until she swept away with a rustle of crimson silk that he realized he still hadn't told her about Tante Louise and the human.

* * * * *

Although a multitude of lights glittered out on the river, all moving toward Isle Delanuit, the streets of the city were deserted. Aurek listened to the sound of his own boots slapping against the cobblestones of the esplanade and didn't bother trying to convince himself that he was alone. As he approached the dark mouth of a particularly noxious alley, three shadows emerged from the masking night.

Aurek sighed and stared at the slouching figures. "What?" he asked with little interest, breath pluming on the chill air.

Somewhat taken aback by his attitude, the shortest of the three made a quick recovery. Steel gleamed suddenly in his hand. "You gots money? Give it here."

"No." Pulling off his gloves, Aurek shoved them into his pockets and began to bring his thumbs together, fingers spread. There was no longer any need for circumspection.

"No?" Only the apparent leader carried a dagger; the other two held spiked cudgels they seemed anxious to use. "You stupid, rich man?"

"No," Aurek said again. But before he could release the fire, the trio suddenly disappeared beneath a half dozen giant rats and three or four times that number of their smaller cousins.

Although there were no actual wererats among his guardians, it seemed obvious that Louise Renier intended him to reach the Chateau with body and power intact. For the second time that evening, the laughter in his head exactly echoed his mood, and Aurek laughed with it as he continued past the screaming thieves and up onto the arc of the nearest bridge.

*   *   *   *   *

In the ballroom of the Chateau, Dmitri blinked as the whirling dancers broke into a kaleidoscope of shapes and colors that made very little sense. Music and voices beat against his ears in rhythms he couldn't seem to understand. He swayed, slopped a little wine down his jacket, and gratefully found a wall to lean against. Although he'd felt fine when he left his room, by the time he'd made his way downstairs his head seemed stuffed with cobwebs once again.

He saw a brilliant red gown flash in and out of the dance, and his expression softened. Louise. She'd been worried about him, but when his body had effortlessly followed the patterns of their dance, instinct accomplishing what reason could not, she'd seemed reassured. Which was a good thing, for though he didn't want to worry her, he wasn't leaving her here alone without his protection.

Frowning, he wondered what he was supposed to

be protecting her from. Doesn't matter, he thought, hand brushing the dagger, I'll protect her from whatever it is.

"Drunk so soon?"

"Yves!" Dmitri grinned happily down at his friend. "Drunk? No. This is my first." Frowning, he scrubbed at his jacket with his free hand. "And I've spilled most of it."

Yves's nose wrinkled. He could smell the drug on the human's breath and see the effect in his eyes. Why Louise—because it could only have been Louise or she'd have killed someone the moment she'd noticed her pet's condition—would want to make Dmitri Nuikin stupider, he had no idea. Nor did he care.

Nor, however, did he want Louise to have things her own way. It was an amazing feeling, almost completely overwhelming what he had previously considered to be a well-developed sense of self-preservation.

His lip curled as he remembered white fur in cold water. Louise had been having her own way too often of late.

"Come on."

"Where are we going?"

"You're going outside to puke."

Dmitri looked confused. "But I don't have to puke."

"You will when we get outside," Yves told him, digging his fingers into Dmitri's elbow and steering him through the crowd. When Louise had removed Chantel, she'd removed one fifth of the protection provided by his circle of friends—and that was an acceptable reason for him to retaliate. It might be too late for vomiting to do Dmitri any good, too much of the drug might already be in his system, but it was a start.

A few moments later, Dmitri looked up from his

knees, one hand clamped around his stomach, the other bracing himself against the ground, a steaming puddle spreading into the dirt in front of him. "Why did you do that?" he asked.

"It's a long story," Yves grunted. The puddle smelled of bile, wine, and the drug. "Come on."

"Now where?"

"Back inside." The wererat effortlessly heaved the much larger man up onto his feet. "You look as if you could use a drink."

"You're not going to hit me again are you?"

"No."

"Good." Dmitri spat to get the taste out of his mouth and allowed himself to be led back into the ballroom. He didn't understand why he wasn't more upset about being hit. He felt that he should be, but it didn't seem worth it to pursue the feeling. Except for the pain where Yves had punched him, and a burning senstion in his throat, he felt surprisingly better than he had. Sound and color still whirled his thoughts about his head, but he found it easier to hold them in place. "I think the cold has cleared my head."

Georges, Annette, and the twins waited just inside the door, their expressions identically confused as they stared from Dmitri to Yves and back again.

Dmitri blinked happily down at them. "Hello. Where's Chantel? Jacques said he was going to bring her in to see me, but she never came."

Yves pushed him back against the wall, grabbed a glass of punch from Georges, and shoved it into Dmitri's hand. "Chantel," he snarled, "is dead."

"Dead?" He clung to the thought, fighting to hold it still long enough to release a meaning. "Dead?" Everything whirled a little slower. Chantel was dead? "She was my friend," he whispered. "What happened?"

"Ask Louise," Yves told him, mouth so close that hot breath lapped against Dmitri's ear.

Dmitri's head snapped around, searching for Louise in the crowd. By the time he turned to Yves again, all five of his friends were gone, and he was alone by the wall. "Ask Louise," he murmured to himself. He could see her across the ballroom, a slender column of red surrounded by a circle of guests. After emptying the glass and setting it carefully back on the sideboard, he made his way toward her.

* * * * *

"I thought we weren't going to do anything," Georges muttered as he got himself another drink to replace the glass of punch Yves had given away.

Yves smoothed a hand down the tattered ribbons on his vest. "We aren't."

"But you . . ."

"Just suggested the little Nuikin talk to Louise. I don't want her to feel as if he's not paying enough attention to her."

Georges shook his head, unsure if understanding or ignorance would be a better defense. "You implied she had something to do with Chantel's death."

Yves smiled viciously. "She did."

"Are you trying to drive him away from her? There's no point, you know; Chantel is beyond caring."

"I know." Yves watched Dmitri cross the room. With any luck, he'd still be disoriented enough from the drug that he'd blurt out an accusation and Louise would take his head off, simultaneously removing the irritating object of Chantel's fascination, messing up whatever plan Louise had going, and really irritating Jacqueline—who would take out that irritation on Louise. "Come on." He took a candle out of his cousin's hand and tossed it under the table.

"Where are we going?"

"Closer to the door." He caught Annette's eye as

the dance spun her past, then nodded toward the far end of the ballroom. Waiting until she whispered the information on to Henri—or Aubert, they were too far away and there were too many other family members masking the scent for him to be certain—he gripped Georges by the elbow and began to move them both in the direction of the exit, secure in the knowledge that what one twin knew the other soon would. "When things get interesting . . ." Digging his nails into his cousin's arm, he cut off an incipient protest. ". . . and they will, I don't want any of us trampled in the rush to safety."

* * * * *

"Louise, did you know that Chantel was dead?"

Jacqueline turned and fixed Dmitri with a basilisk stare. "I beg your pardon?"

Dmitri felt his face burn as he stammered an apology. "It's just," he continued, trying to explain, "I mean, the dress, and well, you're twins . . ."

"My son assures me that I'm more beautiful than my sister."

"Your son . . ."

"Yes, Jacques. I'm sure you met him during your stay. He told me he was taking Chantel to see you when she died. Now if you'll excuse me, I believe this is Monsieur Egout's dance."

Dmitri bowed and murmured something as Jacqueline swept regally away. His thoughts were spinning again. He had to talk with Louise.

* * * * *

Louise saw Dmitri standing by her sister and snarled silently to herself. He had to be far enough away from both of them when Aurek arrived in order to confuse their identities. Which wasn't going to happen if he was deep in conversation with Jacqueline!

She relaxed a little as her twin moved into the dance on the arm of an elderly cavalier and began to snarl again when the stupid boy scanned the crowd then started heading directly toward her. With one hand on the statue of Aurek's wife, safely tucked in a pocket hidden within the full folds of her crimson skirt, she hurried around the edge of the room, her expression moving guests and family alike prudently out of her way.

Dmitri turned to follow.

Where were those idiot friends of his? Why couldn't they distract him? Eyes narrowed, Louise swept her gaze over familiar faces and finally spotted Yves and the others standing together just inside the door. She raised a hand to beckon them closer but let it fall again without completing the gesture as a tall, gray-clad figure appeared in the doorway. Smiling to herself, she headed to where the pattern of the dance would deposit Jacqueline when the music ended.

* * * * *

Standing on the edge of the dance floor, Aurek stared about the ballroom, noticing nothing and no one except Louise Renier. Lips pressed into a thin white line, he set out on a course to intercept her.

* * * * *

Searching for Louise, a quest that had proven to be surprisingly difficult, Dmitri pushed his way around a weighty dowager whose feathered turban had momentarily blocked his view.

"Young man!"

He stopped only because the old woman had a

surprisingly strong grip on his coat.

"You bumped me." The dance had ended, and in the quiet her voice rang out over the murmur of the other guests. "I demand an apology."

On another evening, the amused stares of a dozen people would have been a painful embarrassment. Tonight, Dmitri barely noticed. "Madame, I most humbly apologize." He bowed as well as he was able, considering her hold on his coat, then yanked the fabric out of her hand.

Once around her indignant bulk, he spotted Louise easily. Or he spotted Jacqueline easily. They were standing together, heads bent, both smiling. Then one of them moved away.

But which one?

* * * * *

Totally unaware of his brother's presence in the ballroom, Aurek saw the sisters together, saw them separate, and found it unnecessary to try to tell them apart. The moving twin caught his eye and nodded once.

Louise.

He walked closer to Jacqueline. Shoving his right hand into his pocket, he rolled the tiny iron rod up into his fingers and began the first of the four segments of the spell.

* * * * *

Aurek? Dmitri watched his brother cut through the crowds and recognized the rigid set of head and shoulders. Aurek was furious. And he was heading right toward . . .

Louise!

It was happening just as she'd said it would! His

hand on the dagger hilt, Dmitri began to frantically push his way through the protesting aristocracy of Pont-a-Museau.

* * * * *

Jacqueline, who had been watching her sister through a thick fringe of ebony lashes, saw Louise nod and turned slowly to face in the same direction. Although they couldn't have known why, the guests were instinctively parting like flesh under a razor as Aurek strode toward her across the ballroom floor. She wrinkled her nose at the scent of his gathering power.

When he was close enough, she lifted her eyes to his. "I don't think so," she said softly.

Claws clicking against the polished wood, hundreds—thousands—of rats suddenly poured out of cracks and holes in walls and floors and even the ceiling, every single one of them heading directly for Aurek Nuikin.

Townspeople screamed and began running, some toward the doors, some in circles. The family didn't waste time screaming—they just ran.

With Georges by his side, the twins and Annette following, Yves led the way out of the Chateau. He could hear cries of panic coming from the ballroom behind them as the door proved too narrow for the number of people who wanted through it. Lips curled up off his teeth in amusement as the panic turned to shrieks of pain. Under these circumstances, the family wouldn't allow a few humans in the way to delay them.

He'd miss Chantel but, in sobering up the little Nuikin, he'd done what he could to avenge her death. He'd be a fool to risk more, and she'd have been the first to tell him that.

As the five raced along the landing toward their

boat and safety, Yves shoved a servant, who dared ask him what was going on, off the dock.

"Company for Chantel," he explained as the dark and frigid water closed over the astonished man's head and cut off the first terrified scream.

It was the kind of memorial she'd appreciate.

* * * * *

Back inside the ballroom, Dmitri froze as a small brown body landed on his shoulder and launched itself toward his brother. Rats? He didn't understand.

"Mama!"

The piercing cry from the balcony turned only two heads, Dmitri's and that of the woman he thought was Louise. Unlocking her gaze from Aurek's face, she glanced upward, scanning the second level. When she raised her hand, and the small head shoved through the banisters withdrew, Dmitri realized that Aurek had attacked the wrong twin. His brother wasn't facing Louise; he was facing Jacqueline!

Desperately, Dmitri searched the frenzied crowd for Louise.

She wasn't far. Her lips were pulled back off her teeth in a fierce anticipatory smile, and her hands were curled into fists. She was staring at Aurek and her sister with glittering eyes.

Eyes . . .

Dmitri's thoughts began to whirl again, but this time a pattern emerged through the weakened influence of the drug.

Blood matted the white fur, and one dark red eye stared sightlessly at the ceiling. He had the strangest feeling he'd seen that eye before.

"Ask Louise."

"He told me he was taking Chantel to see you when she died."

. . . his gaze slid sideways to the body of the giant rat. Something was wrong, but he couldn't seem to figure out what.

He hadn't killed that rat. Its neck was broken.

Louise was the only other person in the room.

"Ask Louise."

". . . taking Chantel to see you when she died."

"It was young. The young seldom take the time to think things through."

Chantel was dead.

He had the strangest feeling he'd seen that eye before.

"Ask Louise."

Chantel had white hair and eyes so dark a red they looked almost brown. Louise had killed a white rat with eyes so dark a red they looked almost brown and referred to it, directly after, as "she."

"Mama says only a wererat can kill another wererat."

"NO!"

*   *   *   *   *

The single word cut through the other sounds in the ballroom as though they were flesh and it a sword.

Three of the four segments of the spell completed, Aurek jerked around at his brother's cry. He was alive! He was safe!

"Dimitriiiiii!" The name turned into a howl of pain as the first of the rats reached him and sank chisel teeth through the negligible protection of his trousers into his calf.

"Aurek!" Dmitri clung to his brother's name, used it to pull himself further out of the trap he'd found himself in.

How much of what Louise had told him was a lie

and how much the truth became unimportant. Aurek needed him. His brother needed him.

If Louise was a wererat, then Jacqueline was a wererat, and one of them had to be controlling the rats. Jacqueline was closer. Drawing the dagger Louise had given him, Dmitri threw himself at her sister.

"Dmitri! No!" Thinking only to protect his brother, Aurek yanked a rat off his thigh, stomped on another, and brought his thumbs together. Ignoring the pain, ignoring the spell he'd nearly finished, he grabbed for focus and concentrated. Spreading his fingers, he spun around until Dmitri was no longer within the parameter of the spell and screamed, "Burn!"

Rats shrieked and ignited as jets of searing flame shot from his fingertips.

The ballroom quickly filled with clouds of greasy black smoke.

Coughing and choking, eyes squinted almost shut, Louise didn't know how it had happened, but it was all going wrong. Her carefully constructed, cunningly complicated plan was tumbling down around her like a house of cards!

No! This is my chance! Kicking a burning rat aside, she pulled the statue from her pocket and raced toward Jacqueline. If she couldn't use Aurek's wife as a hostage, the statue would still make a dandy weapon smashed down on the back of her sister's skull.

Large hands closed, with a crushing grip, around her upper arms. She snarled and kicked but couldn't break free.

When the smoke cleared a moment later, Jacqueline and Aurek faced each other across twelve feet of open floor. The burned, smoldering bodies of dead rats fanned out behind the wizard. The silent, watching bodies of live ones fanned out behind the Lord of Richemulot.

Jacqueline held Dmitri in one hand, her claws dimpling the flesh of his throat. A trickle of blood ran from her thumb down under his collar. Dmitri no longer held the knife. It lay gleaming on the floor at Jacqueline's feet.

Aurek held Louise, a hand enclosing each arm. Louise held a small porcelain statue in both hands. He couldn't change his grip or she'd drop the statue, and as much as she wanted to smash it, she knew it was the only thing keeping her alive.

Glancing quickly around the room, noting a pile of bleeding bodies in the doorway that were all that remained of the guests who hadn't escaped, Aurek inclined his head to Jacqueline. "We seem to be alone." His voice, a little hoarsened by the smoke, was remarkably steady.

"The others have fled lest they be implicated in the attempted coup." Jacqueline smiled. "Rats, as it were, leaving a sinking ship. Tomorrow they'll deny they were ever here." Then she sighed, and the smile disappeared. A glittering green gaze fell first on her sister, snarling in Aurek's grasp, and then down at her own trembling captive. "So the little Nuikin races to his brother's rescue; it seems that you mean more to your family than I do to mine."

"That's not true!" Louise cried. "I was running to defend you when he grabbed me."

"Don't be a bigger fool than you have to be, Louise." Exasperation and anger mixed equally in her tone. "You're making the family look bad." Her fingers tightened slightly. Dmitri whimpered.

Cornered and desperate, Louise twisted around until she could stare up into Aurek's face. "Kill her," she growled. "Kill her, or I'll drop it!"

It was an empty threat, and Aurek knew it. If she dropped Natalia while he held her, she knew she was dead the second the statue hit the floor. The moment he released her, and she could scurry to safety, Natalia's life was forfeit. It no longer came down to whether or not he could trust Louise. Natalia's life wasn't the only life he had to worry about. "If I attack your sister now, she'll kill my brother."

"Who cares about your stupid brother?"

Aurek stared across the space at Dmitri, who was staring in horror at Louise as though he were seeing her for the first time. "I care," he said quietly.

Dmitri swallowed in spite of Jacqueline's grip. His eyes filled. Tears spilled down his cheeks and trickled over the back of Jacqueline's hand. "I've been such an idiot, Aurek. I'm so sorry."

"It was as much my fault as yours. I should never have pushed you away."

"Touching," Jacqueline murmured dryly, "but I don't think you've picked the best time for an apology." Her eyes narrowed as she studied Aurek's face. "A simple scholar?"

Aurek's chin rose, and a muscle jerked in his jaw. "It's all I wanted to be. But because of my foolishness—my pride—in believing that research for the sake of research exempted me from the responsibilities of power, my wife is trapped alive inside that statue and my brother's life is in your hands." He inclined his head. "I have nothing more to hide. We are at your mercy."

"You always were," Jacqueline told him, her voice cold. "This is my domain, and nothing happens I do not know about. Something *you*, Aurek Nuikin, at least should have remembered, since I warned you in the beginning. I expected better from you, and I gave you every chance to confide in me." Her expression held no mercy. "If you hadn't tried to pass yourself off as something you weren't, I might not have torched the workshop."

"You . . ." He saw again the ash, the total destruction of hope, and his vision darkened.

"Perhaps you should have told me what you were looking for when you asked for my permission to search. Did you think I have no feelings? Did you think I would take advantage of your love's helplessness? Did you think I have never loved?" She almost shrieked the last question, but a heartbeat later the slip of control might never have happened. "Had you confided in me, I would have known the workshop was important to you and not merely a part of my sister's plotting."

"It was her!" Louise squealed. "She burned the workshop! Avenge your wife! Kill her!" She felt his fingers begin to loosen and started to struggle.

He couldn't risk it. Couldn't risk his Natalia. Not even to destroy the one who'd condemned her to remain in her living hell. "No." He tightened his grip.

Jacqueline's lips curved up off her teeth, though the expression could in no way be referred to as a smile. It was impossible to tell if she approved of his choice or thought him a fool for making it. "As it happens, I have no real interest in either of you. Shall we trade hostages?" Opening her hand, she moved it from Dmitri's throat to his back and pushed him toward his brother.

* * * * *

Louise read her fate off her sister's face, saw the suffering she would endure at her sibling's hands, saw the pain to come. This human who held her would hand her into her sister's grasp, pry the statue of his wife from her fingers, collect his brother, and all three of them would go off to a happy ending.

Leaving her to suffer the torments of failure all on her own.

Oh, no. She shook her head, her own lips curling

back. That's not going to happen.

Shrieking with fury, she flung the statue into the air as hard as she could.

"*NO!*" Aurek watched it rise—up, up—and stretched out his hands to catch it as it fell.

Crimson silk pouring off her as she changed, Louise leapt for Dmitri, claws curved to rend and tear. He had betrayed her! He, at least, would die!

* * * * *

An enraged wererat moves almost too fast for human sight, but for Aurek the attack on Dmitri and the fall of the figurine toward the polished floor occurred agonizingly slowly. He watched muscle and ebony hair sheathe Louise Renier's body. He watched her muzzle lengthen, a tail appear from under the fall of full skirts. He watched Dmitri freeze, eyes stretched wide with horror as he, in turn, watched his death approach. He watched his beloved Lia turn end over end by the smoke-stained ceiling—end over end over end until she began to fall to earth once more.

And he watched Jacqueline Renier watching him, and realized that this choice was his alone. She would not help.

The wererat's claws were a breath away from Dmitri's face.

This choice . . . How could he choose?

And then he saw a way.

The first three segments of the spell had already been completed. Thrusting his hand into his pocket, he pulled out the iron bar and threw it at Louise Renier's feet. It tumbled through the air, mimicking the end-over-end movements of his Natalia's fall. When it finally hit the floor, invisible bands of power closed around the shrieking wererat. It wouldn't hold for very long. He could feel it weakening even as the last band snapped into place.

It didn't have to hold for very long.

With Dmitri safe, he lunged desperately forward, his hands outstretched to catch the falling figure of his wife.

It seemed . . .

. . . to go on . . .

. . . forever.

Then his fingertips caressed the porcelain one last time as it dropped just beyond his grip and smashed into a thousand little pieces at his feet.

Time started moving at its regular rate once again.

Aurek dropped to his knees. The howl of disbelief that tore up through his chest slammed into the grief that closed his throat and emerged as a tortured whimper. Ignoring the damage to his hands as the shards sliced through palms and fingers, he gathered up his Natalia and held her close. Reflected in every drop of his blood, he could see the face of the laughing wizard.

* * * * *

After a time, how long a time he had no idea, Aurek realized he was alone with Jacqueline in the deserted ballroom. Truly alone. Even the laughter in his head had been replaced by an empty silence—but then, the joke was over.

They stared at each other for a long moment, the wererat and the wizard.

Aurek wouldn't, *couldn't* speak first.

Jacqueline slowly shook her head. "I had your brother bandaged and sent back to your townhouse to pack," she said abruptly. "You're a smart man, Aurek Nuikin. You know that I should kill you both for your participation in my sister's little coup attempt."

Aurek stared up her, suddenly aware that should she wish to do just that, he could not stop her. Could never have stopped her. From the beginning, he had been as much in her power as any other fool who chose to live in her domain. He bowed his head.

"Instead," she continued, "I offer you safe passage to the border."

"Why?" His voice seemed to belong to someone else. Someone he didn't know.

Her gaze dropped to the broken statue still cradled in his bloody hands. "I too have loved—and lost." For a heartbeat, the emerald glitter left her eyes, and her expression softened into something that might have been pity. "Go home, scholar. There is nothing left for you to learn in Richemulot."

 # EPILOGUE

Heavy gray clouds hung low in a cold sky and masked the rising of the sun. Dawn brought only a pale light to Pont-a-Museau, barely enough for the hired coach to find its way along the esplanade to a townhouse near the center of the city.

Muffled in a heavy, multi-caped greatcoat, the coachman clucked encouragement to his horses and tried not to think about the stone that had fallen from the last bridge they'd crossed. The condition of the bridges were why he usually refused to bring his coach onto the islands, insisting instead that those travelers wanting to hire him take the omnipresent canalboats to the dock he maintained on the southeast shore of the river. However, when Jacqueline Renier had sent a purse of silver and a request for his services, it was an offer he couldn't refuse. And the money, as generous as it was, had little to do with his acceptance.

Stopping the team by a haphazard pile of luggage, he lowered himself laboriously down from the high seat, spoke to the nervous servant on watch, and sent him to hold the horses while he began tying on the trunks. Bits of protruding clothing spoke of hasty

packing. Hardly surprising, he thought, when Mamselle Renier was arranging the trip.

He'd just finished tightening the last knot when the
door to the townhouse opened and three men
emerged. One, the largest—though all three had
probably towered over their neighbors—wore the
clothing and manner of a personal servant. The
other two were supposed to be brothers. The coachman couldn't see the resemblance.

The older brother had a wild shock of silver-gray
hair and a short beard the same color. There were
dark shadows under his red-rimmed eyes, and he
walked hunched over, as though he were in constant
pain. The younger brother, a serious-looking man
who seemed to be carrying the weight of the world
on his broad shoulders, helped him down the steps
and toward the coach.

When they drew closer, the coachman saw that the
older man carried a box tight against his chest,
clasped protectively in both hands. It was the box, or
rather the way he held it, that caused him to walk as
he did.

The servant reached the coach first. "You are to
take us to the border?" The Borcan accent was thick,
but the words understandable.

"I am." The coachman narrowed his eyes as the
servant began inspecting the coach. "It can meet yer
approval or not," he said, turning his head and spit-
ting into the river, "but yer riding in it anyway."

His passengers had as little choice as he did.

Apparently they knew it, for the servant nodded,
left off his inspection, and merely opened the door as
the other two arrived.

"Step up, Aurek," the younger man murmured.

The wild-haired man made no response, but he did
as he was told. As he stepped up into the coach,
something in the box rattled like broken glass or china.

As the coachman wondered why anyone would bother carrying debris from one country to another, the younger man met his gaze and held it. "My brother is not well," he said as one hand rose to touch the bandage that protruded above the folds of his cravat. "I'd appreciate it if you could make the journey as smooth as possible."

Long hours spent driving alone over empty roads had given the coachman much time to think and made him—he liked to believe—a bit of a philosopher. This young man had the look of someone who'd been plunged into the darkness of his own soul and barely made it out the other side. When the wounds of the journey healed—wounds that had nothing to do with the dressing on his throat—they'd leave deep scars that he'd carry the rest of his life.

Which won't be too long if we don't get moving. The coachman shook himself free of philosophy and nodded. "Smooth as possible," he agreed, which was an easy enough promise to make as he had no control at all over the condition of the roads.

With his passengers safely stowed inside, he climbed back up onto the box and took up the reins. "Let 'em go," he called out.

The servant holding the horses' bridles released them and took off, as though anxious to be away—not that the coachman could blame him, all things considered. Having the attention of Jacqueline Renier fixed on his master's household had to be unnerving for the poor lad.

There was room in front of the townhouse to turn, but only just, and for the first few moments all the coachman's attention was taken up by the complicated maneuver involved in getting the team and coach headed in the right direction without dumping them into the river.

When he finally got them moving slowly along the

esplanade, he felt the weight of a watcher between his shoulder blades and, without thinking, turned. A huge ebony rat, the largest he'd ever seen, was sitting on the roof of the townhouse staring down at him. He swallowed, mouth gone suddenly dry as it met his gaze.

Taking the reins in one trembling hand, he raised his hat and bowed as deeply as his position allowed. Then he swiveled around in his seat and worked very hard at forgetting what he'd seen.

It was the only way to survive in Pont-a-Museau.

As he moved the horses forward as quickly as possible, he heard the disquieting sound of laughter from inside the coach.

Elminster:
The Making of a Mage

Ed Greenwood

From the creator of the FORGOTTEN REALMS® world comes the epic story of the Realms' greatest wizard!

Elminster. No other wizard wields such power. No other wizard has lived as long. No other book tells you the story of his origins. Born into humble circumstances, Elminster begins his life of magic in an odd way – by fleeing from it. When his village and his family are destroyed by a being of sorcerous might, young Elminster eschews the arcane arts. Instead, he becomes a journeyman warrior and embarks on a mission of revenge . . . until his destiny turns in on itself and he embraces the magic he once despised.

Elminster: The Making of a Mage, in hardcover, is coming to book, game, and hobby stores everywhere in December 1994!

TSR #8548